Atlas

The Book of Death: Volume III
Nicholas Gagnier

Cover Design by Temys Designs
ISBN 978-1-7328610-5-3

Also by Nicholas Gagnier

Mercy Road
Founding Fathers
Dead's Haven
Olivia & Hale

• • • •

<u>The Book of Death</u>
Leviathan
Underworld Earth

• • • •

Embers of Aloessia

ATLAS comprises the third volume in **The Book of Death** series, which is a spin-off of the **Olivia & Hale** series, making this book the seventh story set in the universe that inspired it.

This recap will introduce characters, concepts and events in a limited context, who are relevant to the story you are about to read.

The **Olivia & Hale** series, as the precursor to BoD (as The Book of Death will henceforth be referred to as), introduced the central protagonists and concepts through four loosely interconnected, standalone novels; *Mercy Road, Founding Fathers, Dead's Haven* and *Olivia & Hale*. During these disparate stories, we met **Harper Whitaker** and **Tim Hawkins**, who later became connected through Tim's sister **Grace Hawkins**.

It also introduces **the Shroud**, a purgatorial realm between life and Death, presided over by a being named **Reaper**. Out of boredom or for other reasons unknown, Reaper took two souls captive following their worldly deaths in the poem *Genesis*. Using a basin-like reincarnation device called **the Timestream**, he offered **Olivia** and **Hale** (surnames unknown) their lives back if they would participate in a game.

This game consisted of twenty-eight incarnations from birth to death, a target only Hale would later reach. Due to Reaper's manipulations of time and space, Olivia was imprisoned in the past and Hale was told she was dead. After completing the twenty-eighth death, Hale was challenged to stab a dormant Reaper, posing on a stone slab adjacent to the Timestream. When he removed the mask following the deed, the corpse was, in fact, Olivia's.

With nothing left to lose, Hale challenged Reaper, but ultimately took his place as Death. Drowning a woman named **Ariel** whose powers facilitated Reaper's game against her own will, Hale sought to destroy the world out of bitterness, while Ariel respawned in the real world.

During Olivia's time-space imprisonment, she was reincarnated as **Nancy Whitaker**, and had two children, **Harper** and **Charlie**. Following Hale stabbing Olivia, Nancy's real-world form instinctively killed herself. The novel *Mercy Road* follows young Harper as she recovers from Nancy's suicide, unaware of the larger cosmic events at play. It is during this emotional fallout, she and her peers rescue **Grace**, a sex slave from her neighbor's cellar.

In *Olivia & Hale*, Harper returns as an adult when she awakens with five others in a purgatorial realm called the Shroud. One of these others is **Tim Hawkins**, Grace's brother. After surviving an outlaw town Hale ultimately destroyed (*Dead's Haven*), Tim was forced to enter a portal to the Shroud. As Harper and Tim realized their underlying connection to Grace, the reincarnated Olivia's final conflict against her old friend manifested, revealing Grace to be Ariel, the woman Hale drowned after becoming Death.

When the dust settled, Tim Hawkins took Hale's place; and inheriting the locket that sustained Olivia's ghost, Harper went home to her love **Michaela**. But upon returning to the real world, she quickly died of a neurological disease and was claimed by Tim.

IN *Leviathan* (Volume I), Tim travelled back in time to discover what happened to those who abducted his sister Grace when she was nine years old. Upon learning of the FBI agent working Grace's case in its final days, Tim began surveying her life from its beginning, making himself known in her younger years until becoming a regular presence in adulthood.

Arriving at her inevitable death, Tim and **Ramona Knox** learned the child abductions were a hoax concocted by a senior FBI agent, employing a group of former altar boys to do his bidding. Tim reversed Ramona's death, physically merging with her to grant other-worldly powers, while warning it could produce unintended butterfly effects. Following her revenge, and the case's resolution, Tim and Ramona attempted to separate, resulting in the latter's indefinite incapacitation.

Twenty years after that fateful decision, the world is a remarkably different place. *Underworld Earth* opens following a series of butterfly effects that undid most of modern history, including the September 11th attacks, the Obama presidency and the Iraq War— replacing it with new conflicts, balances of power and outcomes. In the midst of this, a deadly plague escaped the Center for Disease Control on Mother's Day 2018, wiping out 99.9% of the human population on Earth, and charging the newly immortalized Harper with undoing Death's mistake. Guided by an angel of Atlas named **Gabriel**, the Phoenix set out to eliminate seven reincarnated individuals, including the comatose Ramona— some good, some bad, some outright rotten.

After being betrayed by Gabriel, Harper had completed five of the seven deaths entrusted to her. As the man who calls himself Death surrendered to the Grand Council of Atlas in exchange for Ramona's freedom, Harper learned of the final name— her reincarnated older brother **Charlie Whitaker**— and refused to be the one to kill him...sentencing Earth to permanent inhabitability.

"But has there ever been
something so great as love, quite
so comfortable with sin?"
Atlas proverb

• • • •

CAST ABROAD THE RAGE of thy wrath: and behold every one
that is proud, and abase him.
Look on everyone who is proud, and bring him low;
Tread down the wicked in their place.
Job 40:10 (New King James Version)

I ALWAYS IMAGINED THE afterlife as a soulless place.

Death gets a bad rap — human beings are easily afraid of things we don't understand. It is why people created religion and stories and rationales, backing up irrational confirmation we know nothing about what lies on the white light's other end.

Ever since I was a little girl, a strange man has visited me. I rarely had control over when he appeared— usually, it happened as I was hurt or traumatized in a way only children can find themselves; quite often, by their own doing.

My parents died when I was two. My father was a certifiable addict who ingested a bunch of terrible substances, and brought my mother and I to a gravel pit in western Virginia. When all was said and done, my mother— also a natural trainwreck— was on the ground with a bullet in her head. Daniel's body was found beside her, similarly disfigured from a gunshot to the temple.

I was the only survivor.

After a year in the foster system, I was adopted by my mother's sister Maya. That woman would raise me into a rookie FBI agent — she was the mother my own never was, tutoring and disciplining and nurturing me through the formative years. She had violent boyfriends, a cigarette constantly between her lips and the sass I inherited from her, but things were okay.

When I was five, the suited man began visiting me, and nothing about my life would ever be normal again.

• • • •

IN THE SUMMER OF NINETY-five, I graduated at the top of my class from Quantico, the FBI's elite training facility in Virginia. At this point in my life, the man who introduced himself as Death under a kitchen table when I was five-years-old became a constant presence. For years before that, he had only shown up in times of crisis, sometimes going years without making contact. Just as I began to believe his appearances were symptomatic of deeper-seated issues, he would appear again.

By the time I began at the Bureau in late summer — shortly before being assigned the case that would change my career— Tim was at my side for all of it.

I gave everything to bring down the Jordan West crew— a grown group of former altar boys who partnered with a senior FBI agent named Stephen Hardwick to abduct young children across the nation. In the end, it cost my life. Hardwick burned me alive and left my charred remains in a dilapidated Georgetown warehouse.

Until that point, the man who calls himself Death had only spoken of his realm. Beyond his casual appearances from nowhere, I assumed his claims were exaggerations designed to keep me in a state of awe and wonder.

After my death at Hardwick's hand, I would be forced to believe him. In a room with shimmering illusions for walls, a thousand holes poked into its black veneer like stars, I couldn't deny what my eyes saw. The floors were slick, without color or hue, shiny as the waxed tiles of any department store. The room's exact size was hard to distinguish, because those multi-plane walls seemed to immediately end and go on forever simultaneously.

I developed a place, he once told me. *A safe middle ground before people come to my world, where we can meet for the first time. On average, a person dies every 1.2 seconds, somewhere in the world. I personally greet each and every one of them.*

"Hello, Ramona," said the man who calls himself Death — whose power over human souls leaving their earthly vessels held the key to my success or failure in rescuing the young girl taken by the West crew.

"Tim? Where are we?"

"We are in the Arcway," the suited man replied. In all the years I have known him, his dress has never changed; the part in his hair and the length of his beard remain identical to our first meeting. "My creation. It is the step before entering my realm, where you will await salvation or damnation."

"Does that... mean I'm dead?"

As Tim explained the chain of events that had brought us to this point, I couldn't help wondering why these cosmic forces had any interest in Ramona Carol Knox— the little girl with dead parents who had no business growing up to be an FBI agent, but did anyway.

Mostly, I wondered what bliss ignorance would have brought me instead.

"Why are you telling me all this?" I asked.

"Because," Tim replied, "I am no longer willing to stand by, Ramona."

And that is the last thing I remember.

Nephalim

PART ONE

WHITE LIGHTS.

The initial wave of suppressed glare behind my eyes poisons the comfort of endless sleep. The lids over my slumber flutter, provoking mouth corners to twitch, fingers to bend. Breaths begin short, tiny assaults on capillaries in the lungs. Tolerance grows, like a rose blossoming, easing its pistils into glare it has been indefinitely sheltered from. It turns my cognition left, then right. The chasm splits over my darting eyes, allowing in more shadows of light than existed before.

And then, like a computer booting up out of deep hibernation, streams of consciousness unravel. Memories return as a flood—sound inhibits my senses, but can't conjure visuals to accompany it.

When I started with the Bureau, back in the seventies, it was simple. Black and fucking white. Bad guy popped up, we put 'em away. You get yourself on a Most Wanted list, we took you the fuck down.

Light is intrusive in its mannerisms, simply feeling entitled to impose itself on the status quo. Soon, pain blooms where those images should manifest. It begins in my head, travelling to knees which feel like they haven't moved in ages. Distant curiosity implores me to wiggle the connected toes. Nothing changes, and mobility remains uncertain. My legs feel like meat in a grocery store bunker, cold slabs on a sheeted surface.

Then, something changed. The Wall fell in Berlin, the Cold War ended. I don't fucking know. Point is, bad guys just weren't so easy to find anymore. People were more educated than ever, and the politicians kept squeezing our budgets. More and more, my brothers in blue were handed pink slips, told to clean out their desks. There just weren't enough heads to bust anymore.

Kaleidoscopic films between my eyelids shade the solidifying outlines with confusion. Light is the color scheme of a growing berth at the base of nascent consciousness — I continue experimenting in darkness I have long felt most comfortable with. Fingers twitch as shifting shoulders turn my neck. All are mildly unsuccessful, and none prove worth the expended energy.

That's the problem, Knox— you still think this is about children. It's about sustaining a failing black market which pays dividends to the real one...upholding the standard of living we have become accustomed to— life, liberty, and security.

How did I end up here?

Considering movement worth another try, fingers attempt curling into a fist. The interlaced colors comprising vision run together, forming blotches that interfere with cohesive sight. I don't know how long I've laid in this bed, nor do I have the slightest inkling where I am. Making out pearl-tinted blinds, my irises distinguish blues from less dominant whites, a bed rail from broken medical equipment whose monitors and displays are unserviceable and blank.

A hospital room. Vaguely aware of the air mask over my face, there is no respirator down my throat. An IV feed is the only flesh-intruding measure they implemented, but it has not delivered drips or fluids through the cords in some time.

And then, it dawns on me.

Why is it so quiet?

Struggling to recall why I'm in the hospital— and why it feels I've been asleep for a long time— frustration yields a tepid fist. It is short-lived, but progress. My eyes feel heavy, and I could go back to sleep, but I need to know more.

Come on, Ramona.

Ramona.

As my own name registers, context begins to creep back in. Like waking from a bad dream, reality floods back quicker, all the answers to how I ended up here at my disposal.

I've already lost two of my best agents to this individual, Knox, one voice says. *I have a city in panic over whether kids will come home after school. They disappear from parks, grocery stores and museums. All it takes is their parents' heads turning, they're gone.*

Emily.

The girl whose disappearance led me to the exposure of my partner was found safe. I remember that. But what happened after?

Outlines of the room gain more clarity. Color consolidates strength, red and blues rightfully dominating those they play superior to. The regular sounds of intensive care never replenish— beeping monitors, the shuffling shoes of passing nurses and droning orderlies coming by to change the sheets — leaving my room deafened by silence. Like the slow drip of a morphine feed, it pulses over the expected cues of tired doctors and hurried specialists beyond the room's door rushing to stem the tides of the dying.

My eyes are exhausted by the rush of stimuli passing through them, and close to regain strength. I can't remember how I got here, or the amount of time passed since the voices running together spoke those words.

I have to get out of here.

That might be easier said than done. Ligaments ache trying to make a continuous, consistent fist. My toes don't wiggle on command; even a turn of my head yields nothing but more soreness and centimeters of progress.

Giving up for now, my eyes grow too heavy, and I fade to black.

· · · ·

CONSCIOUSNESS ARRIVES slower the second time. My surroundings have reverted to blur. Wisps of insanity build— shadows that aren't there, silhouettes even less likely, and the sound of *chewing.* The audio cues are short; saliva squished between cheeks tells the helpless woman to intuitively recognize the room is no longer empty.

The moist movements occur from behind me, and instinct kicks in. Panic transcends earlier difficulty turning my head— I immediately regret moving so quickly as sharp pain reverberates through the muscles surrounding my carotid artery.

A homeless man sits on a plastic chair at my bedside, tipping an aluminum can from a hoisted position into his mouth. He is dressed in a ragged brown jacket and sweatpants. Straggly, gray strands fall out of a dirty tuque onto his shoulders. His cheeks are patchy, with no gums behind his unshaven lower lip to stem sauce under the can's aluminum rim, spilling into his lap.

Seeing my head turn, the intruder realizes I'm conscious and lowers the can. He does not react, rotating his lower jaw counterclockwise, squashing beans under his tongue in lieu of molars to chew it.

"You're awake," he says.

Good. You're awake.

His words recall another conversation, as I was roped to a wooden chair — shortly before the warehouse over my head went up in flames.

"Who are you?" I ask. My voice carries the question on little more than rasp. "What are you doing in my room?"

The man chuckles.

"Capitol's gotten dangerous since the plague. Lots o' dead out there."

"Plague? What plague? And again, who are you?"

"Name's Wilson," the homeless fellow professes. "Had a first name once. Not much use for it now. So yeah, you can call me Wilson.

"Must have been asleep for a while, weren't you? Wouldn't have seen the shitshow America's become. Some strain escaped that Center for Disease Control! Next thing, everyone I knew was dead."

Dead?

"What do you mean, 'everyone'?"

"What it sounds like," Wilson replies, scraping the last of the beans into his mouth and clamping down. The squishing behind his pressed lips does nothing to avert the revelation's casual horror. "President Smith, the whole Cabinet. Congress. Cops. Citizens. I can go on, if you like!"

Unable to promptly respond to the old man's information, I rack my brain for any kind of corroborating timeline.

"So how long have you been nappin?" Wilson asks.

I don't pay the question mind. Rolling my neck back to the position it will no longer ache with unfortunate angles allows me to scan the walls, furniture and ceiling, questioning everything. But as eyes rest on the wide-set window, answers are further than ever.

How didn't I see it before?

"Help me up," I tell Wilson. My hand finds more confidence in estranged strength, yanking the IV needle from the web of nerves and veins it obscures. The tubes fall by my bedside, and I pull my useless limbs to the edge.

"*What*? No, listen lady! You need to rest now, hear?"

Wilson may be a squatter in my current accommodations, raiding the hospital pantry for something to snack on without his bottom teeth, but giving orders is not among his rights. If he won't help me, I'll have to do it myself. Thankfully, the homeless man is not without conscience, standing from his chair. I struggle to lift myself up off the mattress— balance proves unsuccessful, and I fall onto my stomach, almost toppling off the side.

"Sure you want to do this, miss?" he asks.

I don't answer, continuing to struggle. Wilson grasps my shoulders, guiding me back to a flat position.

"Now, listen here, miss! You aren't going anywhere! God knows how long you have been like this, but your ligaments have shortened while you were asleep. Ain't going nowhere without extensive surgery!"

"Yeah? You a doctor?" I groan, settling into defeat.

"Former RN. Back in the days they didn't have too many men doing the job." Wilson circles the bed to a wheelchair near the open door. The semi-private room has no other patient occupying it, so few will judge my ass hanging out of a hospital gown as the old man helps me into it. He slowly lowers me into the mobile device, keeping hands under my armpits until I'm comfortable. Moving to the chair's rear, he wraps palms around the handles, and begins to push. "Why are you here?" I ask, though unable to see his toothless grin or dirty clothes. "Hiding in a hospital?"

Wilson pivots the wheelchair to the window, bringing me closer to the sight my tired eyes covet. A squeaky wheel under my right foot revolts in its bracket, drifting the chair left as Wilson veers the other way, overcompensating for its crooked trajectory.

"Things ain't good in D.C., miss. Plague got loose and killed most. Ones who didn't die at first did later, or did the killing. Point is," he says, "there ain't many good 'uns left."

"The hospital is the safest place, then."

"Yup. Here, we're at the window, miss. Just like you wanted."

Using Wilson's reluctant support, my bare feet touch the floor, straightening out. The old man supports me from the back— my fingers curl into the radiator on level with the window as I soak up the horror beyond our little room four floors above street level.

The United States Capitol—once a testament to Neoclassical architecture and seat of the strongest nation on Earth— lies in devastation. The National Mall's signature monument has crumbled in the distance, collapsing to the ground in giant halves. The Capitol Building's landmark dome is crumbled into the interior structure, and what remains of its white facade has been charred and blackened with time and violence. Streets below the window are awash in empty cars; many of their doors are left ajar, but there are no bodies in them— just windows through a journey their occupants never completed.

And then, it begins to come back to me with more clarity.

By reversing your death, we can stop Hardwick and Royce from selling Emily Rickard. But so too will it change everything.

Tim.

The man who calls himself Death— who I met under a kitchen table when I was five years old, and told me darkness was no different than light— just a little harder to love— saved my life. He reversed my murder at Stephen Hardwick's hand, warning that saving Emily would have dire consequences.

We are tampering with a natural order.

I did this.

People who have died could see their deaths prevented or reversed. For better or worse, it could change the entire course of history.

Tim warned me, and was right. By stopping Hardwick, I condemned the world to die horribly. One little girl's life— at the time— seemed too great an expense to ensure humanity had a chance at survival. Unhooking my fingernails from between the radiator grills, I sink down into the wheelchair. Wilson watches the connecting threads behind my eyes as they drift from the window.

"Miss?" Wilson says. "Are you alright, miss?"

Are you willing to take the risk with me, Ramona?

"This is my fault," I confide in him, prompting an inquisitive expression.

"How you figure, ma'am? Unless you 'was the one who released that nasty sickness, I don't see how you could be to blame. Been asleep after all, haven't you?"

There is no way I could make the toothless man eating beans at my bedside understand. Rather than offering a drawn-out, confusing explanation, I return to the argument's merits, but only in my head—

Before I can begin linking runaway thoughts— *saving a little girl ends in apocalypse?*— a set of bullets cross the room. Both strike Wilson in the chest. He falls over dead as my gaze lifts to their source.

The silhouette in the doorway has already seen my horrified expression. Disregarding Wilson's blank gaze, the figure carries a silenced pistol, moving toward me.

For all the (*years?*) I have been asleep, the Quantico training that trained me for a career with the FBI is rustily embedded. Adrenaline, on the other hand, is not. The masked intruder reaches halfway between the door and my wheelchair; I lunge over the assistive device's side, hitting the floor. The man's momentum did not account for my reaction— he barely has time to process I'm crawling on my stomach. As every ligament rages exhaustion, I grab his calf, sharply pulling up. The man's head arches back with his rising leg. He loses balance, falling to the floor beside me, head smacking off the unmaintained linoleum.

Again, his habit of movement is my struggle, but arrogance is the ingredient for my surprise mobility. His outstretched fingers reach for the gun that fell by Wilson's corpse. My own hand slaps his away as I vault my useless legs over him. We struggle like that for a moment, each trying to gain supremacy over the other. My hand wraps around the pistol's handle first, yanking the barrel upward. The attacker clasps his hand over mine, aware he's already lost to a cripple.

The released gunshot shatters his face, propelling the man's head aside in a bloody mess of brains and balaclava fabric. I topple over him onto the white floor. A growing pool spreads under his skull, tarnishing its unwaxed surface.

What the fuck was that?

The intruder could have back-up, and I am the equivalent of a sitting duck. Wilson's eyes are equally empty under the windowsill. The rest of him is obscured by the hospital bed. I secure the weapon at its foot, disregarding the wheelchair. Elbows pull me forward until

I reach the wide-open door, peering past its threshold into a long corridor. Its throughway of floors littered with garbage and debris is abandoned; clearly, nobody has been treated or worked at this hospital in awhile.

If my assailant has friends nearby, only the pistol will afford protection. I advance into the hallway, dragging useless legs behind me. Formerly dark hair spills down my face, allowing a glimpse at shades of gray it embraced in my slumber. The hospital gown catches on the floor, exposing my bare legs and buttocks as I scurry to the hall's end.

The two masked men stationed around the corner never see the woman crawling at its precipice. The bullets that split their heads, sending them to the floor, assure me of that. The elevator they guarded is out of service; its stainless steel doors tease the fact that I will have to descend the stairs, whether my legs work or not. The floor is empty now, at least. Hoisting myself over the same floor as the hospital room I awoke and was almost murdered brings me to a thick red door. It warns me that opening it will prompt an alarm, but I have to take the chance. I reach for the push bar well above my compromised position, and miss. Swinging upward again, the bar lapses inward by an inch. Arms fall back to my side, but I am not so easily defeated.

Rolling on my back positions weak legs underneath the bar, and all my dormant strength is required to lift them above my head. The first time misses, the second pushing it a little farther in than before. The third unlatches the door from its frame. One foot to hold the bar in place, the other lowers, pushing its creaking weight ajar. I did it. My other leg comes down, reinforcing the foot propping open the door. Heavy metal pins the ankle wedged between it; I lift my torso from the floor, ignoring cracks in my static spine, thrusting a shoulder into it. Reversing myself, I creep between the cracked door and its frame; it latches as I collapse in the stairwell beyond it.

I don't know how I ended up at the end of the world, but it surely waits for nobody. I edge toward the descent; each flight is littered in plaster and trash like the hallway before it. The railing helps in pulling myself to a seated position; the floor is cold between my legs, but its stairs are the only way out of this nightmare.

The next landing brings footsteps pounding up from the bottom. The multiple voices wear heavy boots that compete with their words for volume. I reach the corner of the subsequent flight, positioning myself against the wall facing downward, and point the silenced weapon at my arriving targets. The intruders' conversation is halted by three bullets exiting their barrel. Each connects with my would-be attackers in a critical place— throat, eye and heart, respectively. Twenty minutes after waking, six people are dead; five by my hand, putting the clip at empty. Casting the spent weapon aside, three floors remain. I grab two of the fallen's revolvers as garbled communications filter from radios at my victims' hips. I don't bother pulling off the balaclavas off their faces— I wouldn't likely not know them, and their identities would not help one iota.

I can do this.

One flight lower reveals no assailants. One lower, and I wonder if that is the last of them. Lowering myself past each flight, the dual weapons may not be needed after all. It doesn't mean I grip them any looser.

When I was young, my adoptive aunt's violent boyfriend threatened to beat down the door after being locked out of our apartment. Maya ushered me under a table with a yellow patterned tablecloth.

And that's when the suited man who called himself Death first appeared to me. He never really said when or how he became the celestial being that confronted the terrified child, hugging her rough-housed stuffed bear. I have bits and pieces of his history, but all that matters is the voice in my memory.

You don't need to be afraid, Ramona.

Racking my brain for who could possibly be after me— the FBI agents I betrayed before falling unconscious, the numerous enemies made during my tenure— constantly brings me back to the suited cosmic being; the last face I saw before blackness devoured my soul, and Death had come for me.

Who are you? I once asked him, sitting beneath that table with a patterned yellow tablecloth.

My name is Death, he told the five-year-old whose eyes were widened at the sound of Maya's screaming male companion, pounding on thin wood as she pushed furniture in front of it.

But my friends call me Tim.

It is because of that man I am here now, terrified for my life.

You don't need to be afraid, Ramona.

The bottom floor brings relief. I return to wiggling along the landing. One final flight remains, which would bring me below ground. With no plan to be cornered, I shimmy to the emergency door. Unlike the three floors above, it must be pulled. A few tugs open it far enough to wedge my wrist between, and my arms do the rest.

The hospital's ground level differs from those above in a few key ways. The twin sliding doors are frozen open, allowing warm air to flow into the lobby. Other than several mounds of bones suggesting multiple people died here, and were long forgotten, it is still abandoned. A number of skulls accentuate the evidence, and I try not to glance at them on the way past.

The third and most important difference lies beyond the open doors. Several more men pace in the lot just beyond the hospital's emergency room entrance. Their faces are also covered; one lifts a radio receiver to his veiled mouth, trying to hail their companions upstairs. And at their feet, a black box with a plunger and handle is attached to wires leading inward. In the old days, they might have sent a remote signal using a detonator. Post-apocalypse, the comical cube is attached to wires that pivot through the entrance, past rows of seating. I follow them from my hiding spot near the nurse's sta-

tion— the red and yellow sheathing splits off in different directions.
I trace the jaundiced wire with my eyes, past rectangular cuts of electrical tape hanging it further up the wall— at its end, grey piles of putty are affixed to strategic positions, ensuring maximum destruction when they detonate.

C4.

There is not enough time to disarm the explosives. Their mission is obviously killing me, and my only hope of escaping is—

Tired of receiving no response, the leader orders his men to operate the device in front of him. One fellow steps up, wrapping his hands around the red bar atop its plunger— forcing it to fully depress. The resulting explosion against my skin is excruciating; its blankets of orange and red blind understanding while the small hairs of my arm sizzle. Flesh is cooked off the bone, and the world in front of me evaporates inside a pulsing fireball. Unable to see the men who sentenced me to this fate, I scream for what seems like forever.

But it is my mind, wandering back to the man under that table, who brought me to this point I could be so easily assassinated.

I think, in times of great crisis, we turn to the best and brightest of us to lead the way.

The inferno subsides— a result of several levels of a hospital coming down, crushing what few nerves remain. It only reinforces the fact I signed up to Hell, and the man who called himself Death personally escorted me to its door.

After that, the only sentiment I know is darkness.

CHAPTER TWO

I AM NOT A MONSTER.

As a child, one of my favorite books was *Where the Wild Things Are*. Maya diligently read it almost every night between the ages of six and eight. During those years, I met the man who called himself Death twice— once when I fell down a ravine behind my house, and when one of my pets left us.

I don't remember what I loved so much about this damn book. After my parents' murder-suicide, I can only recall a yearning for independence. I loved the aunt who saved my life to pieces, but the idea of waking up in a strange land, surrounded by otherworldly creatures, was all too enticing.

Opening eyes to linoleum floors and matching walls, a distant hum of electrical tracks should immediately identify my surroundings, and yet it takes a full minute after sitting up to co-relate the train tunnel with a subway station.

Wasn't I just in a hospital?

There is something more eerie about the air here. It feels lighter, invasive; like someone brought it from another world, and its properties do not mesh with the environment. The subway station is empty, but something else is off. Other than heavy silence, it looks like any other underground platform. Advertisements framed in paid promotional brackets advise a fool and their money will soon be parted. A row of payphones sits at the bottom stairwell, leading up into the world at large. A black stickered rectangle, caked over green bricks stretching to the ceiling, informs me that my current location is West 34th and Broadway.

Am I in New York?

That would be a fair way from the Capitol I have lived my entire life. The sites of D.C. were distinguishable from my room's window, even with the destruction levelled against it.

There is only one explanation for how I could have gotten here.

"Tim?"

My voice echoes down the humming tunnel. Like a thrown boomerang, it comes back to me. No train is travelling down the concrete tube; only the pitch of my nervous voice returns, and not even the distant sound of a vehicle on fixed tracks dares follow it.

Last I remember, the FBI turned on me after exposing one of their senior agents as complicit in the abduction of children. Long story short, he and a few others used a group of former altar boys to take kids from grocery stores, museums and any public place they could potentially get away with it. Learning of that revelation almost cost my life. In fact, were it not for Tim, I would not have survived the assassination attempt.

"Tim?"

Again, the name returns nothing, and my eyes drift to the row of payphones to my left. Behind them, silver railings and concrete steps hug the far wall, with a decommissioned escalator separating them. My memories are more accessible, no longer dimmed by the cloudiness of waking from near-death. But there is no sign of my guardian angel who saved me from the FBI's dark underbelly, then granted powers I could not explain.

How long have I been here?

Exhaling, I take my first steps up the multi-flight staircase. Every heightened surface brings me closer to answers, and farther away from questions— at least, until I reach the top.

The scene above the tunnel is New York City, but nothing like I have ever seen. The Empire State Building— if that is indeed what it is— curves in its center, forcing the building's peak to perform a one-hundred-eighty degree angle, making it look like an arch. The point most people would assume to be the top is pointed to the road. Its general shape defies most logic or expectations. Above its bending body, the sky has adopted a dark shade of purple. Black swirls slowly rotate in the violet canopy, reminding me of a *Twilight Zone* episode.

What the hell is this place?

I have only been to New York once, on a graduation trip in high school. Maya encouraged me to go, despite not really being able to afford it. The woman sacrificed so much more than I gave her credit for, and I was able to join my peers on the trip.

Even given that experience, the unsettling skyline is remarkably different from any version of Manhattan I would recognize. Its roads are virtually abandoned— not a car in sight along the intersections. Building windows are dark, as if everyone shut down their lives and moved out of the city.

Trying not to panic, my feet shuffle down West 34th, glancing in all directions for a corresponding sign of life. None of the mobility issues that gripped me in the hospital are in play here. The hospital gown is also gone, replaced with a more familiar dress—a black pantsuit and blazer, like those often donned as a rookie FBI agent. Shoulder-length hair sways with turns of my head, but no longer possesses ashen streaks as a rogue strand escapes the ponytail trailing behind me. I pass several stores before reaching Macy's on the corner of 34th and Broadway but like everywhere else, the iconic department store towering over the intersection is locked tight.

Turning right at 7th Avenue, my subconscious compass carries me from point to point like connecting-the-dots. Somehow, my feet know where I am headed better than I do. Soon in Times Square, I gawk at a scene that should be instantly familiar, but rings hollow and foreign instead. For miles around, Manhattan is desolate. I don't know if the plague Wilson inferred to did this, but am certain it would not turn the sky purple as it currently stands.

This makes no sense.

And then, a voice behind me confirms everything I suspected to be true. Based on all my previous interactions with the man who called himself Death, who led me into a comatose state while the world fell around me, this is his world, not mine. This is the afterlife he warned about, and there is no escape from it.

"Hello, Ramona."

The words evoke a shudder down my spine. Turning to the source— the bearded man was not there to greet me in the hospital ward where armed men came to kill me, nor upon my entrance into his strange world— I shouldn't be as spooked as I am, but scramble back from his empathetic frown and cool demeanor.

Alliance with him has only brought me pain.

"Get away from me!" My shoes run the other way while my head is still turned to him, almost tripping me. The strange world revolves and trembles as I regain balance, sprinting back the way I came. The man who appeared under a table to me at five-years-old does not give chase that I can see or hear. The weird horizon is lost on me— buildings blur together in my dash for freedom. Pacing breaths lends realization that my chest does not burn and my legs do not tire. Neither revelation does much to comfort me.

I have to break free of him, once and for all.

Blocking out logic that dictates I should hear him out— that he has been around all my life, and never harmed me— flight overpowers every remaining intuition, and I care for nothing more than escaping him.

We have to begin the separation process, Ramona.

Bolting down West 45th, the purple sky swirls with my pounding heart and unstable vision. Roads ordinarily filled with cabs, limousines and Manhattan's traffic through the heart of America's most notorious metropolis are dormant. Skyscraper windows are devoid of light or life, promising no escape between them.

Will it hurt?

The memories run together like slapping feet on the pavement beneath. Turning up 5th Avenue, my brain tries to corroborate memories of him as a child with the man whose merging with me left my body in a vegetative state.

I will run forever if it means escaping him.

Several blocks pass by— aside from the weird sky and lack of other human beings, it really *is* New York. Reaching the Rockefeller Center takes the same amount of time as it would in the real version; perhaps slightly faster, since the street carts and sidewalks are empty. Slowing in front of the landmark, whose rink is long untouched and its double door entrance pitch black beyond, I look for any sign of the man who calls himself Death.

You can probably stop calling him that. I have seen the extent of his terrible powers. From the looks of it, his realm is not much better.

We have to begin the separation process, Ramona.

Will it hurt?

Immensely.

None of this would have happened if I had just told him to go away.

I should be out of breath, have to hold my knees to regain oxygen. Maya was a smoker, and the years trapped inside a cloudy apartment in the seventies, when everyone and their mother smoked inside, should have compromised my respiratory system. It never did, but that should not make me Superwoman. I should not be able to sprint twelve blocks and be fine—

"Ramona," Tim says, appearing behind me. I scream at the suddenness with which the suited man appears, scrambling back from him. "We need to talk."

But I've heard everything Death has to say, and paid for every word. I tell him to leave me alone. Turning up 6th, hoping he has enough respect to listen this time. But I am in his realm now. He can appear and disappear and stalk me until I listen to him.

He's going to have to work for it.

• • • •

WHEN I WAS ABOUT SIX or seven, I loved *Where the Wild Things Are.* Long after Maya tired of reading it to the little girl who survived her parents' murder-suicide, I begged her to read it to me before bed. I always thought about being spirited away to a whole other world. Despite not being a reader or terribly interested in television, something about that damn story captured my heart. I went to sleep afterward, happily dreaming of waking up in a strange place. I would be befriended by its monsters and learn to love its darkness, and it would love me in return.

I am sure this monster has perfectly good explanations. He is the Devil, and knows the words I want to hear. Befriending me as a youngster, manipulating me through every major period of my life to ensure his ulterior motives were satisfied; it was all a game to him.

I can't trust anything the man says.

Central Park filters into view under the strange sky; its green shrubberies and trees are less lively, more like plastic ornaments sprinkled throughout to give the illusion it's the real deal. Taking care to check my twelve and six, I advance into it. My hip feels lighter, missing the service weapon I carried with the FBI, and had become accustomed to. Guns won't save me now — I am at the mercy of Death's realm, if that is indeed where we are.

You're not thinking about this rationally, Ro.

Maya's voice surfaces in my memory, forming the only soundtrack to Central Park's irregular state. The purple sky reflects off green grass, lending the blades' tip a brownish hue where the perception connects. Condominiums and high-rise towers surrounding the greenspace are uniformly blank; no worker drones or bodies traverse lit halls from a distance— almost as if the buildings themselves are props.

Of course I'm not thinking rationally, Auntie. Did you see what he did to me?

He saved your life.

Only to ruin it. I'm not arguing with personifications of a memory. I have to get out of here, away from the man who masquerades as a caring figure. Breaking into a trot, the park's massive center offers even fewer answers than its edges. All the best escape routes are unobstructed, and there is no sign of my celestial pursuer—

"You don't need to be afraid, Ramona."

The particular phrasing of Tim's words grind my feet to a stop. They pull my flailing heartbeat back to the Earth. So many ways to retort to the first words he spoke to me, hiding under a table at five years old; but turning to face him, unleashing any, I am capable of none.

You don't need to be afraid, Ramona.

Not to say I don't recognize the snaking pillar of darkness, floating vertically at eye level. It saved me during the FBI's attempt to stop my rescuing Emily Rickard. It appeared in the sky, flipping vehicles and disabling helicopters to protect me from afar. But to see it up close, moving in parts while stationary in others, is something else to behold. Its head tendril is glossy and shimmers as light bounces off its surface when it lands a certain way. In every other manner, it is a cloud, made out of inexplicable material. It hovers, dancing with the air.

All of my former comebacks lost, my feet turn the other way, sprinting back the way I came. Uncanny, limitless stamina ensures my legs don't tire or my arms don't ache, swinging at my sides as I bolt out of Central Park.

I could deal with the apparition, appearing at crucial moments of my life. Sometimes, I benefited from his presence, even if I could never really explain it— like his all-knowingness or bringing me back from the dead.

The whole undead, abandoned Manhattan is kind of a deal-breaker.

I don't make it far beyond the stone wall into the empty lanes of Central Park West before I am stopped by another of Tim's manifestations, this one far more threatening. The being is humungous, towering on giant arms like a gorilla. It is made of the same material as the cloud, but has no eyes or face in general. It must be twenty feet tall, and bows over its front haunches to inspect me.

Other than my childhood years, I have never been easily scared. But the sight of a giant golem widens my eyes before I dart right. The uncharacteristic scream from my mouth echoes down empty blocks. The monster does not follow me.

I run forever, thanks to unbridled endurance I suddenly possess; run until I see the Hudson, glistening under a violet canopy. I run until I can't see smoke or golems or the man who calls himself Death, who I allowed to taunt me for far too long.

Now he is a monster, and I see what terrible things he is capable of.

My name is Death. My friends call me Tim.

I should have told him to go away the first time we met, and Jeremy was trying to beat the door down, and Maya screamed for him to go away.

Would you like to be friends, Ro?

Some part of me knows he has a rational explanation, like he always does. Devils and monsters often wear a friendly face, and this Devil has everything to gain from being calm and collected, nothing to gain from presenting as his darker forms.

My name is Death.

He said it so often, so...*nonchalantly* over the years. He played to my childhood loss of Daniel shooting Tiffany in a gravel pit. I sat in a car seat, only yards away. So, when the strange man in a suit constantly appeared to a child on the verge of tears or abject terror, I found him a calming presence. Little did I know, he was just looking through my life like hitting rewind on an old VCR. Popping in earlier and earlier, until my memories solidified with his subtle interventions, all leading to my inevitable murder by Stephen Hardwick and Ryan Royce.

He knew, and did nothing to stop it.

I run, and would run forever, but my advance is stopped by a descending darkness. It covers my eyes and prevents gasps for air I may not necessarily need, but want to draw anyway. It is sudden, halting my progress toward no particular destination, only away from an apparition who can morph into unexplainable beings.

The darkness pulls. It welcomes and provides a coaxing effect in contrast to the purple sky above my head. It soothes my pounding chest, and I would think I was dead if my mind wasn't racing a mile a minute. But it does, and this can't possibly be what dying entails.

But it is, and I am in the land of wild things.

CHAPTER THREE

THE EARLIEST MEMORY in my fledgling consciousness has nothing to do with the man whose sperm fertilized my mother's egg. That egg hitched a ride to the lining of Tiffany Stewart's uterine wall, even as she was drinking and smoking nights away in her D.C. apartment. Most of what I know about Tiffany stems from old photos, and what Maya was willing to tell me about her. It mostly consisted of bitter criticisms while I was a child. Over the years, her bitterness levelled out, and I learned about my birth mother in a more objective light.

Even pregnant, Tiffany was fucking three guys, telling each she was shacking up with only them. There is no way to know if Daniel Knox was my true biological parent, and I remember nothing of the drug-addled drunk who killed Tiffany as I sat feet away, then himself.

Most memories are of her sister Maya, who raised me on her own accord and goodwill. Maya grew up in poverty and never made much of herself, but worked at the soup kitchen on weekends, down the street from a lavish Capitol lifestyle of politicians and dignitaries. She collected food stamps and somehow, by the grace of God, afforded the ground-level Stanton Park apartment we lived in until she died.

The darkness which enveloped me in Tim's realm lifts to a completely different environment. Gone is the violet sky with weird black swirls, and the same pantsuit worn as I came down on Emily Rickard's abductors.

The room in front of me seems to be a long hall, both travelling forever and immediately closed off from outside influences. Everything from its oblong panels to the inmate-style crewneck and pants I've adopted is white. The walls themselves turn as autonomous, translucent cubes. Glimmers of gray-like lead shade the cubes' edges— there are both several and none, reminiscent of three-dimensional pictures I used to study in grade school, trying to find their layered secrets.

Where am I?

And then, a voice responds. It is female, but hollow like a robot. Its inflections echo through the strange chamber— willing to reveal the answers to all my questions, or none of them.

"Hello, Ramona Knox."

Her arrival is sudden but non-threatening, despite not belonging to any being I can see. No idea whether this has anything to do with the place I just left— and hopefully never return to—but maybe I can get some damn answers.

"Who are you?"

The voice falls silent, having made itself known while seemingly incapable of answering basic questions. The glare its presence returns is blinding and other than my own pink hues, it would be uniform.

"Hello?"

"*Who* I am is a human construct. *What* we are is paramount to understanding principles of the Light."

"The Light?"

"Yes. Think of chemistry, if you will. The Light is nitrogen in a hydrogenous basin, which makes oxygen needed to sustain most life in the universe. It was born from Darkness, and only comprises a small concentration of celestial power. Those whose duties facilitate its use, or through possession of certain artifacts, can wield the Light's true power, but it always comes at a steep cost. For every reaction, there is an equal and opposite reaction.

"The majority of the Light's power is protected by the four-member Council of Atlas. Another percentage is used to power Atlas itself, and another yet for Earth. The aforementioned artifacts that are imbued with it allow its bearers a range of powers surpassing their physiological limitations."

Might as well start with the obvious questions.

"Where am I?" I ask the voice with no body, speaking in an echo chamber of strange shapes and hollow imitations at making conversation.

This time, she is quick to respond.

"Do not consider *where* you are, but *how* you are. To exist within Atlas is a state of being, not a location."

"A...state of being?"

"Yes," the disembodied being says, echoing through the chamber my entire existence has been relegated to. **"Are you aware of the concept of Heaven?"**

"Heaven?" I ask. "As in...God's heaven? Adam and Eve's God, who kicked them out of Eden over an apple?"

"The apple is symbolic. It represents obedience. This is a metaphor your human leaders have used to explain the concept to the lesser-minded to maintain order— something you have seemingly failed to grasp in your time observing such protocols."

Did it just...insult me?

"The Atlas," it continues, **"also desires control, although for reasons not of ego, but order. It governs the state of all things, from quantum physics to morality for complex life in the universe. This is achieved through a network of proxies and individual agents carrying out its commands. If there is an anomaly, these failsafes ensure the continuity of survival by eliminating the threat within a margin of 0.0001% failure."**

I groan at this mundane orientation. My career as an FBI agent relied on pinpointing pertinent information within a mound of it. This being is not briefing, but providing lengthy exposition to things beyond my understanding over concrete answers.

"So what do I call you?" I ask, steering the conversation to something more personal. "If someone designed you, they must have given you a name, no?"

"I was given no such thing. I was designed to be an infinite presence, and prime residents of Atlas for entry. But supposing this attempt to establish a relationship is based on human principles, you may refer to me as the Avatar."

"So I'm not stuck here?" Enticing as lopsided squares of minimal exposure are, I have no desire to be locked in this room.

The Avatar pauses.

"That is correct. Every organic lifeform is equipped with a unique genetic sequence, or identifier. These sequences are composed of billions of numbers. Some are enshrined, and cannot be changed; others are variable and subject to environmental factors."

"What does that have to do with Atlas?"

"When combined and taken into account, these factors all determine the individual's path after death. For as many as Atlas can hold, it cannot hold all. Thus, solutions were taken long ago to prevent bottlenecking by dispersing souls to different realms."

"Like the Shroud?" I ask, invoking the name of Tim's world. The man who calls himself Death showed it to me, having spoken of it for a long time. The conjuration of an emptied Manhattan is fresh in my mind, though it likely has little bearing on the bigger picture.

"The Shroud was designed as a stopgap between life on Earth and Atlas, to protect the supreme realm from nefarious or troubled souls who might present a threat to its safety. It is mostly self-contained, and poses little threat to either Atlas or Earth."

"So...that genetic sequence thing. Does that mean I was supposed to come here to begin with?"

"Negative," the Avatar replies. "You have been summoned by the Grand Council. Its subpoena supersedes your genetic markers, which would place you in the Shroud."

Where all the nefarious and troubled souls go. Of course. Almost convinced I was not a monster, the Avatar's nonchalant revelation is a point against me, placing me in a world of them.

I run with the wild things.

"Summoned for what?"

"You will need to speak with Maester Siskett for that. I am not privy to the Council's wishes."

"Maester Siskett?"

"Yes. I believe you two have already met. This concludes the Atlas orientation."

"*Wait*! I have other questions!"

The being's bass fades. I call out to the Avatar— there are so many things I want to know, and it has most, if not all of the answers. Its silence refuses to affirm or deny whether I'm a monster, other than revealing I was meant to walk among them forever.

What changed?

The room around me begins to shift. It brightens, then dulls; flares with raging light, and fades to brilliant darkness. My breaths linger in the silhouettes of vapors; then, the room's end wall begins to lift. Rolling upward like a garage door, light spills beneath the widening crack. It grows, casting wide curtains onto geometric walls, now flat as any wall elsewhere.

Sunlight tunnels in, rendering the room little more than a metal box, and much smaller than I initially perceived. Golden glare aches against my corneas. The glare transitions, so bright my hand has to shield them from its intense spread over the dark room.

The first steps into whatever lies beyond the fresh entrance slows my brain from initial understanding of the panorama on whose rounded border I emerge. The reach beyond what the Avatar called Atlas is a field of stars and constellations. Streaks of purple, green and yellow dance overhead, tiny beacons repressing star systems that lie centuries away by conventional travel.

I emerge from the equivalent of an industrial shipping container. The box is beside other boxes like it, equally open and empty as the dark space behind me. It purposely exits onto the breathtaking vista, but falling from its ledges would mean death as humans understand it.

The landscape beneath my feet is an immaculate patch of green blades, providing ample softness. Beyond the box surrounded by other boxes, that patch turns to gold hues of cobblestone. Thirty feet down that cobblestone looms a massive golden gate. A bronzed skyscraper dominates the star-studded view through chasms in the cast iron bars, birthing hearty shadows over the city beyond it. The prominent tower hosts twin statues on its east and west flanks— one poses like the Greek mythological figure Atlas, while the other is a winged warrior kneeling in respect of the centerpiece skyscraper it complements.

Unable to cross the gate's threshold for now, I focus on the immediate area. A small militia on my side of the enormous gate recalls the Red Army at the Cold War's peak, lined in perfect rows— six in a line, twelve on either side of the gate. Identical sanguine robes and winged helmets remove any tenet of individuality among them, conscripted to protect the access point from invaders with standard-issue spears. The wall attached to the spiked bars is gold but also iron, and at least two hundred feet tall. It stretches far above the gate itself; from my place at its summit, I could not see if more of these red-robed warriors wait from above. The phalanx on either side does not so much as sway or flinch. Each side mirrors the other, positioned to align on either side of the gate, allowing about twenty feet between the closest man of any row and the one corresponding in the opposite troop.

A short elder with curly grey hair waits between those troops. His robe is brown and though he smells of lavender as we approach each other, it does not look altogether clean. His fingernails are long but immaculate and all his teeth are intact — the man I met eating beans as I awoke from my coma in a hospital bed is unmistakable in resemblance.

"Ramona Knox." The elder's voice is raspy, as if he has smoked all his life. "I have been expecting you."

"You have?"

"Yes. Allow me to introduce myself. My name is Maester Siskett, and I am a humble servant of the Grand Council of Atlas, into whose realm you have now entered."

"I thought your name was Wilson," I tease. "Pretty sure I saw you die, didn't I?"

Siskett frowns. The teeth make him appear more human, and don't move like dentures when he follows up with a polite smile, asking me to accompany him. The enormous barrier shifts with no one evidently operating it. Loud creaking intrudes on the otherwise serene atmosphere; the spiked bars gravitate inward at a volume they must hear through the entire city. It opens fully, overcompensating for our microscopic scale. Siskett and I have passed its threshold well before it reaches its full expansion, and begins to close behind us.

The main cobblestone road cuts up to the skyward tower sur-rounded by stone angels, where it encircles the reinforced iron wall around the skyscraper.

Identical white buildings with no obvious purpose dot the curbs. The people in and around them are people like me. It takes me a mo-ment to notice the sky has changed from an interstellar panorama, replaced by a more conventional assembly of clouds over light blue.

"You must have many questions," Siskett says. We pass people from all walks of life and time periods. Some dress like they come from a different century, and speak to each other using archaic words like *thy* or *ye*. Others adorn clothing and adhere to customs I have never observed. Their garments are like foil, appearing more futuristic- which implies the Atlas exists on a plane that transcends the flow of time.

"Many might be an understatement," I reply.

"No doubt, the Avatar is meant for less exceptional individuals than yourself," he explains. "There is only so much customizing one can make to an artificial intelligence."

"She said— it is a *she*, isn't it?— I wasn't even supposed to end up here. I was supposed to stay in that Shroud place."

"Like I said— as with many things, there are conceptual limits to even the most creative devices we've come up with. The Atlas has many resources, but alas, those limits remain."

"What do you mean I'm exceptional, though?" I ask the monk-like figure escorting me down an otherworldly road, no idea what I did to earn the favor of its overseers. "And where are you taking me?"

"Ah," Siskett smiles. "Those questions are separate, and yet, have a singular answer."

"What does *that* mean?"

The elder chuckles, and the sight of him falling dead to a masked assassin flashes before my eyes. Siskett cares nothing for it, and does not ever quicken or slow beyond his regular snail's pace.

"It means, that is for the Council to know and for you to find out. Patience, child."

The condescension is annoying, but it seems I have no choice. Rather than trying to rectify this floating city in the sky, my mind drifts as we arrive at the Spire of Atlas. The tower's protective outer wall is decorated with more soldiers in winged helmets, patrolling its ramparts. Others guard the ground level with spears at the ready to defend the building. The stone angels loom over either side of the wall, residing behind sections of a brick-and-mortar running all the way around the plaza's far edges. Arches along its thirty-foot wall lead into the back corners and various sections I would quickly be lost within.

Siskett blathers on, revealing the Spire's history; but wondering how many years were lost asleep in that bed, or how the man who calls himself Death fares after I bolted from his dark manifestations barely heeds the elder monk.

"The original Spire was silver," he explains as we approach widening gates in the outer wall. These are not barred, but solid iron blocks scraping against the ground as it shifts inward, revealing red felt carpet beyond the growing chasm. "In the second Age of Creation—"

"Second Age of Creation?"

"Yes," he replies, and tells me to stop interrupting. "It would stretch from the beginning of your world's Jurassic period, to about the death of Christ. Alas, the Third Age is young, yet."

"You're saying *Christ* was real?"

"Oh yes. Not as powerful as your texts make him out to be, but a fine envoy for humanity."

"Jesus was an envoy of Atlas?"

"Unofficially. I wouldn't have called him quite a Nephalim— who are a league of angels here in Atlas— but more of a shaman, seeking humanity's salvation. He really believed in your kind."

I have so many questions— like what specifically separates a second Age from a third, or when I get to speak with God himself. But before I can ask any of them, we pass through the thick solid gates and up the ascending carpet. The gold Spire of Atlas stations two of the winged-faced sentries at its double doors. My white crew neck and slacks stand out against their red robes and glinting helmets, marking me a prisoner to this elder's custody.

"So be straight with me," I say. "Am I about to be sentenced to some kind of eternal damnation?"

Siskett scoffs. We pass the guards and the double doors, and suddenly, I am too spellbound to hear the answer.

The hall inside the Spire possesses none of its exterior's golden flair. The floors are a purity of white that match the Avatar's chamber.

The walls extending from its foundations are also white at the base of impressionist paintings reaching high into the dome above. They begin half way up the spherical ceiling whose climax disappears in a tunnel of ever-evaporating glare. My eyes canvass parts of a visual history I'm too short to absorb in full, but puts Michaelangelo's Basilica to shame. I spot the Burning Spire— a silver ingot inside a bright pillar of flames on one side of the dome about twenty feet up. Another illustration depicts some sort of celestial being lobotomizing a spherical shape I can only assume is Earth.

Rejoining my escort and another, similarly-clad monk awaiting our arrival beyond the inner doors, my sight catches on a final painting etched not high above the Burning Spire. The dark figure flickers like a mirage in the desert of my emotions. Its horned head is complemented by deep crimson pupils that snarls at me over extended claws. Wings unbefitting of its size make the demon logistically incapable of flight, but are raised over its sunken, cavernous shoulders.

"Ramona," Siskett says, pulling my attention back to Earth. "This is Grand Maester Barrett, the head of our Order."

My eyes fall on the second elder, who must be even older than Siskett. Barrett's head is devoid of pigment; spots inhabit his receded hairline like a skin cancer patient, radiating white like the floors beneath him. His robes are shoddy as Siskett's, who tells me that he will leave us to get better acquainted. Once my original escort has vanished beyond the Spire's doorway, Barrett hangs his head with a slight smile on his lips.

"I sense you crave answers, child."

My former trepidation at this giant building falls away at his soft-spoken voice and eased posture. If I am due for some kind of hellacious punishment, Barrett does not let it show.

"What's with the demon?"

The question slips out before I am aware of asking it, and find my eyes constantly drifting up to its dark composure, casting long shadows over the commission's brighter imagery.

Barrett's smile widens.

"You are a student of history, then?"

"If you count reading the back of my history textbooks in high school for spoilers," I joke. The elder frowns, unable to relate. "Nevermind."

"The demon's name is Ziz," Barrett says, glossing over my nervous humor. "Although sealed at the First Age's end, his cult of followers were responsible for the Spire's burning at the end of the Second Age."

"So basically every time you beat him back, a new Age begins? Sounds like you guys live in a cycle of fear, doesn't it?"

"It is more nuanced than that. Each Age of Atlas represents a spectrum of social, technological and cultural change. Of course, change rarely happens without causation, which is what Ziz's forces represent. The threat of his return is always a consideration, but hasn't been a real concern for the Council in quite some time."

Despite Wilson/Siskett's assurances it is too simple to grasp my unique situation, my conversation with the Avatar returns to me as Barrett speaks.

Every organic lifeform is equipped with a unique genetic sequence, or identifier. These sequences are composed of billions of numbers. Some are enshrined, and cannot be changed; others are variable and subject to environmental factors.

"So what's the deal, then?"

"Pardon me?" the elder asks.

You have been summoned by the Grand Council. Its subpoena supersedes your genetic markers, which would place you in the Shroud.

I wasn't worthy enough to be placed here on my own merits.

"You obviously pulled me here for a reason. So no, Maester. I don't really crave any answers other than knowing what that reason is. I am not a child, but a grown fucking woman who would like to know why weird artificial intelligences think I belong in the realm of freaks, and I'm only here because of some weird subpoena!"

If Barrett is taken aback by a mortal's petty anger, it doesn't show. He doesn't flinch, nor does his finely trimmed beard bristle. He pouts momentarily, weighing the wealth of knowledge against his disposition of sharing none of it.

"Have you heard the story of David, Ramona?"

"Sure. He beat Goliath, became king."

"The Bible is a book of many diverse revelations. You have already seen how its words can be twisted by perverse souls."

"What's your point?"

Barrett sighs, annoyed having to explain such apparently basic things. In this city of golden gates and mysterious Maesters, nothing about this is basic. The world I know is gone, every explanation with it. From the moment I told Tim to reincarnate me, we set in motion a chain of events my home will never recover from.

I am complicit.

"You were a remarkable agent for the FBI. Yes, the Atlas knows very well of your exploits, Miss Knox. The Council is many things, but susceptible to change is not one of them. And seeing how you and our *infectorum mundi* were responsible for the Breach, it puts us in a unique position to make use of your mind and skills."

"Okay," I say. "First of all— *infectorum mundi*?"

"It means world-killer, as members of the Council have taken to calling him of late."

"And the Breach?"

Again, Barrett sighs at my ignorance.

"It is the term given to the catastrophic effects of the World-Killer reviving you. Obviously, it was compounded by several third-parties, making it irreversible, but its origin can be traced back to your return to the dead."

"So you're basically saying I owe you one?"

"Please," the Maester says, clearly offended by my oversimplification. "The Atlas does not resort to the petty transactions you mortals are so fond of. The Council has undergone a great deal of trouble, Miss Knox. Much of it lies with the *infectorum mundi,* but you also played a part.

"I will not split hairs with you. The Atlas faces a grave predicament, and seeks to utilize your talents and help us."

Escorted into the chamber I will face down celestial judgment for my actions, my old friend Tim's words return to me, replaying over and over in my clusterfuck of emotions until they finally, at last, mean nothing.

You don't need to be afraid, Ramona.

I wish they did mean something, because I have never been so damn scared.

CHAPTER FOUR

DESPITE VISITS FROM the man who called himself Death through my early life, many memories have nothing to do with him. The suited figure was only disposed to show up in times of crisis, as if I wouldn't have made it through without him. The reasons were varied— a broken leg, a lost animal companion, as I sat in a little white room after being caught shoplifting. They all followed that similar theme.

Tim was only interested in my sorrows and fuckups.

Most of my first memories are of Maya, who sat in the chair across the kitchen table from me. One leg folded over the other, a blue plume of cigarette smoke trailed from the stick between her fingers. I never took up smoking— insane, considering everyone I grew up around smoked— but the dancing smell of menthol filled the small room with sweet, distracting columns of monoxides washing above the words I struggled with.

Why can't I get this? I asked her. She was never the most emotional individual. Hugs were scarcely abundant, and nothing less than grievous harm brought her running. There wasn't a wall to Maya Stewart, thrown up to keep the world out. She was a simple woman who liked to smoke and watch *Wheel of Fortune*, but did not react to the insecurities of her fostered niece.

Am I stupid or something?

This place— Atlas, a wonder of gold and white pillars with red carpets and stone roads and stars above and below— renders me the equivalent of that six-year-old child. But instead of Maya and her menthol cigarettes, it is a robed elder who ignores my juvenile bewilderment, leading me into a chamber beyond the Spire's towering entryway.

The painted tower before the auditorium announces its authority to the city it rules. The inner chamber is more subtle — its ceilings are pitched lower than the iron ramparts running around the Spire, keeping undesirables out. Its central location makes sense, like placing the Joint Chiefs at the heart of the Pentagon, rather than on the outskirts. But this is no Pentagon or White House I've ever seen. It puts the most timeless Greek and Roman architecture to shame, with carved stone pillars forming a circle around the room's centerpiece, connected by a stone ring that links them.

The carvings depict many of the same events painted into the Spire's ceiling— the rise of Ziz, his downfall; the Nephalim uprising and the Burning Spire. The ground is soft beneath my feet like grass, but inspection proclaims this some kind of sorcery, as the surface is a dark marble. The ceiling is a dome; nowhere near as endless as the room before it, but its illusion of stars sparkling overhead reminds me of the Arcway where I was reincarnated.

The floor depresses into a rotunda in the room's center. The entrancing pillars precede two short steps downward on all sides, leading to a circular platform. Two steps up the northernmost side, five enormous chairs loom over the audience.

Barrett is silent, stopping before the beings who sit within those chairs. The second from the far right is empty. The other four are occupied by distinctive figures; one dressed like a Viking occupies the far left, with hollow white irises and a fiery beard. Another in the shape of a man is aglow, his flesh like glowing lava, his eyes yellow like a cat's. A woman with a head of snakes sits between them, hands gracefully in lap. Her skin-tight dress makes it hard to tell where the scantily-clad chest ends and beige fabric begins. The empty seat on the Fire Man's other flank divides him from an old man on the end with a flowing white beard. His hair and robes are a purity of white most people would probably associate with God Himself. His eyes remain closed, chin pointed to the ground, either waiting for the next item on the agenda to surface or too senile to keep up.

The Council's members are all enormous— the Viking alone must be twenty feet tall. All are unmoved by my presence. I am a fly on the wall, and they are inexplicably able to swat me from existence. My eyes drift to the empty chair as Barrett steps ahead of me to address this league of supreme beings.

"Your Eminences. I present Ramona Knox, as your summons requested."

I'm still waiting for someone to tell me this is a dream. The Maester bows his head, stepping out of the central circle toward the back of the room, leaving me to their judgement.

The room darkens like dimmed lights before a matinee, and everything falls quiet. The only source of light manifests from the Fire Man's glow. The red effect pours onto the snake woman's head, giving the creatures' snapping jaws another menacing layer. Some catch on others, and retaliate by biting the offending snakes' necks. One dies in the altercation— its severed head falls to the floor between her and the Fire Man. It struggles for last breaths before dissolving to ash and evaporating. The snoring old man at the end takes no notice of these proceedings and I find myself suddenly missing Barrett's presence.

Hell, even Tim would be welcome right now.

I shouldn't have run away from him.

"Ramona Knox," the Viking says, standing from his equally uncompromising chair. The floor groans under the enormous being's weight. Each step trembles the ground beneath my feet, and his voice booms through the auditorium. **"You are in the presence of the Grand Council of Atlas, standing on charges against the cosmic realms; as an accomplice to the World-Killer, and in failure to heed the infallibility of the natural order. How do you plead?"**

The amicable conversations with Maesters Siskett and Barrett are not present here. I have broken some sort of higher law, and Barrett's words return to me.

The Council has undergone a great deal of trouble, Miss Knox. Much of it lies with the infectorum mundi, *but you also played a part.*

"Guilty," I say, without a second to consider the consequences. "I was given a responsibility to save a little girl's life. The opportunity to do that arose, and I took it to save her. With all due respect, that was the job I signed up for, and I would do it again."

I don't know how much gods know about humanity's darkest depths. Even the most nonchalant, inattentive creator must have some idea we're a lot of fucking assholes. But from the moment the FBI told me to stop Jordan West, I gave everything to accomplish it— right down to my life.

The Viking is silent for a moment. The elder on the end rouses; it is short-lived, and he soons lowers his chin, returning to dozing.

"**Venicia.**"

The being's command hails the woman with a head of snakes to attention. She is smaller than him, but no less breathtaking; her dress ripples in standing to join his side.

"**Explain it to her**," the Viking commands.

The serpents doubling as strands of hair fall still when she speaks, hands clasped at her waist.

"Forgive him," she says, gesturing to her companion who takes his seat. "The Habinar is the chief justice of this Council. He is bound by duty to dispense rulings along lines which may no longer be relevant."

"What does that mean?" I ask. The Habinar, as Venicia christened him, lifts his peach-colored nose, looking over its end at me, clearly unimpressed with the present circumstances. Likewise, the Fire Man does not stir for inane questioning of matters beyond my understanding.

"It means this Council faces whispers of a greater threat than any we have ever faced. The Breach was only the beginning of a chain of events that have spun beyond this Council's grasp on basic security over Atlas, if there is a shred of truth to these rumors.

"This infrastructure has weathered eons of conflict," Venicia continues. "We have withstood demonic invasions and uprisings in the ranks of our very own Nephalim. Mistakes have been made, but control was ultimately maintained."

"Then," I reply, "what use do you possibly have for me?"

Venicia and the Habinar share a glance before she resumes. The snakes draping to her shoulders are nothing like her kind eyes and gentle voice, but vicious creatures that reflect the hard choices their kind are faced with.

"I will not lie, Miss Knox. This Council— despite its misgivings with the World-Killer and his accomplices— has watched your life with great interest. Our agents have analyzed your relationship with Death, and deduced investment in you was perhaps the most apt of his choices. Your handling of the Jordan West case gives the majority of this Council faith in your ability to help us."

The Fire Man has been quiet before now, other than his provision of light through the auditorium. The accent is unfamiliar from his silhouette of a mouth, which has no tongue and is completely black beyond non-existent lips. The closest I could place it is French.

"Venicia puts it lightly, mortal. The Seat of Atlas has consulted its sources, and the information coming from the ground level is...disturbing, to say the least."

Venicia does not appreciate the Fire Man's interruption— the snakes swing like little pendulums turning back to cast her glare at the slouching elemental being in his oversized stone chair.

"While Muerkher has a point, this is not yet a crisis. We are merely employing the most rigid of precautions."

The Fire Man scoffs.

"*Precaution*? We are talking about a coup against this Council, Venicia! The whispers aren't mistaken! The same ones who warned us about Tomas, yes? The children and varmints of Atlas, who predicted the Nephalim uprising! Are you say their warnings are circumspect?"

"Not at all, Muerkher," she retorts, not glancing back this time. "But panic is not a desirable trait in uncertain times. A steady hand must catch the whispers, or we risk empty air."

"Spare me your poetry, woman! This was your idea. I am *tentatively* backing your motion to involve this troublesome mortal, so tread carefully! You have Apollo's vote," the Fire Man says, pointing to the sleeping one, "but I'm not sure he's lucid enough to remember it!"

"Hold up," I interrupt. "So the sleeping guy is *not* God, right?"

At the look the three conscious beings and an empty chair return, this may not be the time for my insipid questions. I shake my head at the floor, and they resume fighting.

"So what do you suggest, Venicia? We send her against these rumors? You want to place our odds of survival in this little... *thing*? Seriously!"

"And what do *you* suggest, Muerkher? We sit idly by, waiting for these rumors to become fact? Or should we signal to our potential enemies we know of their plan, when we send the Royal Guard kicking down doors? Aumothera's sake, are you trying to start a city-wide conflict?"

Aumothera?

"No," Muerkher says, the lava-like glow brightening in intensity with each challenge from his peer. "But we might dispatch actual Nephalim to deal with this, rather than someone with no knowledge of how Atlas works, Venicia?"

"Considering the last uprising was thanks to Nephalim—"

"And how long are you going to bring up Tomas as a reason to sideline our most important line of defense?"

"Really, Muerkher?" Venicia snipes, finally snapping her gaze to his smug pout and crossed arms. "And should we get into *Gabriel*?"

The glowing man falls quiet. There is some truth to her invocation of this name. But it is a line in the sand for the Habinar, who has sat quietly by as they argued.

"The question seems to be whether we can trust this woman. She has been the cause of such trouble that were it up to me alone, she would warrant eternal damnation.

"Considering the threat this Council faces, I am compelled to break the tie." The Habinar stands once more, joining Venicia's side, towering over both of us. **"Let the mortal prove herself. No Nephalim has ever won the faith of Atlas without some kind of test— let her make amends before coming to a final decision."**

Venicia thinks on this.

"I agree. Muerkher?"

The Fire Man unhinges the left side of his jaw, moving the black hole that stands for his mouth.

"Very well. But make it challenging, at least?"

"It will be an appropriate task, but so too will she not be alone." She hangs on Muerkher's puzzled frown, letting him stew in wonder. "We will send Luca."

"*No!*" The Fire Man's face bunches, brightening his complexion even further. "That is cheating!"

"We can tell him to evaluate her," Venicia says. "Luca knows this city better than any Nephalim, and can wield a sword like few others. But he will not offer operational support. Is that sufficient, Muerkher?"

The Fire Man relents. Receiving a nod of encouragement from the Habinar, Venicia refocuses on me. She is sort of beautiful, were it not for the head of savage creatures that hunger for each other's blood.

"Very well, Miss Knox. You have been given a great opportunity to redeem yourself in the eyes of this Council. Maester Barrett and Luca will dispense the task expected of you. Should you be successful, return to this Council, and we will take the next steps."

Venicia and the Habinar take their seats. Muerkher's surface dims as the overhead lights resume, casting artificial cones of light over the rotunda. The Council members return to a dormant state; the Habinar's head falls to the side as Venicia, still clasping her hands around her lap, closes her eyes. Her head points to the floor, its snakes also fallen still. Apollo, who snoozed through the entire exchange, never moves.

Stunned by the events of the last few hours— if time is even a concept in this strange, wonderful place— I barely notice Maesters Barrett and Siskett behind me, waiting to travel wherever it is they dispense orders in the world of immortality.

"Are you ready?" Barrett asks.

For Aumothera's sake, not even close— whatever in the world an Aumothera is.

CHAPTER FIVE

I WAS NEVER A PRIME candidate for falling in love. Like anyone else, I was subject to my fair share of romantic movies that play on rainy Sunday nights while you drink entire bottles of red wine by yourself. You steal glances at the emphysematic aunt you must take care of; she took you in when a monster shot your mother at the bottom of a gravel pit.

You were only two, and faced a lifetime of punishment in the foster care system because both your parents were miserable fuck-ups. That woman saved you, and now slept as you hopelessly watched sappy films with only her oxygen-starved snores for company.

Those movies were all the same to some degree. There was a flawed, hunky man who seemed incapable of holding down a modicum of relationship-material values. Enter the independent dame with a questionable disposition who's been hurt one too many times. She's a career woman, because any movie with a shred of common sense makes her more than a kitchen-bound housewife. They meet and immediately dislike each other. They keep crossing paths— soon enough, all the whores in the world can't compare to her. All the unfulfillment of her career is offset by him, and we're off to the fucking races.

Other than the career-woman template, I was completely beyond those stereotypes. The only men I attracted were flies looking for shit to land on and lay all their eggs of insecurity. My only other companion was a celestial being who came and went as he pleased, manipulating me all the way.

The World-Killer, they call him now.

I doubt Maesters know much about romantic subplots; all mine are hay-wire, better left unmentioned. The last man I dated turned out to be complicit in a child abduction scheme. But now I'm in Oz, planes of existence away from Ryan Royce's vile associations. In a wonderland they call Atlas, I am Alice, tumbling down the rabbit hole of the supreme realm's dimensions.

The city of Atlas is divided into uneven districts called quadrants. Their proportions put each closer to an eighth of the circular floating city which, as Siskett and Barrett take turns explaining, are usually named for a major landmark within them.. There's the Observatory District and the Coliseum District which is home to the contradictorily-named Arena.

The Cathedral and Coliseum Districts sandwich the Observatory behind the Seat and Spire where the Council resides. The three northern neighborhoods are surrounded on either side by two more districts called the Light and Dark Quadrants— home to the angel statues symmetrically guarding the enclaved Spire.

"The Dark Quadrant," Siskett explains, "is also home to the notorious soul prison, Stone Mountain."

Entering the Atlas's Observatory district, the winding stair is low to the ground, immaculately kept despite the horizon beyond it. There is no blue sky over the Observatory like above the Spire, but a panorama of stars leading down into an endless nebula.

"And the Light Quadrant?"

"Mostly residential," Barrett answers as we draw closer to the domed structure at the pathway's peak. The building's open iron doors are similar to the Spire, leading through a short hallway before arriving at a second set. A stone fountain is set on a plateau halfway up the staircase — its spouting centerpiece is the same god depicted in the Spire walls, offering cupped palms from which water plunges to the frilled basin below it.

Ascending the stairs, a silhouette emerges between the spread doors on the paved hilltop leading inside. I squint to see them, but cannot make out the newcomer.

"Ah, there's Luca now!"

The first thing to come into focus is the giant broadsword with a golden hilt. It protrudes outward from his hip where the blade is sheathed on a sheepskin belt. The armor matches his compatriots at the gates of Atlas, though without the winged helmet. A set of bleached wings protrude from his shoulder blades. They are magnificent, arching away from his golden blond hair and down. He looms over all of us— nowhere as large as the Habinar or Muerkher, but at least eight feet tall.

"Hello, Luca!" Barrett cheerily calls as we make our approach. Wary of strangers, I remain in back, trying to be observant. "Has the Council informed you of today's task?"

"Yes," the blond man says, hand rested on the enormous hilt pointed in front of him. "Everything is ready, Maester."

Barrett turns to me.

"Luca is one of the Council's most trusted generals. He is not a Nephalim, due to personal matters that have barred his line from taking up the privilege. He holds special status as the Council's military advisor."

"I see."

"Luca will be assessing you today— seeing if your skills can be useful to the Council's predicament."

"And what will this...assessment consist of?"

The angel grimaces.

"I understand you are new to Atlas. Therefore, I have no way of knowing how much misinformation you are in possession of. So you might be slightly in the dark. All I can tell you is, much like your realm, there are...competing interests at work."

"'Competing interests'?"

Barrett takes over— Siskett has drifted to the background, nothing more to offer than his company.

"As we discussed in the Spire, Atlas has a storied and conflicted history. We have spoken somewhat of Ziz, and the ever present threat he poses to all Creation—"

"His followers are the more dangerous threat," Luca offers. "They are of many factions. For a long time, the Council was preoccupied with the common population—terrorist cells, religious fanatics and cults in service to Ziz. But since the Third Age began, the Nephalim uprising that led to the Spire's fall is a heavy consideration."

"And that's not even considering the latest events," Barrett interjects. "The Nephalim have been badly compromised. There are too many factors operating against them to trust them with protecting the Council any longer."

"What have they done that's so terrible? I mean, these are supposed to be your best men, aren't they?"

Even asking it, I am flooded with memories of the FBI's "best men" as they sided with Stephen Hardwick, gunning down their non-complicit colleagues when the truth came out.

"The Nephalim were largely responsible for the Spire's burning," Luca begins, but is interrupted by Barrett.

"*One* Nephalim, Luca. It does not change the fact, however. Despite being forged from perfection, they are still partly human, and can never be perfect."

"Indeed," Luca concedes. "Many of them have fallen to depraved ambitions or insanity. Tomas led the uprising to free Ziz. Gabriel stopped him, at great cost to himself—"

"But even Gabriel has now disappeared," Barrett adds. "Worse, he may be partially responsible for the current situation on Earth. Then there was Jonah, who was entrusted with the remains of Aumothera— which you may know as the Shroud."

That's one mystery solved, at least.

"The point is, I have no doubt the remaining Nephalim are men of integrity," Luca adds, "but they are too deep. They have been subject to politics too long. Sides have been taken, one way or another. There is no way to assure loyalty to their corrupted brother doesn't remain."

"That is correct. Which brings us to your trial, Ramona."

"Yes. You and I will venture to Devil's Corner to deal with a Whisperer who may have information."

"Alright," I say at last. "What is a Devil's Corner, and what the hell is a Whisperer?"

"Devil's Corner is a district of Atlas," Luca frowns. "It is home to many nefarious cults and criminals."

"So you allow cults and criminals in Atlas?"

"Like we said...competing interests. They weren't always criminals, but have proven notoriously difficult to rid ourselves of."

"Alright. And the Whisperers?"

"Information dealers for the Council," Barrett offers, "but not always working at the Council's behest. They are underhanded, extremely self-serving. If they feel threatened, Ramona, they will lash out."

"And why would they feel threatened?"

"Because," Luca says, gripping his hilt tighter in discomfort, "this is no underhanded backroom deal, but a conspiracy of an unprecedented magnitude, and we must uncover it before we have real problems."

"What Luca means, Ramona," Barrett says, "is these Whisperers fear for their souls. This is much worse than Stone Mountain threatens them with. Whatever has them scared, they will not cooperate lightly. You must find this Whisperer, and make him tell you what he knows. We will station Royal Guard nearby, but they are operating on a need-to-know basis. They know virtually nothing about this operation."

"It's a risk," Luca says, "but we can't be certain they are to be trusted. Do you understand, Ms. Knox?"

I do. But looking beyond the Observatory, into a wasteland of twilight and questions beyond my ken, I can only nod.

"Very good. Maesters, we will rendezvous with you later. Miss Knox and I have a Whisperer to hunt down."

• • • •

JUST AS THE ANGEL DESCRIBED, Devil's Corner is a hodge-podge of sketchy figures, hooded faces and dark alleys. It sits west of the Spire, and has two entrances, just as its sister neighborhood God City does on the Spire's eastern starboard. We enter by heading west out of the Observatory District. The adjacent Cathedral District shares none of the warped nebular vista, despite bordering the same northern end of Atlas. Just like the sky over the Spire, an illusionary blue gives impressions of a flawless day.

"And that is the Cathedral," Luca explains. The church-like structure is smaller than its cousin Observatory. Its facade is better maintained— though it may have something to do with not sitting at the foot of infinite space, being shrunken by it. Several youngsters help a Maester in the late stages of life to his feet, limping into the Cathedral. Another robed elder sits on a tree stump, teaching another group of youths from a leatherbound book.

"Home of the Maesters' order. The Cathedral used to house the Avatar of Light. After the invasion by Ziz in the First Age, the Council had the Avatar moved."

"To those weird boxes at the gate?"

Luca chuckles.

"No. We would not place the Avatar in a place it could be so easily compromised."

"Siskett told me it was an artificial intelligence."

"The Avatar is so much more than that. The Maesters underplay its significance— without her, the world would be covered in eternal night. In creating her, the Council placed all its eggs in a single basket, so to speak."

Luca explains the Light's essence used to be divided into three, and was held by certain members of the Council. This led them to become targets; thus, the Avatar was created to both house and personify the Light.

"Make no mistake," Luca warns. "Were the wrong people to control the Avatar, all of Creation would fall at risk."

"Like Ziz?" I ask. We pass down a cobblestone road shouldered by gardens of lilacs, petunias and tulips swaying in the artificial breeze. I don't mean to keep mentioning him— ever since I saw the paintings of the Burning Spire, he has fascinated me. Luca shakes his head. We pass through a stone gate with two Royal Guards on either side. Their spears' blunt end are held to the road, pointing lethal tips skyward.

"Of course. Many newcomers to Atlas are interested in the Dark Lord. We have not seen his face in thousands of years, and yet, his presence is everywhere. Many worship him in private— others...less privately."

"And does the Council do anything about this?"

"Of course," Luca says. "We remain vigilant. Kicking doors down is somewhat of a last resort. The Atlas values order; inciting people over rumors is counter-productive. Here we are. Devil's Corner."

Stone gates through the Cathedral district's southern arch see the transparency of outer Atlas regress into snaking buildings and the alley-like streets on either side of us. A dark cloud overhead paints the district's slick streets in a coat of glare. Numerous figures pass each other with few words, moving about their business, eyes to the ground. There are almost no Royal Guard— the quadrant is left to fend for itself, as if it once proved too troublesome.

"Keep your guard up," Luca cautions, hand on the hilt of his oversized sword. "This is not a welcoming place, Miss Knox."

"Please. Enough of the Miss Knox business, okay? Call me Ramona. Tell me about the Whisperer."

"Fellow named Gossamer. Unsure of a surname. Maybe it is his surname. In any case, he is a snake."

"What makes you say that?"

"Once a soul comes to Atlas, they have two choices— remain in Atlas for good, or eventually pass onto the White Light, seeking eternal peace. Most choose to go eventually, unless you are the Council or a Maester. Time has a way of shrivelling the most persistent souls who endlessly stay here."

"And Gossamer is one of them?"

"Yes," Luca replies. "He has remained here for hundreds of years, when the strongest and most foolhardy usually last a few decades. It has made him wicked, even among Whisperers, who are known for underhandedness."

We pass a mother in ragged clothing, breastfeeding her suckling infant, cross-legged against a soiled brick wall. Her eyes are sunken, and her bottom lip peels at my curiosity as she lifts her head, revealing a row of blackened teeth. Others like her are similarly rundown, reminiscent of crack addicts. Veins protrude from gaunt arms where healthy limbs should conceal them.

"Why do these people look so rough?" I ask the angel. Luca seems to glide beside me as we turn down the right side of a forked road, where more snaking streets await.

"This area has been overrun by worshippers of Ziz. Those who choose to remain here are at the mercy of his draining essences to sustain a minimal strength. Rather than accept his fate and sleep, the demon is fitful, aspirations stoked by his followers.

"I see the look on your face, Ramona. The one asking why we don't just crush them out of existence. But that is a slippery slope, isn't it? Once the witch hunts begin, it's hard to say how far they go."

"So instead, you quarantine his followers."

"In a manner of speaking. Those who should not be here are wel-come to leave, but I fear other factors keep them. Associations with cults, family, et cetera. It's really all we can do until there is firm evi-dence to round them up."

"Okay. So what does this asshole look like?"

The obscenity clearly puzzles Luca, but he says nothing of it.

"Whisperers wear black robes and masks. Many are like Gos-samer, and have chosen to remain in Atlas beyond reasonable expira-tion, so they cover their faces. Gossamer is known as Fox, due to his mask."

"So he's wearing a fox mask?"

"You could say that. Come on." I scale my pace to match his as Luca leads us to an intersection of thin buildings with stained win-dows and we pass through its shadow-laden alleyway to reach the next one. More sunken people stand on adjacent street corners, not particularly helpful or productive to their cause. Families huddle to-gether and old men pull wagons full of crosses and literature. One yells as he pulls the bucket on wheels, praying for the return of Ziz like Devil's Corner itself is on fire.

Luca peers around his cover— one of the S-shaped apartment (*condo? crack house?*) buildings offers the corner with a perfect view of his target. Peeking over the man's giant shoulder only affords a glimpse of my own.

Down the road stands a man in a black robe, and I understand Luca's hesitancy regarding the mask. It looks like a child carved it, more closely resembling a badly-beaten bulldog. Leather slippers poke out the robe's bottom, and he rarely sways, preferring to prac-tice standing perfectly still.

"There," Luca says. "That's Gossamer. For the sake of simplicity, I should remain here. He will see me coming a hundred yards away, and panic. Rightly so, as I have arrested him on several occasions."

Guess these people have never heard of wearing a disguise. Resolved to avoid eternal damnation, I keep my mouth shut.

"Alright," I reply. "What's the play?"

Playing law enforcement for a realm of existence I couldn't fathom days ago should feel strange, but is just a given. With his chiseled jaw, loose blond hair and light gray eyes, the angel strikes me as handsome.

"You must get Gossamer's attention. Tell him you're a courier on behalf of the Red Brotherhood. He will ask you to prove it, so tell him 'the red wind blows in the west'. It is their code phrase, used to communicate with the Whisperers."

"How do you know that?"

Luca grimaces.

"Because I used to be one of them. Now go."

"Wait!" I say. "What do I say after that?"

The angel is already gone. Muttering, I shake my head and break from the wall, crossing cobbled road to where the cloaked figure waits on a raised sidewalk. Men with the devil wagons drag their eternal sense of duty on, and I have to navigate them to reach the Whisperer. He is even stranger-looking up close, with purple markings— tattoos, like Mehndi art— long settled over his naked hands.

"Whisperer?" He is slow to face me, as if I've crossed some moral line approaching him. "I have a message from the Red Brotherhood."

The reply is raspy, like he hasn't taken a drink of water in weeks. Gossamer tells me to prove it. Looking into the crude fox mask, I tell the man that the "red wind blows in the west".

"*That*," the Whisperer says, "has not been the Red Brotherhood's communique in a few months. Who sent you? Really? Tell me, or you will deal with the Crimson League!"

Shit. Luca gave me faulty intel, and he's tipped off. There's no time for another reaction— I cock my fist, slugging Gossamer in the mask. The thin plastic crumples inward. The Whisperer screams with the sound of his popping nose, clutching his face cover— it falls away, revealing a pruned face. Beady black jewels serve as eyes above albino skin dripping fresh blood from the Whisperer's nose. There is almost no hair atop the head cowering behind his snaky arms.

I kick out; the force of my foot snaps his brittle kneecap, bringing Gossamer down a notch in humility. Thrusting my elbow into his exposed jaw sends him to the ground for good measure.

"Now," I say, as he writhes at my feet, "I might be new here sir, but I have learned one thing for certain. And that is, certain men think they have all the answers. Information is a medal to them. They wear their possession of it on their sleeve, but don't tell you what it means. They hoard it, but only to use it as a status symbol.

"From what I understand, Gossamer, you and your brethren are such men. You deal in whispers and silly little secrets, then turn around and weaponize them if it suits you. So let's make one fucking thing clear right now."

Gossamer's cries have attracted the attention of several people. Many are ordinary citizens of Devil's Corner, namely the old men pulling wagons past the Whisperer's corner. But others— wearing red cowls and the opaque sneers behind them, who weren't visible a moment ago— slowly draw around us.

"I know you have information on a threat to the Council, Whisperer. You can help me, or make the next step uncomfortable."

"*You* are the one who will be uncomfortable! Wretched wench! Who do you think you are? **The Crimson League will eat you alive!**"

One of the cloaked figures reaches the corner where Gossamer cowers under me. A hand grabs my cocked arm, yanking my attention off the Whisperer.

"Is there a problem here, woman?"

The eyes of Gossamer's friend are unlike any I've ever seen. A deep red film infects natural hazel, giving the irises a menacing glow.

The skin around them is rough and sunken with the texture of scales. His fingernails dig into my suspended wrist, slightly piercing the flesh of my arm.

"Not at all. Care to let go?"

"You are threatening a Whisperer," the cloaked figure informs me. "That is not taken lightly in many places, least of all here. State your business, or face summary execution."

"Summary execution? I thought I was already dead."

The cloaked figure smirks. Gossamer fidgets at my feet, gloating at my new predicament.

"You must be new here. Death is still a very real prospect in Atlas, but it is more than death. It is purging every trace of you from existence. Your relatives won't remember you. The world would never know you were here."

"Joke's on you," I quip. "I haven't made that many impressions on people."

Before the cloaked figure can scowl at my lame humor, a gruff voice commands him to release me. With his gleaming sword drawn, Luca offers an offensive stance. His white-knight complex stands out in the drab and dreary disposition of Devil's Corner— many in the surrounding area are familiar with the angel, and scurry away before they can be implicated.

"Ah," the cloaked man says. "I should have known."

"Let her go, Demetrius."

The man whose sharp fingernails dig into my wrist guffaws, releasing his grip. Pulling back my hand, several marks are embedded in its skin.

"Have you come to rescue your pet, Luca? Maybe you should train a gerbil better before you send it after the snake."

"Your friend is a snake, alright," the angel retorts. "He is only lucky to call vermin like you his friends."

Demetrius giggles. The retracted lips reveal a mouthful of broken, jagged teeth.

"Your insults have no value here! The Crimson League will not stand for this harassment from the Atlas, let alone an agent who couldn't cut it as a Nephalim. Isn't that right, Luca, son of Tomas? Hmm?"

The taunt is clearly meant to rile up the angel, but Luca remains calm.

"I do not wish to fight you, Demetrius. Despite whatever delusions you and your friends may have, I have better things to do. So make a choice, but make it fast."

The cloaked figure jeers at me, but ultimately concedes. His reinforcements are dispelled by receding shadows, bringing the other red hoods into focus.

"Very well, Luca, son of Tomas. Your father may have been a traitor, but he didn't raise a fool. Just...keep an eye on your pet? Wouldn't want the Whisperers to think Atlas has come for their secrets."

"Wouldn't dream of it," Luca says, motioning me to walk with him. We return the way we came, moving quickly to establish distance from Demetrius.

"So that's it?" I ask. "You're just going to let him win?"

Luca chuckles.

"On the contrary, Ramona. Demetrius gave us everything we need."

"He did? Because all I got from that was that he wiped the floor with you."

"It is more nuanced than that. Demetrius is a small fish in a large sea. It also includes the Whisperers, but the fact the Crimson League is white-faced over our intervention can only mean one thing."

"Which is?"

Luca shakes his head, sheathing his sword as we return toward the Cathedral. "It means we would be wasting our time on the Crimson League. There is a better source of information if they are involved. Come. There is no time to waste."

• • • •

LUCA'S MISSION LEADS up and over the Seat of Atlas. We retrace our steps past the Cathedral and Arena Districts. The Arena is quiet in the distance— each district seems to have a unique shade of sky overhead, and the Coliseum District's swirling purples remind me of the Shroud where I awoke to Tim's pleas. The thought is soon wiped away; another arch brings us down into God City— Devil's Corner's polar opposite, and simultaneous fraternal twin.

The sky is a pleasant blue here. Concrete gardens sprout remarkable varieties of blue, purple and yellow flora stretching outward beneath thick trunks lining the cobblestone road. Purple-leaf plum leaves and crabapple trees create the illusion of a lively grove under which the district's nobles pass. Dressed in gorgeous white and silver robes, their hair is brushed and clean, beards groomed and much better versed in social etiquette than the low-brow stares and scowls in the western district.

"You really think we're going to find our man here?" I ask Luca as he scans passing faces for the one he knows.

"The Crimson League is running scared," he explains, "but their involvement points to one man who may be able to help us."

"Seems too nice a place for such lowlives to conspire."

"Much like your own world, there are benefactors and beneficiaries. The true conspirators operate in shadow. The Crimson League could never pull this off by themselves. It is proven that one of the senior Maesters has ties to the criminal underworld in Atlas."

"And the Council just lets him run around, doing whatever he wants?"

"They have never found a smoking gun that he is actively helping them, or Quorroc would have long been thrown in the dungeons.

Wherever the Crimson League operates, he is never known to be far. If we can bring him in, it will avoid a confrontation with Demetrius, but help us understand the League's current plans."

Luca slows, and my eyes follow until they see what he does. An elder dressed like Barrett and Siskett sits with a group of youngsters. Many of the children can't be older than ten, gathered at his feet as he sits perched on a bench under one of the crab-apple trees.

"You ready?" the angel asks.

"It's your show, boss."

Luca says nothing, gripping his sword's hilt and walking ahead to join the elder entertaining children with the wildest lore he can muster for them. He speaks with his hands, something that does not stop with Luca's approach. Quorroc immediately notices the angel and stands to argue, waving those frail hands about in protest.

After a few moments of hoarse rebuke, Quorroc agrees to accompany him. Both men pass me without a word; the angel keeps a hand wrapped around the Maester's arm, who looks ready to squirm out of Luca's grasp. I feign a smile at confused children watching their favorite storyteller carted off. None return it.

Whatever challenge the Council saw in pairing me up with Luca feels short. Tired of the kids burning holes through my forehead with Bambi eyes, I follow Luca and Maester Quorroc toward the Spire. The elder limps; the angel pulls him along.

With such capable soldiers, it is hard to establish why the Council actually needs a failed FBI agent.

Sooner or later, their reasons must become clear.

CHAPTER SIX

WHEN I WAS YOUNG, MAYA kept a host of male companions. Many were short-lived, not good for more than a lively night and some diminishing returns later on. A few became violent when Maya's antadonic outlook didn't cater to their ideas of control and mistreatment of women. Some were able to hide it better than others, and it took my aunt longer to establish the *seance* would not work out. All of them became angry as they realized the jig was up. They all mistreated her to some degree— those fellows were just better at hiding narcissism than their brasher peers were at withholding violence.

And still, there was the odd one who *almost* stuck around— who was *nearly* good enough to envision taking a shot at a real family. Of course, we would never be a real family. I was still adopted, and any attempt at trying to pass for something genuine would be forever hindered by imposter-hood.

But to an eight-year-old— an orphan being raised by her chain smoking, somber relative at that— *any* family was a good family. Any man who might come along, and be the diligent, doting figure I wanted my own father to be was welcome. There were almost-those and those I really wanted to fill that void, but something always ended it.

It wasn't until adulthood that I learned such a thing could never exist. My own relationships— Ben Crawlstead from high school, Kevin Breckinmeyer in college and Ryan Royce as a fledgling agent at the Bureau— only reinforced my inability to love and be loved by men.

So many years past that stupid, irresponsible, childish dream, Luca and Barrett escort me before the four celestial beings to decide my fate. Muerkher and the Habinar remain seated. Apollo is still firmly asleep, snoring in his chair. The fifth is empty, and Venicia is in full control of these proceedings. The snakes of her head are still, as if warned not to make a scene. Her pale skin benefits from the Fire Man's natural light as the room darkens.

"Luca," she says as we enter the middle rotunda. "What have you learned?"

The angel of Atlas grimaces— and at this moment, Luca, son of Tomas, should be nothing less than a Nephalim. He plays the part, despite family history that prevents him taking up the mantle.

"The Whisperer was protected by the Crimson League, Your Eminence."

"The Crimson League," Venicia repeats. "Quorroc, then?"

Luca nods.

"I have brought the Maester in for questioning. As you can imagine, he is none too pleased— yelled the whole time about being framed."

"Let him work it out of his system," Barrett advises. "Quorroc will talk if he wants to go home tonight."

The Habinar speaks from his chair. His ire is unmistakably earmarked for Venicia, but he does not remove his beady eyes from me.

"I warned you about this."

"Yes, Habinar," Venicia says. "I cannot argue that. Quorroc has played too many games. We must find out what he knows."

"We stand ready to hand Quorroc over to the Arbiters at Stone Mountain if he is unwilling to cooperate. I don't think it will come to that," Luca promises, "but I have no intention of letting him have his freedom without something in return."

"Quorroc is a crafty old lizard," Muerkher remarks. "He will say whatever must be said to point you away from him. The information will be correct, no doubt, but only accomplish so much."

"That is also true," Venicia says. "And what of the woman, Luca? Does she exhibit the qualities for what I'm considering?"

Luca glances at me. I squint, trying to figure out their endgame, buried somewhere within cryptic conversation.

"Yes, my liege," Luca replies, turning back to the snake-haired woman. "I believe she does."

Muerkher shakes his head.

"I still say this is preposterous."

"Your concern has been duly noted," the Habinar interrupts from the end. **"Venicia is right. The Nephalim have been sidelined too long, to our collective detriment. We cannot undo Tomas' actions, same as we can no longer change Gabriel's. The Nephalim need a new face, so that they may regain their honor."**

"Yes, my liege," Luca repeats. "I fully agree."

I can't help but feel like an imposter. *He* should be the one rebranding the Nephalim, not me. I am the smallest of mortals, who happened to expose the greatest hoax in FBI history by a fluke—friendship with a celestial being who manipulated me from the beginning.

"Very well," Muerkher concedes. Venicia instructs the Fire Man to wake the dozing elder to his right. Muerkher snaps his pointed red fingers— Apollo begins to feel his seat warm, waking in senile anger.

"One more time, Flame Head!" the old man shouts before reverting to a dozed slump. Muerkher reaches over, shaking him. Apollo rouses, looking around, asking what he missed.

"Step forward, Ramona."

With a reassuring nod from Luca, I inch forward as asked. The glow provided by Muerkher's complexion is absorbed in a circular path of light around my feet, drenching my shoes and legs in a cone that soaks me in glare from head to toe. Inside that cone of light, thousands of stars— if not millions— line its seams and center, casting nebulous streaks into dazzling combinations of green and yellow, pink and blue. Inside its swirling center, bright rings of light loop around certain combinations until the middle outer edges resemble photos of the Milky Way galaxy.

"The Nephalim," Venicia says, "are a noble group of warriors whose members' actions have led their integrity astray. For that reason, they have been sidelined from their sworn duty to protect this Council from the multitude of threats it faces. But today is a new day, the start of a new era, and that begins with you.

"To be Nephalim is to dedicate your life to the security and safety of Atlas. Moreso, it is to be a tool of this Council, whenever asked, in whatever measure we see fit to defend this realm. It is not a political post, nor a glorious one."

Muerkher rises from his chair, joining Venicia's side. The light cast by his flesh is no match for the illusion stemming beneath my shoes.

"To be Nephalim," the Fire Man continues, "is to exist for Creation's greater good. It is to uphold the commandments of Atlas, and see justice done against its transgressors."

Following a moment of silence, Muerkher clears his throat, calling on the sleepy elder. The flowing white beard and bow-legged walk are somewhat comical as he joins his peers.

"To be Nephalim," Apollo rasps, holding up a bony, impotent finger, "is to...is to..."

"Defend against shadow," Venicia reminds him.

"Defend against shadow! Defend against shadow! To be Nephalim, yes. You must defend the shadows."

"Against the shadows," the Fire Man corrects.

Before Apollo can amend himself, the Habinar steps between Venicia and Muerkher, puffing out his enormous chest. His custom double-headed ax drags behind him.

"To be Nephalim is to stand with the greatest protectors of the cosmic realms. Evil has a way of infiltrating each, from Atlas itself to the remains of Aumothera. It is your duty to stand

against this darkness; to be the last man or woman standing against it. And when its tendrils overtake the world, you will be our last line of defense."

"These are the expectations," Venicia says.

"To defend the realms—" Muerkher continues.

"And stake your soul on its survival."

"To set an example for our allies—"

"And put a second thought in the heads of those who would endanger all of Creation."

"Do you understand, Ramona?" Venicia asks.

I don't completely, but it is hard to argue with twenty-foot beings charging you with defending all of existence. With a supportive glance from Luca, I nod.

"I do."

"Then it will be done. By the power of this Grand Council, you are hereby appointed a Nephalim."

"Enforcer of realms," Muerkher says.

"Guardian of the light," Venicia adds.

"Eternal protector of all Creation," the Habinar finishes.

With his final words, the path of light closes around me, burning my skin as it seeps inward, absorbed within darkness I have always welcomed.

"Congratulations," Venicia says. "No mortal has ever crossed the line between living and Nephalim. But that is a sign of the trust this Council has placed in you. You must restore the Nephalim to their former glory, so they might protect Atlas once more."

"Your first assignment," the Habinar says, "is to accompany Luca to question Maester Quorroc. No doubt he can shed light on this conspiracy."

I will save my doubts for the angel at my side. The funnel of light has completely disappeared, leaving the room solely lit by the Fire Man's glow.

"I will not let you down," I promise.

• • • •

THE NEPHALIM ARE HOUSED between the main gate of Atlas and the Seat, in their own district called the Barracks. Makes sense. Barrett says he must return to the Cathedral to brief the other Maesters on my appointment as Luca and I make out for the Barracks.

The sky has taken an overcast tone over the God's Road, but I try not to let the gray detract from Atlas' beauty. The large golden gates where I emerged from my conversation with the Avatar still seem huge, but are not our destination.

"He likes you," Luca says as we stroll alongside each other. I am more comfortable with the angel— his presence is a calming one, and he is not hard on the eyes, either.

"Who?"

"Barrett."

"He does, does he?"

"The old man is among the longest-serving Maesters. He has spoken for years of going off to seek the White Light, but something kept him, I think."

"Something?" I ask. "Like what?"

"Hard to say," Luca replies. "Barrett has seen many terrible times during his tenure. Maybe, he was waiting for something to restore his confidence in Atlas."

"The Maester is not confident in Atlas?"

The angel smirks, but does not reply. We pass through the God's Road, almost knocking shoulders with denizens strolling up and down its lengths. Just after the arch leading to Devil's Corner is a smaller stone gate, manned by two Royal Guards.

"These are the Barracks," he says. "It once held political prisoners before the Council built the prison in the Dark Quadrant. Interrogations still occur in this sector, but Stone Mountain ensures they cannot escape afterward."

Luca explains many of the structures in Atlas were composed in the Second Age— there's the Stone Mountain prison and the angel statues on either side of the Seat. The Arena is one of the original structures untouched by Ziz's original invasion of Atlas, but it was damaged during the Nephalim uprising.

Inside the Barracks, red and white temples built along the sides remind me of feudalist Chinese architecture. A pair of Royal Guards is stationed outside each. A stone-laid courtyard divides the six temples on either side by tens of feet. At its top lies an enclosed staircase leading up to a central administration building reminds me of the FBI headquarters in Washington. It betrays the surrounding Far East aesthetic for a six-story brick structure. The Nephalim headquarters is defended by twin platoons— perfect rows of upward-pointing spears wait on either side.

"Lots of security here," I remark.

"The Nephalim have not been in a good way for some time. One reason for the security is keeping them within their bounds, while someone else might tell you they are mistrustful now. There is no black and white answer."

"And I'm supposed to fix this?"

The angel chuckles.

"One day at a time."

• • • •

ACCORDING TO LUCA, Maester Quorroc is held on the second floor of the central building— but first, we must deal with the formalities. The main administration is called the Obelisk. Many questions reserved for my companion are answered in its lobby's hand drawn tapestry.

Flawless depictions of the Nephalim's history painted on the Obelisk's walls show its angelic warriors in golden armor; depicted fighting a multi-eyed demon that resembles an octopus in one slide, a giant serpent in another. In a further tapestry, they battle what looks to be a rotting alligator. But the one at the top— much like the Burning Spire and Ziz— has all my attention.

The creature is massive, with a snarling grin of razor sharp stacilites meeting the stalagmites below them. Yellow eyes pour darkness from its soul, out of the painting, over the room. The snout between its tiny, terrible eyes and the even more terrible teeth is long and accentuated by seething nostrils. A long barbed tail obstructs massive haunches as the creature confronts the much smaller Nephalim of yore.

A dragon.

"A Behemoth," Luca explains. "Defenders of Atlas before the Council turned to less volatile creatures like men. But even men have a beast or two inside them."

"What happened to them? The Behemoths?"

Before Luca can answer, a similarly-dressed angel approaches from the main hall's western quadrant. The man joining us has cropped dark hair in contrast to Luca's, but they are otherwise similarly built.

"Luca," the newcomer says. "Who have we here?"

"Pol, this is Ramona. The Council has designated her the newest Nephalim."

"Bollocks," Pol says. "A woman can't be a Nephalim! This is...blasphemy!"

"Afraid not. The Nephalim have been viewed in a negative light since my father's rebellion. You and I both know they cannot forever be defined by the actions of a rogue few."

"And appointing women as Nephalim is how the Council seeks to solve this?"

"When you put it like *that*, Pol, it seems you *want* the Nephalim to remain outcasts."

Pol relents. I don't amount his attitude to misogyny, so much as a wariness of outsiders. I could have been a red-headed lumberjack and he would have taken issue.

"Very well. I suppose she will need to speak with the High Priestess. Seraphina will want to orient her in the Nephalim's procedures and expectations, no doubt."

"That is all well and fine, Pol," Luca says, "but right now, we are on an urgent task for the Council, and must make haste. We are here to speak with the prisoner brought in earlier. Maester Quorroc. You know he is here?"

"Yes. The Guard brought him in an hour ago. I was here, wondering what purpose the Council saw in keeping one of its scholars locked up."

"Merely for questioning, Pol. May we pass?"

The dark-haired angel mockingly bows, holding out his open hand.

"After you, my liege. Just make sure to see Seraphina on your way out."

• • • •

MAESTER QUORROC IS a small man. Not in the physical sense— at nearly six feet, the robed elder's sleeves hang over his hands. Bad posture diminishes a considerable chunk of his height. Thin arms lend doubt to whether he has the upper body strength to pull an empty kiddie wagon, let alone fight another human being. His beard is white and scraggly, and something in his smoke-colored eyes suggests a petty, defeated soul lives inside them.

The portal used as a one-way mirror to a doorless room on the wall's other side is like nothing I have ever seen. A young fellow with long, braided hair stationed in the room's far corner uses his strange brand of sorcery, conjuring a rippling blue mirror against the opposite brick wall. In its transparent imagery, Quorroc waits with eyes closed.

"Can he see us?" I ask.

Luca shakes his head.

"Negative. Elion here is capable of powerful illusions, allowing glimpses and passage over short distances. But he is not powerful enough to transmit in both directions. Some of the more experienced Magi may be able to, but Elion is young, yet."

Add Magi and their weird powers to the list of questions for later. I return to Quorroc, whose slight smile teases knowledge of something.

The man is all too willing to bide his time.

"So how do you want to play this?"

"Why not show him what you're capable of? After all, you are one of us now, hmmm?"

The intrusive voice pulls my attention from the Maester. A woman— whose very height could only be described as freakish— with red hair and a square jaw appears in the doorway. Elion's mirage fades as he stands at attention, arms by his sides. A robe that matches her hair trails behind her as she glides in through the open door.

"High Priestess Seraphina," the woman says. "Spiritual leader of the Nephalim, Goddess of Unparalleled Beauty and Keyholder of the Light.

"I understand you have recently taken the Oath. How stunning and brave, isn't it? In the Nephalim's darkest hour, the Council should appoint a *woman* to save us from ourselves? How romantic! But then again, there are *some* who might be displeased by such a sudden elevation to power, hmmm?"

Glancing at my companion only merits a sullen nod. History between them is evident, but the Priestess pays little attention to Luca, so fixated on me I think she may be coming on as she leans in. Warm breath caresses her lower lip and protracted tongue, sliding over it as she whispers in my ear.

"I have waited for this day for a long time, dear. The whispers have foretold it. The Light is never wrong, my child. Do you hear them?"

Seraphina pulls away, and I am simultaneously spellbound and repulsed as she turns to Luca.

"Does this not insult you, son of Tomas? The Council has hurt many in their rush to judgement. Why not you, hmm? Does it hurt to see such a soft, beautiful creature take up your father's mantle?"

Luca, who is solemn at best, remains tight-lipped, unwilling to let her get the best of him.

"With due respect, High Priestess, my father was a traitor to Atlas. He incited rebellion against the Council, and was rightly put down."

"A bold assertion. Some might say he was framed by Gabriel and the Council. For his own son to take the side of plotters and schemers shows how adept they have become, hmmm?" Seraphina doesn't wait for his muted answer, turning to me. "You and I will speak later. Best of luck with the scholar."

The High Priestess departs, leaving Luca and I studying each other for meager consolations— and Elion, unsure exactly what he should do now.

• • • •

THE ANGEL AND I AGREE that his presence could put the initial interrogation on edge. None of us want to prod the old Maester any more than necessary, and Luca opts to observe from the drab brick room.

Quorroc watches me pass the liquid entryway the Magus creates, inspecting my dry clothes on emerging from its aquatic barrier.

"Travel by portal takes some getting used to," the old man proclaims. Seated at a steel table, on a matching chair, the Maester does not seem uncomfortable, nor panicked. "Eventually it becomes second nature."

From afar, the hunchback seemed miserable. His voice is quite pleasant, with a sing-song quality unbefitting of his body language. Wasting no time, I pull the chair across from him outward, taking a seat.

"Do you know why you're here, Maester?"

Quorroc chuckles.

"I assume it is because you are Atlas's newest pawn. The Council has given you something to prove. Because let's face it— appointing a woman to the most prestigious post in all of Atlas is a desperation move."

"Or," I say, "a sign that the way things have always been done, no longer work. So, why don't we cut the crap, and I'll tell you how it looks from where I'm standing?"

"Please," Quorroc smiles, "do."

The old man's attitude hearkens back to another suspect I once interrogated— who looked into my eyes and told me God had appointed him and his friends the vile messengers of morality.

Quorroc has a lot less going for him.

"Your ties to the Crimson League are well-known. Your fellow Maesters don't trust you. The Whisperers are running scared because they know the information in their possession is nothing less than incendiary. The High Priestess didn't waste a breath exonerating you, and a man who doesn't even qualify to be a Nephalim thinks you're involved, Maester? And I believe him. Know why? Because I've been in Atlas all of five minutes, and you have the same look other holy men that I've come across all wear. They dress up in it, like a pretty girl to be taken to the ball, and it is very hard to be mistaken for a noble cause."

I let the tallied facts settle. Quorroc mulls over my assessment, but does not panic.

"Very good. That is quite the theory, madam. Unfortunately, you may have gotten some of your more precarious wires crossed, so maybe I will tell you how it looks from where I sit, currently."

"Please do," I mock.

"The Nephalim," Quorroc says, "as an organization, have fallen on rough times. I don't know how versed you are in Atlas's history, but the man on the other side of that wall? The Nephalim's son? There is more to the story of the Burning Spire, if you would hear it."

"Sorry," I retort, unwilling to hear the old man's blatant manipulation. "I'm sure Luca has a very good reason for whatever might have happened in his past. What's the expression? 'Sins of the father'..."

I am blissfully ignorant of whatever procedures the Council has in place for protecting prisoners. America always saw her outlaws treated with minimal respect — that level is clearly below what the Maester expects. The old man stands with speed unbecoming of his age. The echo of his metal chair being pushed under his robe screeches its legs over the linoleum floor so loudly, it's a wonder everybody inside the Obelisk doesn't hear it.

"Now listen here! I will not be treated like some common criminal who belongs in Stone Mountain. For Aumothera's sake, what have I done to deserve this?"

Unfortunately for Quorroc, his outburst doesn't unnerve nor startle me.

"Sit down, Maester." Quorroc calms himself, settling back into his seat. "I can appreciate the gravity of what you're saying—where I'm from? Institutions are almost constitutionally flawed. Men who shouldn't be able to get away with heinous acts do, and all sorts of things are politicized to keep them in control. Color of your skin? Sexual orientation? Bad credit? Any of these things can end a career before it ever starts. So before you go throwing your misogynist, outlier comments my way, please know I have spent my entire life dealing with nothing less.

"You're not going to hurt me by stating my sex, sir. You will not change my mind by throwing around your perceived injustices, or sway me with semantics. If you want to provide information I can use to actually protect the Council, you can save yourself a lot of trouble. Maybe....the White Light?"

Invoking this fills Quorroc's smoky eyes with terror. He shakes his head, trembling hands reaching across the table as he reconsiders this new information.

"No....you wouldn't! It's supposed to be voluntary!"

My gamble worked. The Maester is running scared now, and a boogeyman called the White Light is all it took.

"We don't have to speak of that, anymore," I reply, "*if* you tell me what I want to know."

And so, Quorroc does.

· · · ·

LUCA WAITS WHERE I emerge from the cell. The portal becomes corporeal, rather than a faded window I can only deduce is there through faith. I pass through it, smiling at the boy Elion as he closes the doorway behind me, sealing Quorroc within.

"Pretty impressive, Nephalim," he says. "Though, just for the record, Quorroc is not wrong. Nobody has ever been fed to the White Light as punishment."

I smile at him and Elion. The boy smiles back, the angel remaining stone-faced.

"There's a first time for everything."

CHAPTER SEVEN

I AM NOT A MONSTER.

There hasn't been much time to process everything that's happened since waking (*twice*)— first in a hospital room as a homeless man ate beans and was shot by masked assailants. Then, I woke up in a subway station; New York was purple and Death put on his monstrous show-and-tell. From there, I was transported to this land of disgruntled angels and a Grand Council of gods— one of whose members is snoring through the proceedings.

Hell, I could go back further— to the Capitol, and Emily Rickard, and the legion of law-staining FBI agents kidnapping children to satisfy the high crime rate, justifying their jobs. I was one of them, until I found out, and suddenly I wasn't. A man with a voice-masking filter called me in my office, had me break a key suspect out of the Hoover Building and bring that man to his friends, where I would find out it was all a sham. They burned me alive in a warehouse; I laid eyes on a much simpler, gentle version of Tim's realm for the first time, nothing like that weird conjuration of New York City. He reincarnated me, I woke up in a morgue, and my life would never be the same.

Stone Mountain is hardly stone, and even less of a mountain. It is a tower, and Bastille would be a better name. The Dark Quadrant's main attraction— located in the northeast of Atlas, in a district as dark and pitiful as Devil's Corner in the west— is more iron and metal than stone. Black and white shadows swirl around the free-standing pillar. Windows carved into their sides are black holes into nothing. There are thousands, tiny rectangles with human cries escaping each in a long and wailing and terrible whine.

There are no alleys here; only a wide plaza around the tower, manned by more Royal Guard. The Dark Quadrant's citizens aren't quite as down in the dirt as Demetrius' people, but starved for status nonetheless. Shantytowns and slums surround Stone Mountain, and its occupants give the prison a wide berth.

"Why are there weird screams coming from it?" I ask Luca. He nods at certain Royal Guards along the way, letting my question linger. Both our eyes drift up to a dark cloud at the tower's peak. It swirls like a Fourth of July thunderstorm as the screams grow louder the closer we draw.

"Stone Mountain, as you might have guessed from the name, is unbreachable. It is a soul prison. Even if a break were attempted from the outside, the prison would simply claim them on entry. Nothing that goes in, comes out," he explains.

The looming doors creak outward, as if there is an invisible sensor. Nobody grunts to push the iron doors open, but they open regardless, revealing blackness, insanity and death between them.

"And you want us to go in there?"

Luca chuckles.

"Fear not, child. Stone Mountain is only a threat to the enemies of Atlas. The Royal Guard holds the outside perimeter, but Arbiters—the prison's wardens— serve at the Council's pleasure. They will not harm us."

"If you say so."

Stepping past the final line of Royal Guards, my heart jumps, head sweats, hands bunch as I may be finally realizing my little darkness is nothing compared to actual darkness, so thick is the shroud as those giant doors close and we are sealed within it. Screams pouring out the thousand tiny windows are muted, and not even a passing breeze remains.

Hollow tones of a low-powered relay results in bright glare poured from the room's corners, crossing beams over a central hooded figure. Its arms are bone, scrubbed clean and whitened. The robes drape some sort of levitating effect— with no apparent feet, the figure appears to float, cones of light grafting over his shapeless body.

He is everything I would have expected the man who calls himself Death to be— a Grim Reaper, embracing a scythe as the jailor floats in the room's center.

"**Greetings**," the being says. "**State your business**."

"Greetings, Arbiter. This is Ramona— the Council's newest Nephalim. Forgive us this intrusion."

"**A woman? As Nephalim?**"

Even the FBI was more progressive. Fewer people questioned the woman assigned to lead a national case in 1995. In comparison, everyone in Atlas seems to balk at my appointment.

"I have to defer to the Council on that matter, Arbiter. In the meantime, we urgently need to speak with one of your prisoners. We are investigating rumors of a coup against the Council, and needless to say, would appreciate the Arbiters' discretion."

The faceless being does not count emotive body language as his strong suit, remaining absolutely still as Luca explains. When he is finished, the Arbiter thinks a moment before replying.

"**Do you know how many prisoners are held here, angel? Two hundred million. And do you know why a single prisoner has never escaped these walls?**

"**The Arbiters are soulbound to answer the Council's request. But do not question our discretion so carelessly. To do so may provoke us— your departure depends on our disposition toward you both.**"

Luca nods.

"Understood."

"**You will now be transferred to the Shadow Commons. For the sake of transparency, I ought to tell you that your every move will be watched. Every word will reach our ears. Do not sully this opportunity.**"

Luca repeats that he understands.

I say nothing.

• • • •

TRANSCRIPT

NOVEMBER 21st, 1995

The following is a classified transcript of the testimony of the Acting FBI Director, Howard Paynes, and the United States Intelligence Committee. Also present are Acting U.S. Attorney General Christopher Rosenburg, Director of National Intelligence Kenneth Dearson and Undersecretary of Defense George Roth. Sitting committee members include Nadine Lewis (D-RI), John Redding (D-OH), Xavier Lamb (D-NY), Matthew Ambrose (R-TX), Walter Syms (R-NC) and Nicholas Bluth III (D-WA)

BLUTH: Mr. Deputy Director, you served at the time of Director John Hazel's death, is that correct?

PAYNES: Yes, sir. I served as Director Hazel's deputy for almost six years of the nine John was in the job. Might I add what a loss the intelligence community has sustained, and take a moment for John, if I might.

BLUTH: Motion accepted. Let this committee observe a moment of silence for John Hazel, who died serving his country against a domestic terror threat.

AMBROSE: Mr. Deputy Director, could you inform this committee what occurred on the night of September 27th?

PAYNES: Well, the reports have all been submitted—

LAMB: We would like to hear it from your mouth, Mr. Deputy Director.

PAYNES: (clears throat) Very well. I have to begin by saying this was an unauthorized operation, being carried out covertly by one of our long term operatives, Agent Stephen Hardwick.

LAMB: And what is Agent Hardwick's status now?

PAYNES: Deceased.

AMBROSE: Mr. Deputy Director, I am having a very hard time understanding this. According to you, and reports the Bureau has submitted to this committee, Mr. Hardwick was responsible for operating a child trafficking ring, drawing resources from national security and municipal law enforcement to sell children as young as 8, all to maintain some image of productivity at the FBI?

PAYNES: That seems to be the case, Mr. Senator.

BLUTH: Unbelievable.

REDDING: Mr. Deputy Director, you still haven't answered this committee's request. How did this come to your attention, and what exactly occurred to cause sixty million dollars' worth of damage to Washington D.C., the Bureau headquarters, a dead FBI director and multiple law enforcement casualties?

PAYNES: You would not believe me if I told you, sir. As I said, it's all in the FBI's reports.

BLUTH: Try us, Howard.

• • • •

THE SHADOW COMMONS— as christened by the Arbiter— reminds me of Tim's version of Central Park. The sky is black, rather than purple; silhouettes are hazy, rather than firm. Outlines of spruce and elm trees have seen color siphoned from between their outlines. The shapes are there, but blankets of static have stolen their liveliness.

The transition from the Arbiter's chamber to the Shadow Commons is almost seamless; darkness rose up from the floor like pulling off a mask, revealing the Commons' facade beneath.

"Don't worry," Luca assures me. "Just an illusion."

But my eyes fall on the face brought before us, standing where the Arbiter was. Once again, the transition between one subject and another is seamless. The gruff face and tousled hair that replaces the cloaked Grim Reaper figure is instantly familiar, immediately repulsive and completely unwelcome. His hands are shackled, but not in iron— the same swirls of shadow dancing around Stone Mountain's exterior encase his wrists. He seems frozen in time, unaware of our presence. Silhouettes of trees and hedges sway in the haunted wind behind him, flapping like the heart against my ribs.

"I don't understand," Luca says. "What does this man have to do with anything? This is who Quorroc said had information on the coup?"

As much as I want to throw up, laying eyes on this monster, I cannot understand it either.

. . . .

TRANSCRIPT

DECEMBER 3rd, 1995

The following is a classified transcript of the testimony of the Acting Director of National Intelligence, Richard Gacy and the United States Intelligence Committee. Also present are Acting U.S. Attorney General Christopher Rosenburg. Sitting committee members include Nadine Lewis (D-RI), John Redding (D-OH), Xavier Lamb (D-NY), Matthew Ambrose (R-TX), Walter Syms (R-NC) and Nicholas Bluth III (D-WA)

REDDING: Mr. Director, thank you for speaking with us today.

GACY: Of course.

REDDING: Can you explain for this committee, the events of the last two weeks?

GACY: Yes, sir. On the evening of November 27th—approximately six days after testifying to this committee— Howard Paynes went into his office, pulled a .45 out of his drawer and put the gun in his mouth. His assistant, Madeleine Green, found him the following morning.

LEWIS: Are we certain this was a suicide?

GACY: (clears throat) Yes, sir. Paynes was a career man. Divorced, no children. Our assessment is the death of John Hazel and the outcomes of multiple internal investigations was not a result Howard was willing to live with.

LEWIS: I would like to know more about the agent who exposed Stephen Hardwick. It is my understanding that she suffered some sort of attack in her home, which may or may not be related to the investigation. (shuffles papers). Ramona Knox?

GACY: Yes. We are not quite sure what happened there. Knox appears to have lucked into some sort of paranormal loophole. That could also have something to do with her condition.

LAMB: Where is Agent Knox now, Director?

GACY: She is under 24/7 observation in a local hospital, sir. Her condition doesn't seem to have changed. I will continue to monitor her progress, so we might question her once she wakes.

LEWIS: If she wakes, Director.

GACY: Yes, ma'am.

REDDING: Who is leading the FBI now, Rick?

GACY: We have appointed Melvin Parks as Acting Director, with Phil Fontain assuming the role of deputy in Howard's place. Profiles are being assembled to put before the President, and confirmed by Congress for something more long term, but I believe Melvin and Phil will guide the Bureau through this tumultuous period.

AMBROSE: I hope so. Fifty-six people died on that September night. We want to make sure this kind of incident can never occur again.

GACY: Of course. I understand, sir. These are good men, the best men. I have nothing less than complete faith in them.

REDDING: This is your last chance, Director.

* * * *

LAST TIME I SAW STEPHEN Hardwick, I had just been reincarnated inside Tim's death tunnel that he called the Arcway. After being burned alive, I came back to life, confronting the agent in front of half the FBI and John Hazel. Hardwick murdered Hazel, ordering the agents in his court to fire on me.

I chased him. Limbs of shadow broke out of my back. Four on each side, like a spider. They carried me on stomping tendrils to where my new form smacked him aside, causing fatal internal bleeding. Then, with permission from the bevy of law enforcement and federal agents giving chase, I left the scene, confronting his soul in the Arcway. I shot him again and again— and Tim kept reincarnating him— until he was ready to talk.

There wasn't enough time to ask Death what became of Hardwick. He's lost a good amount of the excess weight he carried.

Bristling hairs of his grey beard cling to a gaunt face, afraid to show the sunken cheekbones beneath. In a brown jumpsuit matching a Maester's robe, the frozen expression makes him look like a statue.

Of all the souls in the universe, how is this the one who supposedly has the information I need?

He will never cooperate.

"How are they treating you?" I ask— for lack of anything, anything at all to break the horrendous, awkward silence hanging between us. Luca does not so much as breathe, trying interpreting the mutual death stares on both sides.

Hardwick scoffs, looking to the dancing insinuation of hedges. Their mass shrinks to a pin-sized hole that light would be lucky to penetrate, before growing into a basin that would welcome home all the darkness the universe could hold. Rinse and repeat.

"Bold," Hardwick says, his voice weak from eternal bondage; the Arbiters are undoubtedly watching his every move. "Bold to assume you and I could have a civil conversation."

"That's a bit rich, isn't it? *Jordan*?"

Hardwick chuckles at the invocation of his mortal crimes. Jordan West, the larger-than-life persona who kidnapped children across the country, was eventually exposed as Hardwick's crew— and Jordan West, the enigmatic, unapprehendable criminal was revealed to be long dead, never a criminal at all.

"So," Hardwick says, "what are we doing here, Knox? Surely, you're not pulling me out of eternal damnation to have tea, right? No, your friend sent me to this twisted place, and I was forgotten. Days, months, years. Everything I worked for, destroyed."

"*Everything* you worked for? You mean the families broken, Stephen? The little girls and boys whose lives were ruined? *That* was everything, right, everything you worked for?"

Hardwick shakes his head.

"I'm not going to sit here and justify myself to you, Knox. You won, okay? Just...let me rot."

"I can't do that."

"No. Of course not," Hardwick says. "Because I have something you need. I know it. You know it. And unless you're in a position to barter, don't even waste your breath. We have nothing further to talk about."

This must be the most miserable of places, and Stephen Hardwick deserves every morsel of it— but despite his crimes, I wouldn't wish the screams from the tower's exterior on my worst enemy. Tim's strange world was punishment enough. Stone Mountain is a level of pettiness I wouldn't have expected of the man who calls himself Death.

"Luca." The angel, whose head was pointed at the ground with the utmost disinterest, snaps to attention. "What is the scope of our influence with the Arbiters?"

Hardwick's entire expression changes. I never break my sightline with him.

"Not much, I'm afraid. The Nephalim have lost a good deal of clout all-around. But, given your standing with the Council and my good word, I am sure these matters can be made minimal."

The self-satisfied smirk is wiped away, replaced with the look of a man hearing freedom is floated. Hardwick isn't jailed on a dimebag charge and locked up for ten years in a red state— the worst American equivalent for justice I can imagine— but sentenced to be here past a reasonable date.

This is his heavenly judgment at stake.

"The game has changed, Stephen," I say. "You know me. Whatever I need to do to get the job done."

"You always were a pain in the ass, Knox."

"Help me, Stephen. Do you want to get out of here?"

Hardwick nods.

"A woman came to see me," he reflects, eyes drifting to the ground.

"A woman?"

"Blond. Tall. Pretty. Reminded me of my ex-wife a bit. Not the first one. The second. Tits like a boar."

"Stephen? I don't need a description. I need an identity. Because so far, all I have are a washed-up scholar, and a hooded man who buckles too easily being hit by a girl."

Hardwick shakes his head.

"I don't know her name."

"What did this woman want?" Luca asks.

"To know about Knox."

What? Why me?

"About me? I haven't even been awake a full day! When was this?"

"Couple months ago. Not sure, really. Time is messed up in this place."

"It's an effect of the Arbiters," Luca explains. "You will be free of it soon. Try to remember what you can."

And so, Hardwick does.

• • • •

"THIS DOESN'T MAKE SENSE."

Outside the prison, I struggle to shake off the cold remaining in my bones. We told Hardwick to sit tight, that we would negotiate his position in good faith with the Council. Hardwick knows the drill.

Luca's giant broadsword swings at his hip as we walk away from the Dark Quadrant, into God City. The streets come alive with friendly faces. Their smiles and banter and casual greetings pull my attention like children at the hem of a dress. The sky is bright, and the houses are like something out of a Dr. Suess book. We pass a small market where people can trade services and buy goods— I'm unsure what use material possessions have in Atlas, but don't spot or smell food among them— and turn down an alleyway.

"It doesn't matter," the angel replies as we emerge out its other end, arcing left through an arch onto the God's Road. Evidently, Luca does not want to debate Hardwick's information with anyone but the Council.

"It's so life-like, isn't it?" I ask, changing the subject. "This...place. God City."

"Ah, yes. It has few of the troubles other districts have, but nor is it burdened by violent symbols. I suppose...it is easy to stop seeing after a while. The beauty of it."

I chuckle, and Luca asks what's funny.

"There was this place I used to go to be alone. Rapids Bridge," I explain. "Might have been better had I ever had someone to go there with, but it wasn't that kind of place. It was mine."

"What are you saying?" Luca asks. Sentiments of any kind are lost on him; I tell him never mind, just as we pass through the Spire's giant doors.

What I might have said— had I been brave enough to continue— was that God City reminded me how I felt, once upon a time, standing on some stupid, secret location everyone and their mother knew of. It didn't matter if the bridge was public; the little girl with freak parents, who died in a freak incident, didn't feel like a freak there, on that little bridge carved into the District of Columbia.

And just like some parts of Atlas, it wasn't because it didn't make me feel like a freak.

On that bridge, I might have never even been one at all.

CHAPTER EIGHT

"A Behemoth?"

The Habinar's voice echoes throughout the chamber. The Viking glares between his equals. Muerkher is stone-faced. The snakes on Venicia's scalp are back to snapping at each other. Two on the left side of her head get into a bloody altercation, spilling red droplets onto the goddess' shoulder. Apollo is awake, though his brown eyes are glassy. He sways from side to side, making me think Muerkher woke him.

The fifth chair, as usual, is empty.

Beside me, Luca holds his head high, but the eyes point down. Like a dog used to seeing its owners yell about something unrelated, the angel waits for their argument to conclude.

"Restraint, Habinar," Venicia urges. "As far as we're aware, these are unsubstantiated rumors."

"Rumors? I swear on the Seat, you have grown complacent, Venicia! Since when do we approach any rumors surrounding Behemoths with carelessness? Ziz waits in the wings, ready for us to let our guard down!"

"While I don't profess to love the man, he is not wrong," Muerkher adds. "We have grown careless, thinking one woman could take this on!"

"We are rebuilding the Nephalim, Muerkher," Venicia says. "That will take time. Ramona has already made headway, and we may prevent another uprising by getting ahead of it."

"Uprisings are the least of our worries," the Habinar scoffs. **"Few who could outright control a Behemoth, other than Ziz. He has already proven willing to subvert his imprisonment, influencing others."**

"But the question remains," says Muerkher. "Does Ziz possess enough strength at this time to control a Behemoth? Might this be a third party? Then there is the matter of this woman, who is acting as the party's agent. On some level, she was aware we would choose Ramona—"

"That wouldn't make sense," Venicia counters. "How could this agent have known Ramona would wake? We certainly haven't announced it to the world. There are maybe five people outside this room aware that she is a Nephalim to begin with— something that, while we might not seek to change that, someone else on the outside might."

"Quorroc?" Luca asks.

Muerkher shakes his lava lamp of a head.

"No, Quorroc may be underhanded, but he is not plotting the Atlas's demise."

"I agree," I interject. Until now, I have listened and observed, waiting to have enough facts at my disposal before submitting any kind of declaration. "Quorroc is a product of his environment. He might wheel and deal to the Crimson League, but the old man literally knew nothing other than Hardwick's name."

"And what do you make of your former partner, Ramona?" the Habinar asks. **"Is this someone we can trust?"**

These supreme beings don't need to ask. They know exactly how I feel about Stephen Hardwick. But however supreme they are, someone is gunning for them, and pulling out all the stops.

"Absolutely not. He is a monster of the worst kind. He has ruined hundreds of lives, and lied about it with a straight face." *Easy, Ramona.* "That said, the greater good requires him to go free. That's my personal issue, not yours.

"Whoever this woman is, that gave Stephen this information— he said she came asking about me. Which means she knew I would be here at some point. She knows about my professional relationship with Hardwick, and left a trail only I would be able to follow."

"In other words," Venicia says, "bait."

I nod. The serpent woman says the Council needs to debate this latest chain of events before proceeding. Luca and I are dismissed, the auditorium lights turn on, and the four return to a resting state.

One could only be so lucky.

· · · ·

LUCA LEAVES ME AT THE Gardens— a half-district of green-space nestled between Devil's Corner in the West and Atlas's main gates. He was quiet after our meeting with the Council, chewing thoughts over Hardwick's claim.

All I can envision at the mention of Behemoths are paintings in the Obelisk's lobby, seen right before we spoke to Quorroc. Luca is clearly uncomfortable with the subject. If my leaders had once utilized merciless, fire-breathing beings on webbed wings, I would be nervous too.

Unable to rectify allegorical monsters with everything I know to be real, I try to focus on the Gardens. A giant hedge maze— which ought to have twisting, confusing passageways to the center, and God help you getting out— is surrounded by long brown trunks supporting millions of flowers in everlasting bloom. The grass beneath my shoes is soft and coyly curls under my weight, even if I can't shake the Shadow Commons' soulless blades before it.

"It is beautiful, isn't it?"

The soft-spoken voice exercises great care not to startle, only join me in observing it. Taking my side, the robed elder Siskett stifles the groan in his joints, covering up a cough.

"Yes," I reply. "Beautiful is probably the word for it. Too beautiful. Almost too much to be true."

Siskett chuckles.

"You are probably wondering if this is all a hallucination, hmm? A frantic mosaic of pretty shapes and colors. Of course, it is not perfect. Nothing in Creation is."

"It might have crossed my mind."

"Everything you have seen, Ramona...think of your life— the one you had back on Earth— as the beaker in which your personal formula was built. The Avatar told you that every soul comes with a unique code— an identification system, if you will. Walk with me, Ramona."

Wrapping his hand around my bicep puts the onus on my balance to assure his own, and he looks much older than he did at the gates, or posing as a homeless man in my hospital room. We circle a corner of the oblong hedge maze, pacing ourselves to accommodate his rheumatic ailments.

"This code," Siskett explains, "is always evolving. There *are* predisposed traits— an inevitable shortcoming of basing production on limited models. So, the Avatar telling you some people are automatically filtered into Atlas— while others are sent elsewhere— is not entirely untrue. That code, were it to remain in a static, unchanging state, would indeed suggest predisposition when it comes to placement."

"I'm not following," I reply.

The old Maester stops, hovering against the hedge maze for further support. He spots a bench down the bristling organic wall, and suggests moving to it, rambling as we do.

"That code has the great capacity of flexibility. It is not easy. Many people feel they are on predetermined paths, only to fizz out and be relegated to the nature of their personal code. Others face trauma, such as you did. *Trauma* is the single greatest catalyst for transforming that genetic sequence. It can take the best men and turn them into monsters. It can take a young vagrant, transforming him to revolutionary. The code can change, Ramona. The code can change. But it is very, very difficult."

"Are you saying my parents' deaths changed some sort of DNA sequence?"

We reach the bench. I help the Maester lower himself. His back pops, and he cries in a small yelp of pain. His knees creak, and he rubs them.

"Forgive me," he says. "I fear the White Light has been sending signals, calling me home. And I am just too old, and too stubborn to listen. So I can't really ask you to sit here and take an old man seriously, but here it is, Ramona:

"What happened to your parents was tragic. But that's not what I'm talking about."

"All due respect, but can we get to the point, then?"

Siskett smiles a little bit, and I doubt any White Light or Behemoth could tame life in the old man's eyes.

"Many humans choose to worship personal beliefs, do they not?"

"Sometimes."

"And how do they choose to present this worship? Meaning, how do people communicate with their gods?"

"Prayer?" I ask, tired of riddles.

"Rituals. Prayers are part of it. Prayers. Confessions. Hymns. Study. Rituals, Ramona."

"Okay?"

"But," Siskett continues, "ritual, over time, becomes complacency. The prayer is there, but its words ring a little less genuine. People go to houses built in their agreed-upon god's name to revel in boredom and habit, rather than reverence and interest. More lose the habit altogether, only attending on special occasions, like Christmas or Easter mass. It is the ultimate about-face— a half-hearted attempt to appease rituals, not gods. It is to achieve an attendance record, not a communal spiritual experience.

"Society becomes more secular, because *productivity* becomes the new ritual. *Rationale* becomes the new ritual. The archaic, faith-based ritual was never formed on genuine love, but fear and boredom and the need for contextually-appropriate answers in a void of questions. Why are we here? What is our purpose? As soon as we had rationale to form the science-based ritual, humans simply abandoned one for the other, and were no more fulfilled for the change."

"Because both are rituals."

"That's right," Siskett says. "Your genetic code— the one that dictates where you belong in the afterlife— can be altered. But many people fall into that ritual of life, never seeking to transcend their limitations. By exposing your partner, and saving leagues of children, you did something few ever manage. To break the ritual."

I chuckle, unsure what prompts me to open my mouth, confiding in this kind old man, for the first time I've trusted anyone since waking.

"I feel like...even though I have no regrets for what I did...I don't know. Maybe my death was the lesser of evils. If Hardwick had gotten away with it, the world might have been better off."

Siskett smiles, then returns to rubbing his sore knees.

"That may be true. The Council would *definitely* agree with that outlook. But things being what they are, happen for a reason. Earth will bloom once again. Whether it can sustain human life is another question. But it will always recover.

"Which, I suppose, brings us to the matter of your friend."

"Hardwick?"

"The *infectorum mundi*," Siskett replies. "The World-Killer."

In all the excitement surrounding the city in the heavens, becoming some sort of celestial investigator and coming face-to-face with my old nemesis, I almost forgot about the man who calls himself Death.

"What will happen to him?"

Siskett shakes his head.

"There is to be a trial. I am sure Luca will tell you soon, if the Council doesn't themselves. It was to be done quite some time ago, but this threat has postponed the proceedings."

"I don't understand," I say.

"After your accident, the World-Killer disappeared. Perhaps he understood the magnitude of what he had done. Maybe it was simpler than that, and he was afraid. By all rights, he should be. But he made a deal with the Council, which is the only reason you are still not in that hospital bed."

"What sort of deal?"

Siskett asks me to help him to his feet. The old man winces as I oblige him, finding balance after a moment and hobbling alongside me.

"I'm alright, child. As to the deal, it is not my place to reveal these things to you. I am just an old man who has been here too long, susceptible to carrying too many secrets. I am sure all will be revealed in time. There is something, however, I would ask of you."

"What is it?"

Siskett stops, leaning on my arm for further support on our way back to the God's Road. The Maester groans with each step, worsening with every second he spends here.

"It has been my great pleasure to serve Atlas all these years. I have been here so long, my hair has gone three shades of grey, two shades of white and I've amassed more aches and pains than I can shake a bloody stick at.

"I am having a party of sorts. A small get- together. Some friends, and nothing more. Would you come?"

I have never been a social person, often choosing to hole up in some sort of confined space, drinking wine or pouring over paperwork. Christmas parties never missed me, because I've never been to one. Friends were a scarce commodity past the age of ten, and my only companions afterward were Maya and Death.

At one point, Tim took her too.

"Of course," I smile. "Would be my pleasure."

We part, with Siskett limping back to the Cathedral on his own. I drift toward the God's Road. Part of me yearns to return to God City, with its quaint little houses and friendly faces dispersed throughout the district. That same part yells at me to avoid places like Devil's Corner and Stone Mountain (hell, even the Obelisk and Seat). But indulging in the nicer parts of this city, while disregarding its ugliness.

All my answers lie in the darkness Atlas hides. If I'm not careful, it may very well devour me whole.

. . . .

CHAPTER NINE

THE GATHERING FOR MAESTER Siskett is held— to no-body's surprise— in the Cathedral district. Luca and I have passed through it, zipping between various areas of the Atlas, at least ten times. Its central location between the northeast and west makes it an ideal shortcut from one district to another, but this is the first time I've seen the old church up close.

Just prior to the gathering, I found myself in God City— wandering the small market, admiring its status symbols for sale. Everyone in Atlas is beyond biological function. There are no racks of meat or smell of overripe fruit pervading the scenery. There's no faint smell of sewage, wafting from some backwoods district. Instead, the wooden stalls hocked jewels and fake dragonskin armor. It looked more like newt skin than dragon, despite its merchant's assurances it was real. My hands traced its rough textures, not a scale or sign of supreme reptilian beings in its makeup, but I politely declined.

"Smart," Luca said from behind me, and I nearly jumped out of my skin.

"Jesus. You scared the shit out of me! How did you know where I was?"

"Wasn't hard. You seemed pretty enamored when we passed through here before. Piece of advice— anyone who tells you they've seen a dragon in the last four thousand years, or wants to sell you something to do with dragons, is selling you lies."

"I will keep that in mind," I said. We gravitated away from the corner market, back between the rows of brightly colored houses. "Where did you disappear to?"

"Updating the High Priestess. She fancies you, you know."

"Does she?"

We passed through the gates of God City, back onto Atlas' central road. The people here are a mix between the mutts of Devil's Corner, intermingling with Royal Guards and a small injection of God City folk.

"Be careful around that one, Ramona."

"Yeah," I said. "Seems like a shady figure."

"Shady is putting it lightly. Seraphina has ambitions that extend beyond the Nephalim. Their ostracization has only seen those ambitions boiled in resentment. Tread carefully."

"Thanks. So, what's the next step?"

"The Council is still debating the next step. The Maesters have requested our presence for Siskett's little party. The Council themselves will be present, as is customary when a Maester meets the White Light."

I should have guessed. The way Siskett moved and spoke— as if something greater than I could see ailed him— should have been a red flag.

"Is that what's happening?"

"Yes. Siskett's final assignment was to retrieve you from Earth, and bring you to Atlas. Since the Nephalim uprising, the Maesters have been pulling double duty researching ways to protect the Council. Siskett has aged quicker than normal."

"I see. Where are we on Hardwick?"

"I am sure," Luca replies, "the Council will strike some sort of agreement with the Arbiters, and he will be released into our custody."

Part of me regrets not leaving that monster in that prison to rot for all time. Knowing I will have to babysit my former nemesis leads to the question of whether I can kill him after this is over— inflict one final round of retribution.

That's not who I am.

But when it comes to Hardwick, I am no longer entirely sure, any more than I am that the man who calls himself Death is worthy of exoneration.

• • • •

THE CATHEDRAL OF ATLAS is an interesting structure. Destroyed in the invasion by Ziz during the First Age, and rebuilt in the Second, it stands out like a sore thumb among other districts and buildings the city's original architects seemed fond of. It is brick, rather than iron. It has turrets, rather than towers. Its stained glass windows don't depict angels or God or the fucking Virgin Mary, but the passage of time beyond its windows. The massive church's interior is awash in gargoyles and angels statues who would protect Atlas from such darkness, were the streets not soaked in it.

It is here that Maester Siskett will meet the White Light— whatever that entails. The room is filled with a garden-variety of the Atlas's denizens. The Council are seated at an oval table that has been pulled over the drab green carpet running up the room's center, draping the steps before arriving at a sept few openly worship. Several Maesters and the common rabble are assembled around them. Their members are more life-sized here, and I can't help wondering if they are projecting themselves into the modest chairs, paling in comparison to their thrones. Apollo dozes, as usual, but there are only four chairs instead of five.

The mystery of the missing god continues.

The walk from the Cathedral's giant iron doors to the top of the room is filled with people. Even in the realm of the dead, old habits die hard. I stick close to Luca as he cuts up the crowd to where Maester Siskett is seated behind the Council. There is not a plate of food or wafting smell resembling it. The people of Atlas converse, but not over food or sweets. None of the Council takes part in such vanity. Venicia comes closest, having swapped out her usual red dress for a white one. She looks bored, affixed beside the snoring Apollo. Muerkher appears unimpressed as the Habinar boasts to lowly immortals gathered around his end of the table.

"**Bless the stars! I cried**," the Habinar says— a group of children have gathered round, mothers watching from afar. "**When that Nephalim rose up, so did the Habinar. I retrieved my axe and struck down those who tried to storm the palace!**"

Luca looks away from the bragging god, steering to Venicia's end of the table. The Habinar continues, enticing the rabble of Atlas with tales of the Second Age's end.

"**It was there, their leader sought a showdown with the Council. We had bestowed heavenly privilege upon him, and this was how he repaid us? No, the Habinar does not stand for such betrayal!**"

Like Luca, the serpent woman has little patience for the Habinar's romanticized history. But his voice booms louder than the silence that follows it, and we must wait until he finishes speaking.

"**I challenged Tomas, the Nephalim who would overthrow us, to explain himself. And he could not, other than drawing his weapon against us! Such are explanations of the weak, children. If you must fight a war with swords, it is because you have no wits to fight a war of words!**

"**He drew his sword, I drew mine. We clashed. I'll admit**," the Habinar says solemnly, "**Tomas almost got the best of us that day. Weren't it for Gabriel, Tomas' brother-in-blood, we might have perished! The sword struck the ax from my hand. Gabriel wielded it, and drove it through his brother-in-blood!**"

The children cheer loudly, then settle, and we are able to speak with Venicia without competing for volume.

"Ah," the goddess says. "The Council's newest Nephalim. So glad you could make an appearance, Ramona. Luca." She eyes the son of Tomas. "That must have been hard to hear."

Luca shakes his head.

"Old history, nothing more. Has the Council decided on a course of action?"

"Yes," Muerkher says, eavesdropping. "There was a great deal of debate, but the decision was made to release Mr. Hardwick into the Nephalim's custody. How he is utilized, handled and what ultimately happens to him rests with Ramona."

Bad decision. Placing Stephen Hardwick's eternal judgment in my hands brings back all the deception and evil one man can embody. Making a mental note for later, I allow the Fire Man to continue.

"The next step will be identifying this woman who came to visit your prisoner. It is mutually agreed she could have been leaving a message of some kind, and its recipient was intended to be you."

"The Maesters are already looking into it," Venicia adds. "Once this business with Siskett has passed, the matter will have their full attention."

Before we can continue, the air grows cold. It flows up the Cathedral's center like a sharp winter wind piercing D.C. in January, arriving like long, slender fingers caressing my shoulder.

"Of course," Muerkher mutters.

Creeping up behind us, the Nephalim High Priestess dons a stunning green dress with golden planks fanning out behind her head. Her smile is twisted as the cold working its way down to where petty darkness lives between my legs, mocking its mere existence.

"Seraphina," Venicia smiles, but the gesture is accompanied by clasped, diplomatic hands. "To what do we owe the pleasure?"

The voice that reaches my ears is a high-pitched whine, reigniting my gut feeling that this woman is terrible news.

"A Maester meets the White Light, and you don't invite the old guard anymore, serpent woman? You consolidate all of the Nephalim's power into this...*doll*?"

"Don't tell me you're jealous, Seraphina?"

The High Priestess scoffs.

"Some nerve. Nevermind it was a Nephalim who saved you! Gabriel risked everything to protect you ungrateful gods, and look what has happened! We are cast out, exiled— forced to watch you replace us from afar! Isn't that right?"

"Gabriel turned out to be a traitor as well, if I recall," Venicia snipes. The snakes on her head eye Seraphina out one side, snapping their jaws malevolently.

"How dare you! Ungrateful gods! That's all you are! How about rebuilding from within? How about paying the dues of those who *bled* for you?"

A hand reaches out, grabbing the High Priestess' flailing wrist. Luca pulls her arm down— Seraphina glares at him in disbelief, yanking the hand back.

"Don't touch me, boy! You are not even Nephalim! It was your flesh and blood who got us into this mess— a petty little boy who is outlawed, *exiled*!"

"Yes," Luca says. "Just like you."

"I am no such thing!" Seraphina protests. "I am the Nephalim's High Priestess! Its functional leader! And yet, I've been cast out! Cast out by an earthling bitch and her pet outlaw, backed by a group of ungrateful gods!"

"Luca," Venicia smiles. "Please see the High Priestess out."

· · · ·

SOME TIME AFTER LUCA escorts Seraphina from the gathering— she screams and yells insults the whole way out the door— Maester Siskett clinks an empty glass. The Habinar, whose exuberant recountings of Atlas history have dropped off, cranes his shrunken neck to look back at the transept where the elder is perched. Candles around the room are blown out as silence befalls the church. Luca and I remain off to the side as the raspy-voiced scholar begins his final speech, his face illuminated by Muerkher's glow below him. I lock eyes with Maester Barrett, stationed closer to the Cathedral's elevated perch where Siskett stands, and we share a nod.

"Thank you all for coming," Siskett says; his voice is clear throughout the church, settling into the history of great speeches and sermons likely uttered long before his. "You know, I have been doing this job for somewhere in the quadruple digits, if we're reduced to speaking in years.

"It was all those millennia ago, a very old friend came to me," Siskett explains, smiling at Barrett, "and asked if I would help him build an Order that could inform the Council of whispers between stars plotting against them. We would have to search the universe, Creation permitting, for the answers that could afford this realm protection.

"I am glad to have accepted. It has been a fruitful journey. It was not perfect! Like any profession, there are members who would undermine its reputation with foulness mistaken for righteousness."

Siskett clears his throat. All eyes are on him— an old man at the tail end of Creation, being called home. In the complacent quiet, he wipes a tear away.

"We have learned a great many lessons together! We have faltered, and learned together! And when the White Light calls us home, it understands why we fought for our vision— *why* we stayed behind. So to you all, I give my parting advice;

"Remember the lessons of the Second Age. What transpired may have been inevitable. The demon Ziz is everywhere. It was on us to be vigilant in every corner we hold. We were not, and suffered terrible losses within our camp. But we held the line, and overcame it— a reminder to never disregard the darkness, which would see this realm dislodged from the universe's workings."

Just as my mind wanders, wondering when the main event will come, an odd sensation shifts the ground beneath my feet. Siskett continues his farewell speech, and I contemplate whether events of the last few days have me hallucinating.

Two things dispel that notion. First, the dead or undead souls of Atlas have no need for sleep. Even if I felt the impulse to rest my head, I am unsure whether I would drift off at all. The people of Atlas are perpetually on their feet— glaring in a window of one of the Dr. Suess-like houses in God City, there wasn't any furniture to sit, a table to eat, or any sign of beds. I have seen peasants in Devil's Corner, but nobody slept in the corner, other than the baby on his mother's breast.

The second confirmation arrives in a shared glance with Luca. Neither Barrett or the Council members notice. Nobody in the crowd does a double take, either. Siskett continues rambling as the inquisitive staring contest with my angel companion intensifies.

"And when the White Light calls thee home, thou shalt look back at thy home, and assess its safety!" the old man recites. Another shift under our collective feet causes Barrett to look up from the floor, and Muerkher glances around.

Whispers travel the crowd, asking about a storm in the forecast. The pit of my stomach lines up with Siskett's enthused, raspy preaching, and I can no longer fight the knife in its lining, stabbing butterflies floating inside it.

Something terrible is about to happen.

"We have to evacuate," I tell Luca. "*Now*!"

Atop his perch, Siskett is so caught in his sermon— so focused on the White Light that will steal him from this world, bring him home to repentance— he doesn't see the turning heads or hear the Council members' whispers to each other.

"What was that?" asks someone in the crowd.

"Is that an earthquake?"

"**Something is behind the Cathedral!**"

"And White Light!" Siskett screams, raising his robed arms to the turrets above. "**Grant us reprieve!**"

The elder's final plea is cut short by an avalanche of breaking bricks and shattering stained glass in the wall behind him. I am not sure which takes him out— the assembly of debris pouring inward at fatal velocity, or the enormous scaled paw that kicked it inward, stomping down where the old man stood. The foot is attached to massive shoulders which break apart the wall further up as a pair of yellow eyes follows the claws inside. People scream and flee at massive webbed wings with the span of a Boeing 747 folding in on themselves as the creature squeezes between the widening gap of its own making.

The Council is gone, confirming my projection theory— it's a good thing too, because the crumbling Cathedral's pieces plunge several feet, crumpling the center of the oval table they were gathered. It snaps in half, buckling toward the ground in the center, a large brick broken within its disaster.

I could have made out the accusations and labels of Atlas citizens, fleeing toward the door, but the world has slowed. This monster makes all the ones who came before it pale as its cat-like eyes focus on Luca and I.

The angel slowly draws his broadsword, holding it level with both hands, blade edge at an outward angle.

Without a weapon, I am frozen.

The dragon leans forward on its front haunches. Warm air pours from quarter-sized nostrils that dance and ripple around their edges. Pulling back, it arches its neck upward and screams, backing away into an attack position. Like a lion ready to pounce on its prey, the dragon begins a graceless trot in our direction, spreading its massive wings.

"It's a Behemoth!" my companion exclaims, backing in the opposite direction. **"It's going to destroy the Cathedral—"**

Luca darts left as the beast plows between us. I cut right, smashing into a pillar on the room's eastern side. The Behemoth charges into the opposite wall, sending more bricks tumbling down. The structure groans. I spot Maester Barrett across the room, crawling on elbows and knees. Siskett's body is lost in the rubble— against my better judgement, I break to save Barrett.

Pulling itself from the jimmy of bricks and collapsing stone, the dragon bleeds from its neck. In the corner of my eye, Luca drives his sword into the Behemoth's side with a scream. It matches the sound several octaves higher, backhanding Luca, sending him flying into the wall Barrett crawls towards.

A piece of the roof collapses above me. The shards are chaotically choreographed to the shattering stained glass windows, nearly flattening me. Were I not constantly moving forward, drawing back, darting sideways and pushing on, one or more chunks of the imploding ceiling would take me out.

Free of the pest that is Luca, the dragon turns its cat-like eyes onto Barrett as I reach the panicking elder. It raises its back haunches from across the room, huffing, drawing air.

"That's a Behemoth, Nephalim!" the Maester screams. Before I can thank him for stating the fucking obvious, a stream of flame escapes its open mandible. Wide nets of fire advance from the dragon's lungs. Barrett screams as the scorching breath grazes us, dropping off; any closer, its outburst would have rendered us burnt toast. Sensing its failure, the dragon sucks in another breath, and we won't be so lucky next time.

A screaming figure runs up its tail and backside. Before I can assign the flailing shape to Luca— bringing his broadsword down into the dragon's neck before it can cook us alive, its scream pulls me back from fear as the head is nearly severed from its body.

Thrown from the dragon's back, Luca hits the ground in a roll. The Behemoth thrusts its muscular tail into the far wall as a desperate, final act of self-defense. With most of the Cathedral's supports suffering a dragon carved through them, the angel yells at me to get Barrett to safety. The dragon frantically seizes, swinging at anything in reach as I place my hand at the Maester's waist. His arm finds my neck and I pull him to his feet.

"Ramona! Get him out of here!"

Luca dodges the dying monster as its massive paw takes out another section of brick on the western side and most of a window frame set within it. Debris and glass is pulled inward, landing near the sept where Siskett died in a heap of settling sediment. Countering the charge, Luca brings the sword down on the dragon's crown. Eyes roll into the back of its scaled head as it collapses in a circular, counterclockwise motion. Wings sweep, tripping Luca as Barrett and I clear their gigantic reach.

The church trembles on its final supports. Reaching the collapsed entryway, I push Barrett toward his freedom, yelling to get away from here as fast as he can.

The dragon is dead, but Luca is not in the clear yet. I inch closer, ignoring his protests as the roof buckles above. I wouldn't hear Luca anyway, screaming at me to leave him. Covering my head with both hands until sure the roof will hold, I advance over the vibrations of snapping structural integrity.

"Give me your hand!" I yell.

Luca doesn't hesitate. Using all my remaining strength, I pull the angel to his feet. His wings are dirtied and his hand wraps around the giant broadsword, yanking it from the Behemoth's skull, breaking into a sprint toward the doors.

The Cathedral gives way. We clear them beneath a relentless avalanche white powder which ensnares Luca and I in a rising cloud that spreads well beyond the wreckage. Split-second glimpses at the evacuated crowd who ran to safety when the dragon broke through the rear wall choke beneath blasts of brick and concrete aimed for the shins, consuming me in a sand-colored tunnel.

Thrown onto my stomach — and caught within the subsequent wave of ricocheted materials that bury me alive— I don't see Luca before the cloud of rising ash becomes darkness overtaking me.

I can only hope my companion fared better than I did.

CHAPTER TEN

WHITE LIGHTS.

When my eyes open, they are not ready for the glare that pours in my nose and mouth, suffocating me. Closing them does nothing— Light will simply find its way in if it wants to. This time, when I concede to the peel in darkness becoming a gaping wound, I expect to see Wilson, scooping canned beans into his mouth without the teeth Atlas provided him. But there is no rigid green chair, nor a man eating canned goods in it, nor a hospital room in the United States Capitol. There are no beeping heart monitors or creepy, destabilized hallways abandoned in the plague, never to be waxed again.

A king-sized bed is overseen by a canopy of wood beams. The fine-pulled sheets and blankets are lovingly made, with thread counts that must be in the thousands. Pillows against my back prop up my torso; a white cone drenches my concealed feet from between gently billowing drapes across the room.

What happened?

My hair is loose. It smells clean, washed of the cloud that covered Luca and I at the Cathedral— the last thing I remember. Hands reach under the covers, grasping frantically at my leg. Fingers feel for bandages or breaks of any kind; they are bare but unhurt, and my toes wiggle on command. Other than a T-shirt covering everything above my thighs, I have nothing on beneath.

And in a chair across from the bed's empty side, a robed figure stares blankly at the floor.

"Barrett?" I croak, snapping the elder's attention to me.

"By the Light, Ramona!" he smiles, and I could swear tears form in the old man's eyes. "We thought we had lost you."

So many questions wait on the tip of my tongue, but a parched mouth stops them like a dam holding violent water, only transmitting single syllables.

"Council?"

Barrett smiles again, nodding tearfully.

"Safe. We predicted such an event. Not of this exact nature, mind you. No one really saw a Behemoth getting back into Atlas, especially not one so agitated. It must have been starved before someone let it loose.

"Don't worry," Barrett urges, seeing my frown. "These things can wait until you're up and about. Had it not been for our quick thinking and your quicker actions, we might have all perished."

There's something he's not saying.

"Barrett?"

"Yes, Nephalim?"

I don't want to ask, but feel compelled to.

"Luca?"

The smile falls off his face— I can feel it dissolve. My face is flushed, and I suddenly regret asking.

"Luca gave his life to save the Council. His remains were too mangled to save, and he has passed onto the White Light, Creation keep his soul safe."

The news is a punch to my gut, worse than any physical injury would have been. I could have walked on through that. Luca was my safety net in this strange place. News of his death both affirms I can die here, and saddens me greatly.

"The man settled his family's debt," I sob, fighting tears. "He should be honored for his sacrifice."

Barrett leans over the bed, clasping his hands with a sigh.

"I can understand the sentiment, Ramona. But his father did untold damage to this realm, endangering Atlas—"

"And you already killed him," I snipe back. "Retribution was served the moment the Habinar bested Tomas, and saved the city. But that wasn't enough, was it? What's the expression? Sins of the father, Maester?

"I don't disagree, Nephalim. But that family's legacy is determined by the Council, on the guidance of every living person in Atlas."

"I don't care. You tell those fuckers hiding in the Seat that man made the ultimate sacrifice for all of us. We would all be dead if he hadn't. If the Council wants my continued investigation, cooperation, whatever— they will do what they have to. You clear Luca's name, and you make this right!"

After a moment, Barrett nods.

"I will bring the topic of a posthumous honor before the Council."

"Good. Next, I want Stephen Hardwick released into my custody. Right now. Then, we're going after Seraphina."

The Maester processes this plan, connecting Seraphina's ejection from Siskett's farewell party to the Behemoth that intruded less than a half hour later.

"You think the High Priestess had something to do with this?"

"You don't?"

"I just don't understand the connection," Barrett says, "if one exists at all."

"Simple. Luca didn't trust her, and I trust him more than anyone I've met here. He knew things, Barrett. He lived his entire life in Atlas, and knew Seraphina is bad fucking news.

"I don't know what part she's playing yet, Maester, but she's involved in this somehow. The High Priestess has been stewing in her anger for years—pretty much since she lost any grasp on power following Tomas' rebellion.

"Hardwick told me a woman came to see him. She knew who I was. She wanted to know more. I don't know, maybe she can see the future or something. One way or another, she knew I would come here eventually."

"And what evidence are you basing this on, Nephalim? Remember, I have no power over you. Only the Council does. Confide as much or little as you want. I'm just struggling to connect it all."

I scoff, sinking down the pillows.

"So am I. Believe me— I'm not looking for some link between Seraphina and the Behemoth. It's just there. She intervened right before Luca and I interrogated Maester Quorroc. She is a woman, and likely told Hardwick about the dragons. And finally, the timing between Venicia kicking her out of the Cathedral and the dragon is too coincidental."

All this evidence before him, Barrett offers no further questions. Before leaving, the Maester asks if there's anything else I need.

"Yes," I say. "Can you get a message to someone for me?"

• • • •

THE GARDENS— ONLY DAYS ago, the late Maester Siskett and I sat on a bench here— are serene. I have lost track of time staring at the giant hedge maze. Its green needles beckon to step forth into its abyss, lose myself in its twists and turns. I do, but only from the outside; the twists are my thoughts, and the turns are conversations repeatedly playing among them.

Trauma is the single greatest catalyst for transforming that genetic sequence. It can take the best men and turn them into monsters. It can take a young vagrant, transforming him to revolutionary. The code can change, Ramona. The code can change. But it is very, very difficult.

So much has happened, all of it madness. Never in my fleeting, mortal life did I imagine dragons fighting angels. Chasing down child abductors seemed far-fetched enough.

Piece of advice— anyone who tells you they've seen a dragon in the last four thousand years, or wants to sell you something to do with dragons, is selling you lies.

My eyes well at the thought of Luca. Siskett was due, ready to go off and seek his White Light. In comparison, my angel companion was young, so much time left to disprove his family's tarnished legacy. From every corner, Luca weathered criticism over Tomas' betrayal. It mostly slid off, but would catch under his skin once in a while, make him frown in a way that broke my heart— even if we didn't know each other well enough to say that little number out loud.

"You called?"

The voice behind me is immediately familiar and true. I don't know if it was coming out of a coma, or the strange world I found myself in before Atlas—whatever had me spooked in the Shroud is absent now. Turning to face the bearded man I have known my entire life, his presence is suddenly comforting.

"Yes," I say, standing to meet him. Our feet are only yards apart, yet he has never felt so distant. "For what it's worth, I'm sorry I ran away from you."

Tim smiles, says it is alright. He motions to the bench, and we take a seat together. The Gardens are beautiful from here. The blossoms are perennial while sending down its pink and purple petals to litter the grove. Unlike before, no yelling children run by, daring to step foot inside the giant hedge maze but never crossing so far that their mothers would scold them.

We are alone, only Light itself observing us.

"How are you settling in?"

I smirk.

"Quite the transition."

"From grown men abducting children to angels and dragons? I would say so."

"When you spoke of all that, to do with...your world, I guess— I wasn't even sure it was real. I'm sorry if that's hard to hear."

"It is quite the tall tale," Tim admits, "but Atlas is not my world, Ramona."

"I know."

"Just like you, this is my first time standing in it."

"I know that, too," I reply, admiring luscious grass leading up to the maze's entrance. "Siskett told me you surrendered."

Tim nods.

"That's right."

"My freedom, for yours."

"That's right, too. I won't lie. The night we separated, I was scared— terrified we had made some inconsolable mistake."

"In a way, we did, right?"

"I stayed scared for a long time," Tim says. "When I returned to the present, I tracked you down, even as Atlas had its agents searching for me. And I just waited," Tim admits. "There was a chance to fix it, but it's gone now."

"What do you mean, it's 'gone now'?"

He sighs— his way of preparing a grand omission, or revealing one. He has manipulated me to no end, but saved my life, and I trust him more than anyone.

"The Atlas sent an agent to eliminate some of the reincarnated individuals. Their deaths were undone by our choice, and she was tasked with eliminating seven names to undo the apocalypse."

And so Tim tells me what happened while I was asleep— how an angel of Atlas code-named the Phoenix strived to fulfill her task, restoring the world; how the Atlas and Tim both betrayed her in different ways. By the end, it feels like the most honest conversation we've had.

"Jesus," is all I can say.

"There's more," Tim says, "but that brings you up to speed in general, so you're not lost during the trial."

"Siskett mentioned that, too."

Tim sits forward, clasping his hands. I have never seen this celestial being exhibit fear. He was even calmer than I was during my raid on the FBI.

There is no trace of that man remaining.

"I don't know what the outcome will be," he admits. "I could face the White Light. I could be sent to Stone Mountain. Whatever the outcome, none are good."

"The Council is preoccupied with this Behemoth threat, if what Barrett says is any indication."

"And?"

"Maybe I can put in a good word, if you're willing to help me."

"No," Tim says. "Do not waste the Council's goodwill on me. I have run from my mistakes long enough, Ro."

"Listen to me— if a handful of gods can't understand why we did what we did, they'll just have to accept it. I am not about to sacrifice you just so the Council can make some example of you, Tim. If anyone is going to kick your celestial ass, it will be me. Got it?"

The man who calls himself Death smiles.

"Very well. What do you propose?"

And so, I tell him my plan— every last detail matters. When I finish, Tim mulls it over.

"And you think this will work?"

"I *know* it will work. Seraphina is in league with the Crimson League, and I intend to make her watch the Nephalim return to relevance. Just wait."

We sit in silence for a while, watching strong winds knock more blossoms off their branches, sending a lavender storm whirling down. They spin like all my doubts at work, released above the hedge maze of my pessimism.

If Seraphina is responsible for the Behemoth attacking the Cathedral, and Luca's death by extension, then it is my sole purpose from this moment to expose her misdeeds — no matter what it costs me.

I am not a monster.

CHAPTER ELEVEN

DAYS IN ATLAS DON'T seem to pass like those on Earth. The passage of time becomes unremarkable. My meeting with Tim in the Gardens could just easily have been days ago as it has been hours.

Were I to estimate how long I've been here in Earth time, it's somewhere in the area of a week. On the first day after waking from a coma, I died in an explosion, wandered a weird world with purple skies and spoke to the Avatar. I met the Council, punched a Whisperer and met an angel whose family history black-marked their line, preventing bestowment of their traditional title upon him.

On the second day, I became a Nephalim while Luca was forced to watch, visited Stone Mountain and resolved to never return to its shadowlands— complete with shrieking souls pouring from its thousand creepy windows.

On the third day, a dragon trampled a Cathedral, and Luca sacrificed himself to save the people inside. Lord knows how long I was unconscious after that. Barrett said a couple days, but it felt more like a month.

Since then, time has stopped and started as I await opportunities to draw the High Priestess into an admission of guilt. I keep my ears open while wandering Atlas, listening to conversations between its denizens. I pass the Dark Quadrant, eyes pointed down but picking up snippets in my travels.

Did you hear the Council—

Who does that new Nephalim think she is?

Dragons are coming. Was dragons that killed Luca, wasn't it? Big beasts, huge as the Spire, their screams echoing throughout Atlas. Dragons are coming, they're the apocalypse and they're here in numbers now, waiting to emerge.

The rumors are far and wide, varied and confused, each more outrageous than the last. The content doesn't change from God City to Devil's Corner; only the degree of sunken eyes and ratty clothes. Passing through the district I punched Gossamer recalls the angel's words.

This area has been overrun by worshippers of Ziz. Those who choose to remain here are at the mercy of his draining essences to sustain a minimal strength. Rather than accept his fate and sleep, the demon is fitful, aspirations stoked by his followers.

Could Ziz be responsible for dragons returning to Atlas? If Seraphina is the demon's executor, that makes her extremely dangerous. Devil's Corner makes sense to cover for intel. But the Whisperers know my plainclothes approach and the Crimson Dawn members recognize me as I pass by.

Luca is no longer here to protect me.

Stephen Hardwick will have to do.

• • • •

I ARRIVE AFTER STONE Mountain's iron doors have ramshackled shut, and the Arbiters are withdrawn back into their black hole. Coming across the man I would give anything to leave in its twisted innards—but fate has bestowed I cannot— his eyes are closed, drawing in fresh air of the Dark Quadrant.

"God City is cleaner," I inform him. My presence startles Hardwick, sapping the moment of any victory. I feel no remorse for it.

"Wouldn't know," he exhales. "I just got here."

"Guessing you didn't observe much on the way in, huh?"

Hardwick shakes his head.

"I didn't see any of it. One second I was with your friend, the next..." He winces, knowing I won't pity him. "Nevermind. What's the game with this place?"

Of course Stephen Hardwick— master strategist, American traitor— would see a game in it. The persona I first met — who cared about people, and didn't believe in torturing suspects— does not exist.

It was all a facade.

"There's no game, Stephen."

"Relax," he says. "It's a joke, Knox."

"Yeah, well— you killed the whole camaraderie thing when you tried to murder me. Let's start walking. I'll fill you in on the way to the Spire."

Our journey takes us through the Dark Quadrant and up to the Observatory, cutting down behind the Seat of Atlas. I tell him about my final confrontation with his crew in Washington, my merging with Tim and subsequent coma; I talk about Wilson and the hospital and waking in the Shroud. And by the time we approach the Spire's entrance on the southern end, I have briefed him on the Avatar and Seraphina as well.

"Quite the story, Knox. You've been busy."

Despite the part of me that should be repulsed by a man who stole children out from under families and sold them— on some level, I've missed him.

That is disgusting in itself.

"Never dull with me."

"I'll say," Hardwick quips as we enter through the Seat's enormous doors. "So what are we doing here, Knox? What's my role in this?"

Before I can reply, his eyes fall on the sky-kissing dome and paintings depicting Ziz. The same wonder that engrossed me takes hold of him— and that's before the Obelisk's dragons. Far as forces to reckon with, they haven't come up yet.

Think I'll leave that last part a surprise. Allowing him a moment to stand in awe of the Spire, neither do I have any desire to let his question linger.

"Whatever the fuck I say it is," I snipe, walking past him toward the Council's chambers. "We shouldn't keep them waiting. Let's go."

"Is that a demon?" he asks, still gawking at it.

"Now, Stephen."

· · · ·

LIKE PAINTINGS IN THE Spire dome, Hardwick shares the same plethora of emotion I did entering the dark chamber. There is no Barrett or Luca to lead me — now, I shepherd someone else before my cosmic masters, bound by Oath to do their bidding.

My former partner's eyes glaze over the beings, dormant in shadow. As my feet reach the center rotunda, they wake one by one— except Apollo, of course, who continues to doze away, rumbling from his sinuses. Hardwick glances to the empty chair, like I did. He absorbs the sight of a thirty-foot Viking, a woman with a headful of snakes and a man whose skin is literally made of magma. I did all that, too.

But now I am confident in front of them, the last Nephalim they can trust.

"Ramona," Venicia smiles as she rises from her stone chair. "It is good to see you up and about."

"Thank you," I say. "The feeling is mutual."

"This Council owes you our lives. Luca too, may he rest with the Light. His loss was a terrible one for Atlas, and will no doubt embolden its enemies going forward."

The Habinar cuts to the chase.

"Are you ready to get back to work, Nephalim?" he asks, sitting forward. The massive ax handle rests against his chair, pointed against the backrest behind him.

"Yes. I have already taken custody of my prisoner, and with your permission, would like to propose my theory, Your Eminences."

Muerkher gestures to me.

"Please."

I pace as I talk, putting all the facts before them. Hardwick looks lost, but less than he would have been if I hadn't briefed him. The Habinar, Venicia and Muerkher absorb every assertive statement, twitching at the emphasized bits I practiced on Barrett. They weigh morality against comfort; and when I finish, it is a moment before any of them speak.

"What you propose, Nephalim," the Habinar booms, **"is nothing short of instigating civil war within Atlas."**

"The axe-head is right," Muerkher says. "Making such a public and denigrating statement would turn what remains of the Nephalim against us. They have their allies—"

"The cost to Atlas would be catastrophic, Ramona," Venicia finishes. "Do you have evidence of this claim?"

"Not yet. But I can get it."

"How?" Muerkher asks.

"We hold a public event. But it has to be big— bigger than Siskett's party. We don't invite the Nephalim. Seraphina will undoubtedly balk if they're not there in some ceremonial capacity, and see it as a further affront to the Nephalim—"

"In which case," the snake-haired woman says, "she will resort to extreme measures."

The Habinar shakes his head.

"I don't like it, Venicia. We barely contained the Behemoth at the Cathedral— and it was destroyed. What happens when it's a plaza full of people?"

"I'm sorry," I interrupt. "I didn't mean to insinuate we invite a dragon into open Atlas. We hold some sort of get-together. Something that would grab Seraphina's attention, and feed into her paranoia—"

"The Atlas ball," Muerkher says. This draws Venicia's gaze to the Fire Man with a look of wonder on her face. Then it clicks, and she shares his line of thinking.

"That could work. The ball was held annually through the Second Age. There hasn't been one since Tomas' uprising."

The Habinar does not agree.

"It was bad enough we had to put down a tradition because of the Nephalim. Now you want to sully one by inviting Seraphina to attack it?"

"Only to give us the proof we need," Muerkher says. "If a Behemoth attacks this time, we will be ready for it. And we will know exactly where the blame can be laid."

Venicia returns to a smile.

"Can you agree to *that*, Habinar?"

It is a long time before the Viking responds.

• • • •

"DO THEY ALWAYS FIGHT like that?"

Though Hardwick is bewildered by the scene he witnessed, I leave the Council chambers somewhat disappointed, having hoped to save the revelation about dragons for another day. Maybe I'd allow one to come within a hair of eating him— but the plan takes precedence, and it is a moot point now.

"Well," he says, "you were right."

"About what?" I ask. The front doors open— I'm relieved to leave this way, sparing myself a glance of the ruined Cathedral where Luca died— and fresh air finds my airway. I halt at the threshold, just collecting its sweetness in my chest.

"Never a dull moment with you." Hardwick says. "So what now?"

A week into being a citizen of the supreme realm, I am still lurching one scenario to another, trying to find the perfect breath. It doesn't exist, of course— expectation has a way of doing that to beautiful things.

I'm not sure why I confide in him, even after everything we've been through together. At the same time, I find myself somewhat short on friends lately.

"I don't even know who I am anymore," I muse aloud. "I lived my entire life, trying to atone for my stupid parents. To... do the right thing. Trying to be someone they might have been proud of, if they would have stopped for a second to care; stopped doing enough drugs to register they had a child who needed them.

"I turned myself into this cold-hearted bitch, but...on the inside, I really did fucking care. Too much."

Hardwick nods, every condolence soaked in shame over his actions.

"You were the best of us, Knox."

Squeezing my arm, he leaves me to grapple with fragments of who I was, and who I'm supposed to be.

In between lies the person I am, and I resent her for everything.

CHAPTER TWELVE

THE ATLAS BALL IS HELD in God City, in a building called the Illumitory. I struggled to repeat the name as it was first said— looking at the massive palace now, it's a wonder I didn't spot it earlier. So focused on the quaint houses and humorous, twisting roads, the castle looming over the district didn't grab my attention. It does now.

Like the Seat, the Illumitory's primal draw is its massive dome arch, defining the castle turrets and surrounding towers. Royal Guard stroll its ramparts, looking out for any threat, rather than Nephalim to perform their rightful security role.

Just as we planned.

The glistening black one-piece Barrett somehow conjured from nothing is uncomfortable on my shoulders. The further discomfort of ladies in prettier dresses than mine have me resort to taunting Hardwick about a similarly acquired tuxedo.

"Gotta be honest," I say, boxed in by Atlas' rich and famous as we enter the palace. "Always wondered how you would look in a suit."

"Put a cork in it, Knox."

"Relax," I grin. "Looks good on you."

The Illumitory's main room is massive. Its dome matches the Spire's audacity, but with no painted tales imbued along its innards. Galleries emerge as balconies on the second and third floors. Small parties gather on them, overlooking the main rotunda and centerpiece interior fountain. A gold chandelier hangs over the water-spewing stonework. Its kneeling angel pours streams from tunneled eye sockets onto a small plate. It overflows into a basin that drains at the angel's feet. A massive sword like Luca's (*dammit Ramona*) is carved in the stone figure's side.

Twin staircases at the top of the room lead to a conjoined flight that subsequently travels up to the second floor. The walls are marked by carved columns with angels etched on one side and demons chiselled into their symmetrical opposites. Each of the balconies is equipped with railings that have the same painstaken carvings.

"Quite the party," Hardwick remarks.

"I'll say."

My eyes drift to the stairs. The Council stands on the second platform, accompanied by several Royal Guards — also strategically placed on the main floor, which contains hundreds of people— and Maester Barrett. Deeming them safe for now, I refocus on the multitudes of bodies in the rotunda. Taking note of some familiar faces— being an open event, I would be surprised not to see representatives of the Crimson League. Demetrius and his robed cronies loiter in a far corner, while a group of Magi occupy one of the above balconies, Elion among them.

It is here we will draw Seraphina out, proving she was responsible for Luca's death. If she unleashes another Behemoth, we will be ready. Hardwick taps me on the shoulder, whispering that he's going to scope out the room. I let him leave.

All I can do is wait for a sign, and it's showtime.

• • • •

SERAPHINA ARRIVES RIGHT as expected. Several nameless Nephalim, and Pol — the angel who greeted us at the Obelisk before we met with Quorroc— tail her into the building.

Hardwick notices her immediately, tapping me on the shoulder. Turning my head, I see what he sees— the tall woman glides through the door with her entourage. A gold dress replaces her red one, and her hair is wound like Carrie Fisher in *Star Wars*— buns around the ears — but I doubt she would get the reference.

"That the one?" Hardwick asks.

"Yep."

We were not alone in noticing her, either. The crowd disperses into two groups on the far sides, forming a clear path to the central staircase where the Council waits on a banister landing. The music—an awkward fusion of what sounds like jazz mixed with ska— stops at the sound of the High Priestess' clicking heels, sucking all warmth from the room as she glides to its top. Venicia is stone-faced at the intrusion; Muerkher scowls, and the Habinar is emotionless as Seraphina closes the distance between them.

"So here it is!" she calls, inching closer to the Council. She passes Hardwick and I standing in the front row on the left, and we are unworthy of the stolen glance. **"The coup is complete!"**

Seraphina advances up the room — smiling at those she knows, scowling at others — until arriving beneath the staircase. The Nephalim with her don ceremonial armor and swords — wings folded at their back, hands steady to draw in the High Priestess' defence.

The Council members say nothing, so Seraphina continues.

"When Tomas went against you, I was among the first to warn you. When the Crimson League floated whispers of further rebellion, *who* confirmed it? The threat to your own lives came at further cost to those who protect you!"

The Habinar speaks — in person, he is much closer to Luca's size — and for the first time, cold objectivity has spiralled into genuine annoyance.

"And how do you explain the dragons, High Priestess?"
Seraphina chuckles.

"And *why* would I know of the dragons, Your Eminence?"

"You are the sole individual who has an issue with us, Seraphina," Venicia says. "Of it, you have chosen to make a public stand against this Council, and innocence is yours to prove."

This angers the High Priestess — sinks her lip into a scowl and furrows her brow.

"How dare you? Do you give any consideration to these accusations, hmm? Have you thought of the consequences of your words?

I wouldn't expect you have — such are the impulses of ungrateful gods."

"Mind your tone, Priestess!"

Beside his leader, Pol appears torn. Seraphina will go to extremes to protect her reputation, but destroy what remains of the Nephalim's to do so. Her long dress drags behind her, never dirtied by the floor it's pulled across.

"You are so quick to cast your allies out, Your Eminences. Had you not, I would have told you all — I have *nothing* to do with the Behemoth that destroyed the Cathedral. I might have shared what I know as well!"

"And what *do* you know, Priestess?" Muerkher inquires. "I would urge you to play your card and prove your allegiance to this realm."

"How dare you?" Seraphina repeats. "Since the First Age, I have served you. Since the Second, we have lived and died for you. There were traitors, much like you have experienced your own turncoats. The *infectorum mundi*, perhaps?"

At the mention of Tim, I cringe.

"That is not a matter that concerns you," the Habinar says. **"This Council will deal with the World-Killer in a timely and efficient manner—"**

"Behind closed doors!" Seraphina says. "Meanwhile, you cast Tomas out! You fed embers to the kindling that set his rebellion aflame! On Gabriel's word alone! Cast out his son, limited the Nephalim's influence and put all of Atlas at stake!"

"That is enough, Priestess!"

"And to make matters worse, you elevate the World-Killer's accomplice to one of us! She, who endangered the realms to begin with! Where is she— your precious pet?

"No matter," Seraphina concludes. "You will soon understand that at the end of it all, this Council has sealed its own fate. You have emboldened the Crimson League, allowed dragons back into Atlas and cast aside your most important line of defence — what happens next will be on you."

The Priestess turns, pulling her entourage the way she came. Her eyes find me this time, leaving a smile in her wake that chills my spine. And when my own eyes fall off her luscious red hair and swanky walk, returning to the Council, they catch sight of someone else.

A blond woman across the room is fixated on me. I have never seen her before. Her dress is black, contrasting pale white skin and pink lips lifted in a smile. The look on her face isn't one of curiosity, but *knowledge*. Trying to dispel the strange *deja vu* washing over me, I glance back to the Council — the Habinar grumbles to himself, while Venicia and Muerkher speak quietly.

"Well, that was close," Hardwick mutters. "Almost expected a swordfight."

Venicia's flushed cheeks make the snakes appear pale. Sensing the goddess's anger, the serpents don't risk it by agitating each other. The room returns to a quiet babble as the crowd recovers from the confrontation. The space cleared for Seraphina is filled in with people, all gossiping about what they just saw.

And then something clicks.

A woman came to see me.

Hardwick, at the Shadow Commons.

Blond. Tall. Pretty. Reminded me of my ex-wife a bit. Not the first one. The second. Tits like a boar. I don't know her name.

My brain jumps into overdrive, straightening my posture where I'm frozen in place. Eyes flirt left to right, right to left, scanning my recollection of that conversation.

"You alright?"

What did this woman want?

To know about Knox.

I completely glossed over that description. Other than Venicia, the Priestess was the only high-profile woman I knew of when the dragon attacked Siskett's gathering, and poor demeanor made her a prime suspect.

Blond. Tall. Pretty. Reminded me of my ex-wife a bit. Not the first one. The second. Tits like a boar.

I was wrong.

"Knox?" Hardwick asks.

Pulled from my daze, my focus shoots back to where I saw the blond woman smiling at me.

When was this?

"Ramona! Talk to me, dammit."

Couple months ago. Not sure, really. Time is messed up in this place.

The woman is gone.

"We have to get to the Council," I say.

"What?"

"Now, Stephen. If what I just figured out holds any water, we may have been wrong. Come on."

I don't wait for his questions, and begin to cut through bodies, gunning for the staircase. Pushing people aside, eyes fixated on the gods I'm sworn to protect with my soul, my mind is everywhere else.

"Knox, slow down!"

There may not be much time —

The thought is interrupted by the sounds of gunfire. It breaks up nervous conversations, sending screaming people to the ground. Bullets and shotgun shells hit the chandelier, exploding its tiny gold ornaments, sending glass raining down over the marble floor.

Bodies drop — either dead or out of self-preservation— around us as armed men with masks filter through the palace doors. Without projections to hide behind, the Council has no means of escape from this band of marauders. They are not Nephalim or Crimson League; no dragon tails the balaclava-clad militia in red trench coats.

"Everyone on the fucking ground! Now!"

My stomach meets the floor, hands splayed in front of me. Hardwick assumes the same position as the aggressors advance to the front of the room. Their weapons are myriad — from handguns to semi-automatics— and I can't help but wonder exactly how one goes about acquiring firearms in Atlas.

It doesn't matter. The Council is under threat.

I have to save them.

• • • •

"Everybody on the floor! Now!"

The Illumitory falls quiet at the intruders' entrance. The indelible chatter and awe of the scarcely-used palace are replaced by scraping elbows along the floor, soft whimpering. Women in bejeweled gowns try to keep their garments from becoming dirtied. The male hostages, less focused on style in a critical moment, glare at our assailants. A sea of nervous glances are exchanged as a hundred bodies meet the ground in surrender.

Beside me, Stephen Hardwick clasps hands over the back of his skull, craning his neck to catch a glimpse of the Council. My eyes follow his, but the intruders' masked faces and semi-automatic weapons obstruct my view of the staircase. Seraphina, who stood between both waves of people during her confrontation, is whisked aside by Pol. The Nephalim unsheathes his sword, white feathered wings extending from openings in his red robes. The blade gleams; glare from the chandelier is cast off its edges as Pol acts as a human shield for his Priestess.

"I demand to know the meaning of this!"

I don't see the Habinar from the floor— only hear his booming inflections over the silhouettes blocking my view of the Council. The attackers don't respond. There are eight that I can see, all outfitted in the red jackets and black masks. Their weapons held low — once the majority of attendees have lowered to their stomachs with inter-locked hands— lead me away from the assassination theory.

These people want something from the rulers of Atlas, and they intend to have it.

One of the taller aggressors commands another to grab a captive; the man is too slow, and the leader waves him off, preferring to do it himself. The woman he pulls up by the straps of her diamond gown screams, trying to escape him. Still holding his sword in front of Seraphina, Pol is met with multiple sights trained on him. The angel has obviously never seen guns *in* Atlas, but is probably well-travelled enough to know what they are.

"Don't even think about it," one of the intruders tells Pol. "Winged freak."

How are they doing this?

The Council waits quietly as the woman is held at gunpoint. The barrel of a shotgun creeping along her soft pink cheek causes her to hyperventilate under the threat of death.

Guns aren't native to Atlas, my brain reminds me. *Since when have you seen them?*

Before I can ponder it further, or study the masked assailants— for a sign of identity, affiliation or any other clues— the leader an-swers the Habinar, holding the weeping woman against his chest. His forearm just over her throat pins her to him, binding their ulti-mate fates.

"Greetings, Your *Aminance*." The mispronunciation of *eminence*, coupled with a English accent and silhouette of a grin under the bal-aclava— which only means one thing.

They didn't manifest from osmosis. Somebody let these assholes into the supreme realm, guns and all. They're not dressed like its denizens and call hostages things like freaks and mutants, leading me to assume both a lack of education and unfamiliarity with Atlas on their part.

"And to what do we owe the pleasure of this interruption?"

The leader chuckles.

"Do you really not know, Your *Aminance*?"

Venicia steps to the bannister, joining the Habinar at its threshold. To their respective left and right, the twin staircases begin.

"Speak your intentions, or surrender peacefully. Dare I say, you will not enjoy the third option!"

Next to me, Hardwick glances above us— looking for an escape, a weapon, anything to defend ourselves.

The leader giggles, pressing the woman's posterior into his crotch area. The girl is no older than I am, in a glittering blue dress with her hair in a bonnet, wincing at the violation.

"Oh, no intentions in particular," he says in the woman's ear to stifled cries. "Ain't that right, sweetheart?"

The Habinar tenses his giant shoulders, gripping the ax he never leaves home without.

It may be all that saves us now.

"What do you want, then?" Muerkher asks, the most diplomatic among them.

"Aw," the masked leader says. "Y'all have a party, and don't invite the little guy, 'uh? Typical of big, self-important freaks who run everything, i'nnit it? Naw— we're gonna help make your big ol' smash a bit more interesting. Now, everyone on the ground floor to the center 'o the room!"

The underlings shepherd a hundred people into a huddle on their knees, alternating sights on all sides of the room. A rough hand meets my shoulder, pushing me ahead. Their gruff accents are mixes of Russian, Southerners and New York Yanks. Hardwick sinks to his knees in front of me, shoved down by one of the masked underlings. The leader and another hostage-taker keep sights trained on the Council as Seraphina and Pol kneel in the room's center next to us. The woman in the leader's grip rejoins the main group, collapsing into sobs. Some of the other attendees huddle around her, trying to offer meager comfort.

"Now, we was sent to collect the Avatar's central unit, or somethin' like that — somethin' I'm told you freaks 'ave access to."

"The Seed?" Muerkher asks. "Why?"

The leader shrugs — his body language suggests a look of perplexion behind the ski mask.

"Like I fucking know! My crew took a job, and we intend to collect!"

Theory confirmed. Somebody sent these wastes of life — someone with access to the Council — and now all of Atlas is under threat.

Seraphina must be working with Ziz's agents.

No Ramona, my brain retorts. *She looks just as terrified as anyone here.*

There is no sign of the blond woman who smiled at me like she knew something was about to happen. Scanning the crowd, I wonder who she is. Did *she* let them in?

Somebody inside Atlas is working against it. But first, we need to deal with the hostage situation, or there won't be an Atlas to save. A short glance past the collective of heads, shifting to the room itself, I look for weakness— anything I can use to gain the upper hand. Canvassing corners, floors and walls, I eventually land on the room's center.

The chandelier glistens in streaks of gold light bouncing off its shattered pieces, the remains of which cake the floor around us. It would provide a momentary distraction, give us a chance at disarming them — but would mean a hundred people killed when it landed on them.

Hardwick sees the lightbulb go off, and asks what I'm thinking.

"I have an idea. Just wait."

The captors circle in predetermined paths. They never stand still, constantly moving around each other, studying their hostages for signs of rebellion. The leader continues bartering with a Council denying they can access the Avatar's central unit — it is long embedded inside the being.

"Bullshit," the leader says.

A booming voice overtakes the Illumitory's silent undercurrent, piercing every pause between their negotiations. It startles me from watching the underlings' patrols for movement patterns.

"The Council is correct." Like a loudspeaker, the Avatar's feminine voice comes from nowhere and everywhere. The leader jumps back at her sudden intervention, looking everywhere around him.

"What the fuck was that?"

"To remove the Seed would short-circuit Atlas, but also kill the person who claims it. Since every action in the universe has an equal and opposite reaction, nothing could occur without a trade. The Seed, for the thief. Light for darkness."

The man in charge visibly panics at first, calming as he remembers there are men to give their lives for him.

"Think you can impress me with your little technol'gy, dont'cha?"

As he is distracted, and the subordinates who hold our group at gunpoint have had their all-consuming focus pulled away, I lean into Hardwick's ear.

"When I call out to you, move this group away, understand? Fast as you can, as many as you can."

Hardwick frowns.

"What's your game, Knox?"

The aggressors rebound from the Avatar's interruption, and I can no longer communicate. Flashing a glare that tells him to do as he's told, I return to watching the Council.

"**Now,**" the Habinar says, "**if that is everything, I suggest your retreat back to whence you came, or face the wrath of the supreme realm.**"

The man snickers.

"Supreme realm? What's 'o supreme about it? Seems like a shit-hole to me—"

One man passes my twelve. Another two are at my two and ten; two more at five and forty. The final one is still unnerved the most by the Avatar's sudden announcement, drifting away from the group.

"I'm going," I say. "Wait for my signal—"

The subordinate at my five notices my whispering to Hardwick, barking at me in a thick Russian accent to stand up and approach him. Keeping hands at head level as I approach him, I move slowly, letting my arms tremble, lip quiver — as expected, the satisfaction in his beady brown eyes tells me everything I can't see about the rest of him.

"Something to say, сука?"

My Russian is rusty, or I might return an equally intelligent re-sponse. The leader's paused speech informs me our confrontation has drawn some heads. All my attention is on the Russian underling who might be able to shoot me in the face; but his ignorance of Atlas is my advantage.

They have no idea that biological function is irrelevant here.

"Yes," I feign as wincing. "I have to pee."

The man exhibits a frown that pulls the balaclava's brow down-ward. His eyes dart over my shoulder to the Brit. I don't try to watch their exchange — to succeed, I have to be committed.

After a moment, the Russian refocuses.

"Fine. Where's the bathroom?"

"Right here," I say, cocking my arm back. The fist connects with his eye and he keels over, clutching the pulsing socket. Without hesi-tating, I grab the barrel of his shotgun, pointing it to the ceiling. The

Russian's finger tenses — the escaping cloud of smoke and shells ricochets, sending the hostages behind me into fits of screaming and crying. My knee thrusted at the man's abdomen dislodges his hold on the weapon, and its newly freed butt finds the right side of his jaw.

"Stephen, now!"

Sights at eye level spin on my heels to face the Council. In my peripheral vision, Hardwick yells at the crowd to help him rush the men to their left. My audacity inspires Pol to climb to his feet, drawing the sword on his hip.

"Nephalim! On me!"

My trigger finger lapses. The captor at my two, readying to shoot me, never sees a Nephalim's sword cut right through him. The leader inadvertently dodges the shotgun's fury — its shells are buried in the staircase below the Council's feet. The stampede led by Stephen Hardwick flattens both guards on my left. The two men scream before falling silent, presumably beaten to death by the braver souls like Hardwick.

Six are down, leaving only the two nearest the Council. I pull back the chamber, but don't check for shells, and am shortly informed by an empty click when I try to fire. Ditching the shotgun, I roll backwards as an automatic stream of gunfire from the surviving underling bursts marble floor at my feet. Bullets eat at the circular fountain as I take cover behind its basin, and it rains down limestone shards around me. A bullet strikes one of the Nephalim — he falls to the floor as Pol takes one through his wing. His sword clatters to the ground, and the bullet stream momentarily ceases. The leader is armed with dual pistols, but the assault is lessened as his colleague reloads the magazine.

Landing from the roll puts me into a crouch, and within arm's length of a fallen subordinate's weapon. Securing the handgun coincides with the AR-15 being reloaded, but my position puts me out of their sights.

A glance at the stairway assures me the Council evacuated to a higher floor when the gun battle started — communication between the surviving attackers assures it.

"Fuck! They escaped, Linus!"

"You idiot!" the leader yells between breaks in the gunfire. "No names, Benny!"

"Bit late now, ain't it, cocksucker?"

Tired of wasting bullets on a stone fountain, Linus and Benny advance beneath the chandelier, weapons pointed outright. The doors behind me open, and the panicked crowd escapes into open Atlas.

The top of their heads appear over the stone fountain's wall, and I point the .45 at the checkered ceiling.

Six bullets pass through the chandalier's center, shattering tiny gold ornaments into more fragments than Fourth of July fireworks in the capital. One strikes the chandelier's central support, severing chain links from the bracket that suspends it high above. The main fixture plummets alongside the busted torrent of jagged edges. It lands on the carcass of the fountain's central figure. Rogue shards splatter around the basin, splintering into a million cubes that wash outward from the point of impact.

The last thing I see before my nose touches the floor, hands hugging my head in the fetal position is Benny and Linus shrieking at the wave of lacerating droplets coming to impale them.

No longer aware of the smattering shower consisting of ricocheted glass, I sit up in the wreckage. The fountain is gone, beyond the bowl that recycled water into its spout. The bracket creaks well above a sea of cubic knives coating the floor in every direction. My arms ache with the blood down my bicep — the only thing that prevented sharing Linus and Benny's fates. Their bodies lay, spread-eagled and bleeding from a hundred new orifices on the fountain's other side.

Trying to regain any semblance of balance, my feet are eventually able to sway more than fall among the dead. Wincing at the fire down my arms, I stumble forward, taking baby steps towards a barely-stifled rage.

Somebody let those fuckers into Atlas — and that is the *only* lead I need to follow.

CHAPTER THIRTEEN

• • • •

"RAMONA," VENICIA SAYS. "I don't know what to say. We are once again in your debt."

Back in their rightful thrones, the Council is solemn. Even Apollo is awake, looking fully concerned. It is the first time I have seen anything more than a dozing look in the old man's eye, and I wish he felt secure enough to just go back to sleep.

Muerkher scoffs.

"It was *her* plan that put us at risk in the first place, Venicia!"

"Are you seriously questioning her loyalty, Muerkher? The woman has saved us not once, but *twice* now! First the Behemoth, now these...insurgents." Venicia seems satisfied with the word replacing a worse one for them.

"Yes, but we would have never held the ball without her recommendation."

I stare at the ground. Hardwick didn't accompany me, leaving me as their sole audience. Barrett is also shaken, and opted to take a moment for himself. I have no desire to insert myself into the argument.

Muerkher is not wrong.

The Habinar, who has quietly mulled this newest development as his peers argued, finally breaks his silence.

"For once, I am on the Nephalim's side. If we had not held the ball, we would have been ignorant to this. Somebody in our court is feeding the source of our problems information. I anticipate these two attacks are connected, and there is an agent of Ziz among our confidantes."

"Who?" Muerker grunts. "We don't have time to chase conspiracy theories, axe-head. Seraphina is clearly in cahoots with our adversary—"

Venicia shakes her head of living creatures.

"I disagree. Three of her own were injured in the attack. If I know anything about the Priestess, she would not knowingly put her men in danger."

"And still, I think she knows more than she is letting on."

Venicia homes in on me.

"What do you think, Ramona?"

"**Yes**," the Habinar says. "**This is your plan, Nephalim. Advise us on the next steps.**"

The newfound respect from the Viking is temporary — the threat to them is profound and merciless in its pursuit, and there is no time for warm and fuzzy.

"I may have mischaracterized the High Priestess, but that doesn't mean she's completely innocent. Her behavior made her a high-profile target, and I stand by my initial assessment. However, I agree that somebody within your inner circle may be providing information regarding your defense strategy — this being based on insider knowledge of both Siskett's gathering and access to the ball. But there's something else."

"What is it?" Venicia asks.

"At the ball, just before the attack, I saw a woman. I had never seen her before, but she was there five minutes before the attackers arrived, and I didn't see her again after that."

"And you think this woman is somehow connected to the conspiracy."

I nod.

"It's possible. There seem to be a lot of hands in this cookie jar, if you'll forgive the expression. Luca said Ziz's followers stem from many different factions — but they're working interchangeably, almost seamlessly to hinder us."

"So what are the next steps?" Muerkher asks.

"We need to find the coordinating agent who is holding all these forces together. Luckily, we know their goal — to steal the Avatar's central processing unit—"

"Which would be the end of Atlas," Venicia concludes for me. "This goes deeper than I ever could have imagined. Tomas' rebellion was one thing, but this is sophistication unlike anything we've seen. There are Behemoths and outlanders, Maesters and gangs wrapped up in it.

"I don't know where it begins, but I tell you: it ends *now*. Find these people, Ramona. Find them, and keep the Avatar safe."

"I have every intention of doing so," I tell them, bringing a smile to the serpent woman's troubled expression.

The Habinar interrupts.

"There is another matter, and one the Nephalim should be aware of."

"What is that, Habinar?"

The Viking sighs — not the least peaceful mood I've ever seen him in, but far from untroubled.

"The *infectorum mundi* — the World-Killer. Seraphina's claims that we are protecting him have provoked…unuseful chatter among the rabble. At a time like this, such a perception is dangerous. We will have to try him soon, in a very public manner."

The news shouldn't have been unexpected — I have to stifle sadness nonetheless. The Habinar is not wrong. The idea that the Council is protecting the person responsible for Earth's demise only places their own lives at further risk.

"I understand. I am sure Tim will accept whatever fate you deem appropriate."

"Very well," the Habinar says, with a new vulnerability to our interactions I can appreciate. **"You are dismissed, Nephalim."**

"Miss Knox," Venecia says. "Speak with me in private, if you would."

• • • •

THE SERPENT WOMAN LEADS me to a set of stairs outside the chamber I wouldn't have ever known existed. Positioned behind a sliding panel in the Spire's painted walls, the dark stone passage winds upward. Its walls are unmaintained, in contrast to the rest of Atlas. Spiders dart between cracks into the grooved blocks, crossing paths as they scurry out of the way.

The goddess leads — though it is dark and I can scarcely see, she doesn't seem as tall here, nor a projection. The Council must be able to seamlessly transition between hologram form and their true manifestations, placing them much closer to humans in size and vulnerability.

As we come to the top, and the Light I sorely missed in the stairwell soaks me in its full power, panoramic windows look out over all of Atlas. The circular room offers a three-hundred-sixty degree view of the supreme realm. From the massive gates where I met the Avatar, to the Observatory overlooked by interstellar panoramas to the north; everything between is visible. God City's colorful rooftops stand out like an acid-infused architect built a miniature Santa's village. The snaking apartments of Devil's Corners are matched in dreariness by the dark clouds over the district, and the Gardens offer a view of the swirling purple blossoms and giant hedge maze's center, containing a bench and yet another stone fountain.

"Wow," I gasp, simultaneously drawn to every sight, both light and dark. "It's gorgeous."

Venicia smiles, but it is broken as the Cathedral in the northwest. "I remember when I used to feel that way. Time has a way of rubbing beauty off the most timeless surface. You can look at something that was built to be forever youthful. Perfect. And it is.

"But over time, you start to see flaws in the perfection — little strategic folds to cover all the things its creators didn't want us to see. It is an illusion, like anything you stare at for too long, trying to make sense of. Flawlessness warps and erodes, like anything else in the storms of time."

The goddess is troubled by all the things she has seen, and rightfully so — the snakes atop her head are contemplative, rather than obnoxious; mourning, rather than adding to the world's violence.

I say nothing, affording her a rare moment alone, saying aloud to herself things that are meant just as much for me.

"We have tried to lay the blame for our mistakes at the feet of others for too long. For all her pettiness and ranting, Seraphina is not entirely wrong. We refused to take any responsibility for the Nephalim uprising, or using Behemoths in the first place. We always moved forward, letting others fall on the sword; ignored elements on the fringes until they constituted a crisis."

A question comes to me — to this point, I have never been alone with any of the Council members. They have always faced me together, and my questions were met with conflicting responses.

"Seraphina said Gabriel was responsible for the uprisings. Not Tomas. Luca seemed to adhere to the more common narrative — that his father led the Crimson League against you."

"What are you asking, Ramona?"

"I'm asking if there's any truth to it," I reply. "Right now, the Priestess is on a very ambiguous line. She could be innocent just as easily as she might be guilty. If it's the latter, she's definitely not working alone. But I need the truth, Your Eminence. If she's not involved, I'm wasting a lot of time here."

Venicia sighs.

"Maybe we put too much faith in Gabriel. I know we did. But he loved Tomas like a brother — to make the kind of accusations he did warranted immediate intervention. We panicked, and took the least righteous course. Sent agents to round up Tomas' wife and Luca, who was only a boy. It was the Habinar's call, but I was just as guilty for supporting it."

"And that's why Tomas stormed the Spire," I finish. A sour taste rinses my mouth, and I recognize it as anger. "To save his family."

Venicia nods.

"Did Luca know that?"

The serpent woman shakes her head, and suddenly, I don't want to hear anymore about Atlas' past. All I want to do is to fulfill my duty. Venicia's guilt is her cross to bear, not mine.

"So," I say, "*what* are you asking me to do?"

The goddess bestows a look unlike any I've seen from her. It is fear — not necessarily toward the storms at her doorstep, but judgment for her part in nurturing its size.

"Determine Seraphina's role in this, once and for all. I don't care how you do it, or what my compatriots think. If she's truly not involved, we can bring the Nephalim back into the fold."

"And if she's guilty?"

"Then things are much worse than we ever imagined. This stays between you and I, Ramona — am I clear?

"Yes, Your Eminence."

"Good," she says. "Do you have any idea how you are going to approach it?"

One second, she doesn't care how I do it; the next, she wants to know. If the serpent woman is giving me *carte blanche*, then my circle has shrunken to me, myself and I.

"I'll figure it out. Do we still have the weapons from the attack on the Observatory?"

Venicia frowns.

"Why?"

"Because I'm going to infiltrate the Obelisk, and make the High Priestess spill the goods. Back Seraphina into her own corner, she'll have nowhere to run."

"And you plan to do this alone?"

"No. I'll have help. I'll bring Hardwick."

The goddess ponders my proposal. There is no more relief in one option than failing to do anything, which is incidentally another, and one I have grown tired of.

"Be careful, Ramona. The Nephalim will not hesitate to cut you down if they see you as a threat to the High Priestess —"

"—who are also in disarray. Several were wounded during the attack on the Illumitory. Pol is out of commission. I think the two of us can outsmart those still standing."

"Very well," Venicia replies. She is no less world-weary for my feigned confidence, but accepts the proposal — to put the Nephalim's rogue elements in their place, once and for all. "See Barrett for access to the remaining weapons. He will need to be brought into the fold."

"Okay." I trust Barrett more than most, and don't anticipate his inclusion is a problem. "Thank you, Your Eminence."

"Just...be careful, Nephalim. Seraphina is a powerful enemy, and already distrusts you. There may be no coming back from this."

I smirk, taking one final look through the panoramic windows, admiring Atlas before I learn to recognize its darkness.

"If the High Priestess *is* guilty, that will be true. For what it's worth, I don't believe she is — just a bitter old crone who's stewed in her resentments too long. Arrogant? Definitely. But plotting the demise of Atlas? I'm not as certain as I was."

At this point, I could basically say that about everything.

• • • •

AFTER RETRIEVING HARDWICK from some generously donated quarters at the Barracks, I double back to the remains of the Cathedral. It is the first time I have looked at the wreckage since the dragon destroyed it. Rubble is scattered in conflicting directions. The stone columns poke out of the debris which no god had time to order cleared away. The dust is settled, waiting to be kicked up by any ghosts that traverse the ruins, grabbing sentiment by the leg.

Barrett waits for us by the wreckage. The old scholar is troubled as any god over the destruction and assault on his Order, the Council he serves and Atlas in general. His eyes are glued to the remains of everything he built; a man at the end of his tenure, debating greater questions with the semi-permanent sunset over him.

"Maester?"

He barely turns, acknowledging our arrival with a grunt — a shell of the cheerful man I met on my first day here.

"Did Venicia brief you?" Again, the response is muted, filled in by Barrett's clicking tongue and slow-drifting gaze.

"All of this violence," he says. "We were given everything — the pinnacle of Creation. Privilege of shaping the universe, and safety from darkness. Yet, all we do is squander it."

Much as I would like to stand here and appease Barrett's self-pity, if those Nephalim recover, this operation will become much harder.

"Venicia said you knew where the remaining weapons were kept from the Illumitory attack. I need them, Maester."

"Why?" Barrett asks. "If I give them to you, how much more vi-olence do we risk? How far does it go, Nephalim?"

"Until it stops," I reply. "Until this city is safe and the Council can sleep with both eyes shut. I gave my word to protect them, and *everything* I have done is in service to that, Maester. I don't want vio-lence anymore than you do."

Finally breaking fixation with the ruins of his Cathedral, Barrett faces me with a wince.

"Very well. I will do as asked. But I do not endorse it, under-stand?"

Neither do I, Maester.

Neither do I.

• • • •

THE REMAINS OF LINUS' crew are held in a cellar below the Coliseum district. It is the first I have ever laid eyes on the Arena up close— a massive circular stadium where angel heroes once put on displays of might for peasants of Atlas — and much to the Council's delight. Barrett explains on the way that few venture here anymore. It has the stink of the old ways, counter to the gods' progressive new image following the Nephalim uprising.

The cellar is attached to a small gatehouse near the physical arena. It is not much more than a trapdoor in the ground, but Barrett didn't want to risk any of Linus' benefactors retrieving their worldly possessions. The air is filled with dust, the cavernous room soiled by mortal corpses strewn over its uneven floor. The collection of spent weapons is the same as the pile of functional ones. Hardwick and I approach the small mountain that once represented the largest threat on Washington's streets. Now there are dragons and angels and nothing will ever be normal again.

My partner secures a handgun, inspecting the chamber to ensure it's loaded, then does the same with an assault rifle. My hands canvass the assortment of deadly contents, settling on two pistols and a shotgun with a leather strap, fastening it around my shoulder.

Behind us, Barrett speaks.

"I sincerely hope you will exercise restraint, Nephalim. Arrogance and foolhardiness has been the cause of enough trouble."

"Believe me, Maester— I agree wholeheartedly. With any luck, we're closing in. And believe it or not, I am trying to exonerate her. She's just too thick-headed to take a reasonable out when she sees one."

"I hope you're right," Barrett says. "Good luck, Ramona."

I am not a monster.

CHAPTER FOURTEEN

. . . .

THE BARRACKS ARE MORE tense than it was leaving them after collecting Hardwick to meet Barrett. It likely has to do more with the fact we're about to make a scene. The Royal Guard has withdrawn from the district. Groundskeepers and lesser angels without the distinctive Nephalim robes (some don't even have wings), glare at my holstered pistols and the rifle in Hardwick's grip. Ignoring the temple-like buildings down the Obelisk's flanks, we march through the corridor between their opposing arrangements. The central building is my only fascination now, our pace brisk approaching its walled stairway.

Two higher-ranking angels barricade the doors, keeping their spear bottoms glued to the ground. Like those in the courtyard, they study the combustible weapons not native to Atlas as we approach.

"Gentleman," I say. "We have a standing appointment with the High Priestess."

"I don't think so," the Nephalim on my left says. "The Obelisk is closed to outsiders."

"I don't understand," Hardwick says. "Aren't you one of theirs?"

I roll my eyes.

"You would think so."

The second guard speaks.

"The High Priestess does not recognize this woman as Nephalim. She is an interloper, and will never be accepted by the order. Please retreat beyond the Barracks, or we will be forced to call reinforcements."

Unbelievable. He addresses Hardwick the entire time, acting like I'm not present. My fingers tense around the shotgun strap, and Barrett's request for civility becomes less likely.

"If Seraphina wants to exonerate herself, she'll speak with me—"

The first guard interrupts.

"The only audience the High Priestess owes is to the Council itself. Make all the threats you please, woman. She is done with the likes of you."

Whatever dream of smashing the angel with my shotgun's blunt end is superseded by Hardwick swinging his own into the Nephalim's face. The man collapses at my feet, clutching his bleeding jaw, but tries to get back up. I kick out, bringing the top of my foot into the bridge of his nose. The angel's nasal cavity shatters, and he falls still in a heap.

Putting the other angel in a chokehold, Hardwick pulls the angel's sword from its sheath with his spare arm, holding the rifle over the guard's throat. He casts the blade down the stairs; it clatters every few steps before settling at the bottom.

"I got him, Knox. Let's move."

I enter the cleared doorway; Hardwick pushes his hostage through the frame behind me. The guard grunts, manhandled under the threat of death. All the Nephalim's demons are on full display with the painted walls as I raise the shotgun barrel. We advance into the hallway where several members have drawn swords after hearing the commotion at the doorway.

"*Stop right there!*"

"**Not another step!**"

"They've got a hostage! At ease, men!"

Pol pushes past the frontline, who don't quite ease as ordered, continuing to hold their swords outward. Pol disregards his bandaged wing and arm in a sling to intervene, met with cynicism by his brethren and us.

Hardwick and I keep our weapons raised — Hardwick to his captive, mine to anyone who walks in front.

"Are you alright, Nephalim?" Pol asks the man in my partner's grip. At his disgruntled nod, the angel raises an open palm, standing between his brothers and my shotgun. "We can resolve this peacefully, Miss Knox."

"Is that right? You're going to take me to Seraphina?"

Pol grimaces.

"The High Priestess is unavailable. She sustained shaken nerves at the ball, and has been holed up in her chambers since."

"Well, let's go knock on her door, then. I can be fairly persuasive when I want to be, Pol, and I'm all out of small talk with the woman."

Our negotiator ponders this a second. His dark hair is ruffled, and he looks tired of his order's political games.

"Release the boy, and I'll take you to the Priestess," Pol says. He wheels, using his good arm to signal his compatriots. Within a second, their swords are lowered.

"Nope," Hardwick says. "Kid's the only thing that keeps you from cutting us down. I'll let go when you come through for Knox."

I look back at my partner, and tell him to release the hostage. This earns a scowl from Hardwick.

"The hell, Ramona."

"Let him go, Stephen. Fair is fair."

Hardwick mutters something, but obeys. The young angel rubs his neck, stumbling to the other Nephalim. Pol is good to his word, and beckons me to follow him.

"Your partner stays here," he commands, and I tell Hardwick I'll meet him later.

"Sure?"

"Yeah. I got it from here."

"Fine," he says. "But keep your guard up."

Hardwick's eyes canvass the paintings above the platoon of Nephalim. He keeps the rifle raised, backing toward the door as I am led away by Pol. The strap of my shotgun finds a shoulder, and bit by bit, I lower my guard, rather than raise it.

Time to make Seraphina spill the goods.

• • • •

THE HIGH PRIESTESS' chambers occupy an entire level at the top of the Obelisk. A special elevator in the back bay of the building is required to take us there, but there is no metal box like in the real world. The glowing red platform with no handrails shudders as it moves — Pol is calm at its rocking ascent, while I sway back and forth like an idiot to maintain balance.

Seraphina's lobby is a nondescript room with thick metal doors, engraved with the dragon-themed seal of the Nephalim — a serpent with a Behemoth's face atop it. Two sentries on either side of the double doors immediately notice our intrusion, informing Pol that the Priestess is not taking visitors.

"I understand," the senior Nephalim says. "Unfortunately, we have a slight emergency—"

While Pol might have no problem weaving the tale of his predicament to everyone he encounters, I don't have time. Emulating Hardwick, the butt of my shotgun smashes one angel in the jaw as my foot is thrust into the other's shin, sending him to kneel. The one suffering a broken mandible meets my wheeling foot as the weapon crashes into the second.

Pol glances down at his wards in horror.

"I could have diffused that, you know."

"Sorry," I reply, arriving at the crack in the doors. **"Seraphina!"**

There is no answer on the other side, nor a discernible device to knock with. They don't budge meeting my shoulder and offer nothing pressing my ear against them. Pol watches intently as I bang my fist on the metal and continue calling the Priestess' name.

"Are you sure she's in there?"

"Yes," Pol says. "Seraphina is known to go into deep meditation. It becomes nearly impossible to reach her in these trances, if at all. We may be forced to wait until her session concludes. It could be a long one, so brace for a wait."

I don't care if she's at fucking Seaworld — I'm getting through these doors. I raise the shotgun, firing dual shells at the door. They bounce off metal and ricochet into the far corners, leaving a trail of sparks. Pol and I duck as they ring off one wall, throttling toward the next, almost taking both of us out.

"Are you insane?" the angel yells. "That's six-inch metal!"

"Sorry," I repeat, and prepare to resume banging on the door when a massive shift occurs beneath my feet. The doors creak voluntarily; a loud whine rings in my ears and doesn't cease until both are opened wide.

"Leave us, Pol."

The shrill inflections float out of Seraphina's chamber. Pol nods as I look toward the chamber where our final confrontation will ensue.

"Come in, Miss Knox," the voice invites from the disembodied corners of my dread.

Keeping the shotgun raised, I advance inside, unsure if either of us will re-emerge.

· · · ·

SERAPHINA'S CHAMBERS are impressive and colorful. Exotic rugs run the room's length. Bookcases filled with ancient texts in leather-bound tomes line the walls. Seating consists of large cushions spread throughout the room, which is dimly lit and adorned in bead curtains throughout. Candles provide most of the illumination — their arrangements remind me of the way a serial killer might lay them out before performing some sick, sacrificial ritual.

The High Priestess waits cross-legged on one of the circumferential cushions. Its texture looks to be animal skin of some kind, and Lord knows what makes up the stuffing. Seraphina seems to be more lost in despair than meditation — her eyes are sunken, ridges of her unforgiving jawline darker. The red strands of her long hair are frayed.

"Have you come to gloat?" she groans. "You would have been wiser to wait until I had my face on. Not my most flattering look, hmmm?"

I don't lower the shotgun, slowly advancing toward her.

"It's time we had an honest talk, Priestess. I would buy you a drink and do it in a more civil manner, but your attitude has made that a bit challenging. So if you want to clear your name in this conspiracy, I suggest you put aside whatever problem you have with me, and cooperate."

Seraphina scoffs.

"Don't flatter yourself, Miss Knox. My issue is not with you any longer, hmm? It is with truth."

"Truth?"

"Yes. That my usefulness in this political hierarchy may be outlived. I have been here for a long time, Ramona. I have seen things that would haunt me mercilessly, if I had not learned to block them out, hmm?'

Seraphina has nothing to do with any of this. The shotgun lowers at this realization — the woman has been defeated so long, any attempt to defend herself is heresy.

"When the uprising happened," she says, "I knew it was my fault. I saw what Gabriel was becoming — the Council trusted him, and he was too willing to sacrifice others in their eyes to get his way. I saw how he treated Tomas, who loved Gabriel like a brother. But Gabriel only loved himself, hmm?

"I shouldn't have...fought them after. I should have done it *before* all this happened, and I was irredeemable — after I failed to protect Atlas."

"What about the dragons?" I ask.

"The dragons," Seraphina scoffs. "My weakness. All because my outbursts were ill-timed, I am forever associated with their return. I can't tell you about the dragons, Ramona, hmm? I can't tell you, because I have no more information about them than you do."

I was right.

"If that's true," I say, finally pointing the weapon all the way down, "you need to stand with us now. Let the Nephalim earn their way home — not with resentment and petty politics, but honor and pride. Stand with the Council against this threat."

Seraphina chuckles.

"And what's to say the Council doesn't turn us away, hmm? We are disgraced. Forever on the fringe of Atlas now — just another gang of thugs."

"What's to say they do?" I counter. "The Council needs you, Priestess. Will you stand with us?"

The disheveled leader says nothing, but doesn't need to — there is a slight relief to her expression, as if the world's weight has lifted from her shoulders, and she tries not to let the long-coveted exhale show.

The Nephalim stationed downstairs eyeball me walking past them as I leave, exiting onto the stone staircase. I try to suppress gratification at being right for once. The journey to coax Seraphina into civility was long and treacherous, and part of me is glad to have her allegiance at last. My circle of allies is building, our foothold into every level of Atlas more secure with each confrontation with its factions.

That self-congratulations is cut short by the lone figure standing alone in the courtyard as I approach. The blond woman from the ball. She waits with a crooked smile, as if she expected me — as if someone told her I would be here. Only a handful of people knew— but here she stands, in a white t-shirt and jeans, almost as tall as me and dressed for a day at the mall, rather than manifesting at the most inopportune times.

Her smile grows wider as I close the gap. There are maybe two hundred paces from the Obelisk and the barrier separating it from the God's Road, but each step is heavy and my heart revolts at the sight of her.

Did she let Linus and company into Atlas? If she did, who told her how to access the Illumitory or the Council? I reach the center where she stands, and the world between us rings with deafening silence.

Who is this woman?

I don't speak first, but neither does she. And when our staring contest stumbles into the snapping beams of patience, I finally ask the question on the tip of my goddamn tongue.

"What do *you* want?"

CHAPTER FIFTEEN

THE WOMAN LEADS ME to Devil's Corner. She is silent through the walk. Blond hair in a loose ponytail, her clothes are simple in comparison to the ball.

Instead of panicking, I resort to taking in my final view of Atlas, if she does indeed plan to murder me.

Her destination is unremarkable — a tall, snaking structure reminiscent of all the others in Devil's Corner. From its southern point, the thin building curves out before swinging inward like the letter S. A nondescript glass door on the eastern wall leads into an apartment building of sorts. The lights inside flicker and people slump under graffitied descriptions like **PRAISE ZIZ** and **OUR S ULS OR HE DARK L RD.** The woman ignores the ground floor's occupants, leading me to a cluttered stairwell.

The third floor apartment resides in a less populated hallway. It takes a moment to recognize my surroundings as we enter the frame. The woman closes the door as my eyes fall on the tile entrance, master bedroom door and bathroom. *Deja vu* is instantaneous. Through the swinging kitchen door lies the table where I kept folders of forensic evidence and conversed with a ghost who appeared throughout my existence, offering guidance. An antique rotary telephone on the countertop is yellowed by time and cigarette smoke, and I still smell nicotine on the walls.

The woman says nothing as I explore. I exit out of the kitchen, hands passing over walls, my eyes meeting the mirror in our front hallway whose reflection I could never face. In the living room where Maya lived in a chair for years, hooked up to an oxygen tank until she died, all the furniture is perfectly preserved. The couch where I slept, holding her hand still bears my faint outline. The gray machine by her recliner whirs and beeps, although it was turned off the second they carted her away.

"What is this?" I ask, wheeling to face the woman.

Her lips remain pursed, hands clasped in front of her.

"This is where it all began, wasn't it?"

"Where...what began?"

"*You*," the woman says. "Where you learned you were special, Ramona. Where greater forces found you, demonstrated there was more to the world than you'd been shown."

"Tim."

"If that is what you call a man who sentenced the world to die — all to appease some personal grudge, no less — then call him what you will."

"The World-Killer, then. He's who you're referring to."

"It doesn't matter," the woman replies. She paces to Maya's chair, caressing the spot her head used to lay. "Atlas will soon have bigger problems than one rogue celestial being."

"The dragons?" I ask. "Do you know about them?"

"That, and so much more, Ramona. I have been gifted with an unimaginable calling — the gift of knowledge. That which drives you is in my possession."

"What does that mean?"

The woman smiles, but its arrogance drags more anger out the question than curiosity.

"You have been given a *great* responsibility, Miss Knox. To protect the pinnacle of Creation from threats in the shadows. A noble cause, to be sure. But not all who admire you for your heroic deeds — saving the Council at the Cathedral, then again at the ball — might know you would have never survived the Jordan West case without divine intervention."

"What are you trying to say?" Discomfort is reaching critical mass in my tensed jaw and bunching fists. "And who the hell are you?"

"I am a catalyst, Ramona. Nothing more. Like you, I was given a great opportunity to serve something bigger than myself. The only difference between us? I chose the stronger horse."

"Ziz." The words escape my mouth without braking to consider the velocity of their landing. The woman must have expected I would deduce her allegiance quickly, because the answer satisfies her.

"I was quite pleased when your investigation targeted the High Priestess. She is quite the conspicuous one, isn't she?"

In an illusion of the only home I've ever known, all my wildest failures unravel. The revelations are like fireworks, lighting up my expression with explosions of colorful horror.

I don't know what part she's playing yet, Maester, but she's involved in this somehow. The High Priestess has been stewing in her anger for years; pretty much since she lost any grasp on power following Tomas' rebellion.

Seraphina had no part in this.

"Same goes for the Crimson League. The Whisperers. Quorroc." She clearly delights in how wrong I've been. "I couldn't have timed the Behemoth better. All these forces the Council and its proxies were so sure were involved — the perfect distraction."

"But why?" I ask. "Even if I can never understand, why tell me?"

Even as I ask it, home movies of my human error infinitely playing in my head, the woman wants me to know I've failed.

"When I first came to Atlas," she explains, "I was broken. I had given up everything to right a wrong. But instead of being rewarded — as some may see it — I felt emptied of everything I had ever loved."

I say nothing.

"But time has a funny effect. The longer I was here, the more my eyes opened. I saw the Council's hypocrisy, how they treated everyone who has ever laid down their lives for them. I saw the love that

I someday hoped to reclaim...*taken*. I felt replaced, in every aspect of the word.

"I started...hearing voices — at first, I thought I was going crazy. It came to me in dreams, when I ventured too close to Devil's Corner. In the beginning, I ignored it. But then, the voice became stronger. Beckoning me. It flowed into my thoughts at all times of the day, and I would have gone mad eventually.

"I followed its instructions. It led me to the darkest depths of Atlas, where the sun never goes and even the rats are scared to idle. I went well below the underbelly of this city. There, Ramona, I found what was always missing — a part of my soul that was always kept from me."

"What part?" I ask, suddenly more uncomfortable with my childhood home than I've ever been. After Maya died, I could barely dwell here, but our conversation within its memory tarnishes it, and this moment may never leave me.

"Power," she says. "Of such magnitude, to go back to a time without it would leave me a skeleton of what I am — a weak, dishevelled being that would make the longest-tenured Whisperers look like the belle of the ball."

This agent of Ziz — who has made all of us look like fools chasing a loose group of suspicious individuals — is a bigger threat to Atlas than anyone I have encountered. And yet, wringing her neck would get me no closer to stopping her plan, whatever it may be.

"And what are you planning to do with this power?" I ask. "What's the endgame here? Or is that some big mystery?"

The woman's smile reaches its apex.

"Not at all," she nods. "Let me tell you."

And so, she does.

CHAPTER SIXTEEN

I DON'T KNOW WHAT TO do.

Leaving the weird conjuration of my childhood home — where a suited man named Death first appeared to me at five years old; then, years later, took my aunt's soul — I want to die, and go all the way back to the beginning; let the Habinar feed me to the White Light, let Luca spearhead the investigation. It would have ended with a Behemoth killing him, and the Council would die, anyway.

But my part in this nightmare would be removed.

My feet feel like nothing as I pass leery-eyed Crimson League. I pass the mother with a suckling infant and forget about the persistently murky sky of the district, just trying to outrun my panic.

I have to get to the Council.

They will be at Tim's trial. After Seraphina's accusations at the ball, they couldn't delay any longer. No doubt Hardwick will be in the audience — a public trial was another result of the High Priestess' challenge — to see justice visited on the man who sent him to Stone Mountain.

I will need his help.

The trial is held in the Observatory, thankfully a short sprint from Devil's Corner in the west. The nebulous sky greets me after passing the destroyed Cathedral.

The northernmost structure in Atlas is massive. A giant device atop its domed roof looks outward into the universe that makes the building seem so small. It is the second largest building in Atlas after the Seat, easily dwarfing the Illumitory and Obelisk. The district is filled with people crowded around the building because it is too full to get inside. Many of them are of negligible status — all are poorly dressed, no nobles, Maesters, or angels among them.

"Knox!"

Stephen Hardwick cuts through the sea of people to my left, pushing aside from the west as I traverse north through the bodies, and I beckon him to follow.

"What the hell is going on?"

"We have to get inside the Observatory," I reply, pushing through sets of shoulders. The fifty feet between the gate I entered the district and the Observatory steps are more like Woodstock than a public trial or inauguration.

"Good luck with that," Hardwick says, trying to keep up. "This place is fucking packed."

"If we don't cut through it, the Council is dead." I explain it will have to wait as we navigate up the stream of chattering people awaiting a verdict. Soon enough, I can make out the giant open doors and an inadequate number of Royal Guard to hold back the bottlenecked crowd.

"How solid is this intel, Knox?" Hardwick asks.

I never have the chance to respond — there is a loud crash, followed by a roar, then a second scream ascending the Observatory district's stone wall. I turn my head — arms pushing ahead withdraw, tapping Hardwick on the shoulder. My partner is fixated on the original plan, still trying to advance.

It is not my touch that draws his attention to twin beasts perched on the stone wall, but their second set of bellowing that rings through the district.

"Jesus fuck!"

Behemoths.

The woman said her forces were coming for the Council. I had no reason to disregard her, but the dragons stop my heart every time I see their brown scales and rippling nostrils. A cone of fire escapes one, provoking the second to match its fiery breath. Both outbursts blow like welding torches over the fleeing crowd. Limited entryways into the quadrant prevent them from escaping fast enough. The dragons rest atop one of them, and it crumbles as the population tries to funnel through the other. The result is charred bodies in the hundreds, and the smell of cooked flesh filling the front lawn behind us.

"It's a dragon!"

"*Light help us!*"

"Everybody run for your blasted lives!"

"Knox," Hardwick says. "We have to get inside *now*!"

The scene in front of us is no better. People in the doorway avert their eyes from the trial to the terror behind them, and begin to stampede the other way. Several knock shoulders with me — I stand upright through the first two, before the third knocks me to the ground. The world deviates from light to dark, dark to light.

"Ramona!"

Hardwick's scream is absorbed by pounding feet around my head. One set kicks me, is followed by a chorus of shrieks — whether from the dragons or the crowd running into their treacherous area of destruction, I can't tell. A pair of hands grab my arms, losing grip on them; the second attempt is more successful, dragging me against the sea of fleeing people.

"Close the doors!" someone yells.

"It's a dragon, isn't it?"

"Knox!" Hardwick says. He releases me. I slump to the floor; hair drapes my face, chest aching like I was hit by a freight train. Regaining focus, I sit up, observing a much different scene that the one I just escaped.

The room is emptied of everyone but the Council, assembled atop a marble bench that resembles a half-moon. Tim stands shackled in a gated platform; its spiked gold-picket fence gleams in Muerkher's natural glow. The suit he has always worn is replaced by a white crew neck shirt and pants like what I wore when speaking with the Avatar. Several Nephalim and Seraphina, the Maesters and a handful of Royal Guard are assembled around them.

The terrible yowling of fire-speaking beasts beyond reinforced doors, cooking the population of Atlas alive, is worse than anything Tim and I could have brought upon the world. Even Hardwick waits sullenly beside me, hunched over my knees as we wait for the massacre to conclude.

Breath returns to me, but sanity is long gone.

CHAPTER SEVENTEEN

BY THE POINT IN THE trial Hardwick and I burst through the doors — pursued by mammoth organic flamethrowers, no less — the proceedings had already reached their crescendo. As Tim would tell me later, it was the only latest event of his trial to unnerve him.

I haven't seen Tim much since coming to Atlas — the man who calls himself Death has remained scarce; perhaps sensing he had caused me enough trouble, he wasn't present during the outlanders' attack on the ball.

From what Tim tells me of the day afterward, it is a wonder any of us survived at all.

• • • •

TIM'S RECOUNTING OF his trial begins the night before being shepherded into the Observatory, and standing in front of twenty-five hundred people to make the case for his soul.

Until then, he had stayed in a little cottage in God's City — I may have passed it several times without knowing. Most of the time, he simply stared out a window, trying not to think. And there was enough to think about, if he was of the mind. There was his old life — his wife who died in childbirth; his teaching career, his home and his future. He tried not to think about the grief that consumed him after the nameless spouse died and he was alone; about how one little trip to a backwater Washington town put him on the path to becoming Death.

Most of all, Tim tried to ignore the choice that ended the world— so that when the Nephalim showed up to escort him from God's City to the Observatory, the man who calls himself Death was at peace.

All of Atlas seemed aware he would be pulled through those doors. Hundreds of people waited outside the small apartment the Council had kept him in lieu of Stone Mountain. Some chanted and cried and wanted to touch his hands; others screamed traitor and World-Killer. Tim ignored them all.

"May Light have mercy on you!" one woman cried from behind him. A hand touched Tim's shoulder. The man who calls himself Death closed his eyes, trying to drown out the torrent of yelling and waving hands in his direction.

"*Traitor!*"

"Go in peace, *infectorum mundi*. Peaced be."

As Tim was pulled through the parade of spectators — out of God City, around the Seat and into Atlas' northernmost quadrant — the crowd not only followed through the low arches and stone gates; like a snowball rolling down a mountain, it *grew*. More people of divergent opinion joined the mob, washing down the cobblestone like a wave. Ragged souls on street corners joined the nobles who began this journey with him, sweeping into the Observatory district.

Tim and the Nephalim moved up the stone pathway lined with Royal Guard. The field of stars overhead contrasted their winged helmets. The mob of curiosity funnelled into the lawn where they would shortly die in a dragon attack, following the party right up and through the doors. Tim didn't look behind him, but could feel the heat of their gathering on his back.

Inside the Observatory awaited the influencers who would determine the World-Killer's fate. The Council — even Apollo was awake and somewhat alert — waited behind the large bench from where their judgement would pass down. They were present, rather than in hologram form. The seven surviving Maesters sat left of the bench, acting as a partial jury. On its right waited High Priestess Seraphina, her right-hand Pol, and several nameless angels in her service. The tall woman sneered, but there was a light-heartedness to it, as if she had waited for this moment all her life.

A pedestal erected on the floor before the Council consisted of a short set of steps leading to a gated platform. The Nephalim holding his arm guided him into it, closing its door behind him. The crowd who had followed them did not chatter or whisper; their respect for these proceedings was absolute.

"Tim Hawkins," the Habinar said. **"Otherwise known as the demigod Death — colloquially called the World-Killer, the infectorum mundi, the destroyer of worlds. You stand before this Council on grave charges, son. For the sake of the court, I will list them here—**

"Failure to heed the natural order. Interference in the world of the living. Time-space manipulation. Destruction of Atlas property. Communicating with a mortal. Subverting the death of a mortal. Reincarnating a mortal. Dereliction of duty. Assault on an agent of Atlas. Resisting arrest. Divulging sensitive information, breach of trust, breach of ethics. And finally, bringing apocalypse on the world of the living."

The Habinar's booming inflections dropped off. Venicia spoke — the snakes atop her head were restless, uncomfortable with this state of affairs, and sought to mangle each other.

"How do you answer these charges, World-Killer?"

Tim — who had contemplated his answer endlessly— had promised himself to go through with this moment, and not be afraid.

He could not backtrack now.

"Guilty on all charges," Death said, to multiple gasps around the room. Muerkher hung his head and Venicia sullenly nodded. To their right, Seraphina beamed.

"And have you prepared a statement in your defence?" Muerkher asked. His glowing skin lit the podium on which the man who calls himself Death would either be exonerated or — more likely — punished.

Tim nodded.

"I have."

"Then you have the floor."

The World-Killer closed his eyes, trying to forget about all the people watching him.

When he opened them, he was ready.

"I did not ever ask to be Death," Tim replied. "From what I understand of the role, it was first given to a Nephalim, named Jonah.

"Aumothera — also known as the Shroud, for those not familiar with it — is the former world belonging to Ziz. After the Dark Lord was subdued, Aumothera became an alternate realm; the ultimate eugenics experiment, so that only worthy and redeemable souls could come to Atlas while the rest floundered in this dark world.

"Believe me — I understand the reasoning. This is a sacred place, Your Eminences, free of all the nuances that life in the Shroud entails. Was I wrong to take pity on myself, and allow the curiosity over what happened to my sister beckon me to an answer?

"Yes," Tim continued, "but at the same time, it may have been inevitable from the day I took this job, and nothing less than absolute power passed to me. What I eventually did with that power was wrong — but also human error, and what comes of placing flawed people in this role."

At this point, the room fell silent. He had few allies here, but Tim knew every person standing behind him and outside could relate to his amplified voice.

"I point you to my predecessors, if I may. Jonah was an angel who entered Aumothera first — we know him as a being named Reaper now, and I don't think recounting how he became that way is a matter for this trial.

"Then there was Hale, my immediate predecessor — a man who willingly, *knowingly* endangered the world; who interfered with mortals on numerous occasions. Who wanted to remove the barrier between life and death, and pour Aumothera's horrors into the living realm.

"I helped stop that," Tim said. "Were it not for a handful of us who confronted him, Earth would be ashes anyway! As for the plague...*that* was one of your own who released it, in order to frame the Breach as a worse occurrence than it was.

"I don't say any of this to detract from my actions or mitigate what happened because of it. But I believe that an unfair proportion of blame has been cast on them. I don't say it hoping for leniency, but acknowledgement — there were a lot of individual forces at work here."

There were no gasps or audible surprise as Tim concluded his defence. Every soul in that room studied the Council's emotive reactions at play. Venicia, the most empathetic of them, would have been the most torn; the Habinar, whose cold proclamations often got under my skin, the least. Muerkher fell somewhere between, and was the first to speak.

"I can appreciate what the *infectorum mundi* has put forth. And while this Council has always sought fairness in its dealings—"

Tim scoffed.

"Something to add, World-Killer?" the Habinar asked.

Tim tells me he regrets this particular outburst, especially in light of what happened next. At this point— after months in custody of Atlas, years of fugitive status before that, and his fear of punishment awaiting him— the man who called himself Death shed his trademark calm. It fell to the floor like a mask, revealing the disfigured morale beneath.

"Oh, I know *all* about unfairness, Your Eminences. But while we're on the subject, let's discuss fairness, shall we?"

The Council said nothing.

"*Fairness* was allowing Jonah to be infected by Aumothera, operate it with minimal oversight— leading to his rebirth as Reaper. As this being, Jonah built the Timestream, subjecting souls in his purview to its horrors. Nobody stopped it — *where* was fairness then?

"*Fairness,*" Tim continued, "was allowing these souls to freely roam the living world. Because of that, one of those souls would eventually impersonate my late wife, leading me into Aumothera, where I became Death. Tell me, Your Eminences— *where* was fairness then?

"And *where* was fairness when that same soul manipulated me to a point this responsibility was put on me? This woman had never done the job, and couldn't even explain what I was signing up for! All she told me was that fairness, for all its romanticization, was simply a red herring— the most perfect of distractions for those below to aspire to!"

"So," finished the World-Killer, "speak of Order— speak of Light. Make my eternal judgement based on obedience and perfection, Your Eminences. Quote your visions and your expectations and my human failure to observe them. But do not ever speak to me, or in front of me, about fairness. Everything I have done was predicated on it— a utopian ideal this Council has never supported."

"That is quite the accusatory statement," Venicia said after a moment, first to address Tim's wrath. "You are not wrong, World-Killer— the first cardinal rule among gods is often the first broken. We are guilty of thinking ourselves perfect, when that has rarely been the case.

"This Council has a hefty responsibility to ensure the continuity of all living things. In subverting the natural order, Mr. Hawkins, you have placed all of us at risk."

Muerkher interrupted, but carried on Venicia's train of thought.

"You speak of fairness, World-Killer, but frame it in such terms that we could easily sit here debating its philosophical merits for days. I will not argue there are many moving parts to the degree of your guilt, Mr. Hawkins — where your responsibility ends, and everything else begins, is our decision alone."

Tim nodded.

"I understand, Your Eminence."

• • • •

TO THIS POINT, THE trial had been a polite yet sordid affair. All of Atlas knew about it — from Maesters to the vermin running the cobbled streets of Devil's Corner. Whatever differentiated the classes and castes of the supreme realm was absent; no quarrelling between the distinctive members of the Crimson League and their sworn enemies in the Red Brotherhood took place. There were no altercations between the slinking Whisperers and Seraphina's people, vying for a prize to bring before the Council for small favors.

Everything was simultaneously tense and serene.

That would all change as a pair of overgrown reptiles climbed the stone arches dividing the Observatory District from the rest of Atlas, spewing blankets of heat down on the unprivileged spectators gathered outside. As Hardwick and I entered the crowd from the rear, pushing to the front, the Behemoths' shrieks tore down the lawn, through the open doors.

A moment later, people began to scream and flee.

• • • •

"WHAT IN TARNATION?"

The Habinar is first to react to the bloodcurdling pitches from outside. Even with the doors wide open, walls obscure the sight of monsters atop district walls. More people filter out— only to be met by a blast that missed Hardwick and I.

"We're under attack!" Muerkher cries. "Guards, close the doors!"

Tim tries to exit the bannistered prisoner's box. The gate is waist level, and he could easily jump it, were it not for the transparent barrier that pushes him back. The Council stands from chairs parked behind the marble bench. The Habinar's hand wrapping around the handle of his ax is matched by Venicia's snakes frozen in terror, sensing their larger winged cousins' wrath.

Hardwick and I finish beating against the sea of evacuating spectators, and I collapse to my knees where I was almost trampled in a stampede. The doors meet with such force that the entire building shudders on its foundations. The crowd's screams outside are outmatched in size and fury by creatures raining fire and brimstone down on them.

Time is only measured by my hollow breaths at the dragons' continued shrieking, while all other sounds die out.

"Oh good. Everyone is here."

The collective attention of every soul in the Observatory is pulled towards its eastern end. A set of stairs surrounded by intricate columns lead up into a second-floor alcove. A silhouette descends the steps, something dragging behind them— a dress. Its white entrails follow their owner as she comes into the shuttered Observatory's dim light. The Guard lift their spears while the Nephalim hold their swords' hilts, ready to defend their Priestess at a minimum. The Maesters nervously rise courtside. Each of the Council members displays a unique expression— annoyance from the Habinar, curiosity from the Fire Man; Venicia exhibits anger, with a faint aura of alarm from Apollo.

Trapped in his force field, Tim's jaw drops at a face that is obviously familiar to him. The blond woman who I thought was Seraphina, coordinating Ziz's return—

"*Hannah?*"

The blond woman ignores Tim, advancing toward the Council. Gone is the simple attire and loose collection of hair, now tightly wound in a beehive. Clasped hands at her waist, she is completely at peace with the Hell she rained down beyond the doors.

"We need to talk, Your Eminences," the woman says. Tim's eyes are wide with disbelief as Hardwick helps me to my feet.

The Habinar's hand grips his ax tighter as Venicia raises her chin, inspecting every inch of the woman allegedly responsible for all this chaos.

"What about?" the goddess asks.

The strange woman who conjured an apparition of my childhood home smiles.

"Why," she says, "the future of Atlas, of course."

CHAPTER EIGHTEEN

I WAS ONCE A MONSTER— whether because I was the weaker sex, entrusted to make strong decisions between men who were flimsy in the knees; or because I made hard choices, showing up a roomful of the old boys' club, I was seen and treated like a second class citizen. There are undoubtedly those who would tell me this is just the world's way— made for men, controlled by them, designed to keep everyone else in the dark. Maya would have. She did, whether with words or cigarette smoke between her lips, poisoning all the good men couldn't see— or didn't want.

I was a monster from the time my parents died. In turning that gun onto Tiffany Stewart, then himself, Daniel Knox sentenced me to life outside the village of beloved little girls and their adoring daddies, but also sent me a man named Death who saw the little girl for what she was.

Watching Hannah— this woman Tim knows of, yet whose relationship with her is unclear— I am beginning to realize I was wrong. The only sounds are ambient, like the slight creaking of the Habinar's ax dragged toward him, or the flicker of Muerker's skin intensifying in glow. But it is Venicia whose unravelling calmness unnerves me — the snakes are truly an extension of her fear, shrivelling at her scalp to escape a sense of impending doom.

I have been wrong, because the only monster to ever exist in Ramona Carol Knox was the one she saw in herself. And because she saw it, others did, too. Layering sexism and misogyny over top of it allowed mortal men to amplify that lack of confidence until nothing remained but instinct and determination.

The blond woman suffers no such shortcomings— her shoulders are straight and her head held high, perfectly able to predict what comes next. This woman holds the keys to the universe. She wheels and deals *on behalf* of the true monsters, the real things that jump in the night.

Next to her, I am an imposter.

"Now that we have gotten the unpleasant part out of the way—" Hannah begins.

She is almost immediately cut off by the Habinar.

"Unpleasantness is nothing next to traitors."

Hannah smiles, unaffected by the label.

"I understand— this must come as quite the shock, Your Eminences. Rest assured, the utmost diligence has been undertaken to arrive at this point. The plan had its challenges, as all plans do."

"I assume you will ultimately tell us what this plan consists of," Venicia remarks. "Personally, I'm still trying to figure out your role in all this, Miss..."

"My name is unimportant," Hannah says. "This Council has rarely excelled in deductions, hasn't it? In the interest of laying out the whole picture, let's review just how wrong you have been— though it *is* quite difficult to establish where ineptitude truly begins. If I had to wager, it would be around the time Ziz first rose against you. And why was that?"

Muerkher clears his throat.

Venicia does not answer, and the Habinar is deathly quiet. The dragons' screams have dropped off beyond the Observatory walls, and Tim can only stare at the stranger for as long as he is trapped with a front row seat.

When none of the Council answers, Hannah does it for them.

"Because he was one of you, wasn't he? The infamous fifth chair. Only an arrogant being would keep it as a reminder of their selfish glories—"

"Or," the Habinar corrects, **"as a reminder of the mistakes we made in naïveté."**

"*Naïveté*?" Hannah repeats. "You have settled into your history so comfortably, it must be difficult for you to see past lies."

"What lies do you speak of, woman?" Muerkher snipes. "Level your accusations in a timely manner or hold your tongue! I am tired of these games."

Hannah's smile grows wider.

"Very well— a rendering of truth is in order, for you have all forgotten what it is. And once that truth is laid out, this Council will see it has lost the moral authority to govern Atlas— that in valuing order and complacency over compassion and true leadership, you have invited open season."

As the Council members whisper to each other, Hannah recounts her tale. She begins with Creation, and the Sphere of Light— what I assume is her name for the Big Bang Theory— creating the Seed, a precursor to the Avatar. She speaks calmly and methodically regarding the creation of five gods, three of who remain lucid and in working order. She speaks of Zizikk, whose compassion was unparalleled among his four peers. For every audience, Zizikk tempered the other four, who were prone to malicious power trips. He offered those who kissed the Council's feet with reasonable solutions and pragmatic offers, angering the others. Zizikk was the best of them— establishing the Nephalim in their infancy as an order of true-hearted warriors. He was committed to the defence of not only Atlas, but its most vulnerable.

The Council was angry with Zizikk, the blond woman claims. His efforts made them appear greedy. After all, they coveted control over all Light in the universe, sacrificing innocents to harvest its power. Zizikk warned them against this. The other members ignored him, because he was a weak boy whose place among gods was circumspect at best.

"Eventually," Hannah remarks, "you had driven those beneath you so far, they became monsters. Zizikk saw this, and finally understood— the real monsters were the ones exploiting them, and knew you would never see reason. And why not? You had the Behemoths to instill terror in the hearts of those who loved you— who saw you as saviors, rather than tyrants.

"But Zizikk— the Boy God, so brilliant he had bonded with dragons as more than slaves— knew there was no place for him among you—"

"And rather than mediate," Venicia says, "he absorbed Au-mothera's wastes and sought to unseat us instead."

The remark is clearly meant to rile up the intruder, but Hannah remains calm.

"The irony of Ziz is that he is far better at acknowledging his shortcomings. In retrospect, he considers that move as emotionally charged and unwise. Time has a way of revealing these things to us, don't they?"

"You are speaking of ancient history," the Habinar says. **"Our confrontation with Zizikk is old news. This Council was humbled by that uprising, as we were by the Nephalim—"**

"Perhaps your greatest crime of all," Hannah says. She smiles at the High Priestess, who has remained silent alongside her grimacing band of surviving angels.

"Explain," Muerkher says.

"You know as well as I do that Tomas was no traitor to Atlas. Like Zizikk, he loved this city. He cared more about the people who lived in it than his own personal quest for power. It was *Gabriel* who felt threatened by his brother's compassion. Had you sent Tomas to handle the situation on Earth, it would not be a wasteland! That was all Gabriel's doing— just like the Nephalim uprising."

"You are submitting a lot of statements without evidence, woman," Muerkher says. "There are few left alive from the First Age— all those who could corroborate your facts have long passed to the White Light."

"I think what my associate is trying to say is," Venicia offers, "you have taken an awfully great risk in confronting us in such a manner, based on hearsay! If you can present an argument based on more than anecdotal evidence, you will save yourself and your co-conspirators a great deal of pain."

I was once a monster in the eyes of the world— maybe God himself, if anything I have seen or heard can still attest to a singular, all-powerful being at the center of everything. But in all my postmortem travels, gods are prettier than men and it is my job to protect them from people like Hannah.

Held back by Hardwick from tearing the woman apart myself, I have failed. But it is not until I look at Tim, a certain conversation returns to me from long ago.

I had a wife once.

As that dialogue floods into every part of my brain— infecting sight, sound and memory — my gaze shoots to the pontificating woman who wields dragons in the palm of her hand and destroyed a chunk of Atlas without batting a fucking eyelash, and the words are supreme.

I had a wife once— she was the love of my life.

How did I miss it?

She used to tell me the universe is built on unfairness. In fact, they were her last words on this Earth.

Tim has the look of a man who has been shown up by nobody less than his life partner— a person I had assumed was long dead. Due to her longevity in Atlas, her knowledge of its darkest workings and sudden reappearance, it's safe to assume the man who calls himself Death did as well.

She died. Childbirth. It's a long story.

The revelation has not occurred to the Council — all their focus is on her, and Tim's warnings might not be heeded, even if he could muster the courage to speak.

My point is, I used to think I was nothing without her, he says, somewhere in the distant past. *And when she died, existence became a whole lot messier. But eventually, there came a day when I was forced to be* everything *without her. I had to become something new.*

Finally, in a crescendo of all-out war on my limited set of emotions, I am reduced in equal measure. A ball in my stomach twists and revolts against the organ's lining, and I am five years old, hiding under that table with the suited man.

Would you like to be friends, Ro?

The grownups are playing around us, and I wonder why I ever bothered playing at all.

Hannah is unfazed by the threat of eternal punishment. The Habinar, however, is at his wits' end. He stands, hand fully enamored around his ax. Though not as tall as his projection in the Seat, he is nearly ten feet tall; his weapon drags on the floor, rounding the bench, lurching toward the blond woman who is an insect in comparison. Tim's wife shows no fear at the Viking storming towards her, lifting the ax high by its handle.

"I will warn you, Your Eminence —"

The cleaver rotates through the air in a perfect hundred-degree angle, closing the distance to Hannah with a single thrust over his head. Time slows as the ax reaches its midpoint through empty space, beginning its final descent. As the bellowing scream from the god's mouth is let loose, Hannah's expression is *satisfaction.*

The blade strikes her silhouette. A blinding light dispels outlines of every soul inside the Observatory. The flash is everlasting and my eyes ache from the brightness— a supernova within the court. And when it fades, and the room filters back into my mortal judgement, everything has changed.

The Council is gone. The first sign is a loud bang that rings throughout the Observatory as the Habinar's ax clatters on marble flooring with a hollow wince before settling for good. Muerkher's light is excruciatingly absent from my general awareness, having grown used to the man's natural glow. There is no sign of Apollo, other than some white hairs that blow off the bench where he sat.

And Venicia, whose only remaining presence is a convulsing snake on the bench's surface. It topples off the glossed surface in its struggle to breathe, landing at the foot of Tim's box. The man who calls himself Death looks down at it with sadness as it falls still and dissolves to ash, as if he was the cause of all this destruction.

All the Maesters to the bench's left are gone, save a despondent Barrett. On its right, Seraphina sinks to the knees of her golden dress, alternating between sobbing and screaming—her entire band of Nephalim was wiped off the face of Atlas, scattering to the breeze like Venicia's last serpent.

Hardwick has no words to console my murderous stare toward Tim's wife, the hyperventilating tide of despair washing over me, or the returned screams of victorious Behemoths beyond the Observatory.

"Well, then," Hannah smiles, turning on the bench where she wiped the governors of Creation away in one fell swoop. "I believe we have a trial to get underway."

CHAPTER NINETEEN

THE WORLD IS DEAD, and I have to be alive to witness its end.

Hannah steps over the Habinar's abandoned weapon, approaching the half moon bench. The blond woman disregards both Barrett and Seraphina on either side of her, trying like all Hell to stifle their losses, and rounds the pedestal to where Venicia and the others were wiped from existence.

Tim's eyes never leave her.

"Now that we have dispensed with unpleasantness," she says, and takes Venicia's seat, "I say the *real* trial should begin."

"And who are you to judge?" the High Priestess spits from the sidelines. "Everything we stood for, you have thrown into chaos! Disorder! Ever think of that, *witch*?"

Hannah smiles— that wicked, upturned grin that unravels my deepest, dark reaches; the smile of a winner, like my childhood friend Alison Delahunt used to flash when she won over me in some stupid, juvenile game. But Hannah is no young daughter of a blue-collar mechanic and there is more than her twisted grin if we lose.

"I find it quite convenient, Priestess," Hannah replies, omitting half the title due. "To my knowledge, you have spent two thousand years scheming— plotting revenge, biding your time to humiliate gods whose own schemes were beneath you. Unworthy of, say, basic respect?"

Seraphina's face lights up, yanking it from the shadows it had settled, anticipating despair and rebuke.

"Not to mention the Maesters— isn't that right, old fellow?" Hannah asks, looking at Barrett. The Maester's face does not change. The last of his Order keeps a tongue behind firmly closed lips, but Hannah doesn't linger— her eyes canvass the room, ignoring her former husband. With the Council dead, that only leaves Hardwick and I.

"Stephen Hardwick," she says. "Step forward."

My gaze shoots to Hardwick, praying his lips don't find the upwards curve Seraphina's did at the blond woman's promises of power. His thin frame is a good fifty pounds lighter from his adventures in Stone Mountain, making him a shadow of his former self.

"Yeah, that's me."

"I recall," she cooes. "Do you remember our deal?"

Deal?

"I do," Hardwick says.

"And? Do we still have one?"

What is she talking about?

A woman came to see me.

Hardwick glances back at me, shaking his head. His beard bristles in dead air— quite possibly riled by my storm of emotions— and I recognize a different look than the one he showed in me in Washington, learning of his depraved deeds.

Remorse.

"We do," he says, looking back at Hannah. "Long as you hold up your end. Reincarnation, as we discussed."

"Very good," Hannah says, and dismisses him. Two of the five survivors are in the blond woman's court— both are my fault. I pushed Seraphina too far; put too much stock in Hardwick's redemption. He joins the High Priestess— leaving Tim, Barrett and I as her sole challengers.

A familiar rage boils the surface of my throat. Hannah's eyes drift to me, but she doesn't call my name before diverging to the prisoner in a gated box with force-fielded walls; they hum like laughter, mocking my oldest friend's predicament.

"I suppose that brings us to the reason we are gathered here today. We will dispense with...whatever *that* was, that the Council called a trial," Hannah says, leaning over the bench. "But first, some ground rules— not to bestow undue *unfairness*, as our mutual friend here is so fond of using to shield himself. Let's discuss that, shall we? Then, I will call our first witness."

I don't know what right this woman has assumed. She is neither a god nor celestial. And still, someone has granted her this...*power*, as she called it...were it defined by wiping out beings triple in size.

"Fairness," Hannah says, "is a made-up word— created by those who disagree with the way things are; some form of delusional justice unto those who have the final say.

"Justice was done when the Seed of Light chose five beings to govern the supreme realm. It is done again in evolution— the strong weeds out the weak, establishing a new order for Creation. To rail against this cosmic justice is not a matter of unfairness. It is the song of whining gnats who have never taken the time to outwit their oppressors — to *win* over them.

"I'd like to sit here all day and talk about fairness, but time is short, and the Dark Lord's is far more valuable than ours. That said, I call the first witness— Stephen Hardwick."

Hannah's revelation— that my former partner betrayed me (*again*), and would rather stand with the Devil than make amends— roils every look in his direction, burning with the hatred I have long pushed down. Hardwick stands with his back to Hannah, inadvertently facing the accused, and me.

"State your name for the record," Hannah says from behind him— despite having no stenographer or intention of recording these proceedings.

"Stephen Henry Hardwick."

"And would you tell us about your history with this man?"

"Yes. He is the Devil," Hardwick grimaces.

"Please tell us more," Hannah smiles.

And so, Stephen Henry Hardwick does.

• • • •

HARDWICK'S TESTIMONY lasts nearly an hour. Each minute is an eternity. Words drip off his tongue like venom, poisoning everything good within me and increasing my resolve to murder him when this is all over.

It wouldn't be the first time.

He begins by speaking about his life— growing up in Maryland, where his father was a reverend in the United Church. His mother was a former prostitute and his father Russell converted her to Christianity.

("The religion of charlatans," Hannah says at one point.)

But his mother eventually died, and Young Stephen— as I imagine the little boy with peach-fuzz on his face, skinny shoulders and a head full of idealism— wanted to escape the shadow cast over him since childhood. God was always watching in the Hardwick household, and Young Stephen was only interested in getting far away from Him.

Young Stephen joined the army— both angering Russell, and greatly saddening him. But Young Stephen was meant for more than being the doting son of a church minister, and soon enrolled in the FBI training program at Quantico. He had a natural affinity for the work, and could hit a shooting target like nobody's business. Over time, he became one of the Bureau's most valuable assets.

Russell passed, and his only son forgot to pay his respects. The big guy was upstairs now. His father was never a sentimental man, merely a compassionate one, but Hardwick had despised him for it.

Young Stephen became Old Stephen, the man predisposed to yanking the rug out from beneath my feet every time. He conceived his grand plans, all gone swimmingly until a young female agent came along, dragging her indispensable morality into matters she was beneath— not even realizing until he had her cornered at gunpoint.

Arriving at our confrontation inside Tim's afterlife tunnel, Hannah smiles; she knows about *all* of it. Hardwick's testimony is simply the confirmation she craves.

"And that's when he sent you to the Arbiters, correct?"

"Correct," Hardwick says. "I was taken to Stone Mountain, and left to rot! Twenty years, I withstood those fucks, counting the days until I was let out."

"Something that might not have happened without certain information in your possession, correct?"

Hardwick nods, eyes on Tim.

"Correct. I would likely still be there now."

Hannah thanks him, having wrangled all the biased testimony from Hardwick she will, and says her agents will meet him outside the Observatory.

"Don't have to worry about the dragons, do I?"

"Not at all," the woman promises.

Hardwick bows his head, looking back at her with gratitude. I can't look at him as he exits the self-opening doors. Instead, my nascent rage returns the blond woman calling her next witness. Seraphina beams as she assumes the spot Hardwick stood, but I'm beyond participating in this charade any longer.

I've heard enough.

* * * *

THE HIGH PRIESTESS' account lasts almost three hours, detailing every transgression against her immeasurable pride over three ages of Atlas. She recounts the Council's arrogance, the Nephalim uprising and her struggle to achieve recognition. Seraphina speaks of loyalty— the word occupies every tenth spot in her long-winded complaints— and candor; of responsibility and unity, stating the Council held palaver with none but themselves.

Tim is also less interested in the Priestess than he was in Hardwick. Seraphina's shrill voice echoes with festering resentment that pleases the blond woman— and when she is done, Seraphina is also dismissed.

The High Priestess refuses.

"I would prefer to stay, Your Eminence," the Priestess pleads.

"Very well," Hannah says. "It is time to deliver the verdict then. Miss Knox, if you would join your accomplice before me— this will not take long at all."

I am frozen, disgust reaching deep as Seraphina's toward the Grand Council. Luca is dead. Hardwick has turned on me, again. The Council is gone, Atlas is in ruins, and there is no Earth for any of us to return to, if Siskett was telling the truth prior to his passing.

"Miss Knox? Don't make me ask twice."

Insofar I have stood, like a lone idol against the tides of darkness, listening to the Devil's many mouths. Weak knees take their vulnerable first steps from near the doors, slowly joining Tim's side.

"You obviously have questions. Rest assured, they will be answered in time. The Dark Lord is merciful for those who are willing to help themselves—"

"Like Hardwick, right?"

I had resolved to keep my mouth shut— given the present circumstances, that is no longer possible.

Hannah glosses over it.

"The trial set out by the Council was a mockery of justice. The Council had to balance punishment with its own safety, and keeping their newest protector at ease. Their well-being depended on allegiance to Miss Knox— to cast her friend Death to some heinous outcome would have damaged that partnership, bringing doubt unto their longevity as rulers of this realm.

"Unfortunately for you, I do not have the same considerations— keeping in the true spirit of cosmic justice."

"Excuse me," Tim says. Until now, he has been unable to muster the words to denigrate her. "I think you're forgetting something."

"Please," Hannah snipes. "Inform us."

"You are a biased judge, whose reasons for siding with Ziz I can only guess. But if you did it for the reason I'm guessing, you are no better than every selfish god I've met. Worse, in fact— you don't even have the cosmic title to hold such authority."

His outrage *enlivens* her— all I can think of is the conversation in Maya's illusion of an apartment, speaking as if we had known each other for years.

"I beg to differ," our new judge says. "Follow me, if you would."

The white gown trails behind her as she rounds the bench, walking past us. The force field around Tim's prisoner box dissipates like a released gust of electrical currents powering down. Tim reluctantly lowers his right hand, unlatching the gate. Its gold-cast bars swing outward and his feet touch solid ground. I wait for him, afraid to walk alone, or step on the gown's entrails, sentencing me to worse fates than this one.

The nebulous sky over Atlas' northern most point darkens above the macabre display— whether due to reality or my capsized emotional state is hard to tell. Tim's fingers wrap around my own as we follow Hannah over the dust and ashes of a natural order ripped from its pedestal, put on a bloody display for all to see.

The wall previously enclosing the Observatory district has been pulled down by the dragons climbing its thin collection of stones. Many have toppled off the highest point, meeting the ground in pieces. Bodies on the lawn are bloodied or charred black, sprawling in every godless direction. Most were caught in a direct blast and barbecued to Hell.

And in the lawn's center, a body has been nailed onto crude crossbeams, and the corpse has all my attention.

Stephen Hardwick— the man who stole children, murdered and then betrayed me in the afterlife— lies lifeless on its joists. His hands are bloodied where six-inch nails were driven through them by robed figures surrounding the cross. Bird masks cover their features, reminiscent of plague doctors. Hardwick is naked— his eyes have been gouged out, and thin, gray hairs of his beard flutter in the slight wind.

The twin Behemoths scale the wall above his corpse. They are fast creatures, ascending the broken arch before I have assigned a specific emotion to their proximity.

Hannah looks onward, clearly pleased with her handiwork. She cranes her neck toward Tim, whose lifelong calming presence is a gaping wound, bleeding at his estranged wife's feet.

"Choose your champion, Death. Light has chosen hers."

CHAPTER TWENTY

WHITE LIGHTS— NOT THE kind I have come to know; of opening my eyes from darkness, only to discover Light holds no regard for its own well-being. It was born from darkness, is infested with it — a slow-acting metabolic disease.

It has been several days since the trial ended with Hannah tricking Hardwick into being crucified. His body was left there. I don't know if bodies rot in Atlas, but have no desire to return to the Observatory district to find out.

Not that we could — Tim and I were immediately escorted back to his apartment in God City. The district was robbed of its former spirit. So many lives were lost in the Whoville of celestial creations, the place is a shell of what it once was. The houses are still bright and quirky, but gone are the unique lifeforms who inhabited them. The Illumitory sits in perennial daylight, casting optimistic shadows over a world washed away in them.

The Brotherhood has kept us here for days. I'm sure Tim could evaporate into his cloud form, were he brave enough to try — but the man who calls himself Death was rocked by his trial. The return of his wife didn't help, and all these deaths are on him.

Every ticking timer has a bomb attached, and three Ages worth of resentment and tension just exploded in Atlas. No biological need for sleep or hunger, I have fallen catatonic by the time a nameless member of the Brotherhood comes to collect us. There was some conversation a couple days ago, but it has fallen off as we await Tim's champion.

Do you think she'll come? I asked.

Hard to say, Tim muttered. *She will not come on her own.*

What makes you say that?

He shook his head, and mostly fell quiet after that. Time took on shades of pointlessness beyond its simple passing. The sun never went down beyond the drawn gray curtains — the only thing protecting our sanity from abundant Light.

So, when the Brotherhood come in the form of a lone guard, I almost welcome the break in despondent silence and abject resignation. The shifting door is sudden, and the masked guard beckons us outside.

Atlas has grown worse in the time we've been under house arrest. Several structures lie collapsed in our tour north. The sky is a lovely shade of blue, only now I see it for the illusion it contains.

Tim says little as we walk, and I turn my attention to the escorting Brother as he grunts at me to speed up. With no visible weapons to enforce his commands, maybe I can take him.

"Where are you taking us?" I ask our escort. The Brother grunts a reply (something like *the red wind blows in the west, father*), and tells me to keep moving.

But the Brother's casual muttering revives the phrase in my brain — back to when I first came to Atlas, confronting a Whisperer in Devil's Corner with Luca — and the rabbit hole descends through my memory.

You must get Gossamer's attention. Tell him you're a courier on behalf of the Red Brotherhood. He will ask you to prove it, so tell him 'the red wind blows in the west'. It is their code phrase, used to communicate with the Whisperers.

But when I used that code phrase on the Whisperer called Gossamer, he disregarded it — what had he said?

That has not been the Red Brotherhood's communique in a few months. Who sent you?

These Whisperers fear for their souls. This is much worse than Stone Mountain threatens them with. Whatever has them scared, they will not cooperate lightly.

Barrett.

Atlas has a storied and conflicted history. We have spoken some-what of Ziz, and the ever present threat he poses to all Creation—

His followers are the more dangerous threat.

One by one, all the Maesters have been incapacitated or killed. It began with our arresting Quorroc; from there, Siskett was advised to seek the White Light— by Barrett. He was crushed by a Behemoth.

All the others were killed in Hannah's weird flash.

They are of many factions.

"Ramona?"

Why is Barrett still alive?

The red wind blows in the West.

Because he helped Hannah.

Barrett is the inside player. He fed information to Ziz's agent, provided access and the Council's whereabouts on at least three occasions he was present for. He was quick to put Luca and I onto Gossamer's trail, and must have let the Atlas ball's attackers into the city.

That has not been the Red Brotherhood's communique in a few months. Who sent you?

The communique never changed— Barrett put the Crimson League up to telling me it had. Changing their beloved catchphrase was about as likely as America deciding in God it no longer trusts. Ramona Knox didn't know that— like a naive little girl in Oz, she took its proclamations at face value, and failed in her quest.

"Ramona?" Tim says. "Are you alright?"

The Brother is annoyed at my lack of urgency, and tells me to hurry it along. I tell Tim I'm fine — but inside, I am more terrified than any encounter with Death as a child, my career with the Bureau or anything I thought possible in the land of wild things.

• • • •

THE SOUND IS THE FIRST thing I notice as the curmudgeonly Brother pushes us under the Arena's arched doorway, and over the scant layer of sand-kissing concrete. The open-roof stands are filled with spectators, but none I would have recognized outside of Devil's Corner days ago. Their clothes are ragged, empty eyes a collective cloud washing over us from all angles. Gaunt cheeks and emaciated souls are the calling card of Ziz's worshippers, and they have come through for their deity in strength.

But it is the percussion— those fucking drums — that make my heart sink. Hollow, persistent tribal rhythms of moccasin instruments accentuate each dip in terror's electrocardiography.

Do you think she'll come? I asked Tim in the safe house we were held before the Brother came to collect.

Choose your champion, Death.

The drums pound maddeningly, martyring thoughts I can't hear and dislodging optimism that any of this will have a good end.

Hard to say. She will not come on her own.

Light has chosen hers.

What makes you say that?

Tim's champion is our only hope now.

• • • •

HANNAH WAITS IN THE Coliseum's ground-level pit, well below the full moon of eyes intently watching these proceedings. Barrett and Seraphina wait behind her. Two Brothers work together to create the heartrending rhythms echoing through the Arena.

The world dies on the soulless tide of those drums. Barrett is composed behind the blond woman, none of the warmth he previously showed me in reserve. Over Hannah's other shoulder, the former High Priestess is smug in her content, having wrangled back the respect and position she was due.

But it is the songs of war— of darkness versus Light, the allegiances of each backwards— that will haunt me longest.

Light is the darkness, and darkness is salvation.

Darkness is Light, because Light has forgotten everything it once represented among the endless stars.

Everything except the songs of war.

· · · ·

THE WRETCHED BEATING ceases, enshrouding the Arena in quiet so far from the piercing bass that pushed fear to the top and left me in cold sweats. As Tim and I arrive at judgement, I have never seen a crowd so still. They are everywhere; the stands are filled to capacity, people pushed together in blank reception of cosmic justice. They are conduits, the eyes of Ziz, offering the Dark Lord a view from all angles of the giant ring.

Hannah's mouth corners lift in her trademark condescension as we are pulled to a stop by our escort, and she addresses people seated overhead.

"People of Atlas!" The call echoes through the Arena, bouncing off the stands, barely registering with the zombie faces occupying them. **"For too long, Creation has been held hostage! By schemers and benefactors, angels and their overlords!"**

Hannah's voice drops off. Her blue eyes are empty as the crowd her statement targets— a shell for Ziz to utilize in his quest for supremacy.

There is no response from the crowd.

"But today is a new day! No longer will imperfect gods rule, masking all their imperfections! No longer masquerading as untouchable beings standing on your shoulders, dragging you down! Instead, we serve a new god— one who is humble and merciful; one who will tell you a mistake is something to learn from, not be punished over!"

When she resumes, her words are quieter, no longer thrown as far as a yell can travel.

"But first," she says, "we must close out certain chapters opened by history. Bring out the Phoenix!"

At Hannah's command, an iron gate at the arena's northern end opens. There are no changes in the crowd's demeanor— they do not stir for the Brotherhood's members who cross the gate's threshold, nor the figure shackled between them with iron links.

On the walls of the arena, the beats return, but not because the drummers have returned to pounding on their instruments. This is a different breed of percussion, climbing the Coliseum walls. Three of the winged reptiles clamber over, balancing on the crumbling strip just above the stands on all sides— I count four of the giant beasts, though there could be more lying in wait— the drums are no longer needed.

The screams are an orchestra all their fucking own.

* * * *

THE WOMAN PULLED FROM the gate in chains is blond like Hannah. Her clothes are a ragged assembly of Earthen convention— t-shirt and faded jeans, soiled by her journey here. Her face is smudged, short hair tangled on her shoulder. A silver locket in the shape of a star hangs at her neck, glowing at its seams.

The Lone Brother steps between us, demanding we back up ten paces. The dragons grip the arena's outer rings— their massive claws use the stone strip for balance, pinching chunks of it away, which topple under their massive weight onto the non-reactive audience.

Do you think she'll come?

The girl hangs her head as a squadron of Brotherhood pushes her forward into the pit, wheeling around Hannah's entourage to face her. The prisoner's hazel eyes drift upward momentarily— her only interest is Tim, casting a glare worthy of Death itself.

Hard to say. She will not come on her own.

"Harper Whitaker," Hannah says. "Welcome to Atlas, Phoenix. I hope your journey was comfortable?"

The woman says nothing, continuing to stare at the thin layer of sand at her feet.

"Do you know why you have been summoned here?"

Harper mutters something. Her back to us, all I can see is the back of her head, tilted downward.

"What was that?"

The second time, her words emerge more confidently.

"Go to hell."

Hannah smiles at the refusal to answer.

"Your old friend requested your presence. I told him to choose his champion. To be honest, I assumed it might be Miss Knox here. But that would be out of character, wouldn't it? Death, sending the woman he has protected to no end, to her own? Not likely.

"So instead he chose *you* — someone with little love for his escapades. Someone he knew would be a hard sell. Who knows?" Hannah says. "Maybe he did it, thinking there wasn't a hope in Creation you would show. But once again, Miss Whitaker, he underestimates me— you *will* represent Death, whether you choose to or not. Won't you?"

The prisoner is unmoved by the blond woman. They would be the same height if the shackled girl's posture wasn't as atrocious as this chain of events.

"No."

"No...what?"

"No," the woman repeats. "I will never stand for him again."

"And why is that?"

The woman cranes her neck, glancing at the bearded figure behind her, then back to his wife.

"I think you know why," the Phoenix says. "You'd not have brought me here unless you did."

Hannah's smile grows— like a blossom in spring, its stalk grows, curling the rose in her pale cheeks.

"Ziz said you were a clever girl. No matter— His will be served. So yes, Miss Whitaker, I know all about your relationship with my husband— that he helped you stop Hale; saved you from Gabriel after the Nephalim turned his back on you. You weren't the reason for the Breach— but in refusing to fulfill your task, it made its effects irreversible."

The Phoenix does not react, nor give any indication how she came to bear the title.

"As I said before, Miss Whitaker — you *will* capitulate, one way or the other."

Hannah snaps the fingers on her left hand. The sound produced is unpleasant, and echoes through the Arena like a heavy plank of landing wood.

One of the Behemoths leaps down from its place on the crumbling outer wall; gliding over the crowd, its massive front paws kick up a thin layer of sand. Its sickly gray wings retract onto its back with the landing as another group of masked Brotherhood enter the arena through the south gate. Two guide the group, with another set taking up the rear. The middle pair wields a captive by either arm.

The thin woman screams behind the burlap bag thrown over her head, hyperventilating under the fabric, manhandled by her minders as they pull her forward.

The Phoenix glances between their concealed woman and the creature lurking over Hannah's shoulder, small yellow eyes resting on me. The woman continues shrieking— whatever words accompany her shrill tones are lost to them. She temporarily breaks free, and the Brothers spare no mercy or time in grabbing her off the ground, setting her upright.

The voice rings true to Death's champion, and her gaze snaps past Tim and I, gunning for Hannah's soul.

"What are you doing?"

As during Tim's trial, her shit-eating grin has reached its maximum threshold. The Behemoth behind Hannah snorts, unleashing a stale breath of hot air over us.

"Let's call it, 'providing motivation.'"

A pair of hands grab my arms, pulling me toward the eastern arena wall. The Brotherhood subdue Tim, dragging him the same way.

A robed figure removes the burlap sack from over their prisoner's face, revealing a woman about the Phoenix's age with short dark hair and a loose t-shirt draping thin shoulders. Her eyes operate in a logical sequence once uncovered— beginning with the massive beast they can't explain, then moving to the dragon's owner before finding a face she recognizes.

"*Harper?*" she gasps.

The Phoenix's expression is remarkably changed from its earlier resignation, twisting Harper's face into murderous rage.

"Em," she says. "It's going to be okay."

Her assurances do nothing to assuage Em's terror at the Behemoth salivating over Hannah's head.

"Don't you fucking touch her," Harper warns. Shackled at the wrists, she has little recourse to stop the Behemoth from slinking closer.

One of the Brothers in service to Hannah grabs the Phoenix by her left arm, attempting to pull her away — Harper wheels around, slugging him in the face. The iron shackle connects with the plague doctor mask, crumpling it against the man's face, sending him tumbling back. She ducks another of our captors as he swings above her head. Throwing the connector links over his throat, the Phoenix forces him to an oxygen-starved kneel.

This is our chance.

The Brothers subduing Tim and I release their holds, running to their gagging peer's aid. My fist swings outward, connecting with my captor's neck. He goes down clutching at his carotid artery, wheezing for relief. The other Brother who held Tim back gets halfway to his struggling comrade, looks back at the one I downed. Fear penetrates the obstruction over his features as I run at him, but does nothing to shield him from the kick that collapses him at my feet, lost to these remaining events.

Harper pulls her hostage to an uneven balance, dragging him back under the threat of asphyxiation. Hannah doesn't react to our rebellion. The blond woman lets her cronies meet pavement, holding up a closed fist to the dragon hovering over her.

"**Tim!**" I call back to my guardian angel, but there is no time for a follow-up. Having left both of Em's flanks wide open, Harper drags her captive to the far south end of the arena.

Oh no, she's going to —

Hannah brings her fist down from on high. The dragon advances toward Em, thrusting its neck down toward the ground. A lone scream follows the woman into the open maw, abruptly ended as the dragon's mandible snaps shut, catching Harper's friend between its jagged teeth. A river of red liquid pours down between the mandible and snout in thick globs, staining the sand in coagulated blotches where Em stood.

The Behemoth unhinges its teeth, releasing its victim. All that remains of her is the lower body, collapsing in a heap as the dragon lifts its head high into the air, swallowing her torso.

The horror washing over Harper's expression forces her to release her hostage. The man passes out, clutching his folded jugular and battered mask. The Phoenix collapses behind him, devolving into sobbing as her knees meet the ground.

Hannah doesn't savor the moment— another hand signal turns the Behemoth towards her. The dragon inhales, casting its trademark inferno directly onto the Phoenix. The fire burns long and dances off the ground's surface. The Brother caught in its blast zone screams as endless hell rains down on Death's champion.

When the eruption ends, Hannah's underling lays smoking, a thick plume of gray caressing his corpse. By some grace of God, Harper is unharmed— it could have something to do with the now-gold locket around her neck, blazing like Earth's sun at her collarbone. The hopeless sound of her drawing in convulsing air, crumpled halfway between sitting and lying on the ground, twists my heart like a wet towel, right before I proceed to beat myself with it.

The dragon returns to Hannah's side. She pets it, praising it like a dog who fetched its ball and brought it back, wagging its stupid tail— ready for another retrieval of its master's deepest desires. The blood where a woman named Em stood darkens at her open-toed slippers as the Phoenix buries her forehead in the sand, trying to muffle the depravity of her loss.

Hannah smiles at the Behemoth's massive feet, looking at her thralls in the stands— her zombies, her motherfucking legion.

She smiles, because she has won.

At last, the real monsters have come out to play in earnest.

Behemoth

Part Two

CHAPTER TWENTY-ONE

ONCE UPON A TIME, HAD you told me that Heaven was a city in the stars called Atlas, I would have thought you schizophrenic. Had you confided in a woman who had no business growing to be an FBI agent that the afterlife's supreme realm was closer to any Hell in our wildest fictions or faith-based dreams, I would have referred you to the mental ward.

Maybe people in mental asylums have been to other worlds, and are simply telling their stories, if they can get past the tics and twitches of trauma.

Held back by members of a cult who wear red robes and plague doctor masks and call themselves the Red Brotherhood, they and the dragons are are all that restrain our impulse to murder the blond woman.

At Hannah's gruff command, the beast used to subdue Death's champion is dismissed. It clambers up the lowest set of stands. People seated in the first two rows are crushed under the dragon's front paw — then more as its feet follow. Those around them don't panic, because they're mindless zombies in service to the Dark Lord Ziz.

Harper is pulled to her feet by several Brothers. Her hair is a sand-caked storm of strands. Her eyes are red, mouth pulled in a sorrowful scowl. She doesn't resist the underlings pulling her forward.

The recovering Brothers I sent to a keel secure Tim and I, using more aggression than required to haul their prisoners before the woman. The Brother manhandling my arm jerks me to a stop between the Phoenix and Tim. Harper emits nothing other than a quivering lower lip, baring her bottom teeth.

Hannah — who may have once been Death's wife but now holds matrimony with a far worse Devil — gloats at her sunken shoulders and the remains of her friend Em, whose mangled legs stain the ground only yards away.

"An awful precedent to set," she says. "May this woman's death serve as a reminder to all those who would challenge the new order in Atlas, and seek to defy the Dark Lord's will."

My shock has followed me from the moment two Behemoths stormed Tim's trial. This bitch has broken Atlas like dropping a wine bottle— the only difference is the blood from its broken neck, replacing merlot.

I can't contain my rage any longer.

"Who the fuck died and made you Mad Queen, lady?"

Hannah raises a single eyebrow. Her composure is unbreakable, powered by Ziz's arrogance and fury toward the world.

"Spoken lightly from the mortal whose gallivanting around with my husband caused the apocalypse. You are in no position to lecture me, Miss Knox. I am more powerful than you will ever be, meant for greater things than being Death's lapdog.

"The three of you will be kept under guard for now — due to Miss Whitaker's outburst, her restraints will remain in place until she decides to become more cooperative. Once I decide the nature of the trial by combat, the Phoenix will stand for Death. Until such time, Harper, you will receive adequate training to defend yourself."

Based on Harper's sneer, her trainers may have to face her wrath before anything Hannah throws at us. But she remains silent, occasionally looking at Em's mangled body before closing her eyes.

"Is that understood, Phoenix?"

Harper lifts her head, meeting Hannah's confident stare. The locket at her collarbone thrashes with light embodying her anger, but the face affords her none.

"I have *nothing* left to say."

The Phoenix is unrelenting in refusing the blond woman satisfaction, hardened by the stories Tim has told me about her — how the locket belonged to her mother Olivia; how its passing down made Harper immortal, bestowing powers she never wanted.

"Very well," our captor smiles. "Go with my friends in the Red Brotherhood. They will show you to your new accomodations."

I cast a glare at Maester Barrett. The dramatic sorrow draping his face after the Council's death is absent. He seems almost as pleased as Hannah, mouth corners lifted in a slight smile. Seraphina stifles discomfort with what just happened. Survival dictates action for the High Priestess, but she may have finally met with regret in her moral travels.

Harper's shackled forearms require an extra tug from her Brotherhood escort, while Tim goes along quietly. The man who calls himself Death has barely climbed out of the awe I shared with him over Hannah's reappearance. I was stunned by it, but it has clearly broken him — a man notorious for composure in crisis, who thrived on lording over mortals with his infinite knowledge.

He is reduced to nothing now— just another cog in Creation's sick machine.

• • • •

THE SCREECHING BEHEMOTHS follow us out of the Arena district, yet another layer of security to prevent our escape. The dragons are legion in the skies over Atlas — their collective of spread wings creates storm clouds of their own, flapping powerful currents down over us. Even our escorts are perturbed by the beasts' presence; they have not walked Atlas since the First Age of Creation, and make volatile guardians at best.

My mind drifts as we walk toward the Barracks — now an empty representation of what the Nephalim stood for. But I am the last of them, once again the lone survivor of a massacre, doomed to wander on. My companions on this journey are disquieted and offer no comfort on the lonely road Atlas has become. Little remains of the liveliness when I first arrived in the supreme realm, naive to the darkness that lived within. Like Venicia said in the Spire's peak, I see it now, and may never recognize this city's beauty again.

Over time, you start to see flaws in the perfection — little strategic folds to cover all the things its creators didn't want us to see. It is an illusion, like anything you stare at for too long, trying to make sense of. Its flawlessness warps and erodes, like anything else does in the storms of time.

So much to love has been lost, and now Creation's devils lord over its pinnacle. The Barracks are gutted in pride as we cross into them, lured toward the Obelisk, then whisked left into one of the temple-like buildings that symmetrically oppose each other on either side. Their walls seem darker, shingled pyramids sloping downward from the peak on all sides, but Light has abandoned them as well, and the Nephalim who lived here are ash and dust.

Our escorts are quiet — we don't fight them, allowing them to pull us into the temple's recesses, past a room with more canvas paintings I am no longer enamored with. My curiosity is long sated.

The world runs together from hallway to cellar, to the shared dungeon cell they slide closed behind us. The fringe of illumination from beyond the cellar door disappears as the Brotherhood closes the hatch over a sloped ladder, pulling back its last threads.

All my life I have pretended to love the darkness. But as the door closes, snatching all Light's hope of redemption, I meet its true form. It is not a man who professed to be Death when I was a child, nor monsters like Stephen Hardwick or Tim's wife.

In true darkness, I am forced to meet myself — the reason why I have often avoided squarely looking at myself in mirrors, or going to therapy.

In true darkness, fumbling for walls and the boundaries of our existence, there is nothing left to look for but existing silhouettes, intermingling with imaginary ones. I might stumble onto some greater truth within them, but am saved by a spark to my left, lighting the entire cell.

"Of course," Tim mutters.

The mysterious star-shaped locket at Harper's neckline acts as a flashlight. Its glow reminds me of the cosmic light when I took the Nephalim's oath before the Council; white like all other lights, but dotted with tiny constellations.

The Light around the locket, when it seems lost everywhere else, is alive.

The majority of the Light's power is protected by the four-member Council of Atlas. Another percentage is used to power Atlas itself, and another yet for Earth. Certain artifacts are imbued with it, allowing its bearers powers to surpass their physiological limitations, survive physical death, or other such enhancements.

It must be one of those artifacts.

"You're welcome," Harper snipes. "I ought to leave you in the dark, but knowing you, you can probably see through it."

"I'm sorry about Mic—"

There is no warning to the cocked fist that strikes Tim in the jaw, sending him sprawling on the cold floor. Harper doesn't follow up, retreating to a far corner of the cell, covering the opposite stone wall in the locket's glare. In the second before the amplified picture is lost, I catch sight of something in its projection. It stands out, even in the second-long glimpse before it pours back onto the floor with Harper's frantic paces, and I help Tim to his feet. He rubs his jaw while I stare at the darkened wall.

Tim takes no notice of my wonder, solely focused on Harper as he nurses his swelling cheek.

"Blame me if you want, Harper—"

"Oh, I do! I blamed you when your interference in a natural order resulted in the world going to shit, and my life going to shit with it! I blamed you when you weren't just straight with me, and had to play your stupid, minutiative games, when you *could* have just been honest! But you had to do your godly thing, like all gods do, just playing fucking mysterious!"

The locket pulses with rage. Her shackled hands move violently with her speech, wavering near tears but never quite reaching the devastation she deserves. She holds it back, for some reason — maybe all they have been through together is the softened blow.

Harper falls much quieter, enunciations more pronounced and pointed, riding the wave of a hollow whisper.

"*Everything* I had left to fight for is gone. Gonna go back in time and change that, too? Be my guest. I wouldn't defend your honor if it reversed everything!"

The constellations at her neck dull as she slumps in the corner, staring into nothing. The Light around her collar bone weakens, and darkness is stronger for it, creeping across our flesh and threatening to envelop us once more.

If my eyes saw what I think they did, that locket may hold information instrumental to saving Atlas. I need her to show it to me, but the poor woman is emotionally destroyed by Em's death — coming at it from the good old Ramona Knox angle, shrewd and aloof, will net only hostility.

We need to get out of this cell first.

• • • •

TIME PASSES BY. IT'S all relative now. Minutes bleed into days, because I am dead. Harper's locket provides its restrained berth of Light throughout. Tim is morose, though he seems to possess some sort of regenerative power — the bruise on his face was gone in minutes. We sit in our individual corners for a long time, three spokes on a broken wheel; wondering if anyone will return for us. There must be punishments to dole out and Creation to tarnish, dragons to feed and spectaculars to hold.

Whatever Hannah's endgame is, it's far from realized.

Trying to make peace with the pariahs of the universe, and the gnats employed to ensure their will is done, I think of Maya, and each time Tim appeared throughout my young life; of Tomas' rebellion and Venicia's revelation the blame laid with an angel named Gabriel; of Hardwick and his propensity for betrayal, until he met someone who was far better at its nuances.

I think of all this— until finally, mercifully considering that dwelling on these matters has only deepened my obsession over them, doing little to alleviate them. Lifting myself off the cold floor, I gravitate to Harper. Tim eyes me the entire time.

I slide down the bars next to the Phoenix, who barely acknowledges me. The thick iron bands around her wrists don't seem to bother her, but that does nothing to change the fact I would free her if I held the key.

"When I was two," I begin in a hushed voice, "my parents died. Well, they killed each other— you think that would make it worse. Ask any little girl who lost her family and she'd probably say it doesn't matter whether a drunk driver killed them, or they turned on each other, like mine did. Any little kid would tell you the cause wasn't the important part— only the result."

The Phoenix says nothing, but her fingers pull nervously at the chain between her shackled wrists, and I know she is listening, which is all I need.

"I'm not going to sit here and try to convince you that we have a world in common. Anything in common, really, apart from being in this cell together, with a man who hasn't always done best by either of us."

In the corner of my eye, Tim's face puckers, trying to determine where I'm going with this. But he's not the one who I need to convince.

"That man — who I met long after you did— is not just part of my life. He *is* my life," I say, returning his inquisitive glare. "He first showed his face when I was a little kid, but he was watching over me long before that— before I was anything worth caring about.

"When he told me the truth — about how he was moving backwards through my memory— I felt betrayed. Stupid, for thinking I was special, that he had a genuine interest in me.

"At first, I regretted any sort of alliance with him — and rightfully so. It was too easy to blame, and cast everything gone wrong in my life onto him. It wouldn't have changed the scope of betrayal I faced among the living, or made me any better off without him. I would have died regardless, tied to a chair in a burning warehouse."

Harper tries to keep her expression from morphing— to maintain the composed shock worn since we were dragged into this cell — but it sags. Her eyes drift to our mutual ally, and I continue.

"But then I came here — to Atlas; and suddenly I understood. The man who saved my life might have made a terrible, unfathomable mistake. But he did it to save me. Because, in my heart of hearts, I know he cares about me. On some level, he may even love me. And if I was trying to save the person who meant more than anything, I'd risk Creation itself."

The Phoenix closes her eyes, letting loose an exhale from her tense chest. The chain between her arms jangles, filling the cell with metallic friction. The full light from her locket betrays her emotions, but nothing more than her fixation on Death.

"Whatever may have happened between you," I conclude, "there are clearly worse evils out there."

Not wanting to agitate her further, I leave the Phoenix to her troubled thoughts and dancing chain links to fill the gap between them. Returning to my lonely corner of the darkness — where I always pretended to belong but masqueraded within — the light from Harper's locket only casts the thinnest quilts of light along the floor.

It is inadequate for something so far gone as hope, and I won't even try to look for its fleeting shadow any longer.

· · · ·

TIME PASSES BY SOME more — its increments are ambiguously drawn out like tricks played by my eyes. Harper does not react to its passage any differently than Tim does; both seem to be waiting for something, while I can only continue drawing blanks.

There are few good courses of action. With the Council dead, Atlas at the mercy of Ziz and a blond witch holding our collective fate in her hands, it could well be lost.

Eventually, Tim shuffles down the cell, taking a seat beside me. His hair is out of place. The white clothing worn since his trial is the most disheveled I have seen him in three decades. Sitting together, backs against the bars, our muffled conversation is only witnessed by the hoarse Light from Harper's locket.

"For what it's worth," he says, "I'm sorry for getting you into this."

I snort, too exhausted for hindsight's bullshit. Tears at the precipice are foreign, borne more of emotional collapse than any affinity for having them.

"Please. Even I know that trial was a sham. Whatever comes next is a mockery."

"That's only scratching the surface. Hannah ..."

"*Tim*. Nobody could have seen that coming — your wife being wrapped up in this was an unforeseen outcome to every person in Atlas. Everyone," I finish on downturned lips, "except Stephen. He *knew*. The entire fucking time! And I was so stupid, to let him fool me again—"

"How could you have known, Ro?"

I scoff.

"How could I have known? How could I have not, Tim? The man kidnapped and sold children! He burned me alive! What in my right fucking mind made me think he had changed?"

Tim shakes his head, nothing to offer. I fall into self-aggrandizing spirals — eyes on the woman sitting opposite us, but not really looking at her head catatonically pointed at the floor.

All I see is Stephen Hardwick.

Stop it, Ramona.

I need a plan. We can't just sit here, waiting for the world to end. I use the bars to pull myself to balance. Tim casts me an inquisitive look, but sitting here, beating myself up over Hardwick won't win Atlas back from that witch.

"Get up."

The woman doesn't respond to my command at first, forcing me to repeat it. On its second, more confident iteration, Harper's head lifts. The hair strewn over her face falls to the side.

"What?"

"You heard me. You too, Tim," I say, glancing back at him. "You two have some big problem between you— fine! Kill each other when this is over, then. But right now, we need a truce. We need co-existence, because his wife is about to wipe us off the face of Atlas! So both of you, get up right now!"

Tim obeys. Unlike his uniform as Death — a black blazer that has hints of blue in low light, a white shirt and matching silk vest between them which never creases for anything— his prison whites are dirty and stained at the knees, immaculate nails blackened and grown. His skin is a pale gray, like old people who have been alive too long.

Or the recently dead.

Stop it, Ramona.

Harper, on the other hand, does not obey. Like a slouching high schooler, her spirit is not one of cooperation.

"No."

Unbelievable.

"Why?" I counter.

The Phoenix scoffs.

"Why? Oh, let me see. You want us to kiss and make-up, when you have no idea what he's responsible for—

"I know *exactly* what he's responsible for! He's Death, for fuck's sake! What, do you expect him to go around giving out candy? Of course he's hurt a lot of people, you included —and, from what I know of you Harper Whitaker, you were probably once someone who believed in doing the right thing. That's what I am trying to do here! So get over yourself!"

Harper chews her words. Her hands can only move so far apart, and she uses them to join our level, delivering her death stare.

"Bitch," she says, "you have no idea how close I came to killing you. In your hospital bed? If Tim didn't stop me, I would have fucking succeeded."

I disregard the revelation, glancing back at the wall her light shines onto. It brightens with her anger, making the golden object visible. It is Atlas — a dot near its northernmost tip pinpoints the destroyed Cathedral as its marker.

A map; maybe something that can help us.

"Your locket."

"What?" Harper asks.

"Look," I say, pointing to the wall. Its light swims and wavers as her head cocks to examine it. Tim notices it too. "It's trying to tell us something."

The golden dot at the northern tip of the Cathedral district where the Maesters once lived, destroyed by a dragon Hannah let loose and timed to Seraphina's outburst earns an eye roll from the Phoenix, and she paces past Tim, shaking her head.

"What *is* that?" Tim asks.

Not so all-knowing now, are you, Death?

"An answer," I smile. "Once we spring from here, that's where I'm going—"

Harper returns from where she paced past Tim — and throws her binds over his head. It finds his jugular, and Harper pulls the chains back. Dragging him to his knees as she did to the Brother in the Arena, Tim gasps for breath. The Phoenix has the element of surprise, and it takes too long for my shock to abate.

"What the fuck around you doing?"

"C'mon," Harper grimaces, pulling the chain tighter around Death's bulging neck. His eyes shudder and his hands claw outward, shattering any faith I had in his immortality. "You don't really believe he can die, do you? He's Death. He's not giving out candy, right?"

Tim's gagging pulls me back from the weaponization of my own words. His hands reach for me, face reflecting blue and purple shades I would have never expected of the man who calls himself Death, genuinely distressing my darkest reaches.

"Let go of him!"

The voice from my mouth is dragged down by failure and the snapping beams of my tolerance for death and destruction. But it is too late — Tim's final breaths evaporate. The rest of him breaks away in the same cloud-like form he showed me in the Shroud, black flakes drifting up to nothing until all of him is gone.

Harper's locket flickers. Its allocated Light dies with the rest of Tim's dissolution, and the final rod holding up my frail state is gone.

After all, the only thing I know is darkness.

The only difference now is I'm terrified of it.

CHAPTER TWENTY-TWO

MANY OF MY EARLIEST memories have nothing to do with the man who calls himself Death. Before he became a constant presence in my life, it was never directionless, but purpose seemed to wander anyway. My relationships were few and far between. Maya was the only constant force in my life. She got more and more sick, and I became less and less convinced anything about my introverted love life would change.

Everything before that is a blur, from a time that my petty transactions amongst the living amounted to nothing important — only to me. The first boy I kissed. The day I graduated from high school. The day Maya collapsed, and we learned she had emphysema — all of these moments had nothing to do with Tim. I chalked up the elusive visitor to childhood loneliness, an imaginary friend. I grew up, and he was soon forgotten.

Watching him dissolve into nothing, as Harper pulled at the chain over his jugular, and the exertion against his Adam's apple bulged the veins in his face and his panicked hands clawed for me to help him, all I could manage was a half-hearted plea.

Now he is gone, and I am back in my corner, trying to console my trembling hands. The rabbit hole in my memory is rife with landmines — recollections of Tim in my young life intercut with all the times I thought he might never return.

Harper is also back in her corner, no more comforted for her actions. Her Light returned after a few moments, but she offered nothing more. All I could do was glare as inner clockwork rotated snippets between its gears.

I blamed you when your interference in a natural order resulted in the world going to shit, and my life going to shit with it! I blamed you when you weren't just straight with me, and had to play your stupid, minutiative games, when you could have just been honest!

After a while, though — and short of trying to kill her — it was easier to sink back into self-pity.

You were the best of us, Knox.

I don't know if Tim gave Harper the slip somehow. I wouldn't put it past him. She's resigned to these events and slowly, I find myself treading in the same pessimistic direction.

Everything I had left to fight for is gone. Gonna go back in time and change that, too? Be my guest. I wouldn't defend your honor if it reversed everything!

That map from her locket is the key. Despite every indication I should lie down and die, that necklace is imbued with Light. It knows *something*. If we ever escape from this wretched hole in the ground, that is my only lead. Light willing, I can wrangle the woman into helping me defend Atlas, trial or no trial.

Then there's the matter of Tim's wife. If the man who calls himself Death still lurks nearby — and I have every reason to suspect he does — I wonder where he will draw the line between her deeds and her safety. If he intervenes to save her, things could get ugly.

"He's not dead, you know."

As if she could hear my whirring panic, Harper's low voice pulls me back from self-torment and fleeting visuals.

"What?"

The Phoenix chuckles, jangling the chain links between her spread legs. Her hair is matted and her stare blank, the words from her lips as empty.

"It would take a lot more than an angry lesbian and some strangulation to be rid of him. Don't get me wrong," Harper muses, hazel eyes drifting away from me, out the bars. "I won't be any happier to see him."

"Awfully assumptive to assume that was reversible."

"Maybe. But when you get rid of one screw-up called Death, you know how hard it will be to escape another."

Her confidence brings some relief — my lips lift on one corner, and I nod in understanding.

"I'm sure it wasn't easy for him to choose you," I reply. "From what he told me, things ended badly between you."

Harper scoffs.

"Badly is an understatement. So much happens in this fucked-up universe that I can't rightly explain. I know he's not responsible for all of it. But...what you two did made my personal life kind of difficult for a while.

"Maybe you've come to terms with what that man is," she continues. "He is so different from the Tim Hawkins I first met, I don't know if I'll ever see that man again. It's my fault he became Death in the first place — if I hadn't been so selfish, wanting to go home to Em, it would have been me.... it should have been me."

"What do you mean?"

And so Harper tells me the final piece of the story I haven't heard — how her mother Olivia impersonated Hannah's ghost, pulling him into Aumothera to defeat Hale; how he almost lost his mind without the apparition he had become used to. And finally, given the ultimatum that one of them had to take Hale's place to keep him from returning, Harper allowed Tim to volunteer. It completed what had been stolen from him, but emptied Tim of his humanity.

Our conversation is cut short by a loud banging sound and screams from above as objects are thrown into walls and ceilings. Garbled commands survive the trip between levels as nonsense, followed by a shriek before everything falls silent upstairs.

The cellar door opens, pouring a wide berth of Light into the dark chamber. Footsteps follow it down the ladder. It takes me a second to recognize the gleaming loafers as they descend the rungs. The figure descends, and Harper rolls her eyes as I lapse into a tearful smile.

The man who calls himself Death is alive and well. His dirty prison whites are gone, replaced with the black blazer and matching silk vest. Not a hair on his head is out of place. His hand wields the key to our freedom, a silver little thing with jagged edges.

"Thought I'd make myself useful while our friend settled down," he says, sliding the key in the lock. It turns, jangles and gives, collapsing the tumbler and opening the cell. "Miss me?"

I rush out of the cell door and hug him, taking him aback with the sudden gesture.

"Don't ever do that to me again," I say.

We separate — the awkward patting on my back tells me to cut it short — as Harper lifts herself from the floor, approaching us at the open cell.

"What did I tell you? Good as new," she snipes. Casting only a glare at Tim, the Phoenix pushes between us, wasting no time in climbing the ladder that leads up to the light source. There isn't so much as thanks in passing — part of her was ready to rot here, but with no plans to stick around, Tim and I are left alone.

"You okay?" he asks.

I scoff.

"All things aside, I'm okay. Seeing you strangled, though—"

"Must have been unnerving. It was not my intention to scare you. Giving her the chance to exert some aggression seemed better than fighting her, and potentially hurting you in the process. Not to mention her girlfriend's death has put her in a worse mood than usual."

"See, I thought she was in a good mood," I joke, but the humor slides off quickly. "Tim, that projection from her locket. I'm going to see what it leads to."

The man who calls himself Death responds with a raised eyebrow.

"You really think it could help us?"

"I don't know. There aren't many good options. But if that locket leads to something we can use to defend ourselves — isn't that worth it?"

"You're not wrong," Tim says. "Come on, we should get out of this cellar."

• • • •

THE TEMPLE WE WERE escorted by Brotherhood into a cellar is nothing like it was. The painted walls are torn and tattered where bodies at their base were thrown against it. The dead are all Brotherhood— at least twenty corpses are sprawled across the room, bringing to mind our attack on the team of FBI backing Hardwick.

It seems like a lifetime ago.

The scope of Death's destructive powers never ceases to leave my mouth hanging open. The bird masks are crumpled. Their robes are torn where Tim split them open like he once did against a legion of federal agents.

"Jesus," I say, standing just short of the cellar door and ladder we ascended from. "You're really good at that, aren't you?"

Tim shrugs as he spots a speck on his breast pocket, flicking it off with his middle finger and thumb.

"Only when I need to be. We should go — before more Brotherhood show up."

We step over the bodies, moving past our macabre statement of self-defence, and for a second, we may stand a fighting chance — of convincing the Phoenix, defeating Ziz and saving Atlas. As the double doors open, exiting into the Barracks' courtyard, my eyes adjust to natural Light, and that optimism dies.

The Phoenix is forced to her knees at the passage's center. Her hands are still bound, hair obscuring known disgust. Hannah circles her, twirling a golden dagger in her hand, brushing close to Harper's face before flipping it away from her.

From the arches into the defunct Nephalim headquarters to the stone steps leading up to the Obelisk doors, the woman pulled the full strength of Ziz's army to contain us. The Brotherhood are reinforced by at least five Behemoths circling the courtyard overhead. The groundside forces are armed with swords and crossbows, their bearers wearing the same expression as any man I've ever seen on the other end of a gun.

"Didn't think you would escape so easily, did you sweetie?" Hannah grins. "Arrogance is such a dreadful thing, isn't it?"

"No matter. I knew you were clever enough to weasel out of your accommodations. After conferencing with the Dark Lord, I agree it is somewhat useless to cause ourselves the headache trying to contain you. Come with me, if you would."

"Where?" Tim asks, breaking his silence.

"Why," she smiles, "to the heart of Atlas, my dear husband."

That locket is our only hope now.

CHAPTER TWENTY-THREE

. . . .

PHYSICALLY SPEAKING, the Spire is untouched by Hannah's rebellion. The rest of Atlas is defaced as Tim and I are boxed between the Brotherhood, but the Seat where the Council held palaver still twinkles under the constant daylight surrounding it. It may not have been ruined by its occupiers like the riots we passed on the way to it, or have the misfortune of proximity to the flaming torches tossed through the gates of God City, where turncoat Arbiters pull citizens through smoke and rising ash to Stone Mountain, freed from their moral bond as the dragons swing over districts, torching insurgents from above.

Harper was quickly pulled a different way — now Tim and I are carted through the heart of desperate cries and sundered peace, and the white clouds rising up from the cracked cobblestone of Heaven's central road.

The Royal Guard that once protected the commandeered Spire have perished, either wiped out during the initial assault or numbering among the bodies scattered around it. Of those who remain, the winged helmets are crumpled, robes torched where the dragons flambeed them to death. Hannah disregards the destruction she and her friends have caused, leading the mob through the gates, now open to all of Atlas.

The paintings that once captured my interest are unharmed, unlike those in the Barracks, but I can no longer admire them. I keep eyes straight ahead, burning a hole in Hannah's back as she leads us into the Council's old chamber.

The lights are not dimmed and four of the five chairs are gone, leaving only one where gods once sat and argued. My heart hurts at the other chairs' outlines where they were ripped from the stone floors. Hannah's army pulls us to a stop with them — only Tim's wife advances, climbing the shallow stairs to the spot Creation was once controlled by greater beings than her.

It is not until she wheels around, my chest caves and her power is indisputable. Taking a seat in the lonely throne, Hannah crosses one leg over the other, settling against the stone backrest. Her tiny hands tap the chair's massive arms, that wretched smile fully present. Our escorts move Tim and I into the circle of pillars where I became Nephalim and once theorized Seraphina was the worst that Atlas had to offer.

I was fatally mistaken in that regard. Barrett and the High Priestess are present. The natural order's most perilous traitors are outfitted now — the surviving Maester's robes are gold, rather than their traditionally caked browns. He seems quite pleased with the change; much more so than Seraphina, who shuffles in a disconcerting silver dress which is ill-fitted to her tall frame.

Hannah disregards both of her underlings as Tim and I are shepherded before her. The Brotherhood disperses beyond the central rotunda, leaving the man who calls himself Death and I alone at the Dark Lord's mercy.

"Things have obviously gotten off to an uncomfortable start," the blond woman says from her throne, awaiting no cue or permission from the gods to speak. "Revolution is often a messy affair — that so many lives were lost was an undesirable outcome."

Neither of us respond, earning a smile from Hannah.

"Atlas has been incompetently ruled for three Ages, and a change in leadership was never suggested. It was inferred, as told by Tomas' rebellion — which we all know was a sham created by a fellow Nephalim named Gabriel to siphon more power away from the ruling Council. And do you know where he is now?"

Finally, Tim speaks — the tone is bitter, long soaked like a cloth under spilled chloroform.

"Yes. The Phoenix and I killed him."

"Correct," Hannah says. "It seems Gabriel was emboldened by the Nephalim's downfall. He ceased to represent the realm he was sworn to protect, and only cared about angelic supremacy. Gabriel was corrupted by Light, and Earth paid for his malfeasance.

"Ziz, on the other hand, understands balance." Her right hand lifts, a black shape rising from her flat palm into the silhouette of flame. It bubbles and expands, cancelling out any connotation of natural elements. On the other hand, Hannah's raised fingers hold up a blinding ball. Within seconds, the blond woman encloses both displays in her fists, and they evaporate from the conversation.

"Darkness and Light. One was born from the other. They are a set. One can exist alone, but would be incomplete. The other would not survive in solitude, because that would be like a person without oxygen, wouldn't it?

"The problem," she says, "is that organisms created in the Light forgot to properly include Darkness in their grand plans. And why would they? Darkness is such a wild, misunderstood creature. It holds all of our fears, the underbelly of our faith. Most people would run from it, and soon forget it is the source of everything."

Hannah admires her blank palms which previously held elements of her fascination, turning them over— opening, closing, flexing their power.

"In their misunderstanding, Atlas embraced the Light without regard for its true creator, and the side of Creation nobody was willing to represent.

"Zizzik did. He stood for Creation, when all the other gods and angels harvested Light for their self-interested endeavors. His transformation into Ziz is often glossed over in Atlas' history. I'll have to tell you sometime."

I have no desire to hear this woman's voice another second — she is apocalypse in a pretty dress, recklessly throwing Creation around like a wrecking ball to suit whatever ends she has.

Power, she says in my memory— *of such magnitude, to go back to a time without it would leave me a skeleton of what I am — a weak, dishevelled being that would make the longest-tenured Whisperers look like the belle of the ball.*

"Enough, Hannah," Tim says. "Stop with the games, and just tell us what your plan is."

"You want to know the plan, is that it?" she asks, and turns to Barrett, who nods and disappears as Hannah reverts her attention to us. "Very well."

The angel who returns with the Maester is larger than Luca, who neared eight feet tall and was taller than any Nephalim he was out-lawed from standing with. The newcomer has dark hair and gorgeous wings. His suit is golden steel, jangling as some pieces scrape against others with his stroll. A giant longsword sits on his chain link belt. His hair is knotted down his back, and beady blue eyes look out over a thick beard as he stops next to Hannah.

"This is Mykul," Hannah says. "A creation of the Council who sought to infuse their soldiers with catastrophic amounts of Light in the First Age. Certainly another bit of concealed history, isn't it? We found him in the Obelisk's basement, kept catatonic by the Nephal-im. I had my men free him."

The Council tried to make the angels like the artifacts they had successfully infused with Light. It failed, and they locked their exper-iments away.

"Your champion," Hannah explains, "will battle Mykul for the ti-tle of Death. And whosoever is the victor will retain control of Au-mothera."

"Making this freak the new Death if he wins," I say.

"No," the blond woman chuckles. "Mykul is merely a champion, representing a vested interest."

"You?"

Hannah giggles.

"Please. I have my sights set on greater things than that cesspool. The fact is, the Phoenix will participate — her forfeiture is also yours, Tim —"

"Why are you doing this?" Tim asks. "All this destruction, for what? Do you realize what you are following here?"

My ears perk up, because a theory has bubbled under the surface for just as long, and this is my chance to confirm it. But Hannah shakes her head— we are gnats in her clockwork, and she owes us no justification.

"I will hold your friend — she requires training to make the spectacle worth holding. We wouldn't want a quick death, would we? In the meantime, you are free to go. I will send for you both when the time is right."

With a final wave of her hand, we are allowed to leave — the crowd of plague doctor masks disperses further, allowing us to cut through their numbers. Neither Tim nor I speak passing the Spire's double doors no longer held by the Royal Guard, but groaning Behemoths overhead, putting a second thought in the head of those who would endanger their mistress.

Beyond the Seat, glancing out at all the destruction of the last few days, I have no words, only motive.

I have no consolations left— only bare ambition.

I am going to murder that cunt.

Follow the trail. It has protected me in the past, when going off-road might have ended very differently. I have to follow Harper's involuntary map, and see what lies in the Cathedral's ruins.

But first, there's somebody I need to see.

And it's all thanks to Barrett.

CHAPTER TWENTY-FOUR

I WAS NEVER RELIGIOUS as a mortal. Part of that may have had something to do with my parents' deaths, but they seem like such a small consideration now. God's absence seems to have been the byproduct of ambivalence— if the nature-nurture argument is to be believed, it had mostly to do with Maya being non-religious. She hung about a sham tarot dealer named Glenda, but never attended a mass in her life.

It wouldn't have helped — the handful of Scripture I know is the byproduct of human imagination to comprehend a void. The Atlas was happy to let our fictions take root and inspire the living.

My return to the Barracks is less tense without the mob of Brotherhood pulling me between them. Tim went off in search of something. I told him to meet me at the Cathedral in two hours. It would be long enough for what I need to accomplish.

The Obelisk is haunted by the sterile Light washing over it. No angels and Royal Guard pass each other on its steps, exchanging nods on their respective patrols.

The doors are unlocked, the interior emptied of legendary warriors once responsible for guarding the Council; who failed, and were relegated to the sidelines until Ziz wiped them out. The art is still on display — mighty depictions of Nephalim dwarfing Creation's monsters, of whom I am not one. The visual tales range from Lovecraftian horror to mutant beasts, leading to the one in themselves they were unable to overcome. Different monsters control Atlas' airspace now, answering to a single master, and those mighty warriors are just some creations in a painting.

I came here with purpose — sneaking back into the one place Ziz nor his agent expected me to turn, and don't linger.

Hannah says she found Mykul in the Obelisk's basement, hooked up to tubes like some Nazi experiment.

Contrary to my secular nature, I pray for something of a similar nature.

Some things about people never change. Whether one travels to Narnia or Atlas, key tenets of humanity remain predictable, leaving a trail in the darkest times to something resembling hope. I don't know if hope is still tenable in the supreme realm, given the degree it has buckled and crumpled under the Dark Lord's forces.

There is something about transitioning from impending to full-blown crisis that rocks the most stubborn souls, finally wrangling a concession from humility's long-forgotten wreck. They're not suddenly more helpful or eager to please.

They do, however, go where they feel safest.

That is the case for Elion, the portal caster from when I first spoke with Maester Quorroc. I lost track of him at the ball when Linus and company crashed the party, and have scarcely seen or heard of the Magi since.

The only other place I ever saw one was the Obelisk, and that is where my bets are hedged.

The Maester and Nephalim orders have effectively collapsed. Hardwick is gone, and my only other ally is a murderous woman with a weird map around her neck. She's a start, but I would be insane putting all my eggs in her basket.

After twenty minutes of wandering the ground level — and perhaps stopping to admire marble busts I missed the first two times blazing in here — the second floor was cleared much faster. There are no elevators or stairwells, but ramps that gently ascend between stories.

In a large chamber on the third floor, the Magi number less than five when I expected a full group. The four of them mediate, heads pointed down, thumbs and forefingers forming a circle at the vertices of crossed legs. Purple robes contrast the room's color scheme of stone beige and they sit like monks; a front-facing teacher, with his students' back to me in a line.

Their leader, whose eyes are firmly shut, lifts his head. His hair is fine like threads of silk, but he is old and the slicked-back hair running down his neck has grown sparse. In front of him, a pool of clear liquid manifests from nothing. The puddle grows, expanding into a solid; like a moving worm laying itself flat, it grows to a quarter inch, then a half— and soon, it begins to morph.

The body rises. Pieces branch from the central mass, taking symmetrical forms. The middle fattens, rounding out — eight tiny threads descend from the belly. The oval's point smooths, becoming like the smaller head of a snowman, and a green bulb lights up its thicker end. Before long, the puddle from nothing is some sort of firefly, lighting the teacher's catatonic state.

Osmosis.

My awe reaches its crescendo, and the man opens his eyes. There is no other subject of interest — he is aware of my presence, and exactly where to find me.

"Ramona Knox," the teacher says. His expression is blank, neither surprised or questioning why I've come. "We were expecting you."

Okay, now I'm uncomfortable.

"You were?"

"Yes. Since Atlas has fallen, and the Nephalim fell with it, you are the last true-blooded angel in the supreme realm. We are at your service."

There must be some mistake.

"Um," I chuckle. "I'm not an angel, okay? Luca was an angel. Pol and the others were angels—"

The teacher interrupts me. His students do not turn away from their mediation.

"You have taken the Oath, have you not?"

"I took *an* Oath," I reply. "But I don't have wings or a big fucking sword, if that's what you're saying."

"And was there a light during this Oath taken?"

The weird constellation that closed around me after the Council pronounced me a Nephalim? What does that have to do with anything?

"Yes — it had stars in it."

The old man smiles, the first hint of genuine emotion he has displayed. The glowing insect flutters around his head as he speaks, and I am spellbound by both.

"Then the Oath was taken, and you are Nephalim — one with the Light, and its last sworn defender, by my last count."

"You don't know me," I scoff. "I came to speak with Quorroc. Elion will tell me where he is, if you won't."

But Elion doesn't lapse, nor do his two peers. It doesn't matter — no confrontation would predicate Maester Quorroc rounding the alcove, which is exactly what he does. The frail elder that Luca and I arrested is no worse for wear. His robes are their original soot color, encompassing everything Barrett left behind in his quest for power. If he holds a grudge over my interrogation tactics, it doesn't show.

"Ramona," the old Maester says. "You have come in our darkest hour, child."

Looking between the two elders — one who should, by all rights, hate me; the other is half a monk praying to delusion, practicing osmosis on the way — I have no words but vomit them up anyway.

"Did you know?"

"About Barrett? Yes," he admits. "None of the other Maesters took measures to defend themselves from our leader. He is the worst kind of power-hungry. At least Tomas and Gabriel were brash, their struggle on full display.

"But Barrett — his search for knowledge went too far. He wanted to be the smartest man in Creation. He craved knowledge like others do power. But knowledge has a corrupting effect, much like power does. And whatever he has seen, it drove him to help destroy Atlas."

There will be time to avenge these traitors later. The unnamed Magus teacher wakes his students. Elion's eyes open slowly like the others, also intuitively aware of my presence. But Quorroc is a Maester— perhaps the only decent one left, whose legacy is tarnished by years of humiliation at Barrett's hands. Luca saw him as a troublemaker, but now he may be our only hope of not fighting Ziz blind.

"How do we stop it?" I ask, cutting right to the heart of the matter.

There are no games left to play.

Quorroc sighs. There is more life in his gray beard than either Siskett or Barrett, and the lines of stress don't run as deep. He may have been innocent the day Luca and I arrested him, carted away for nothing more than entertaining children.

"The Behemoths themselves are a force all their own to reckon with. If the gates to Ezzark are opened — their homeworld and breeding grounds — their presence will be infinite. Not to mention the involvement of the woman," Quorroc says, emphasizing *the woman*. "She is the true wild card in the Dark Lord's plot."

"And they want the Avatar," I finish, because the plot's endgame is all that matters now. "All the spectacle and grandiose bullshit aside, Maester — that's what they're after."

"Correct. The Avatar's role is often minimalized, but she is the key to controlling Atlas, or destroying it. We have no way to know what Ziz plans to do with her, but the outcome would be catastrophic for every soul in this room.

"Make no mistake, Ramona. You are now the highest-ranking official that Atlas has. Seraphina and Barrett forfeited their rightful place in the hierarchy by abdicating. All the Nephalim are dead, save you. This means we must protect you at all costs."

"Why would I need protecting?"

The green firefly passes the Magus teacher's amused look. He looks up to Quorroc with a half-smirk and cocked head.

"She doesn't know."

"Of course she doesn't know!" Quorroc snaps. "I am trying to tell her in a way she will not go into shock."

"Ah. Carry on, then."

Quorroc rolls his eyes.

"Forgive him. This is Avalon, the Magi's leader. He is under the impression he has mastered the school of confusion, but all he manages to confuse is our perception of him."

"Nonsense," Avalon replies.

"The point is, Ramona — this is the greatest threat Atlas has ever faced. It makes the Nephalim rebellion look like child's play. Without the Council, all of Creation has been dislodged from order."

I don't need a long, drawn-out explanation. I need to follow Harper's map, save her from Mykul, and kill Tim's wife.

A behemoth task, to be sure. Tim's words echo from a time the worst I had to worry about was men like Stephen Hardwick, operating in the shadows.

"Tell me what I need to do."

Quorroc smiles.

"There is much work to be done. But first, a ray of light in this dark time."

Before I can inquire what in the world the old man is on about, a familiar face rounds the same alcove Quorroc did. The sight of blond hair and angel wings, with a sword in a sheepskin sheathe brings tears to my eyes.

"Luca?"

The angel bows his head. I rush forward and hug him. His red robes are gone, replaced with ragged white matching the feathered wingspan. As we separate, I ask the only question I can muster.

"But...how?"

The angel steps back, joining Quorroc. He is much taller than both of us — a fact I had forgotten but am happy to be reminded of.

"Just prior to your arrival, the Council summoned me," he replies. "Told me they had concerns about Barrett — that he had been reported as working against their interests, citing his search for knowledge. At the time, I had no true indicator to how deep the Maester was, and proceeded as I always have; with extreme caution.

"The morning before the Cathedral attack, I spotted Barrett conversing with a blond woman. It was the first time I had seen her. I reported my findings to the Council, and recommended using their projected forms for the party. Were something to happen during that event, I was to go dark and survey Barrett from afar."

It was all a ploy. It may have been all that saved Luca's life, and despite my annoyance over wasted feelings, I'd rather him here.

At the same time, all I have are questions. They come out aggressive, failing every attempt to sound measured.

"So the ball? The trial? You couldn't interfere?"

Luca sighs.

"The ball was affirmation of the blond woman's ties to Ziz. Barrett travelled to Earth, must have made some sort of deal with those raiders."

"How did they get in?" I have wondered about a doorway between Earth and Atlas since Linus and his friends made their appearance.

"My fault," Avalon says. "The Maester told us they were marked for added security — he met them, said they were headed for orientation with the Avatar. I had no reason to doubt him. Forgive me."

I shake my head. The Magi climb to their feet, the seven of us all that stands against overwhelming darkness.

"Mourning the past won't save Atlas. Beating ourselves up will not bring the Council back. If what you say is true, Maester — that I have some influence over Creation — then my first order is to make Luca a Nephalim. Screw Tomas. Fuck Gabriel. To hell with the old way. We do this my way now."

"Ramona," Quorroc says. "Luca cannot be a Nephalim. With the Council gone, we lack the power to allow him to take the Oath."

"It's true," Luca offers. "There is no point trying to rectify past mistakes. The chance is gone —"

"Give me your sword," I reply.

"What?"

"Give me your damn sword."

He does, and I tell him to kneel before me. I lift the massive sword and rest it on his shoulder with some struggle.

"Luca, son of Tomas — your past does not define you. It might have once, like mine did for me. But you are more of a Nephalim than any of the ones I met."

Quorroc purses his lips, wondering what good this will do. Let him wonder — this is a fight to the death, and alliances are everything. Avalon and Elion stand at ease opposite the Maester, and the room is eerily silent.

Luca is stunned at the gesture, but I continue.

"When Barrett told me you were dead — that you had gone onto the White Light — I thought Atlas had lost a hero. Today, I'm glad it's gained one.

"I don't have weird lights, or some fancy Oath for you to take. What I ask is simple — stand by my side, help me win back Atlas. And in exchange, one day this may all be yours. Light knows, I don't want it. All I ask is that you help me end this threat, and put that bitch in her place."

Effortlessly holding up the heavy blade with his shoulder, he is two-thirds of my height on his bent knee.

"I swear it."

"Do *not* betray me. I've dealt with enough turncoats."

Luca bows his head.

"To the day we fall in battle, sister — I am at your side. Until we win, or Light fails completely, my life for you."

I remove the sword from his shoulder, wincing at its weight as gravity pulls its tip to the Obelisk's floor. Luca returns to both feet, securing the weapon from me.

The situation is no less bleak, but this — the beginnings of a resistance to Ziz's unchecked power, as well as my angel companion's return — gives us a small fighting chance of saving Atlas.

The faint screams of dragons penetrating the chamber's walls, shaking the floors with their sonic bellowing above — reminds us it may be futile yet.

CHAPTER TWENTY-FIVE

THE RUINED CATHEDRAL district is largely untouched from the night of its collapse. So much has happened in a short time, organizing its clean-up seems like a trivial matter in comparison.

It will never be rebuilt now. The rest of Atlas crumbles under the Behemoths' brute force. The populace is zombified, color drained from their faces. I am the highest-ranking remainder of the old order, and my failure to protect the Council may pale in comparison to what comes next in Hannah's game.

The conflicting slabs of broken brick where Maesters once lived is a stain on its perfected landscaping. The gardens still thrive in arrangements of red and pink and yellow, the grass a perfectly-trimmed density approaching the debris. Glass is scattered around buckled stone. A grayed claw poking out from its rubble grave shows no sign of decomposition, and I wonder if its reincarnation is possible, adding to the current set of dragons circling above me.

They are everywhere I go.

All that exists is a stubborn mosaic of chaos, and the victims trapped within. I don't know if Siskett's body was removed, fed to the White Light. He could still be under there.

Maybe the locket was trying to warn of an attack. Maybe there's still some hidden weapon under here.

Perhaps, it means nothing at all.

One of the first decisions I made after making Luca a Nephalim was to leave him in hiding. Barrett has every reason to think the angel is dead, and I want his reemergence to come at the greatest crux of drama, and let Luca take the old man out.

"Such a tragedy," says a voice from my six. So fixated on the destruction, I didn't notice anyone join me. Tim's wife drifts up the pathway from the God's Road; her monsters circle above, but she is otherwise alone. "Albeit a necessary one."

She is dressed differently — closer to my first conversation with her, before I knew her name — and gone is the wicked gown.

"Sorry," I reply. "I don't qualify tragedy by its political merits. I believe that's called terrorism. No offense, but it's something I got into the business of stopping."

Hannah smirks.

"I can see why Tim took an interest in you. He was always attracted to the intelligent ones." Her eyes travel from the top of my head to my feet, dressing me down before drifting back up. "Certainly pretty, too."

"Is that what all this is about? Kind of been wondering, is all."

"Wondering what, exactly?"

She chose to confront me alone, where nobody could lend backup or save me, should she use her living weapons to cook me out of existence. The two in the sky are smaller than the one from the Arena, but will obey Hannah's every word.

"Just how big that jealous streak of yours is."

Hannah snorts.

"Please. I am beyond petty exchanges over my husband's infatuation with you. Keep him — I am sure he will just upgrade once you're out of the picture."

She can lie all she wants. This is, at its heart, about my relationship with Death. If it weren't, Hannah would have never used that creepy conjuration of Maya's apartment to make her introduction into my life; she wouldn't be talking to me now, or trying to guilt me over and over that Tim took interest in me.

"You were gone," I tell her — knowing beneath the facade, this woman does care. "What should he have done? Pretended you were coming back?"

"Spoken like a true mistress."

I shrug.

"Bit far for an affair, really— if it *was* an affair, and not some cosmic clusterfuck I lucked into. So tell me why you came here, or leave me the fuck alone."

For all my baiting and teasing, Hannah's composure never breaks. Pacing away from me, I am only privy to the back of her head as a visual.

"The Phoenix is refusing to take part in the event. She has already injured several of my followers. Normally, I would shrug it off, send the girl to her senseless death. But the Dark Lord has told me that is unacceptable."

"*Ziz* thinks it's unacceptable?"

"Yes," Hannah says, turning to face me. "The Dark Lord thrives on spectacle. He insists the girl be trained, and will hold off on the event until she is broken of this resolve."

"And you couldn't just pick someone else?"

Hannah snickers.

"And overrule my husband's wishes to have this woman represent him? I'll tell you what— if he was a true man, he would have chosen himself; not thrown another into the line of fire. He is a coward. Always has been.

"So," she says, "I am going to make him watch me break his friend's spirit. And if that does not suffice, I will move onto you."

I have never felt more desire to murder someone in cold blood. But I have no guarantee she can actually be killed — achieving death in trying would not save Atlas.

"And what makes you think she will cooperate with me?"

Hannah shrugs.

"Nothing. But if she kills you, it will be one less of mine who died trying. This is not a request, Miss Knox."

"Sorry. I don't take orders from you." Before her brow can furrow, and she can signal her reptilian friends to crush me, I continue. "That said, I will talk to her."

The momentary frustration disappears from her face — that of a child not getting what she wants — and is replaced with her lunatic, bright-eyed grin.

"Thank you," she says, but I'm not done.

"Keep one thing in mind, lady."

"What's that?" she asks.

Closing the renewed distance between us, I pause, our faces almost touching. Her blushing composure is maddening, her proximity poisonous. But my bloodlust is stronger than it has ever been.

"We'll play your little game. But when you inevitably lose, you're going to wish your demonic-worshipping ass had stayed in the shadows where it belongs. You and your boy Ziz are going on a one-way ticket to Hell, bitch."

Hannah's smile falls from the highest corners of her mouth. I don't feel as assured as the words sound, pushing them out with all the confidence I have left.

"I imagine that is a comforting dream to have. Speak with the woman, Miss Knox. Your future may depend on it."

With that, she turns, retreating the way she came. Looking back to the Cathedral's wreckage, only her fading footsteps are allowed to bless my conscious thoughts with her departure. I can't muster the strength to talk to her much longer.

• • • •

THIS THING HAS SO MANY moving parts, and I am not privy to the full picture yet. I have bits and pieces, scraps of solace and threads of disappointment. Between the Phoenix trying to kill Tim, dragons in the sky, extramarital vengeance and freak warriors of the Light, there is no way to imagine a tidy ending.

Returning to the Obelisk, I find Avalon meditating; the other Magi are gone, as is his insect friend. Quorroc is absent. Luca sits in a corner, sword over his legs, head bowed with both eyes closed. He is not sleeping, because nobody here sleeps.

"Hey."

Luca looks up as I join him.

"Ramona — how did it go at the Cathedral?"

I slide down the wall next to the steady sword across his lap, the hands holding it less certain.

"The woman confronted me. Wants me to compel her prisoner to fight. But I don't think Harper will do it."

"This is the one Death has chosen as a champion?"

I nod.

"There's some kind of unspoken resentment between them. To be honest, I don't really understand why he picked her."

"What about the map? The one you said contained some sort of astral projection?"

"If there's anything there, it's under the Cathedral— which is a hulking piece of wreckage. We don't have the manpower on our side to get to it."

"We may be able to change that," the angel says. "It comes with some risk, but will expand our numbers against Ziz."

"What's that?"

Luca grimaces.

"The Crimson League."

"Demetrius?"

"Yes. The Whisperers and Crimson League preached unfairness in regards to the Council's treatment — *my* treatment — of them. The League has never helped its reputation much, but they only followed Ziz out of inadequacy—"

"Not genuinely, like the Brotherhood does."

"Exactly," the angel replies. "They were never good enough to serve the Dark Lord, anyway. He prefers his servants capable, rather than the riffraff in Devil's Corner."

I chuckle, and Luca asks what's funny.

"When we first dealt with the Crimson League, you seemed so sure. That they were involved, I mean."

He nods.

"A terrible mistake that I will forever have to live with. I knew from my years in the Brotherhood they were fanatics. They really seemed to adopt legitimacy for a time. Took on security contracts, offered their services throughout Atlas. Compared to the chaotic League, who openly flaunt dark magic and make reckless statements, the Brotherhood was making gains in decency."

I can't say much in this department. Stephen Hardwick fooled me twice, and I will forever feel responsible for allowing him to funnel me into the blond woman's sights. To sit here and denigrate Luca for his own blind spots would be the ultimate hypocrisy.

Instead, I choose to confide in him.

"I've never been in love," I say, unsure why these words need to be said at all. "At least, don't think I have. Maybe I am now, and that's what terrifies me. Everything going to shit around us only took that inkling of what I knew and reinforced it — that I feel something for Tim, and I know he feels the same for me."

Luca smiles, as if this twist in the conversation soothes him.

"We have a saying in Atlas. 'But has there ever been something so great as love, and yet so comfortable with sin?' My father used to quote it when I was young to justify some of the atrocities committed in the Council's name. I have not heard it uttered in many years."

"Kind of true, if you think about it."

"Meaning?"

"Meaning, I helped end the world with a man most people would have felt terrified of. But he has never threatened me. He's always been there, for better or worse. And now, this whole thing with his freak bitch of a wife is awakening something in me. And I have never felt so scared of anything, Luca."

A moment of silence passes before the angel speaks.

"Does he know how you feel?"

I shake my head.

"Unless he can read my mind, I've never told him." Recalling the conversation in the jail cell, I have spoken of it in front of him, though — I resolve to leave that last part out.

"Maybe you should," he nods. "While you still can."

• • • •

I FIND TIM ON THE FIFTH floor of the Obelisk. While the administration building's living quarters are more comfortable than a jail cell, I have little intention of spending much time here. There is work to be done if we are to bring the League to our side. It will have to be done quickly to bolster our numbers against Hannah's forces. Quorroc and the Magi are one thing, but we need capable bodies to overcome the monstrosities she deploys.

Knocking at the room the Maester told me he had claimed, Tim opens the door to reveal a twin-sized bed and sparse furniture. His beard is no longer as finely trimmed as it was, and I wonder if stress has precluded his default state.

"Can I come in?"

Tim's face is strained with the weight of recent events. He closes the door behind me, and it clicks with finality — we have no more desire to run from each other.

"What can I do for you, Ramona?"

I don't have a clue where to begin — I have never been the warmest of people, and feel ridiculous even now.

"You look tired," I say. "What's going on?"

Whatever I thought would be said coming in here is absent from his face, like he just received the worst news in the world.

The man who calls himself Death grimaces.

"We need to talk," he says.

CHAPTER TWENTY-SIX

DURING THE HUNT FOR Emily Rickard, a man named the Spider called me in my office. At the time, I believed him to be Jordan West, the elusive mastermind behind a ring of child abductors.

One of the most perplexing parts of the West case was — prior to Stephen Hardwick revealing it had been him all along — their leader was never seen. He walked in the shadows while his group of grown altar boys stole children from public places and sold them. That West was actually dead never occurred to me until the revelation was flesh-and-blood.

During the ensuing events, in which I physically died in a fire and was resurrected by my guardian angel, his composure never broke. Even disobeying the acceptable rules of his position by bringing me back to life didn't faze him.

But there is a side to Tim I have seen since coming to Atlas. This is his apex of fear and dread, as he takes my hands in his, and sits with me on the bed.

"What's going on?" I repeat.

His cheeks are pale and his hair tousled — something I never thought was possible. The suit slouches on his shoulder, and there is only life in his twitching lower lip.

"Hannah demanded to speak with me — after we left the Seat."

"She confronted me too," I admit. "When I went to check out the Cathedral district."

Tim frowns.

"She did?"

I nod.

"Tim, I think she wants me out of the picture. And that's fine, if that's what you want —"

He stops me.

"That is *not* what I want. However, you are right. Our relationship seems to form a great part of her motivation. I never expected to see her again — was I supposed to twiddle my thumbs until she magically reappeared?"

"You said she died in childbirth, right?"

He nods. "But then, about six months later, she started appearing. At first, I was sure she was a hallucination. She professed to be a symptom of my grief — but that was a lie. It turned out to be this Olivia woman, using Hannah's essence to appear to me as my wife. That little revelation made me angry for a long time."

"This is the woman you told me caused you to become Death?"

"No," Tim says. "Olivia's impersonation of Hannah led me into the Shroud. It's how Harper and I met. We helped Olivia kill Hale, and I became Death. Voluntarily."

I ponder this information for a second, unable to recall how much he has already told me.

"I need you to tell me exactly what happened with Hannah," I say. "I may have a way to bring her down, but I can't be in the dark on anything, Tim."

Tim nods, and I ask him to tell me what happened again.

This time, he does.

Tim's encounter with his wife was quite similar to mine. After leaving the Seat and parting ways with me as I went off to meet Quorroc, he gravitated to the Arena where all his personal failures had come to roost. Emptied of the spectacle that cost Harper's girlfriend her life, the man who calls himself Death walked the graveyard of his worst impulses. He examined the blood spots Em was cut in half by a reptile's giant jaws; and stared at the spot Harper fell to the ground in haunting sobs.

He wandered for so long, it might have been days before he heard the footsteps behind him.

You have to understand, he tells me. *I looked back at her, and saw the girl I fell in love with as a teenager — who I married at twenty, and lost at thirty-eight; whose ghost drove me to what I am now.*

Nothing of that woman remained, and she didn't ask permission to join him.

"I imagine you're angry with me," Hannah said. "After all, quite the jump, isn't it? From nobody, to holding the fate of the universe in your hands."

"Referring to yourself?"

"Please. I'm not your pet, Tim. You can't dance around me. Remember the girl from Valencia? What was that slut's name?"

"Wendy," he cringed, wondering how long this conversation would continue.

Hannah chuckled.

"You always did remember the pretty ones. Shame you couldn't hold a place for the most important woman in your life. What's the phrase? 'Until death does us part'?"

"Only death *did* us part, darling. I had no way to assume you survived. And here you are — petty as you always were," Tim said. "Hiding in the shadows like a rat, instead of communicating like a rational person? And now, you serve a god who is essentially the Devil."

The woman's gown rifled in the slight breeze washing over her graveyard of decency. The eyes he remembered were glossed over in megalomania, and her movements did not suffer the rebuke.

"Ziz said I would face a test of my faith. He didn't indicate when this would happen, or the form it would present itself. Now, I am beginning to believe that the test concerns you, dear husband. You and your little friends can keep fighting inevitability, or accept the uniform truth."

Tim frowned.

"And *what* is the uniform truth?"

"That I am going to win," she said. "Eventually, you will realize that your only rightful place is beside me, Tim. That all of this — Atlas, the Shroud, the Council? None of it matters. The only thing that matters is *us*."

Her thin hands reached across the space between them, wrapping around Tim's lapels, then cupping his hands in hers. She lifted one to her mouth, kissing the knuckle.

"I have missed you...*so* much. There were days I never thought I'd see you again. And maybe...I made an impulsive choice when I realized where you were, and who you were...*with*."

Her blue eyes dug into his brown ones, pleading to return some kind of sentiment — but like the Phoenix told me in our shared cell, the old Tim Hawkins was erased by his cosmic role.

"If that was true, you would join us against Ziz."

This made Hannah's ordinary smile transition to a bleaker one. Her breaths became short, irises coated by a film of water.

"Unfortunately, that is no longer possible. The Dark Lord and I are entwined. My soul belonged to him from the moment he washed over me, becoming one with my thoughts. He is part of me now — separating from him would destroy me."

Tim pulled back his hand; both of Hannah's dropped to her sides. Envisioning the child who claimed her life on a hospital delivery table all those years ago; that his wife was possessed by yet another leech on her lifeforce angered him. It's no poison infant, whose travel down the birth canal would kill both mother and child, but a Devil nonetheless.

"So what's your endgame here, Hannah? Forcing me to abandon the people closest to me to consolidate your ego? Allowing Ziz to destroy Creation, all to settle a damn grudge?"

Hannah chuckled.

"To do what we have always done. Make the best of a bad situation. But if that is your position, World-Killer, I cannot stop you. Just know this:

"The Dark Lord is everywhere. He is more powerful than ever, and only requires a body to complete the metamorphosis — a conduit whose power can sustain him, but not be so strong they can refute his will."

Tim knew exactly who Hannah was referring to, but did not dare utter the name. He turned to leave, ready to storm past the scene he had been so determined to see again, take accountability for.

This conversation had erased all of that resolve.

"Tim!"

Her call stopped Death in his tracks, leery to face her again — and when he did, Tim wished he'd kept walking.

"If I were you, I'd treasure what time the two of you have left together."

Speechless, Tim turned toward the main arches of the Arena. He didn't look back at his wife standing alone in the massive structure's center, but could swear he felt the giant footpads of multiple Behemoths shake the ground as they touched down, encircling their mistress in a phalanx of webbed wings.

• • • •

"WOW."

The silence between us sits in the dead air, fouling it with the smell of my panic. Everything is on the table now. In one lane is Hannah trying to win her husband back. In another, Ziz is trying to wipe out Creation by destroying or repurposing the Avatar, and wants a body worthy of possession for his reincarnation.

And at the center is Death's champion, who refuses to play her part out of resentment.

"Ramona," Tim says, "this is not likely to have a good outcome."

I nod, hands still in his.

"I know."

"And I need you to know whatever happens, I am not giving into her demands. I am done playing her vile games."

"It may not come to that."

"What do you mean?" he asks. "I don't see how we can possibly stand against them."

And so I tell him about Quorroc — how Barrett betrayed Atlas, allowing its key defenses to short-circuit, and Hannah to pull off her coup against the Council. I tell him about Luca's off-the-books operation, the Magi's involvement, and the plan to recruit the Crimson League.

"That may be a risk in itself," Tim warns. "From what I know of the Crimson League, they may sabotage any resistance we could form."

"Except that the League has worshipped Ziz for an Age, and wasn't brought into the fold for Hannah's assault on the Council. I saw a few being mistreated by the Brotherhood on the way back here."

"But is that enough to turn them against the Dark Lord, Ro? If they see this as a trial of their faith — as Hannah so lovingly put it — they may be too far gone to save."

Pulling hands away, I stare at the floor, hoping for some guarantee of certainty this can all work out. The only chance to save Atlas rests on my ability to organize these disparate forces.

"Maybe they are. I won't need Demetrius and his crew for long — just long enough to sabotage Hannah, and prevent the match from taking place."

Tim says okay, and never have I doubted less that he is with me. Luca is with me. I have a Maester at my disposal and some magicians who can make portals and insects out of nothing. And soon, I may compel the gang of hoodrats who once threatened to publicly execute me to lend their assistance.

If I can bring the Phoenix to our side, we may stand a fucking chance.

CHAPTER TWENTY SEVEN

HISTORY IS FULL OF people whose shifting allegiances sealed events a certain way — ask anyone, and I'm sure they would tell you Lee Harvey Oswald was not born bad. Lenin was no madman as a child; even Adolf Hitler had to traverse the world, learning all the nuances and injustices that inspired the Holocaust. I make no excuses for these people — only wonder what drove them to such lengths.

The woman's motives are clear. She sees salvation in Tim, or Ziz, but not both. I am the nuisance standing in her way, not considering myself a mistress, as she does; not claiming prettier, smarter or better.

Less batshit crazy? Probably.

The Crimson League is the key. My initial adversaries in Atlas are locked out of salvation and damnation, but it doesn't have to be one or the other. Until now, they have protected the Whisperers who held information on the Dark Lord's return; passed each other notes in alleys, playing cards close to the chest — hoping when the time came, Ziz would choose them as his loyal, undying servants.

There is no such future for the League. Their ambitions are delusions, their loss my gain. They are rats and roaches— pests in the shadows the woman never considered twice for the job. The Brotherhood was the more capable, subtle force. They were legitimate, rather than troublemakers— in short, everything the League wanted to be.

Luca and I find Demetrius and Gossamer where we last confronted them in Devil's Corner. The former still wears grungy red robes, eyes reflecting more insanity than rational thought in their red-tinted irises. The Whisperer dons his fox mask, but has made no effort to iron out the concave nose where I hit him square in the face.

At the sight of my angel companion, Demetrius lapses into a mix of terror and disgust.

"No!" yells the League leader, hailing his sentries across the road. "Get them out of here!"

Knowing he trusts Luca about as much as the Dark Lord trusts the League, I take the lead on questioning.

"Relax," I say. "I'm not here to cause trouble for you. We have a proposal."

Demetrius snarls, exposing rows of the yellow, jagged teeth. His robed friends draw closer around us, and Luca finds the hilt of his sword.

"And what does a Nephalim have to offer us? Your kind is no more, angel. The Dark Lord has seen to that."

"Is that right?" I ask. "Seems to me like your precious Dark Lord is far more interested in your Brotherhood friends. For all your reverence, he doesn't seem to want much to do with you, old Dem.

"But we could use your help. I'm not coming to you as some Order I never asked to be part of. After all, what use do Nephalim have for a woman, right?"

As if he has waited a thousand years to hear these words, Demetrius' crimson irises widen. There is no altruism in them, only an insatiable hunger to be included.

"And what makes you believe the Dark Lord would not quash us for helping you? I assume you are not bringing him daisies, hoping to earn His favor."

"Sorry," I quip. "Not a flower-and-chocolate kind of girl. I was thinking more along the lines of fucking his shit up."

Demetrius shares a glance with his compatriots. When he turns back to face me, the hunger has grown.

"And what would such an allegiance offer us? You cannot possibly hope that we would trade our standing in the Dark Lord's eyes for scraps."

Of course the League would conflagrate their delusional alliance to Ziz. I know better, but I have to play Demetrius' game.

"Help me," I say. "Save Atlas with us, and I will make sure you are taken care of."

Luca's lips form a scowl as I barter with the League's leader for use of his men — it is just as distasteful to me.

"You will have to give me a few days to confer with my people—"

I shake my head.

"Offer's on the table, and good for about five minutes before I leave you here. I will not come back, old Dem."

Demetrius snarls at my nickname for him, but makes no mention of it. He says his people will hold a palaver now.

"Do you think they will really cooperate?" Luca asks as we observe their muffled huddling.

"Do you?"

The angel grimaces.

"I have had many dealings with them during my tenure as the Council's military advisor. They do not trust me, and my faith in them goes just as far."

"Don't worry," I reply. "I have every intention of keeping them on a short leash."

Demetrius returns a few moments later. His entourage remains on the road's opposite side, watching their leader intently. Gossamer remains with them — even through the pruned mask of childish making, I feel his beady eyes on me.

"We accept your terms," Demetrius says, drawing my gaze off the Fox's mask. "Tentatively, I might add — we have served faithfully, some might even say blindly. But we are no martyrs; if the Dark Lord will not accept us, we will go where we're accepted. But do not break your word."

The League's leader is no master in the art of negotiation, and still manages to convince me that betraying him would be a fool's choice.

"Trust me— I don't believe I could if I wanted to."

"Very well," Demetrius says. "I will gather my people. Where shall we meet?"

Despite my companion's drawn lips and squinted eyes, he knows better than to offer the same suggestion I want to. But telling the robed figures to get bent— on some hedged grudge that has not aged well — will not bring us any closer to saving Atlas from the blond witch of the wind that blows red in the west— as the Brotherhood is so fond of saying.

For now, we will have to put our stock in them — for the greater good.

• • • •

ACCORDING TO TIM, HANNAH is holding the Phoenix in the Observatory. Whether his creepy omniscience is booting out of the shock that Hannah's reappearance inflicted, or the woman told him, is a question for another time.

The district is well-guarded. Two Behemoths man the lawn, scaly backs poking over the broken stone wall.

The rest of Harper's wardens consist of Brotherhood. Now that we're not fighting for our lives, I can observe them more clearly, and they come in various shapes and sizes. Some are round with poorly fitted robes, while others are bulky and tall, causing their outfits to ride high in the ankles, exposing sandaled feet.

The two stationed by the arch in from the God's Road are the former. I don't see past the weird bird masks with tinted goggles, but learn a couple things from their body types and posture.

They're grunts.

Luca and I share a satisfied grin. Their only weapons are spears appropriated from the annihilated Royal Guard. Left out of the action by their more dominant brethren, these boys look all too happy to man the access point, away from the violent excitement surrounding Hannah.

"Here to see the prisoner," I tell them, stopping short of walking right through them. "At the woman's request."

The guards study me, escorted by a much taller angel who should all rights be dead, too; exhibiting fear in their exchanged glance no mask could ever conceal.

"And him?"

"My bodyguard," I reply. "I thought he looked better with wings."

"Really?" asks the other one, trying to feign confidence in the face of potential conflict. "Because he looks a lot like a traitor's son."

I shake my head.

"Nonsense. He's my manservant. Can we pass?" But they are reluctant, and I can't joke my way past them. "Look, I'm not going to cause trouble. Your queen came to me, insisted I speak with the Phoenix. Now, what do you think she's going to do when I go back and tell her you refused to let me pass, all because you thought I was walking around with a dead man? Think about it, boys."

Another shared glance results in our passing through the gate. The Behemoths beyond the stone arch (*only two, thank baby Jesus*) follow us with yellow eyes over their snouts, expanding and contracting, punctuated by faint smoke out the nostrils. There are almost no other Brotherhood — I guess two dragons would give any jailbreaker second thoughts on their own.

Luca and I pass over the steps where Behemoths chased us into Tim's trial, and a hypothermic chill trickles up my spine. It begins at the second shallow flight leading into the structure itself — the lower-pitched hall between two sets of doors where I was almost trampled in a stampede trying to reach Tim warms with anticipation, but the chill soon returns in a wave worse than the last.

In the heart of the Observatory, a cloaked figure who resembles Stone Mountain's Arbiters barks at a haggard woman wielding an iron sword. I have never figured out why this place is named like it was meant to study the stars that dwarf it — it is nothing more than a glorified courtroom.

"Stop dragging your feet, girl! That woman has caused me enough of a headache!" he says, waving a bony hand from sagging sleeves of a gray robe. A hood is pulled over its head, but there is only dense blackness inside the fabric.

Harper scowls. Her face is blackened with the exhaustion of her adventures, her spirit sooted by loss, and she refuses to lift the sword as we enter the room.

"What's the point?" she says. "They're just going to try and kill me anyway. And we both know it'll fail."

The hooded being scoffs, and I notice that my angel companion recognizes him.

"Semantics, Phoenix. It is in your best interest to do as you're told—"

The being notices Luca drawing closer — mostly glossing over me — and turns to face us.

"So the son of Tomas lives."

Like every other time someone has invoked his traitorous father, it slides off — but there is a new confidence to it now.

"As does the mutant."

"Luca?" I ask, in one of the few times my curiosity has gotten the better of me since coming here. "Who is this?"

The angel's scowl never leaves the hooded figure coaching Harper.

"This is Jonah— or Reaper, which is the name he has taken for himself. Before that, he was the Nephalim assigned to Aumothera after Ziz was banished. Someone had to guard it while it turned into a dumping ground for troublemakers. Instead, he let the Shroud's power corrupt him."

Reaper cocks his head in the only display of emotion the empty hood allows.

"Old history, son of Tomas —"

My hand reaches out and grabs Reaper's tattered gown. He glides towards me, rather than stumbles, but the effect is the same.

"His name is Luca, you sick fuck. He's a Nephalim now — show some respect."

Reaper jolts back as my palm opens, releasing him, and adjusts the Halloween porch costume of a robe with his pointed, fleshless hands. Not a string or tendon remains on them. They are white as my teeth.

"This man is no Nephalim. Just because one decrees another to be so, does not make it true! He has not taken the Oath—"

"But he's taken *my* Oath. That's worth more to me than the light-show I got. And seeing as I'm the highest-ranking person in Atlas left defending it from you degenerates, I'd like to get to the point of this visit. I'm here to speak with the prisoner. *Her* orders."

Reaper shrugs.

"I see nothing stopping you, Nephalim."

"I do." My eyes canvass him head to toe, from the void of his face to the hidden slippers he calls feet.

Fortunately, the hooded being can take a hint, and says he will give us some privacy, disappearing through the Observatory doors to join the Behemoths.

The Phoenix does not react to our presence. Her expression is blank, eyes at the mercy of gravity like her grip on the sword. The Observatory doors close, leaving us alone, and I approach the somber prisoner.

"I'm sorry about your girlfriend. It took me a minute to piece together who she was. I can't even imagine what you must be feeling, Harper. But I don't have the luxury of waiting for you to finish mourning her."

The Phoenix doesn't react, choosing to remain perfectly still in front of her stuffed training target.

"It won't bring Em back," I say. "She's gone because they took her from you. But we can make them pay."

Harper snorts.

"And how on Earth do you propose we do that? You're out-gunned in every respect. The odds aren't in your favor, lady."

"You're right. Chances are, we'll all fail horribly and die trying to take back Atlas. But I don't know about you — I would rather go down taking a chunk out of them."

"Easy to say when you're not the one who has to fight them," she scowls. "At what point do we stop hurting ourselves to harm them?"

She's not wrong.

"Listen to me. I am going to do everything in my power to prevent that match from taking place. If I have to tear down the damn Arena to do it—"

The thought rolls off my tongue before my brain has processed how simple and effective it is. Luca squints like I've suffered a stroke, but the idea has taken root.

"That's it," I say. "Can't have a fight if you don't have the venue to fight in."

"And how exactly do we accomplish that?" Luca asks. "That Arena is fifty metric tons of brick and travertine!"

"I'll figure something out. Always do." I return my focus to the Phoenix, who eyes me with weary new respect. "Over my twice-dead body will you fight that freak. Sound good?"

Harper smiles for the first time since I've met her. It is no ear-to-ear, heartwarming grin, but given time, I can bring her to our side.

For now, she is pissed, with every right to be. The locket around her neck emits its weird brand of illumination, trying to tell us something, pointing to something in the Cathedral ruins.

Given time, maybe she will care to find out as well.

CHAPTER TWENTY-EIGHT

THE GROUP MEETS AT dawn. The supreme realm's last defenders boil down to a rogues' gallery of a Maester and his underworld connections, an outcast angel, a group of portal-raisers, a Whisperer and the celestial being formerly known as Death. They are led by the last surviving Nephalim in name only — a woman with no business being an angel, but who became one anyway.

The Magi said I was the only person capable of saving Atlas— that under the surviving order, little old Ramona Knox is the one to speak to. The forty-some bodies spread throughout Avalon's chamber seem to adhere to that logic. Each steals glances at me— some appreciative and trusting, like Luca and Tim's nods of encouragement; others like Gossamer and Demetrius eye my renewed status from the room's shadowy corners.

The pieces are set. The plan is a risk, but the only chance in cold Hell we have.

"Thank you all for coming," I begin. The conversations pierced by those nervous first words quiet and subside as all eyes fall on me. Standing where the Magi named Avalon conjured a living firefly from thin air, I hope the next part sounds more confident.

"Like me, you probably find the most recent events troubling. I might be new here, but for what it's worth, I'm still struggling to accept the degree of traitors among us. Seraphina, Barrett, the Brotherhood. I look at all your faces, and see that same disgust.

"The Council trusted these men and women to play an instrumental part in their security. The Maesters were given unlimited means to pursue their scholarly ambitions— for that, this newfound knowledge was weaponized against them.

"The Nephalim — the stock-and-trade warriors of Atlas— were given unbridled cunning and strength to defeat the Council's enemies. They may not have been directly involved, even given their poor track record of egomaniacs and mercenary attitudes. But now their leader stands with Ziz."

Quorroc speaks.

"It is possible that given the High Priestess' recent history, this is very much in line with a pattern of self-preserving behavior."

"What are you saying, Maester?"

Luca answers on the old man's behalf.

"I think what Quorroc is trying to insinuate, is that Seraphina may simply be over her head."

Quorroc frowns, as if he didn't need the help.

"The High Priestess is a fascinating, if not predictable example of extreme survival tactics. In every situation, she has played the most advantageous side to her favor. Right now, Seraphina believes that this Hannah woman offers the best deal—"

"And if we can offer her a better one, she might flip." Recalling my earlier confrontation in her quarters, Quorroc may not be far off the mark.

"Precisely, Nephalim."

"If it comes to that," I say, "we will give the Priestess her chance to repent. But if she refuses, I won't be giving her a second." Quorroc nods, and Seraphina's status is thereby a concluded debate. "Any other concerns?"

At the silence of almost fifty people, I accept there is no confusion as to whom the enemy is, and what happens if we fail.

"Make no mistake, people — this is a fight to the death. The Phoenix has tentatively accepted her role as Tim's champion, and every one of us needs to support her by making sure the match can't take place."

Demetrius interrupts from the back of the room.

"Are you saying we can't even count on Death's champion for certain?"

If anyone was going to resist my plan, it was the criminal elements we brought in.

"The situation with the Phoenix is complicated — she has every reason not to help us. For now, we are lucky to count on her support. She will continue feeding Ziz's forces the idea she is willing to fight their champion. If we can act quickly, and compromise the venue, it will cause them to rethink —"

"*Please*!" one of Demetrius' hooded friends yells. "It will merely cause delay!"

"Delay is all we need," I snipe at the outsiders. "Delay will breed opportunity, hopefully allowing us to corner this Mykul character."

"Ramona is right," Quorroc adds. "On the current timeline, we stand little chance of saving Atlas. If we were to cause a diversion — buy ourselves a few precious seconds — our options will greatly expand."

"So what do we do?" Tim asks. The man who calls himself Death on one side of me, and Luca on the other, gives me the strength to see this through. I cannot vouch for the League, but Quorroc promised they would be a minimal liability at worst.

From the way Demetrius is glaring at me, I sincerely doubt that.

"We destroy the Arena," I say.

"How?" Avalon asks. The Magus' curiosity is piqued. "We don't have the demolition capability, nor the manpower to bring a structure of that size down."

"We don't, but Hannah does."

Luca smiles as my idea becomes his own. This replicates through Quorroc and Avalon's faces, followed by Tim. The League members remain unimpressed.

"The Behemoths," the angel says. "Of course. We draw them to the Arena—"

"And have them steamroll right through it."

"This is a dangerous plan, Ramona," the Maester states. "Might I urge restraint from foolhardy schemes that serve to compromise this group. We are small enough to begin with."

It is hard to miss his cynicism — this amounts to no less than a suicide mission for many of us. The somber reality floats among my audience, and their determination softens.

I can't let that happen.

"Every person in this room needs to understand one thing. If we sit back and do nothing, we all die anyway! Do you think I'm standing here, gloating at the fact this could totally backfire? Do you think I want to risk life and limb to save a place that didn't even want me until they needed to be saved?"

The more words escape, the more my eyes burn and my throat closes up. Reflecting on their renewed mortality is no light task, but we're out of time to do it.

Before I have to further implore them, a hand reaches for mine. Tim's fingers close around my own — for a girl famous for being un-emotive, I'm freakishly sentimental, lately — giving me needed support.

"I'm with you," says the man who calls himself Death.

"So am I," Luca remarks. "To the bitter end, sister."

One by one, each of my remaining allies affirms their support. Quorroc and each of the Magi state in some form that they are willing to lay down their lives — Elion does it with a quiet smile. At last, Demetrius reluctantly pledges his crew's to our aims.

The plan is set — to destroy the location Hannah will seek to humiliate us, and use her own pets to accomplish it. Another day's worth of planning remains — who contributes what, which of us lures the dragon— but by tomorrow morning, we could plant a major thorn in the Dark Lord's size.

Whatever makes the woman's life harder is worth it.

• • • •

THE NEXT MORNING BRINGS the details to fruition. Luca and I will draw the dragon by confronting Hannah outside the Seat. This will get Barrett's attention and give the High Priestess a reality check.

She will likely sic Mykul on us before the dragons, the angel advised. *If that is the case, I can hold him off long enough for Ramona to kite the dragon toward the Arena, where Demetrius' people will pull it off her. Death will use his abilities to taunt the Behemoth into the Arena, whereby its entrance alone should compromise the structure's integrity.*

Okay, Tim said. *What about the Brotherhood? We can't discount Hannah deploying them to outflank us.*

Luca grimaced.

They will certainly be a factor. The Brotherhood believes in self-preservation above all. It is why they have done so well in Atlas — they much prefer assassinating you in a dark alley to being cannon fodder.

I think what Luca is saying, Tim added, *is be on your guard, Ramona. Constant checks on your six, three and nine. Hannah will not think twice about crushing us for this. This is all-or-nothing, Ro. We have to push, or get pushed back.*

Those words accompany me escorting Luca up the God's Road. The angel's steps are measured, and much more confident than mine.

Once a gleaming ornament I fell in love with, the Spire is reduced to a symbol of Ziz's depravity. Five dragons of varying size and ferocity circle the tower's peak. The smaller greenscale comes too close to its massive cousin's brown wings, causing the bigger Behemoth to snap its jaws. The smaller one breaks away, screeching like an injured bird.

Luca disregards the beasts, passing the spot where a small army of Royal Guard once stood. The dead wind and empty cobblestone road once occupied by thousands of cheerful souls is deserted. The sword on Luca's belt sways as his stroll carries us to the precipice of Hannah's vile kingdom.

"Ziz!"

The single syllable blasts like thunder in every direction. The angel's wings reach out in full span. Next to him, I feel a gnat; in conjunction to feeling like a mouse to winged elephant above, it is not a good combination.

Luca unsheathes his sword, scraping its tip along the ground. A moment where I think the Dark Lord's forces will not answer quickly dissolves in the whine of creaking gates. Between the parting iron, several silhouettes emerge from the interior.

The blond woman's followers are all distinct and immediately recognizable. Barrett and Seraphina accompany Hannah on either side. Mykul towers over them, a brute by any other name, wielding a massive ax I immediately recall was held by another individual.

The Habinar's weapon.

At their sides, tens of Brotherhood members flank their leader, pouring out the edges of the giant door frame behind her. The majority don't wield swords and crossbows but daggers and cracking knuckles. The freak angel is their damage sponge, the Behemoths their overkill.

Hannah snaps her fingers, recalling two dragons groundside. Their landings bring up dust between the cobbles, pushing tremors beneath our feet as the violently remixed wind settles.

"You called?"

"I asked to speak with Ziz," Luca says. "Not some interloper he hides behind."

Hannah's calm does not break for the angel whose massive sword alone could decapitate her.

"And who might you be?" the woman asks. All my gratification lies with Barrett, who seems appalled that Luca lives. "Oh, that's right. You're the traitor's son, aren't you?"

"Speak your devilry, woman. It will not save you. I have come to hold a palaver with your master."

Like Barrett, Seraphina seems caught in a cycle of disbelief. That Luca lives after everything is her damnation. They have done worse than Tomas ever could have, and his son's survival is the nail in their coffin.

"Ziz is not presently accepting audiences, as he has no physical body to conduct such negotiations."

"Then, you are his agent?"

"I am merely an intermediary," Hannah explains. "The Dark Lord speaks through me, and my eyes and ears are his. So whatever you have come to say, please. Make it quick, or I will have no choice but to retaliate against your regressive attitude...son of Tomas."

Luca's sword lifts, evening out in its aggression, its point level with Hannah's hip. Even with the short distance between him and the woman's skulking followers, Luca would close that gap in a heartbeat if I hadn't implored restraint on his part beforehand. The weapon sways in his grip, but does nothing to quell the storms of panic enveloping us.

Hannah's gaze reverts over Luca's shoulder— the grooves between stones deepen as our eyes lock.

"To say I'm disappointed would be insufficient. I thought we had an understanding, Miss Knox."

Saying anything to the woman's crude demeanor would only embolden her, continue feeding the slow-drip glee that maddens my resolve.

"But then, it's my own fault — never question the impact that delusion has on obedience. I imagine that whatever schemes you have conjured up are well-met with virtue. Heroism is often easy to romanticize, yes?"

Luca's sword twirls in the angel's beefy palm, veering the blade up and around him, effortlessly passing it to the left hand.

"Play your card, she-devil. The Dark Lord is not welcome in Atlas."

Hannah chuckles. She advances past her advisors, stepping out from the Spire's long shadow.

"Really?" she asks. "By whose decree, son of Tomas?"

Luca gives his sword a final, decisive twirl through the air — shades of the Habinar play in my mind as he struck the blond woman, only to be pulverized — lifting it high in the air. My chest tenses, dreading the flash of white that detonated inside the Observatory, purging hope and killing the Council. But as it comes down, the angel's sword is knocked horizontally away. High-pitched rings echo from meeting grades of steel with such force, I am only vaguely aware that Luca is disarmed.

Where Luca meant to cut Tim's wife in oblong halves, the mute warrior freed from the Obelisk cellars circles him on the ground. Mykul's face is hidden by a golden helmet like those the Royal Guard wore, only without the corniced wings. The grunt from his mouth is a cry of dumb rage as the sword in Luca's palm flies several feet into the main roadway.

The angel clutches his shoulder, dislocated by the force with which Mykul struck his blade. The abomination is taller, and much broader in build, but moves uncannily fast. Luca barely scrambles ten feet before Mykul has hands on his armor. The giant lifts my companion off high into the air, thrusting outward.

Luca flies roughly fifteen feet onto the cobblestone. His trajectory does not stop with landing, revolving between skyward and downward-facing before coming to a wistful halt, dust rising around him. His sword lays just within reach, but without the grounding to grab it outright. Mykul kicks out; the tip of his iron boot connects with my companion's rib, and the angel is vaulted onto his back.

"Luca!"

Frozen between their conflict and Hannah's pleased grin, Barrett's disquieting smirk and Seraphina's renewed horror, his name is all I can manage. The grounded dragons circle the mutated warrior, snorting and whinnying like horses in heat, snapping their jaws as Mykul does his work, unleashing his gloved fist at every spot on the angel's torso.

Bending down to where rogue stones decorate the God's Road, I have one chance to save Luca.

"Hey ugly!" I yell. Straightening my back, I pitch one into the closest Behemoth's nose. The creature shrieks as the rock bounces back onto the road, settling near my feet, coinciding with Hannah's order to kill us both. As Mykul retrieves a sheathed dagger reserved for Luca, I push my considerably thinner body between them, temporarily distracting Mykul while yelling at Luca to cover his head.

The quickened, widening strides of a creature the size of a small commercial airliner is impossible to stop once started. I break through their struggle — as does the dragon. It is not too primitive to recognize the flaw in its chase, nor failing to know an ally lies directly in its trajectory. The Behemoth swerves at the last second, arcing its wings left away from Mykul, losing all concept of its own dexterity. The speed with which it lands on its side barely avoids a rolling Luca. The outward-flying claws strike Mykul, squarely in the chest, sharing its airborne aptitude for about thirty feet. He crashes through a nearby building and settles in the crumbling bricks and rising ash within.

"Kill them!"

The world is drowned out by the second dragon giving chase. Thick foot pads crack the road, its wings cutting into house corners as I dart away from them. Every dead heartbeat flays my throat cutting along the Seat's protective outer wall. The Behemoth's haunches bash its structural integrity — not breaking it apart like the comparably flimsy houses behind us, but crumpling its reinforced exterior, slipping and sliding on cobblestone to keep up with me.

Rounding the Seat, my destination lies through a little arch that will eventually open up to the Arena. Leaving the rounded wall's flank is the closest the Behemoth comes to stomping me, diverging in front of its final, terrifying gains.

In my peripheral vision, the gold cobblestones are cracked and concave inward from the dragon's momentum. Passing through the arch's alleged safety, I turn a hard left, lest the storm of exploding brick and stone and plaster rain down on me. Throwing myself to the ground at the base of the district's wall, I cover my head with both hands, bracing for the typhoon.

An angry blast of debris collapses under the Behemoth's entrance, sprinkled all the way to the Arena's southern-facing gate where the trap is laid.

It's up to Tim now. The distance between the arch and the gate is about fifty feet — a stone pathway where the Brotherhood carted us toward it earlier is awash in remains of the district wall. The dragon cannot stop its velocity breaking through. With my eyes still firmly closed where the debris storm fell overhead, most of what happens next is heard not seen.

The Behemoth plows through the Arena's southern wall, but does nowhere near the amount of damage required to level it altogether. What does collapse — a small section of the south stands— is old and gives easily. The beast disappears inside the ring leaving a cloud of dust behind it.

The creature's roar emanates through the district as it comes under attack inside the Arena. Its shrieking protests are followed by a skyward cone of flame unleashed from its unseen mandible, and joined by human cries of those caught in the blast.

The struggling dragon's kin enter overhead, wingspans in the double digits as gusts of warm air follow them toward the Behemoth under duress.

A figure with blond hair is tossed over the wreckage, landing in the Arena's outer grounds with a limp roll. Luca's chiseled face is bruised and bloody, and followed by Mykul's hulking steps over the knee-high carcass of a twelve-foot wall. He is followed by Seraphina and Barrett; the High Priestess glides in behind the warrior, sapped with horror at the destruction.

The dragon's brothers and sisters arrive on the open roof's circular precipice like a flock of pigeons, but they are not harmless birds, they are the true World-Killers. There are at least eight, though more circle above, varying hues of blue and green but united in their affinity for spewing flame. Crowded around each other but making space for all to fit, I realize we don't stand a motherfucking chance.

The phalanx of flame bears down on the Arena's occupants. Screams replacing the captive Behemoth's fill the sky like they do my blood, with horror and sickness and regret.

Avalon. Elion and the other Magi whose names I never bothered to learn. Tim, although he was supposedly in dark form, likely survived. Demetrius and the entire Crimson League.

And Luca, whose blackened eyes and bloody face is lost to these events. Mykul stands guard over him— for the first time, the warrior cracks a gratified smile.

Hannah clasps hands at her waist as the dragons' exhale ends. A plume of black air rises from ground zero. The Behemoths tire of being crowded together and launch themselves into the sky as the blond woman's head slowly turns to where I'm still on my stomach, having barely avoided death yet again. My clothes are caked in white dust. Her cold stare falls on me, but the smile — the wretched, wicked grin that I'm not sure how Death ever loved— is gone.

And I'm not sure which version of Tim's wife scares me more.

CHAPTER TWENTY-NINE

DARKNESS.

My eyes open to its vastness. Like standing in a rowboat, I look at the sky, expecting the full moon or North Star to light the way for nocturnal travellers. But there are no constellations— no Orion or Big Dipper, no Jupiter on a clear night or sunrise poking out behind the clouds.

There is only darkness; it was the first cosmic force to show up to work, and will be the last to leave, turning off the Light once Hell has collected its coat.

There aren't many good explanations for the uniform shadows of my surroundings. I can't see the tips of wiggling fingers, but feel the iron clamps holding my arms to an uncomfortable surface under my back. I can't see clothes, only the pale hint of my white belly, and feel cold across my exposed skin.

Like darkness, nudity is universal, and the chill of a hollow room is unforgiving to my shivering core. It tickles my bare ribs, nestling in the bones of my arms and legs, fastened to a rough veneer that feels like plywood under my shoulders.

How did I get here?

The Arena.

We confronted Tim's wife. It ended badly — most of the resistance was wiped out, torched alive by Behemoths. Hannah and her underlings looked on, and there was no more protest or sound from the Arena's interior.

After that, I was dragged to damnation, kicking and screaming, pounding my fists on Mykul's beefy back plate, making chuffed music of the rhythm with which I yelled and fought him. He carried me effortlessly over his shoulder. My feet kicked at his breastbone, hoping to wind him. The warrior's free hand pulled Luca behind us, yanked over the cobbles on his back. His head bounced left to right as his skull caught on the damaged road.

The inhumane Frankenstein's monster was unfazed by either Luca's weight or my struggle. But Hannah wasn't, quickly commanding her champion to silence me. With the return of rational thought comes sharp pain on my jawline.

The black density is more than darkness. It must be. Even in the darkest recesses of Earth, human eyes begin to see outlines of sanity. Worst case, hearing and other senses take on extracurricular duties. Darkness is artificial here, force-fed through tubes in every pore, pumping me full of it. But this sensory deprivation can also tell me things the Light is deafened to.

My mind can only imagine one place in Atlas where it can exist in complete lawlessness, as the master of its own universe; the only place on this side of the Shroud that welcomes darkness as much as it rejects Light.

Stone Mountain.

My back tenses and palms sweat, lungs hyperventilating through a better part of the revelation's impact. The single experience I have here — as Luca and I bartered with Hardwick for his freedom, in exchange for intel that dragons had returned to the supreme realm—does not spell an easy escape.

For the first time in a while, I allow myself to access the mental dossier with Hardwick's name, replaying our first exchange since Washington in the Shadow Commons' creepy, grayscale park grounds. Nevermind anything to do with the Jordan West case that cost both our lives — everything in Atlas was far, far worse.

It was a brilliant set-up on Hannah's part. She knew Hardwick would be the fume that set me alight, and he was sure that he could weasel his way into a second chance. The path that led us from a Whisperer to a Maester to Hardwick had too much momentum to stop, and I was too stupid to see the only good course of action would have been to go back on my word.

Think, Ramona.

It would be a waste to leave me here. The soul prison is petty on Tim's part, but seems tame for Hannah. The bitch despises me; leaving me to rot would not suit her. She wants an example made, which can only mean one thing — this is a scare tactic.

According to the plan, the Magi were supposed to port the group back to the Obelisk. The dragons seemed satisfied lifting off the ring wall, meaning they claimed someone in the blast.

One or more of the Magi could have survived. The biggest misconception I had about Atlas coming in was that death was not achievable, many having already experienced it once. But as seen on multiple occasions, that simply holds no water anymore. The White Light was thrown around a lot in the beginning, but there's more than one way to get fucked up in the supreme realm.

As for Tim, he would have been in dark form — the formless column of smoke he has inhabited and used to save me on several occasions now — and likely fell away like a piece of rope, sneaking out the back.

Another chill tenses my jaw, clenching fists, pleading with inner Ramona to accept mind over matter. I return to thinking, because aside from those limited movements, it is all I can do.

Time loses meaning somewhere around the hundredth time replaying events. The cold has put my body into hypothermic trance. My sight never adjusted, and there is little to do but wait for the odd, merciful sound.

Eventually, they will come for me— and I ought to treasure every moment alone before they do.

• • • •

AS PREDICTED, HANNAH arrives in due time. It wouldn't suit her petty streak to let me be forgotten. My name must be publicly purged in a bout of violence and spectacle, or her drama loses some of its weight.

Voices outside the cell draw close, wiping away the blissful fusion of disassociated nerves quelling anxiety that my purge from existence is nigh. The voices confer on the fringes of hearing — one belongs to Hannah, while the other contains hints of bass, and can only belong to a creature comfortable in dark, wet holes.

Arbiters. When the dialogue ends, the wall before me shifts, allowing a column of Light that grows to a rectangle as the invisible door slides aside like a hidden passage in its seamless facade.

That low-relay sound of a switch being flipped enables a painful cloud to assault my vision. The room comes to life beneath an unsparing glow. Tim's wife enters alone, without Arbiter or dragon or bodyguard. The fitted gown is gone, in favor of a leather corset with stockings. Cleavage is cleverly concealed by her free-flowing blond hair; and elbow-high gloves on her arm have me wondering if I've stumbled into an adult film. There isn't a way to remove the organic binds— shackles I mistook as iron but are swirling currents of white and black — and cover my indecency.

I have never been sexually adventurous— dry spells lasted years. Random encounters were often rushed, always at their apartment, and I was usually quick to leave. But as my nemesis glides around the upright device she lowers horizontally on its supports, my eyes canvass stone ceiling for solace. Placing her hand on my sternum, Hannah leans over me, smiling.

"Shame about your friends," she says. "So foolish are those who would challenge the Dark Lord. You might have stood a chance, but just *had* to interfere— didn't you?"

Her hand drifts to the soft flesh right of my solar plexus. Her touch is light but firm on my breast, before sauntering down my tummy. Fingernails dance over the navel, stopping to admire its exaggerated flatness. I struggle against her touch as much as the binds allow, fighting non-consensual terror. I have never been raped, placing Hannah's exploring hands at the closest anyone has come.

"He loves you," she muses. "You know that, don't you?"

Hannah's hand drifts lower, but my squirming has stopped, in its own life-and-death struggle against more subtle resignation. Tim's wife does not approve— she slips her hand down and jabs two fingers inside me. I grunt and thrash at the penetration, something rarely allowed and even more scarcely enjoyed.

"It is a pity that you two have come so far— all these unrequited feelings for each other; all the pain and heartbreak and unrealized infatuation." Her fingers push deeper past the labia, spreading the warm wetness further. "All this time wasted just to realize the tragedy of it. But you like this— don't you, Ramona? Yes, bare your teeth like the wild animal you are, Miss Knox. You enjoy me, don't you?"

Twisting my head, to and from, back and forth, a series of low sobs escapes me. Satisfied, Hannah withdraws her fingers. The sticky remains of her methodical humiliation makes me wish I had never survived Death as Tim's wife wipes my fluids on a towel hung off the side of my table.

"Believe me, Miss Knox," Hannah says. "I take no joy in this. Personally, I'm of the mind that women need to stick together in these trying times. We allow boys to masquerade as men— they fuck us and leave at the first inconvenient juncture— and when they tire of that, turn on each other, leaving us to do the same.

"Again, I take no pleasure. But I made a promise, and intend to keep my word. The Dark Lord is a merciful god, but remains cognizant of the necessary steps to his salvation."

"The only steps that fucker will take," I manage through gritted teeth, "will be the ones I knock you both down on the way to Hell, bitch."

Hannah circles the table to a soundtrack of my shortened breaths, stopping at the top, bending over the waist-high base. Her fingers run gently from my wrists to armpit, and I have no more strength to fight this horrible woman. Her comparably wider bust rests at the top of my skull, forehead over my throat. Hannah's bottom lip drags over mine before pulling back and cupping my cheeks in her warm palms.

"But has there ever been, something so great as love, quite so comfortable with sin?" She repeats Luca's quote from the Obelisk in a sing-song voice as her hand strokes my cheek. "But likewise, there's never been a queen, quite so determined to win."

I cannot disassociate long enough to allow her revolting grin of self-satisfaction to go unnoticed.

"You are going to feel some discomfort, Miss Knox. Rest assured, it will only be momentary. After that, you will be free to go."

Seconds earlier, I was resolved to say nothing. I had said my piece, and was determined to say no more — but there isn't a safe place left to go other than the follow-up questions of my hardened terror.

"What kind of discomfort?"

Hannah smiles.

"The kind that follows the greatest pleasure of your insignificant existence, Ramona. The cost of carrying the Dark Lord's future." Her hands cup my face again, and her final words are gentle.

"Close your eyes," Hannah says.

Unable to think of an alternative, I do.

· · · ·

AS THE SOLE SURVIVOR of Daniel Knox's drunken shooting spree at the bottom of a gravel pit, I know a thing or two about trauma. My childhood is a mosaic of flashes and withdrawn personifications.

As I sat, infinitely oblivious to the violence the child carrier faced away from, my idiot mother tried to console Daniel — I imagine she said she loved him

(*please don't do this, Danny*)

as he grunted and paced.

Later, I learned his revolver had the serial scratched off, and was likely stolen. Most of what I know about the crime scene stems from decade-old forensics reports dug up in my early days at the FBI. Everything Maya could not bring herself to describe lay inside that sealed file. Black and white photos showed my father took the gunshot at his left temple, where it lodged on a piece of skull and failed to come out the other side.

Tiffany was shot just above her right eye. One photo depicted the dime-sized entry as seemingly tame. The one underneath showing the smashed jack o'lantern in back where the bullet went out was far more gruesome.

I have no recollection of the physical moment my parents died — burrowing down the rabbit hole to mentally escape the shadows wrapping around my thighs, digging inside me, I am living it.

(*Daniel, please!*)

My mind is a gravel pit where Daniel Knox took his twenty year old wife — warned by just about every reasonable family member, including Maya, not to marry him. The emotional escape route from this moment carries me through that one, because Hell is a hedge maze and anything is better than this.

But has there ever been, something so great as love, quite so comfortable with sin?

The pit's walls are not a drop, but still a steep descent, hardened by the autumnal plunge in temperature. The sky is cloudy without rain, dark without night, wide without wonder as Tiffany screams at my manic father — torn between drunkenness, the drugs in his system and the gun in his hand — to think of the baby. The carrier sits on a downward angle several feet away, but looks at the ascent back to sanity.

The baby? Daniel scoffs. *We can't even take care of us!* The weapon shakes in his hand but points downward. Tiffany can't stop looking at it, nor muster anything beyond basic, sobbing pleas.

Danny, I love you.

You stupid bitch, I want to yell. *Stop trying to save this waste of life. Come home, be a mother to me.*

You stupid bitch, Daniel says in kind, proving everything I said to be true. *You're just gonna turn me in, aren't you?*

Danny, no!

But has there ever been, something so great as love, quite so comfortable with sin?

Daniel lifts his arm. The gun's barrel points directly at her, and Tiffany emits something between a scream and squeal of the most horrible, terrified nature.

He's going to kill her.

A jolt between my legs pulls me back to the table in Stone Mountain. My mind claws away, back to the West Virginia gravel pit, back to my birth mother's final moments.

But likewise, there's never been a queen, quite so determined to win.

I would rather watch this a thousand times than give that bitch the satisfaction. If this is where my mind must go, I'll be Alice, trusting where the rabbit hole takes me.

Daniel thumbs the hammer on the revolver; my mother's hands tremble with her final, stammering words.

Danny, I —

The blast from the revolver's end is a haze of smoke and ear-shattering confusion. I know from the forensics where the bullet went in, mutilating Tiffany's brain before casting the back of her skull into the rocks. In this dream, I only see my mother crumple, knees buckling one way as her shoulders fall another, collapsing in a pile only feet from the maligned baby carrier.

Startled by the killshot, the toddler begins wailing. Daniel takes no heed. Even in his delirium, the guilt of seeing his murdered wife spreads across his face. Tears fill his bloodshot eyes, and he begins to cry.

Before Hardwick, I might have been played by the crocodile tears of a fucking junkie. Before having to wrangle Creation back from a mad god, this scene may have moved me.

If I held a gun, and existed in this dream, I would kill him right now.

"We're done," a voice says, penetrating the closed system of my illusion. "You did very well."

But has there ever been, something so great as love, quite so comfortable with sin?

I look up, but no longer see Daniel Knox in a gravel pit of my worst coping mechanisms, deprived the satisfaction seeing his suicide would have brought me.

"Your clothes will be returned to you, and the Arbiters will see you out," Hannah says. "We will be keeping a close eye on your future development, Ramona."

The door slams as disassociation fades, and the woman is gone. The lights are a small mercy, waiting for the Arbiters to release me from this Hell. My abdomen aches where the shadows did their work, tunneling through a part of me that may never feel the same.

But likewise, there's never been a queen, quite so determined to win.

Alone, naked and bound on the plywood table, all I can do is cry.

CHAPTER THIRTY

IN TIMES OF DOUBT, people often take solace in habit. The comforts of yore prove more durable than modern day medications or therapy — there is something about the ragged stuffed bear you find going through boxes in storage. It reminds you of a simpler time, when you only had to worry when the suited stranger would show up next.

Sometimes, he went so long without visiting, I questioned if I had just been crazy at the time. But the stuffed animal was persistent, a talisman of comfort used to shield myself in uncomfortable situations.

I have no access to those items in Atlas. My past, present and immediate future is here, allegedly impregnated with the Devil's spawn. My oldest sentimental attachments are twenty-some years gone.

For that reason, I find myself back in the Gardens. I can't go back and face what remains of the group I got killed. After limping out of Stone Mountain alone, I wasn't ready to return to the Obelisk.

Not yet.

The flowers are less lively, infected with the same darkness poisoning the heart of Creation; the twisted force that has commandeered my womb for its sick ends. The hedge maze no longer invites me into its winding corridor and forks in the path. Its hedges are sullen, a reflection of my mood.

Pivotal conversations took place here — back when I thought Seraphina the smartest, most conniving woman in Atlas. Now, I am alone, sitting on a bench I shared with both Tim and a dying Maester at different points. There is little solace in the replaying scraps of past dialogue, but anything to keep the thing inside me from getting into my head as well is welcome.

Everything you have seen, Ramona...think of your life— the one you had back on Earth— as the beaker in which your personal formula was built. The Avatar told you that every soul comes with a unique code— an identification system, if you will. That code, were it to remain in a static, unchanging state, would indeed suggest predisposition when it comes to placement.

The Atlas sent an agent to eliminate some of the reincarnated individuals. Their deaths were undone by our choice, and she was tasked with seven names.

Tim and Siskett's conversations endlessly weave together. My eyes don't focus on the browning, winged leaves of the bushy wall; only the men who separately tried to console me then, but can't now.

Trauma is the single greatest catalyst for transforming that genetic sequence. It can take the best men and turn them into monsters. It can take a young vagrant, transforming him to revolutionary. The code can change, Ramona. The code can change. But it is very, very difficult.

Hannah called Harper the Phoenix. The locket both seemed to protect her from the Behemoths, and draw a map toward the Cathedral district. The Avatar told me certain objects are imbued with Light, didn't she?

The trinket around Harper's neck may have a role to play in saving Atlas.

Somewhere around the twentieth time reaffirming this in my head, a bright light flies past me. As I think my mind is playing tricks, it zips by again. This time, my attention catches on its circling green body, dancing from left to right in my peripheral vision. The tiny being buzzes and squeals in wild acrobatics using threaded wings obscured in natural emerald glow.

Avalon's insect — the one created from a puddle on the floor. It bounces and emits its high-pitched whine, almost colliding with a tree branch above. It drops sharply, hovering in front of my nose where I can see its bulbous shell. Its eyes are many like a spider, with a tiny flap below them folded upward in a smile.

It's trying to tell me something.

"What is it?" I ask the squealing creature, holding out my hand. Bow-legged landing gear settles in my palm's creases. It jumps, whines and paces back and forth inside my cupped fingers prior to launching its glowing body in the air.

"You want me to follow you?"

The bug bounces in the air, again narrowly missing the branch above, close to a nod as it will come.

"This had better be good," I mutter. Avalon's creation spurs as I step off the bench, darting toward the hedge maze's opening. It disappears, and I hesitate before following it inside.

The first turn in the maze's labyrinth cuts a sharp right, and leads to a fork. The insect doesn't rush ahead, patiently waiting for me to catch up.

Several turns later, we reach an opening that contains a small fountain and twin benches like the one outside the maze. The hedge walls are adorned in roses whose beauty outweighs any amazement I ever saw in the Spire's dark paintings. Their stalks twist from every corner of the three enclosing walls to the open entry into the labyrinth's heart.

And in the center awaits a sight I thought was forever lost to me. The short woman with a bob cut of gray hair and gaunt cheeks hasn't lost a streak of age in her strands, yet looks far healthier than on her deathbed as Tim claimed her soul to my reactionary protests.

"Maya?"

My eyes well at the sight of the aunt who raised me. Her final years of agony and helplessness, hooked up to oxygen machines are erased from her present form, and my heart uplifts to see the woman I remember.

"Ro."

Forgetting how cold our relationship once was, her aversion to affection and my own cold exterior she fostered, I embrace her. Maya does not withdraw, returning with arms that have to reach up to wrap around my neck. A torrent escapes me, shuddering against my childhood protector. When I am done, and we separate, I am speechless.

"What are you doing here?" I ask.

Her voice is no longer raspy and withered, but full as the surrounding roses. Her white house gown is clean, rather than yellowed, and she smells of lavender, not cigarette smoke.

"I have been waiting for you, my dear," she says, motioning to one of the benches under the rose vines. We take our seats. Maya crosses one leg over another, hunching over her lap like she always did. There is no hand lifted to her mouth, cigarette drifting upward as she mulled the misery of her life.

She seems happy.

"You have?"

Maya nods.

"Your friend kept me safe. To be honest, Ro, I had no idea. All these years, it felt like I hadn't given you enough — I was so bitter about my sister leaving me her mess, I didn't appreciate just how special you were."

A chuckle escapes me, alongside withheld sobs.

"I'm not special, Auntie. Thank you for saying that, but I'm just someone who lucked into something extraordinarily fucked up."

"That may be so," Maya replies. "But if you hadn't, you wouldn't be my niece. You were always brilliant, Ro. It did not surprise me to learn that you might be the only chance that Atlas has."

"See," I say, "all this time, I've tried to figure out why the Council picked me. They had angels to protect them. They had more qualified beings than some mortal. They put their faith in me, and I failed them."

Maya smiles, placing her pruned hand on my knee.

"I love you, Ramona — you are too hard on yourself."

"Am I? I'm beginning to believe I'm not hard enough—"

"Don't interrupt, child. It's rude." Her familiar chastisement eases my soul, and I fall silent. "You don't have time for self-pity, Ro. All of Creation is on your shoulders. Lord knows, it is a terrible burden to carry. But that does not change the fact that every living thing this city governs is counting on you."

I scoff.

"No pressure, right?"

"You were not chosen by some fluke, my dear. The Council obviously saw righteousness that was sorely missing among their inner circle. I hate to think how much worse it would have been without you." At the look of awe I cast her newfound omnipotence, Maya reveals that Tim has kept her updated on my investigation.

Which leads me to the most horrible puzzle piece, the one I have struggled with since leaving Stone Mountain.

"They did something to me, Auntie."

"Did what?"

Looking down at the womb they desecrated, the panic of knowing something lives there now, growing inside me, overrides the urgency of stopping Hannah.

"I don't know. But I feel different now. Sapped of my confidence, or something."

Maya's eyes search my own, intuitively aware I'm omitting something.

"Talk to me, Ro."

I sigh, equally aware how ridiculous it sounds.

"In Stone Mountain...well, for lack of a better term, I was raped. But not by a man. It was...horrible. And when it was over, they told me I was carrying Ziz's child."

Exhaling as the final tense syllables leave my bitten tongue, and finally venture into the open, Maya takes my hand in hers, silent for a moment before speaking.

"I have a confession, Ramona. In any other circumstance, it might warrant anger. And if you are angry with me, so be it. But it may be a blessing now."

I frown, asking Maya what she means.

"When you were about six, you fell in that ravine behind our building. Do you remember that? The one with —

"The trees overtop," I finish. It was the second time I met the man who calls himself Death. Running in the field with my childhood friend Alison, I slipped, tumbling over the side of a sharp drop, breaking my leg. Alison screamed, and I implored her to fetch Maya.

After she disappeared, Tim's voice rattled through the sunken corridor of twigs and root, leaves and Darkness, as I looked up at the sky above.

You don't need to be afraid, Ramona.

"I remember."

"Well," Maya says, "when I took you to the hospital, the doctors ran bloodwork, and you had a separate cyst on one of your developing ovaries."

Maya says I shouldn't talk to strangers.

"I remember that, too. They had to do that surgery."

"What I didn't tell you about that operation was the damage that overgrown cyst did. The doctors weren't sure you would ever be able to conceive. I'm so sorry, child. I grappled with telling you for years. I was scared to put that on a six-year-old. For a long time, I knew it was a disservice to you, bless your heart, and I'd have to tell you someday."

Maya is right — in any other situation, the revelation might leave me angry. I never took to men for longer than a night or two, and might have never known at all.

"It's alright, Auntie," I reply. "If that's true — and by some small chance, applies here — then we finally have a win. It's a small one, but denying Ziz rebirth has pretty big ramifications."

Maya smiles.

"I pray it does, child."

We sit together a while, appreciating each other's company when I thought I'd never experience hers again. I never had an inkling of my reproductive shortcomings, but in this case, it might be Ziz's as well.

CHAPTER THIRTY-ONE

DEAD AIR GREETS ME as I enter the Barracks, where our best laid plans were formed. Every time I return to the Nephalim's former center of operations, its buildings have taken on a new tone of hopelessness. From the moment I first interrogated Quorroc in the Obelisk, meeting Seraphina and Pol and Elion, I have never known what to expect each time I venture here.

The lobby is completely silent. Anticipating being the only soul still standing, my lackadaisical circadian rhythms burst into full gear, little black heart pounding as I reach the chamber doors on the third level.

Pushing them inward, all my fears prove completely unfounded. Waiting for me are Tim, Quorroc and three of the four Magi. Luca is bruised, but no worse for wear otherwise.

"Ramona!"

My name emerges from unscathed mouths. Tim is the first to say it, followed by just about everyone else present. That isn't to say all our allies still stand. Elion's absence gives me a bad feeling. Demetrius is gone, though some of his brethren remain.

Still, more than I hoped for.

The crowd around me parts, revealing the High Priestess waiting at the back of the room. Seraphina's expression is blank; the former Nephalim leader is reduced by her time in Hannah's inner circle.

"We thought the worst," Luca says — the bruises have turned to welts, and I would see Mykul pay for ruining his beautiful face. He embraces me, and Tim does as well.

All my attention remains fixated on Seraphina.

"What's her deal?" I ask. "Has she actually flipped?"

Tim and Luca share a look before the angel replies.

"The High Priestess has been humbled by recent events. She came here, at great risk to her safety, and wishes to speak with you, once you are settled."

"There are other matters to address as well," Tim advises. "We think there is a way to delay the trial, without provoking another confrontation like at the Arena. Again, when you're settled."

The thought of another futile stone throw at Ziz's forces makes me ill. I won't risk another confrontation unless certain we can win.

"I'll speak with Seraphina. After that, Luca and I are going to the Cathedral, and seeing what's under the wreckage."

Tim frowns.

"Ramona, shouldn't we be —"

"Look," I tell them. "We already wasted a lot of manpower going at them head-on. We're outmatched in every corner, guys. The Behemoths have us at a checkmate.

"Whatever lives under the Cathedral — that Harper's locket pointed us to — has some role in this. I know it, Tim."

Luca speaks.

"There may be a better way," he says. "Tim and I have been talking. There's a quicker way to both cripple the woman's ambitions and access whatever is beneath the Cathedral. Speak with the Priestess, then we will reconfer."

I agree, and make my way over to Quorroc and Seraphina. Nothing remains of the latter's former fire, and the Maester speaks on her behalf.

"The High Priestess has come to forge an armistice. She wishes that I remain her counsel until these terms are settled. This is fine with me, as long as you have no issue, Nephalim."

"None at all," I reply. "Let's get this over with."

• • • •

WE MIGRATE TO THE SAME part of the complex I interrogated Quorroc, along with Luca and Avalon. The Priestess wishes to speak with the old Maester in private, and the Magus opens a portal into the doorless room between rooms, closing it behind them.

"I'm assuming Elion didn't survive the Arena," I say, in the first words I've shared with him since returning. Avalon grimaces, shaking his head.

"He opened the portal that we escaped through, at the cost of his life. He was such a good boy, too. Brilliant portal master. Would have been a worthy successor."

"I'm sorry. I wish I'd had more time to get to know him."

Avalon smiles.

"Many thanks. Elion thought quite highly of you." He closes his eyes, receiving some kind of mental signal from the wall's other side. "They are ready."

The portal Avalon opens is purple, rather than the original blue cast by Elion. The light-hued brick wall becomes a box with three chairs and a table, lit by solitary lamp overhead. Seraphina's eyes still fall to the mercy of gravity, glued to the steel top table as I take my seat across from them.

"Ramona," Quorroc says, but I stop the old man before he can begin.

"Let's get one thing straight, Priestess. In peacetime, what you've done would be a punishable crime in my world. No idea the term for it in Atlas, but treason is the word I know. I don't believe you had any part in the original plot to annihilate the Grand Council, but you did side with their killers. And given our prior relationship, Seraphina, you face an uphill battle in convincing me you can be redeemed."

Compared to the firecracker she was before, the woman who towers over the Maester and I is a shell of herself.

"Seraphina is willing to provide a valuable service," Quorroc says.

"Really? And what service is that, Maester?"

"Assassination." Seeing interest piqued through my cold exterior, Quorroc continues. "The woman has been the cause of all these problems. Were the Priestess to administer justice where she least expects it, Ziz will be crippled."

"Fair," I say, skeptical that I can trust the sullen woman that Quorroc represents. "And what assurances do I have your client won't turn on me, Maester? None. She could have been sent here to gather information on how many of us are left."

Seraphina finally lifts her head. Crimson locks obscure the better part of her face.

"Do you not think she already knows? Hmm? She spared every one of you, even after you attempted such a foolish heist at the Arena. The Dark Lord is one with her, hmmm? Speaking to her. And the Dark Lord sees *everything*." Her voice reverts to a whisper during the last sentence.

Still skeptical.

"If that's true," I ask, "does Ziz not know you're here?"

"He might. But Atlas is my home. I have had my grievances, not done as well by it as I should have, hmmm? It grew easy to assume it would always be there, like a child who bad mouths her mother. You expect that which birthed you can withstand your most childish challenges. Push, and see how far your minders will allow you to venture outside the rules. But you don't love them any less for their weakness, hmmm? Their overreactions?

"The point is, Ramona," she says, "I have taken the greatest risk in coming to you. I did not come asking forgiveness, but awareness."

"Awareness of what?"

Quorroc assumes control from the Priestess — Seraphina's eyes drift back to the table, and in that moment, I sense her guilt is real.

Joining Hannah went against everything she stood for.

"If the opportunity to remove the woman presents itself, the High Priestess will act in the best interest of Atlas. It is understood that in the event she is caught, there will be nobody to save her. She will be on her own."

She has no wish to live with it. I can't really fault her — Seraphina will find redemption with or without my blessing.

"I accept," I say, pushing back my chair. "May the Light protect you, Priestess."

Avalon's portal opens in the brick facade. Before either Quorroc or Seraphina can say anything else, I step through it, rejoining Luca and the Magus on the other side.

"Get all that?" I ask. Luca nods tepidly, eyeing Seraphina talking quietly with Quorroc on the portal's other end. "She plans to martyr herself if it means killing Hannah."

"A bold plan, assuming the woman doesn't catch on. What do you think?"

Crossing my arms, I am uncomfortable sending the Priestess to certain death, much as she deserves it. The remorse in her face, both at the Arena and during my interrogations on multiple occasions, will never cease to haunt me.

"I don't know yet. Tell me about this plan you and Tim came up with."

And so, Luca does.

. . . .

"THIS IS THE PLAN."

Back in a room with Creation's last defenders, the mood is less hopeful than before our attempt to destroy the Arena. The people are more tired, their wounds deeper. Few reasons remain to see hope in the situation. None of them were almost forced to carry the Devil's spawn, or have knowledge of Seraphina's plan, but they hurt nonetheless.

The High Priestess slinked back to the Seat, taking her rightful place looking over the blond woman's shoulder before too many questions were asked. I consider her gamble a contingency, and don't inform the larger group of our bargain.

Our forty are down to twenty-five, and we may be down to fifteen before this last-ditch attempt to halt Hannah's death match goes off.

"Tim and Luca will lead the assault on the Observatory where the Phoenix is held. If all goes according to plan, it will be lightly guarded. They'll take three or four men with them. The rest will come with me to the Cathedral ruins.

"The dragons are the biggest obstacle, followed by the angel Mykul. Lesser so are the Brotherhood, who form the main line of defense around Hannah. Quorroc will raise alarms in Devil's Corner, filtering most of her forces that way.

"If we're lucky," I finish, "we'll clear the debris by the time Harper reaches the ruins. If there's something there, her locket will point us to it. Once Harper and I go down, everybody will lose their tails and rendezvous in the Gardens. Do *not* come here. It is the first place Hannah will send her people once she realizes the deception. Does everybody understand?"

Murmurs, concerned glances and unspoken panic around the room are stifled with encouraging nods from Tim and Luca.

"Alright, then. Let's fuck up this woman's day, and bring the Phoenix home."

CHAPTER THIRTY-TWO

• • • •

THEY SAY THE BEST LAID plans are often the first to go awry.

Since coming to Atlas, there has been no plan. I have lurched from one twisted scenario to another, compartmentalizing double-crosses, shifting allegiances, misdirections and personal betrayals. I played my deepest fears with a straight face, cutting through an unprecedented amount of hokum and bullshit to nab my suspect.

I found her, but she was Pandora's Box, and opening her tightly wound secrets destroyed Atlas. It cost the Council their lives, turned Hardwick against me; exposed Seraphina's true colors and annihilated her league of self-serving angels.

Our future now depends on this plan — again, not a real plan. A reaction to the reaction, an action merited by desperation and anger and exhaustion.

Guerilla warfare.

The Cathedral ruins are quiet. Quorroc has yet to raise the alarm in the west, drawing the woman's forces away from the Observatory. Once that happens, Luca and Tim will eliminate resistance, and extract the Phoenix.

It's up to the rest of us to clear this mess in time. Avalon's surviving students work together to create a larger portal than either of them could conjure on their own as Avalon uses some form of telekinesis to lift the larger pieces up. The Crimson League helps me shovel aside smaller pieces, working our way around an adjacent wreckage. With Demetrius gone, their leadership falls to a man named Errol. He is not as mouthy, and mostly responds in grunts.

"Oy!" his companion Homan calls. "Ain't we got somethin' better to do than dig in a bunch o'rocks? What in the bloody Light are you looking for, anyway?"

The handful of men in red robes are whittled down to seven from their original twenty. Errol does not dignify Homan's jabs, nor those in agreement with him.

"Pot of gold," I tell him.

"What's that?"

"Little leprechaun. Lives at the end of the rainbow? Quit complaining and start helping, Homan. That alarm is going to sound any second."

He glares at Errol.

"Is this wench serious?"

Homan's *de facto* leader grunts and returns to hoisting debris aside. The other League members take a cue and return to work as well. My sore hands haven't stopped clawing in the crater of oblong rocks and brick, not even for Homan's bitching.

A sharp wail sounds on the other side of Atlas, followed by a racket beyond the Cathedral district's walls. The Behemoths circling the Seat split off into separate groups, flapping hollow currents down as they arc toward Devil's Corner.

"Light be with you, Tim," I mutter.

In a few minutes, Luca and the man who calls himself Death will storm the Observatory, assuming the Behemoths guarding it join their brothers and sisters in western Atlas. Otherwise unguarded, that will leave Reaper as their only source of resistance. The mutant Nephalim seemed more bemused than loyal to the woman—it wouldn't surprise me if he simply throws bony hands in the air and lets it happen.

I return to the task at hand, casting occasional glances at Homan and Errol. The former's pace has slowed to a crawl, while Demetrius' successor diligently pitches pieces of debris out of the pit. Avalon continues guiding the larger chunks through his students' portal.

Just as I think this is a fool's errand, the Magus calls out.

"Found it!"

Grabbing the ledge of my adjacent crater, I clamber out, joining the Magi by their separate pit. Errol and his men follow — a moment later, we are admiring the trapdoor belonging to the Cathedral's former basement.

"Where'd you put all them big pieces, mate?" Homan asks. Avalon's students close their joint portal, returning to his side.

The teacher smirks.

"Jammed the doors out of Devil's Corner. The Brotherhood will take a minute escaping our diversion. You can't hear it, but they're probably still investigating the alarm."

Brilliant. Even the cynical Homan agrees with a chuckle.

"Where do you think it leads?" I ask, eyeing the trapdoor.

"Hard to say," Avalon replies. "If it leads where I think it does, it is better to only send two or three down."

"And where do you think it leads?"

The Magus shakes his head.

"I'm getting ahead of myself. Best to wait until the Phoenix gets here, than put one's foot in one's mouth."

And so, we wait.

• • • •

HARPER MAKES HER APPEARANCE about ten minutes later. With only the dragons to contend with — the rest of Hannah's forces exclaimed confusion a moment earlier as they realized they'd been tricked — the Behemoths canvass near the Seat. Their beady eyes scan every district.

Our party hides behind the northernmost debris. I see my allies first, chased by a familiar shadow pitching up and over the Cathedral district's wall. It arcs down, swimming along the crushed grass before perking up and materializing as the man who calls himself Death.

As Harper and Luca trail behind him, ducking under the arch, another shadow appears over the walls, prompting me to yell at the League members to open the trapdoor.

Homan has other plans.

"What? That's a bloody dragon, you hollow-headed wench! We'll be exposed to it!"

"If we don't get the door open, we're all dead! Now go!"

Homan relents with a scowl. He and Errol descend in the pit, keeping low to avoid alerting the hovering dragon, fully focused on the trio bolting from the district wall toward our position.

The stream of flame blowing down into the pit hits Errol and Homan, missing the newcomers. The cone burns long and hot, charring their screams to a crisp silence. Both men collapse as the dragon is winded.

"We've got to get that door open!" Avalon yells over the thunder of rising smoke in my conscience.

Tim dissipates to his cloud form once again. The smoke column crosses the district in a diagonal path, and wraps around the Behemoth's back haunches, crossing under the animal's stomach, arcing upward to tie off the wings. The dragon screams at its siphoned mobility, and physics do not allow it to remain airborne.

"Ramona! The door!!"

Harper and Luca join us behind the mess of collapsed wall. At Avalon's reminder, I leap forward into the pit, landing in a roll toward Errol and Homan's charred bodies.

The dragon erractilly swerves through the air as Tim's tendons tighten around it, grazing over Luca and Harper's position, nearly flattening them. The animal crashes through the northern district wall — beyond which lies nothing, just endless blue trailing down to the cosmos below.

The trapdoor gives under my pull, exposing a gently descending tunnel. I wave the Phoenix into the pit as Luca watches over the edge.

"We're going down. Take the rest and pull back to the Gardens. Do not go back to the Obelisk."

Luca nods.

"I'll see you soon, sister."

"Be careful, hear? I don't want to hear you got killed by one of those stupid things. And tell Tim, no more risks."

Harper is already down the tunnel. It leads to something, something her locket wants us to see. I follow her down, over narrow stone steps leading into the heart of Darkness.

Light willing, there will be something to help us defeat Ziz.

Worst case, it's a cruel trick.

I guess we'll find out soon enough.

CHAPTER THIRTY-THREE

ALL MY LIFE, I FELT pointless — whether it stemmed from surviving an event I should have died, or life seemed to assign me no greater purpose, I had to *make* one. Nobody told me to go into law enforcement, or made me feel I was destined to join the FBI. Tim only knew because he first heard of me investigating his sister Grace's abductors, years after her disappearance. He witnessed my betrayal at Stephen Hardwick's hand and from there, manipulated time and space to move backwards through my chaotic youth, until finally intervening.

Sometimes, I wonder what my life would have been without Death's interference. Did I become the first prominent female FBI investigator on my own, or because of him?

Where does my autonomy end and his begin?

The dark tunnel Luca herded Harper and I into is pitch black once the doors close. The floor is a slope beneath our feet. Silver glints offer the occasional, faint dim glow, and we won't make it far in this state.

Thankfully, Harper's locket ignites, pouring its strange cosmic Light between star-shaped seams. The effect is muted by the expanse of a stone tunnel that creaks and drops dirt from its ceilings every hundred yards or so. The Phoenix is mostly quiet as we traverse its span in single file.

"Quite the impressive piece of jewelry, if you don't mind my saying so." My voice echoes down the tunnel, no matter how quietly I speak.

Harper doesn't turn her head for small talk.

"It was my mother's." Her feet keep shuffling, leading the way as the tunnel takes on a steeper slope, beginning to wind downward—a staircase without stairs, too angled to keep our feet on any kind of balance.

I suggest sliding. We take a seat, one behind the other. Harper pushes herself off, descent picking up speed quickly as she disappears around the winding bend.

Spine against the ground and arms over my chest, my body plunges along the curving chute, around and around. Wind kicked up by my joined ankles is pushed to my face, pouring in both eardrums. The corridor spins, keeping me pressed along the side of the tube. Feeling I'm coming to the tunnel's end, a nervous sensation overcomes my concern — I wouldn't exactly call it a fear — of falling. That feeling grows as a black hole grows under my groundless footing.

This tube is a fucking chute out of Atlas. It leads to nothing, a trap for invaders who dared send their men down. The chasm widens quicker than I can come up with a solution to avoid falling out the bottom.

I don't know what happened to Harper, but —

Short of finding myself cast off into open space, a hand grabs my forearm. The rest of my body jolts, then bounces back, slamming against a stone wall. Harper's slender fingers hold onto me with superhuman ease; the locket flares as she effortlessly pulls me onto her ledge.

"Thanks," I say. "Thought I was a goner for a second there."

"Yeah, well, they didn't exactly advertise there's a door down here."

Her statement points my attention to the alcove beyond the ledge with a stone door, blue unlike the tunnel housing it. It is jagged in places and several feet thick.

"Any ideas?" I ask.

Harper shakes her head.

"None whatsoever. You?"

I mimic the gesture.

"Let's see where this thing leads, shall we?"

As my hand compresses against the door, it begins to tremble, shaking the corniced ledge over an infinite drop. The door shifts at a snail's pace into the cavern it conceals. The air is humid and full of condensation, like a boiler room. Stalactites drip overhead as I take lead into the dark recesses, leaving the Phoenix to accompany at her own pace.

Harper and I turn the corner, coming face-to-face with a glowing object through the time-laden columns above and below. Its surface is blinding and has no physical shape — only raging formlessness, swimming in a calmed state.

The Avatar.

After the invasion by Ziz in the First Age, the Council had the Avatar moved, Luca says in my memory.

It never moved, but was here all along.

Siskett told me it was an artificial intelligence.

Laying eyes on its true form, threaded Light spills out onto the floor, casting the same arrangement of stars as Harper's locket.

The Avatar is so much more than that — without her, the world would be covered in eternal night. In creating her, the Council placed all its eggs in a single basket, so to speak.

She is the key to controlling Atlas.

The center flares as we approach it, spreading its glow further down the cave. There is no mouth I can see, but its voice is identical to every time I've heard it —female, robotic and cold.

"Greetings, Nephalim. I have been waiting for you."

The booming voice that greeted me on entry to Atlas and spoke during the ball is unburdened by the events occuring a mile up. It has not been located by Hannah, but that could easily change.

"You have?"

"**Yes**," the Avatar replies. "**You are the last remaining guardian of the Light, Ramona Knox. This meeting has been sorely de-**

layed, due to unforeseen circumstances that have led to the Council's demise."

"What does that mean?" I ask.

"This means I am to instill you with guardianship of the Seed of Light, which will grant you a greater chance of saving Atlas."

"How?" Harper asks, nowhere as infatuated with the hovering light as I am. Her locket dims in the Avatar's presence like a dog heeling to its master.

"The Seed is the central processing unit of the Light— to reduce it to technological terms, its wielder controls distribution of Light. Historically, I was built to house it after the Council learned it was too much for any single individual to hold. Ziz seeks to drain the Seed's essence, but to do so would come with catastrophic consequences to all living things.

"By possessing what the Dark Lord covets, you will hold the power to drive his forces back. This is your only chance of restoring Atlas to its rightful state."

"And the dragons?" I ask. "How do we get rid of them?"

"After Zizikk was sealed, the Council banished its Behemoths to a wasteland world called Ezzark. They bowed to the Seed then, and will do so again — it is their weakness. As with all things that require the Light to survive, too much of it can be fatal to their kind."

This all-knowing device holds all the universe's answers — from the meaning of human life to defeating Ziz and his mistress. It possesses the only weapon I need against the Devil, and speaks with none of the condescension from our first meeting in a metal box.

Harper also understands the Avatar's significance, and *also* has questions, albeit from a far different place than my childish wonder.

"What is *this*?" She lifts the star-shaped locket around her neck with a single finger— the pendant swings in front of her mouth.

"**That**," the Avatar says, "**is one of the most powerful objects in existence. It was once called Mother's Star.**"

The name is not familiar to the Phoenix, who seems to have a troubled history with the locket.

"My mother gave this to me," she says. Her tone has changed from angry to winded, trying to keep ancient tears at bay. "I've been trying to get rid of it forever. It's kept me immortal against my will; granted powers I can't explain. Same as it granted her.

"What I need to know are the prerequisites for passing it on. Answer me that, and you will have my eternal gratitude."

"**And why would you wish to pass it on, Phoenix?**"

Harper gulps, drawing her mouth corners tighter as she submits her answer.

"So that I can die. Like Olivia did."

I look between this sullen, defeated woman and the Avatar as both observe a moment of pause. Then, the bright light speaks again.

"**Mother's Star is an ancient relic fashioned by the blacksmith Piotr in the First Age for his love Meri. Their daughter Athena fell mortally after befriending a demonic trickster named Hiago, who put a curse on the young girl.**

"**Meri was devastated by her daughter's ailing state, and consulted the Council to save her. In the end, only Venicia showed mercy — she allowed the locket to be imbued with Light from the Seed at the cost of Meri's life, and she dissolved before Athena's eyes.**

"**Angry, grown and now in control of the locket, Athena returned to the Gardens, confronting Hiago for the prank that claimed her mother's life. She attempted to put a curse on the demon, resulting in Hiago binding the locket to the girl's soul. It eventually withered her, preventing every attempt to pass the White Light, removing any chance of a normal life.**

"What neither Athena or Hiago realized during this confrontation," the Avatar continues, "was the locket's essence split in two — a dichotomy of Light and Darkness, sentenced to perfect harmony. Its wearer was cursed to feed the locket's insatiable hunger, while being granted powers beyond compare."

"If that's true," Harper says, "then how did my mother come into possession of it?"

"The inadvertent curse put on the locket by Hiago comes with caveats. It *can* be broken. Athena carried it for a thousand years, but eventually dissipated to its growing hunger. According to my archives, it was found by a guard and given to his commoner daughter, a young girl named Dinah, who became instrumental in defending Atlas against Zizzik's forces. For years, Dinah was reported as wanting to be rid of the locket. She was infamous for murdering her sexual partners, earning the nickname 'Mantis' among the troops she commanded—"

Harper rolls her eyes.

"Enough with the history lessons, okay? Can we cut to the chase?"

"Certainly. Let me put it another way — Dinah was only able to pass the locket to her daughter Bethany as she sacrificed herself."

"What do you mean, 'sacrificed herself'?"

"The locket's origin story depicts an extreme act of maternal love. In cursing the locket, Hiago made this a permanent condition of its inheritance. Dinah could not give Bethany the locket until there came a moment the relic recognized she would fall under Zizzik's rebellion, and was bestowing it to save her daughter. Likewise, your mother Olivia was unable to remove Mother's Star until your final battle against Hale."

"Does that mean Olivia's mother gave her the locket?" I ask on Harper's behalf — the Phoenix has fallen silent and teary-eyed at this revelation.

"Negative. The locket went missing at some point during the Second Age. How it made its way to Valhalla, where Olivia came into its possession, is not detailed in my archives."

"Okay, then." I look back at my shaken companion, whose steely hazels are fixed over her shifting jaw. "Tell you what you wanted to know?"

Harper nods blankly, and I turn back to the Avatar.

"Tell me how to use the Seed to save Atlas."

And so, the foreign being made entirely of constellation-stricken glow does exactly that.

* * * *

HARPER AND I RETURN to the surface through a passage behind the Avatar's podium. The Seed of Light in my possession is little more than a perfect sphere of Light that warms my closed palm. I am not sure what part it will play in our coming confrontation with Hannah, but so many parts of her plan have failed — there is no squirming fetus of Darkness in my abdomen, if that counts for anything.

I hold her ultimate objective in my hand. The only question is how to use it against her.

The Avatar's passage offers a kinder slope than the one under the Cathedral, emerging in the Illumitory's cellar. Escaping into God City, the pink and red hues of sunset dance in the district's skies. The city beyond the palace steps is eerily quiet. Not a dragon dots the horizon as we leave the Illumitory's courtyard where the Atlas ball once came under threat from armed outlanders. The Whoville-like houses of my formerly favorite district are emptied of the charming nobles and wealthy spirits who once walked its cobblestone.

Harper is quiet as I lead her out of God City. We keep to the outskirts, carefully working our way counterclockwise around the Seat, where we are less likely to be spotted than we'd be cutting in front of the Spire. No Brotherhood man the God's Road, nor do Behemoths cling to the gold tower's pointed peak.

The greatest damage is done to the Coliseum district section where we lured a dragon, but is nearly matched by the crumbling border before the Observatory.

What took millennia to build was destroyed in a few weeks.

It's time to make our own mark on this cosmic destruction.

• • • •

"YOU READY?"

Inside the Obelisk, the two of us admire the paintings in the administration building's tapestry walls. I smile, remembering the first time Pol said I couldn't be Nephalim because I was a woman.

Harper nods, looking up at the same paintings. "I think so," she says. "You sure about this?"

I chuckle.

"Too much history in these halls. The Council thought it could be saved. But you can't save a soul that's sold itself to the Devil, right?"

"If that's true, what makes you think Tim can be redeemed?"

A gentle calm spreads across my held breaths.

"I think it comes down to what you thought he was guilty of in the first place."

Harper's mouth finds its own version of a smile.

"Man ends the world, and you want to quantify his guilt?"

"Only because as his accomplice, I'm no better than he was. Reincarnating me changed a million little things, speeding up some scenario in which Earth fell. You don't think I feel responsible for that, Harper?"

It's her turn to chuckle now.

"You two are really something else. Are we gonna do this thing?"

I nod.

"Honor's all yours."

• • • •

TEN MINUTES AFTER IMPLORING the Phoenix to do her thing, an alarm sounds throughout the Barracks. The dragons are first on the scene, illuminated by crackling flames reaching out of the Obelisk's innards. They are shortly followed by Brotherhood and Mykul; the angel strolls into the Barracks' courtyard, which is awash in the orange heat pushing the yelling Brotherhood back. Mykul simply observes, joined by a scowling Barrett, who displays shades of frustration he never let slip before his betrayal.

The Obelisk buckles under intense streaks of flame licking its roof and corners, eating the structure's weaknesses while whittling down the stronger points. Embers fly off the spreading mouth, forming new fires as they land on the surrounding temples. A lone spell from Harper's locket became an inferno devouring every building inside the Barracks one-by-one.

At last, the group below is joined by Hannah. The woman glides up the courtyard, stopping beside the much larger warrior as the Brotherhood panic to put out the disaster.

I can't see Hannah's face, but feel the aura of all her plans backfiring under a rebellion that survives its own failures and is still willing to challenge her, unaware they are watching from above.

Bet the bitch wasn't expecting that.

CHAPTER THIRTY-FOUR

IN THE EYES OF HUMAN history, I was a decent agent that got caught up in the dark, underhanded schemes of the FBI's best men. They tried to kill me, but failed. Next they knew, I had destroyed half of Washington, D.C. confronting them to save a young girl from being sold into sexual slavery. My legacy ends being found catatonic on my bathroom floor a few hours later.

I have tried to avoid thinking of that aftermath — with Maya dead, nobody was left to mourn me. The media would have had a field day. Indictments rolled off the corpses that hadn't started to cool. Investigations led to political blame, and the public looked for a scapegoat over fourteen children abducted in broad daylight.

Walking alongside the surviving members of my party, our approach to the Seat is less tense from our first confrontation with Hannah. Several Behemoths have returned to guarding the Spire — two of them fondle the tower itself, perched vertically like house flies while the larger ones circle them.

On one side of me is the Phoenix, with Tim and Luca on the other. Black clouds roil the tower as we reach the metal ring running around the Seat's perimeter.

Collectively stopped in front of the closed gates, there is no answer to our physical presence but the dead wind, cool and restrained like just before a downpour.

"Call them out to talk?" I ask.

Harper chuckles.

"I'm done talking."

The Mother's Star flares — its white blanket oozes over her shoulder, transitioning hue as it moves under her armpit, over her elbow, snugly swirling around Harper's wrist. Its manifestation reaches a symmetrical climax at her merged palms, shooting a star from them that hits the gate, not only splitting the golden bars off their hinges, but rips through the massive doors of Atlas' central palace. One splits in half, its top breaking off into the building's innards. A second blast from Harper's locket breaks the door opposite in three sections.

Thinking nothing of the incensed Behemoths above, or the damage done to a landmark building, she takes lead past the destroyed gates, now toppled in conflicting directions.

Immediately greeted by numerous Brotherhood evacuating the Council's old chambers, the plague doctor masks are gone, revealing a plethora of missing teeth and sunken cheekbones. Wielding everything from batons to bare fists and ninja stars, senseless chatter escapes their mouths as several backflip and parry around us. They are followed by Hannah's usual entourage — Mykul is the first to emerge. Barrett and Seraphina are followed by Hannah herself. The woman looks tired, as if she has been punished by Ziz for her ineptitude in trying to contain us.

Mykul scowls, eyeing Luca. Hannah's squinting resentment is fixated on me, Tim's glued to her. Harper's death stare at the blond woman is only matched by Barrett's incensed staredown of Quorroc. Seraphina stares at the floor, contemplating whether this is her moment to act as the Brotherhood purrs on the sidelines, awaiting their kill order.

"Well, at least you got inside this time," Hannah snickers. "I assume you've heard the definition of insanity — but dears, this will have the same result!"

"I beg to differ."

From the southern tip under the Spire's massive dome to their position near the north doors, the distance between our parties is more than a sword's throw but close enough to change quickly. The Brotherhood have blocked off our escape route, waiting to enclose us in a beatdown of battery weapons.

"And how is that? All you have is Death's washed-out champion — who doesn't even want to participate. So, no real loss. The title will be forfeited, and you'll soon face judgement. I assume you've told your little friends about our...*rendezvous*...haven't you?"

Tim frowns at the revelation that I might not have told him something. Luca's expression doesn't change.

But Harper's does.

"You think your precious Dark Lord is going to save you?" she asks. "I would think again, witch."

For all her failures of late, the woman is not discouraged in the least, and no less smarmy.

"As much as I would love to see it, Miss Whitaker, you people have a poor track record when it comes to interfering in our plans. So let me tell you all what is going to happen — Miss Knox here is carrying the Dark Lord's new form in her womb. Oh, did she not tell you, dear husband?"

I don't need to look back at the man who calls himself Death, already aware of the betrayal spreading over his face at this news, but it won't matter long.

Let the bitch talk.

She's about to have the rug pulled out from under her — I'll allow her the moment of glory.

"I'm sure you two will have a few discussions ahead. Like, how you're going to take care of your new responsibility. I'm sure Ramona never saw herself as a mother, did you?"

"Please," I smile. "Tell us what happens next."

Hannah's eyes narrow at my newfound condescension. Maybe I am being too obvious, but her world is about to come crashing down — and I cannot fucking wait.

"When Ziz's new form comes of age, he will reward you all for your insolence. Do you doubt this? You really shouldn't."

Drive the knife in.

"Well, I'm sorry to burst your bubble. But I couldn't bear your hellspawn if I wanted to. No matter how much you will it, you will never figure me out." At Hannah's morphing expression, I imagine Tim is equally caught between confusion and bewilderment, but all my satisfaction is right here.

"That's preposterous," Hannah scoffs. "Ziz told me it would be you —"

"I guess even the Devil can get it wrong. I was pretty surprised myself, but I trust the source. I'm infertile. Understand that? Your Dark Lord is up Shit Creek — and I'm about to beat his head underwater with the fucking paddle."

She's lost, and knows it.

"Then why are we still talking?"

I chuckle.

"You and I have unfinished business. But I'm not stupid enough to risk my people further. You have the dragons, and I have the Seed of Light."

At the mention of this, the woman's eyes widen — the central tenet of Ziz's journey is in her sights. Barrett pouts, bushy white brow drawing anger on his face. He must have tried to access the Avatar for centuries, and tried to convince it to let him hold the Seed himself.

"Prove it," Hannah says.

I shake my head.

"Uh-uh. You want the Seed, then you're just going to have to take my word for it."

"That is a lie!" Barrett yells from behind her. "You don't even know where the Seed is kept!"

But Hannah believes me — I wouldn't have come here, bluffing about something as foolish as the most important power source in Atlas.

"What do you propose?" she asks. Barrett groans and she hushes him with barely a glance in his direction.

"Honor the original wager," I say. "The Phoenix will fight your Champion, in the Arena, as agreed."

"That's it?"

"Nope. There are new stakes now. If your Champion wins, we give up the Seed, and you can go on your merry way, destroying Creation in any way you see fit."

Hannah smiles.

"And if Mykul loses?"

"Then you'll leave Atlas," I reply, "and take all your twisted followers with you. You'll accept whatever consequences go with abandoning Ziz — if he murders you and strings you up from a pole, that's not my problem, lady. But you will leave, and if you're smart, never fucking return."

The proposition weighs heavy on every weathered face in Hannah's entourage — Barrett seems the most affected, torn between disgust and rage at the prospect of abandoning his quest for power. Mykul scowls on the sidelines, hanging his head, waiting for Hannah to decide his fate. Seraphina has barely looked up, rendered a ghost of the High Priestess I first met in the Obelisk.

"Do we have a deal, Hannah?"

None contemplate the decision more than the blond woman, whose very fate now rests on the choice in front of her.

Ziz said I would face a trial of my faith.

She thought it would be Tim, but never saw me coming from a mile away.

After a moment, Hannah nods.

"Very well. You have proven yourselves to be worthy adversaries — even if you did start out with a weak display. I have nothing less than faith that the Dark Lord will prevail in this struggle, as he has through every other. I accept your challenge, Miss Knox."

"Good. A few ground rules, then. The dragons are to be kept no closer than the Seat during the match. Our champion will have no advantages, other than how you see her now. The same goes for your man."

"Agreed."

"Next, Tim retains the title of Death, no matter who wins."

Hannah scoffs.

"And *why* would I keep a known adulterer and unmitigated disaster of a human being in such a prestigious position, Miss Knox? Your relationship with my husband aside, you have to admit he's not very suitable for the job."

I disregard the snark, bitterness and the contempt of her assessment. She has been wrong about everything else, and is wrong about this, too.

"Because up until the moment he met me, I think he did a pretty good job. I'm like that, you know. Just...cancerous to everything that loves me. And I feel up until the moment you passed on, he was probably a good husband too, wasn't he?

"Just because you're bitter with him doesn't change the fact that your fight is not with him. That's according to *you*, who has chosen to represent *Ziz*. And what does the Dark Lord care about Death, anyway — or the Shroud, for that matter? Face it, lady. The only legitimate fight you have to pick, if you truly represent Ziz's interest alone, is with Atlas and the Light."

"What is your point, Miss Knox?"

I cross the room— risking death at the hands of Brotherhood I pass, Mykul's tense hand at the hilt of his sword, and Barrett ready to wring my neck. None of my entourage follow me past the picket line of reasonable self-preservation. And when I stop, we are almost touching faces, her strands of escaped hair falling between us.

"*I'm* Atlas now. Which means your fight is with me alone. There's no higher power standing between us — it's all or nothing, Hannah. But those are my conditions."

This close, I am reminded of our intimately horrifying encounter in the soul prison, but maintain my composure in the face of hers.

"And what's to stop me from killing you all, and taking the Seed, anyway?"

My smile returns, this time with finality.

"If anything happens to me, my people have instructions to throw the Seed into the White Light."

My gamble worked once before, on Quorroc — no reason it can't work again.

This time, Barrett replies.

"Don't be foolish! To do so would be a fatal error for us all—"

"Think about it," I reply. "If you're going to cheat your way into destroying Creation, it's all the same result. But I'd be more than happy to take that glory away from you. So let's avoid the games, fight with honor, and avoid any more stupidity!"

Feeling the danger of a hundred sets of hands ready to kill me from behind — Mykul in particular seems to edge toward me in peripheral vision— I wait for Hannah to accept with a tepid nod.

"You have my word."

"Then you won't mind shaking on it, will you?" I say, extending my hand. She looks down at it, as if touching it will suck out the devilry that's tainted her soul, then takes it in hers. We shake on the matter.

I tell her the match will take place tomorrow morning, having lost track of when tomorrow morning will be. It seems to be at least twelve hours away.

"Tomorrow morning," she agrees.

I release my hand, and return to my party.

· · · ·

ON THE EVE OF OUR FINAL confrontation with Ziz's forces — one can only hope for finality now — our group of survivors takes shelter in the Illumitory. Debris from the Atlas ball still cakes the floor, and surviving shards of chandelier glass crunch under my feet where I dislodged the main fixture. New damage from Harper's jail-break is evident in the walls and columns. The balcony where the late Council once stood, interfacing with the outlanders who threatened us, is a hole in the ascending staircase. Several corpses mar the lobby — their ends were recent, scattered round the collapsed fountain in spread-eagled positions, and have already begun to bloat.

I guess the dead *do* rot in Atlas.

"Let's settle in," Luca says. "Tomorrow will be a taxing day. We should get some rest while we can."

Harper stares blankly at the dead as Luca and Quorroc gravitate to corners of the room away from them. Tim stays where he is, closing his eyes, and I wish I had something comforting to offer him.

I begin with Harper— our adventures together have endeared her to me somewhat, and I may have better luck offering solace.

"You okay?"

The Phoenix suppresses a bitter chuckle, lowering her head.

"So much is riding on me, it would be delusional to hold onto optimism, don't you think?"

I nod.

"Sometimes the upside is all we have."

"Upside," Harper repeats. "Silver linings aren't my strong suit. One way or another, this is the end of the line for me."

"Did you really mean what you said to the Avatar? That...you want to die?"

Harper contemplates her next words. There are so many ways to explain her nihilistic outlook, but only she can do it justice.

"It must sound crazy. Hell, I'd be concerned if someone was so casual about it. I feel a bit like that Athena woman, you know? Sentenced to be...*consumed*. Eaten away. No gift is worth that outcome, right?"

Suddenly, I understand her in a way Tim could have never explained himself. Like the Whisperers who choose to remain in Atlas beyond reasonable expiration, Harper is the same — but passage onto peace is not in her realm of options.

"For what it's worth," she continues, simultaneously stifling deeper emotion in the waves of her voice, "I don't blame you and him for Em. I loved that girl from the first day I met her. But that piece of me is gone, and I know exactly where to lay the blame. With that fucking cunt — who will rue the day she came into control of those dragons. If it's the last thing I do, I will put her in the ground."

Fighting my own watering eyes, I nod and reach down, grasping her hand. The receiving fingers hesitate, but momentarily close over my own.

"For Em, then," I say.

Her face scrunches from the tide pushing her brow down, her cheeks against it, but Harper quickly resumes control.

"For Em."

Leaving the Phoenix to her final reflections, I move to Luca. My angel companion's bruises have begun to lift from their lowest point as he sits at the room's corner, sword in lap — just as he did on his downtime in the Obelisk.

"Here we are again," I say, sliding down next to him.

Luca chuckles, balancing the sword on his thigh.

"It would seem so. A vicious cycle of being forced together for the greater good."

"I would hardly call it vicious. I don't know what I would have done if we hadn't met, son of Tomas."

Luca laughs — I don't think I have ever heard that level of glee from his mouth, and make a note to remind him to do it more often.

"If there's one silver lining in all this, it will be never having to hear that parallel drawn again," he says. "I spent my whole life in my father's shadow; expected to carry his guilt for all those who remembered what he did. The people in Atlas have a long memory, and live long."

"It wasn't fair that you paid for him," I assure Luca. "There is no more pure-hearted angel in Atlas."

He smiles.

"I owe you everything, you know."

I shake my head, that burning sensation returning to my lower eyelids.

"You don't."

"But I do," the angel argues. "I spent my entire life trying to set the right example — show Atlas that I was not Tomas, and would never let harm befall them. And in that, there was no chance of atonement. I would have toiled until the end of days, nothing more than their errand boy.

"But you — it didn't matter how many gods or Maesters told you I wasn't fit to stand among my brethren; no matter how many smears and justifications, you never fell for it—"

I interrupt with a hand on his much larger bicep.

"People always tell me, I'm a pain in the ass."

Luca chuckles.

"Thank you, sister. From the bottom of my heart."

Laying my head on his shoulder, this man makes me feel safer than I have any right to be. After a lifetime of turncoats, he is the first person I would genuinely call my friend. Not since six-year-old Alison Delahunt would I have assigned that label to another living soul other than my adoptive aunt and Tim Hawkins — the man who calls himself Death.

Looking over our final hours of sanctuary, there is one final conversation I must indulge before everything goes to absolute shit.

I find Tim in the Observatory, having wandered to make his peace with whatever powers he clings to solace. It surprised me to find he had disappeared from the Illumitory.

Wandering the palace's lesser-known halls, searching empty rooms, a green light passed my face. I drew back as it zipped by me again. A low, familiar buzzing jogged my memory to that day in the Gardens when I first heard it.

Avalon's insect. It whooped and squealed in the staircase I nearly ascended as I realized it was trying to hail me.

"What is it, little guy?" I asked, met with more squeamish whines. Its threaded wings fluttered as it bounced left to right, turning and shaking its bright rear end at me. "You want me to follow you again?"

With a high-pitched affirmation, it trailed past my head, green glow bobbing against walls and the ceiling like a toddler with a sugar high. The bug bee-bopped out the hallway, around the corner and through the Illumitory doors. I caught Quorroc glancing at me as I followed it past Avalon, who noticed his friend, submitting a nod — as if he knew where it wanted to lead me.

Outside, the insect continues down the steps and out of God City. I trudge behind its excited, chaotic trajectory.

There are no signs of the dragons or Hannah's gang of cosmic misfits on the God's Road, only me and Avalon's little friend. It squeals past the destroyed Coliseum district wall, dancing to withheld knowledge. Groaning at the distance spent in ignorance, I am relieved when it rounds the arch to the Observatory, following it inside.

The man who calls himself Death faces the nebula dwarfing the structure where the Council perished. His suit is gone— even pointed away from me, the tweed coat and khakis are a remarkable departure for the figure I've known my entire life.

He turns around as I enter through the arch — the beard he has kept for ages is clean-shaven, discarded at our feet like his celestial threads.

"I hoped you would come." His voice is calmer, unlike the heartbeat which pounds and batters itself against my chest. "I am glad our mutual acquaintance could persuade you."

Tim's hand reaches out as I join him on the plateau before the final steps into the Observatory begin, taking mine inside of it.

"Yeah, well, it's pretty hard to say no to something that fucking cute."

Tim chuckles at my deadpan remark. His eyes drift to the crumbled wall before falling into the gap between us.

"There are so many things I have to live with. In mortality, the illusion exists that once you're dead, all those problems are forgotten."

I let him speak, consoled by the moonlight with no moon behind it — alone, as he and I have always been.

"I have made some terrible mistakes, Ramona. But I stand before you now, the very essence of who I am, to convey that you were never one of them. This whole time, I struggled to minimize my feelings. First, due to guilt, for allowing you to come to harm — then, due to my past relationship coming back to haunt me.

"But that is all beside the point — I love you. I have *always* loved you, Ramona Knox. I asked myself, over and over, why I was still here if I didn't; thought, 'there's no way she could ever return it'.

"I would risk Creation a thousand times if it meant saving you once; invite dragons and demons and the ruin of everything. But that's the crux of the argument, isn't it?" he smiles. "I thought we were doing good — that somehow, I could atone for my predecessor's bitterness and cavalier wish to end the world. I thought...I can't possibly be as terrible as Hale. At least he wore his disregard openly. Mine has hidden behind this destructive, tempting thing called love; masqueraded as something beautiful while destroying reality around us. And in that regard, Ramona, I'm no better than Hale was."

I take his other hand in mine — this man who has turned the universe upside down to protect me, ruining my life all the way. My conversation with Maya in the Gardens returns to me, and I repeat her advice.

"I love you Tim Hawkins — but you're too hard on yourself."

The man who has shed Death frowns.

"Pardon?"

And then, Maya's wisdom is followed by Siskett's, as we sat just beyond the hedge maze I would eventually meet my adoptive mother one final time.

"Someone once told me, 'everything you have seen is the beaker in which your personal formula was built'. From the beginning, you have been here when nobody else was. You protected me when the world wanted to swallow me up, spit me out whole. If it weren't for you, I would have died when Hardwick burned me alive. And because of you, I finally have a purpose."

Tim shakes his head.

"No, Ramona — you made your own purpose. I helped you accomplish that, but *everything* you built is to your credit, and has always been. You are the most incredible person I have ever met."

My hand reaches out, touching his cool, shaven cheek. His own hand pulls me in, kissing me. Whatever connotations come from locking lips with Death are absent — his lips are warm as any living person I have shared the act with. There is no hurried attempt to remove my clothes and get inside me, but a slow, withheld passion, as if he has waited decades, and would rush nothing.

The kiss lasts a long time. When it ends, we are not naked in the grass — only in gratitude we still have each other.

CHAPTER THIRTY-FIVE

RECKONING HAS COME.

If there is such a thing as a peaceful morning in the carcass of the supreme realm, it is lost on me. The sky around the Seat is a peaceful, solid blue with lazy clouds nestled in its canopy. The Behemoths are sentries to any outsider who might waltz into Atlas, see us all fighting like medieval savages, and think to put a stop to this madness. They remain south of the Spire as directed, well away from the Arena where the fate of Creation will be decided.

On this clear mockery of a morning, our group emerges from God City to find Hannah's forces waiting. The blond woman wears a golden gown that clings too close to her bust. Her hair is wound in a confident bun, but her eyes are sunken and mascara does little to conceal the cost of her servitude. Seraphina lurks close, sporting white robes and an elaborate halo-like headdress, red strands sharply pulled in twin braids. Like Hannah, the High Priestess looks rough.

Barrett beams beside Mykul, who also seems to have taken on some modifications as Ziz siphoned his soul. Wielding the Habinar's ax, the mutated angel's demeanor is unchanged, but it's almost impossible to miss the wheezes escaping Harper's foe.

"What's wrong with him?" I ask as our groups join on the God's Road. "Doesn't look so good."

Mykul grunts, flexing the enormous weapon as Hannah shrugs off his condition.

"It is nothing you need to worry about, Miss Knox. Mykul is more than capable. Is your Champion ready to fight?"

A shared glance with Harper ends in a nod, and I look back at the blond woman.

"We're ready. We'll set up on the Arena's northern quarter. Your champion can prepare from the south. The fight will begin in an hour. Agreed?"

Hannah smiles, and I take solace in knowing she will soon be incapable of it.

"These are very dictatorial requests when you haven't even proven to be in possession of the Seed."

The smile she receives is equally condescending.

"It's nearby. If you win, it'll be handed over at a time and place of my choosing."

"Very well, Miss Knox. I can only assume your word is your bond. We will soon see, won't we? But do try to remind your friend this is a winner-takes-all fight. If the Phoenix loses, she won't be getting back up."

Harper's face lapses into a spiral I can only call hatred.

"Same applies to you. Light be with you." I say before turning, pulling its last defenders with me. "Not that it would save a traitorous cunt."

With that, we veer toward the Arena where the final outcome awaits.

If Light is with us, we won't have to wait long.

On a clear, blue morning — the pleasant effect spreads to the Coliseum district, whose skies are often purple and moody — the carcass of Atlas carries the sound of death on its acoustics. The stands above fill with Brotherhood and other faces I don't recognize.

Our group of Harper, Tim, Luca, Quorroc, Avalon and his two students— whose names I've since learned are Almed and Eriam — takes shelter in private quarters on the Arena's northern end. Quorroc and the Magi are contemplative. Tim is composed, Luca steady.

That leaves only Harper, whose face is awash in beads of perspiration. Her hands shake in the room's corner, crouched with her back against the wall, eyes closed as I approach her. The Mother's Star brightens as I draw near, alerting her to my presence.

"Need some last-minute encouragement?"

Harper scoffs — the slender hands continue to tremble, the only indicator to how deep her terror runs.

"Unless you have a magic sword you can pull out of a water basin, there's not much you can say to mitigate it."

"Hold up," I say. "A magic sword?"

Harper smiles, shaking her head.

"Had to be there, I guess. But this is a whole different game. Situation, whatever. It's one thing to want to die by yourself — but taking everyone with you if you fail…"

I kneel next to her, and take her trembling hand in mine.

"Listen to me," I say. "You're not going to fail."

"Right. Got a crystal ball?"

"No. I got something better — *this.*"

Harper's eyes widen at the tiny glowing object between my enclosed forefinger and thumb. It blots out of my fingertips, and I have not dared remove it from my pocket before now.

"You want to use the Seed to win? What happened to honor?"

"Fuck honor," I say. "This is Creation at risk. You've been entrusted with our fates — might as well give you the means to win. Here, put it in your locket."

She reluctantly takes it from my grasp, ever so careful not to drop it as she deposits it between the open halves. The Mother's Star closes over it, and emits a bright flash, blinding the room's occupants, drawing shouts from the other end.

When my eyes adjust, Harper is staring at her hands. As if imbued with new strength, the Phoenix flexes her forearm; it no longer shakes as her slack-jawed reaction meets my growing smile.

"Thank you," she says.

"One condition," I joke. "When this is over, you tell me how to get a moniker as badass as yours."

My heart feels lighter at Harper's new confidence, and the relief washing over her. But turning to face my other cohorts, I am met by a stunned Quorroc, who witnessed the whole thing.

"What have you done, Ramona?"

I shrug.

"What?"

Quorroc shakes his head in disbelief — the old man looks between the Phoenix and I like children committing some stupid act, lacking the common sense to make any other choice.

"You cannot join the Seed with a relic of its Creation! You could short-circuit Atlas, and send us plunging to the realms below!"

"Oh really, Maester?" I ask. "And what do you propose when Mykul wins, and that demented woman takes the Seed anyway? Don't you think our survival is worth a little risk?"

"That is not the point, Nephalim. You cannot possibly think to hand absolute control of the Light to this unstable woman —"

I am done being questioned.

"You know what, Quorroc? That unstable woman is our only hope of restoring Atlas. So yeah, I'm putting all my eggs in her unhinged basket, and you know what? If it fails, and goes to shit, and we all die — at least we died fighting. Not rolling over for the Devil's tramp, gagging on our own self-righteousness!

"That said," I continue, lowering my volume, "I understand the risks as you have explained them, Maester. What happens next is on me."

Quorroc is unsatisfied by my cavalier response, but does not argue further, withdrawing back to his corner in disgust. I am joined by Tim and Luca as he storms past them.

"Is he going to be a problem?"

"He'll cool off," Luca assures me. "You made the right choice, Ramona. If the woman wins, there won't be a difference."

"But if *we* win," Tim interjects, "it will be another thing to deal with. Atlas falling out of the sky is just as catastrophic as Ziz destroying it."

Then there's the matter of what it may do to Harper, who is placed at risk by simply carrying it inside Mother's Star. Remembering her deathwish, I say nothing of the woman crouched against the wall behind us.

"We'll cross that bridge if we come to it. Right now, we have to win this fight. Also, we have to consider that the High Priestess may make her move soon."

"There are a lot of balls in the air," Tim agrees. "For the sake of versatility, we should sit at opposite ends of the Arena as Harper battles Mykul. If something offkey happens, one of us will be able to quickly close the gap."

"Okay," I say. "We'll have the Magi wait at a safe distance, and muster there if Hannah doesn't decide to play fair. I'm thinking the Cathedral ruins — they can port us out a safe distance from there."

"Agreed," Luca replies.

The plan is set. Our champion will wield the Light's full power against all the darkness infesting Atlas, and one will emerge the clear winner this time.

Reckoning has come.

* * * *

THE TRIAL OF CREATION'S fate is upon us.

From my seat on the Arena's southern end— the section we lured a dragon into destroying is closed down, but only comprises a small portion of the bottom stands— I lock eyes with Tim in the north, and nod to Luca on the eastern part of the ring.

The crowd of Brotherhood entertains outlanders from Earth, who whoop and yell and throw objects from the stands into the Arena below. Both factions lean over the railings, fragmenting visual signals between our party. The items tossed into the ring range from household items like kettles and pots to more nefarious possessions like daggers and spent ammunition. All were hauled here from the living world and land scattered beneath their jeers and insults.

Not far from my enclave of degenerates in the land of wild things, Hannah is perched on a canopied balcony, on a throne like her chair in the Seat. Her gold dress shimmers in the daylight. Seraphina stands over her left shoulder as the woman stands to address the crowd with Barrett to her right.

"Newcomers of Atlas!" Hannah's booming voice reaches every corner of the Arena, packed to capacity with malevolent souls. **"Today, you are a part of history! It is here, in the court of mythical warriors like Dinah the Great, the future of the supreme realm will be decided, along with all living things it governs!"**

The crowd cheers and stomps their feet like apes, continuing to throw their worldly possessions into the pit. Clattering metal and landing refuse overrule the silence — when it has ceased, Hannah resumes.

"The Dark Lord will not be known as some interloper who whittled Atlas out from under those who ruled it! He will be known as the gladiator who won this city with valor, in the traditions of old! He will have won it back from gods that failed to appreciate their role of serving, not lording over their mortal subjects!"

This is met with more wild cheers from her army of repressed sycophants — whom the Avatar would have not hesitated to send to the Shroud once upon a time, citing a threat to the peaceful aura of Atlas.

They are here in force now.

"This started being about Death's malfeasance! Be assured, he will dig his own grave in time! This is an attack on our free-

dom, to live without celestials dictating when our lives must end! To that, I say — long live our souls!"

Hannah lifts her right arm into the air — it's not the naked limb's trajectory that unnerves me, but Seraphina's eyes following the closed fist as it lifts over the pit, and the woman's trademark grin returns.

"Let the fight begin!"

Cranking gates on either end of the Arena force an exhale from my chest, and I catch the blond woman smiling at me, salivating over the moment she apprehends the Seed of Light.

May the Light be with us.

CHAPTER THIRTY-SIX

IN THE BEGINNING, THERE was nothing — it comprised all except the vomited matter from antimatter, something from the big nothing; scraps of potential in a debris belt of pointlessness. Much like the little girl who survived Daniel Knox and Tiffany Stewart's depraved deaths, it rose up from nothing.

Osmosis, like the puddle before Avalon becoming a living, breathing exoskeleton with a light in its ass and intuition I sorely lack. The Magus' insectoid friend and I may have more in common than I'd like to admit in that regard. We are shapes from the formlessness that birthed us, like the universe that paved the way in unnatural, spontaneous paths.

In the grand scheme, this battle is ours to lose — pushing back at the mammals of Darkness who came down a birth canal they were welcomed at the other end.

Even Ziz — the boy god who befriended dragons, turning them against their malevolent masters, resulting in near-universal banishment— was born with a place in the natural order. Unlike me, the Dark Lord was fostered into his final form, rather than forced into it. He saw the Council's actions, and made a choice to go against them.

The crowd assumes their seats as the blond woman does; stops shifting as the bloodbath they were promised begins. Many of them — all men, following the sole female authority who gave them new life— rub their hands in anticipation, whispering garbled excitement to each other. But the boisterous behavior that preceded their sudden, consuming respect is absent, biting its tongue under the risk of punishment, or simply out of reverence.

In the ring, cool air does nothing to mitigate the stream of sweat down Harper's cheeks. Her outfit— a simple white tank-top and black slacks— is dirtied with fear and apprehension, but her face wears none of it. The locket glows emerald rather than its traditional white, casting green aspersions over the Phoenix's bare collarbone. The effect is still dull, but the woman overseeing this match would not recognize the Seed's effect if it were naked in front of her.

Unlike our side, she has never seen it.

The moment between Mykul completing his series of twirls and flips with the Habinar's double-headed ax and his charging Harper across the Arena is filled with terror and loathing that can only go double for the thin woman facing him. Mykul is three times her size, and about the same disparity in body weight. Watching him effortlessly wield the gigantic heirloom like nothing injects dread into my darkest reaches as the angel charges her with outstretched wings.

Despite his visible ailment, Mykul's wide arc with the ax is completed with maximum gusto, backing Harper into one of the rear alcoves. She scrambles out of its reach on hands and knees, fingers clawing at a thin layer of grains. Mykul pulls the ax up to shoulder level and advances, chasing my crawling Champion down the Arena's middle, lifting the ceremonial weapon above his head with the most effortless golf arm I've ever seen.

The weapon reverberates on the spot the Phoenix rolls away from. Her hand reaches along the threadbare coat of sand, finding a clump as the rogue angel lifts the ax again.

Pitching her fist of grains at Mykul's face sends the much larger man into a fit of screams and grunts, using the base of his palm to wipe at his affected eyes. Harper wastes no time scrambling to where her comparatively paper sword was cast off in their initial struggle.

Seeing their hero easily beaten back by Death's champion, the etiquette of Hannah's followers is forgotten in a volley of yelling, pounding feet and swearing.

She's got this.

The Mother's Star does not react or change for her momentary victory — the emerald glow does not brighten, nor weaken. Mykul rebounds, sending my gaze to the blond woman. Hannah's expression morphs between hope and despair. I can't linger on her, and return to the fight.

Mykul and the Phoenix now occupy the dead center of the ring. The angel stumbles as Harper climbs to her feet. In his heavy suit of armor, Mykul is his own worst liability — the giant swings the ax, and its black coat moves too fast to make out the gold characters engraved in its handle. Its blade passes above Harper's lowering head. Returned to a crab walk, she scurries to the Arena's western side.

Mykul recovers momentum. The angel's eyes are empty, wings are dirtied from the kicked-up earth. He exhibits no fear of the much smaller woman he is tasked with murdering, but does not enjoy the length of time it is taking to best her.

Harper's blond locks beat back and forth with her flailing head as Mykul pitches the ax aside. Rather than put stock in a weapon that doesn't belong to him, the angel makes faster gains over the Phoenix's crawling torso. Harper winces as Mykul bends over her, grabbing the fabric of her shirt from behind. Using uncanny, unlimited strength, he lifts her into the air, pitching her across the Arena.

Thrown into one of the closer walls, pulling down debris from her point of impact, Harper's face rotates over a limp arm. I look up to my right, magnetically pulled to the blue irises burning into my cheek, grinning at me. I disregard the woman, attention returned to my Champion.

Harper shifts on her aching bones, face hidden by the storm of shoulder-length hair. As the Phoenix slowly lifts herself off the ground— first using her arms, then legs, to push herself to a stand— my head lifts, shooting to Hannah. The woman's former confidence is replaced with annoyance, and she nods at her Champion.

Come on, girl— you got this.

The angel lunges, giving little thought to his own trajectory. Harper sidesteps his stomping sandals. Mykul smacks the wall, bouncing off it, landing on his back. This gives Harper the opportunity to put some distance between them.

The angel is already climbing to his feet; his wings contract on his back as if he landed on them like it was a funny bone. Cracking his neck, the woman's champion advances with an unintelligent roar, walking briskly to the northern end Harper is backed into. Mykul sweeps the stones with his hand along the way, wrapping around the Habinar's ax handle, thrusting it into the air with one hand and catching it with another. He brings it down as Harper narrowly dodges the swing, catching in the Arena's creviced wall. Mykul tugs and pulls with all his dormant, brute strength. He eventually gets it out, but the moment comes too late.

From her new position on the western wall, Harper breaks into a cantor, upgrading to a sprint, closing the gap with her adversary. The Phoenix's soles lift off the ground. She doesn't quite bring her leg up high enough, and the angel grabs her ankle as it attempts a kick. He releases at a half-circle; Harper shoots across half the ring, landing hard on her side.

The woman smiles at me, then returns her focus to the match. Hannah stands from her throne of rock and godless glory, casting shrill inflections down at Mykul.

"What are you waiting for?"

Harper winces at the mutant warrior's enclosed boot. But this time, her gasps are stronger than resolve.

"Kill the bitch!" Hannah screams.

Mykul's hesitation is Harper's gain— so focused on his mistress, the angel does not notice Harper's head lift, nor the rogue, static hairs down the side of her head. A powerful glow escapes the darkness between her arms, heart buried in the thoughtlessly dispersed sand.

It is not the flame that broke open the Spire's gates, red with a white center, a blazing hot ball of pure physics. This is untempered

Light — the Seed bounces in the magnetically hovering locket, rising until it is inches from her face. The blanket escaping the star emanates yellow film over a bleached core swirling down the Phoenix's arms. It envelops Harper's body, turning her skin the same volatile glow.

A human sun.

The wave of Light that hits the angel passes through him so quickly, it is nearly possible to watch the giant man dissolve into nothing. A shrill cry escapes the box to my right — only seconds ago, Hannah was so sure she had won.

The Seed fades inside Mother's Star; Harper collapses on her side, trying to cough the inferno out of her lungs as smoke rises off her flesh. The locket fades to the emerald glow it displayed before turning her into a mini-supernova.

In the north stands, the man who calls himself Death sinks in relief among the angered crowd, who have returned to rowdiness on all sides, echoing Hannah's despair. On my side of the stands, outlanders and Brotherhood alike hurl insults and objects, all which fall just short of the recovering Harper.

As Hannah's sole syllable of agony escapes her — unbeknownst to my spinning head and darting vision during the fight — my worst fear comes true. Seraphina lifts a blade she must have concealed inside her wrist, and swings at the blond woman's neck. I only catch a glimpse of the assassination attempt coming off a check on the Phoenix.

I don't know what made her choose to do it at Hannah's lowest moment — she does have one hell of a petty streak going, after all — but the attempt is quickly cut short. Barrett unveils his own blade, driving it through Seraphina's throat with a primal cry. Hannah's head looks back at the confrontation as the knife falls from the Priestess' hand. I can't see Barrett's face, only the hand pushing his own weapon in.

Seraphina drops to her knees — he's talking to her and I can't hear what they're saying over the boisterous crowd's cursing and chanting, but I know exactly what he's doing.

The Maester wants her to know she failed. He withdraws the blade from her windpipe, and Seraphina crumples to the floor behind Hannah's throne. Barrett turns his head back to the events below. Though his white beard is soaked with the Priestess' blood, his expression is quite pleasant — like it never happened at all.

Hannah's is more dazed; first in confusion, then terror, shortly culminating in rage. When she looks down on the surviving Phoenix, the woman knows she has been cheated. She moves her mouth, doling instructions to Barrett. I don't hear her command, but don't need to.

I know *exactly* what happens next.

CHAPTER THIRTY-SEVEN

THE BEHEMOTH THAT HANNAH calls down into the Arena is larger than the one Luca and I faced in the Cathedral. I know this one — it is the alpha male of the dragons that came from Ezzark. It has never intervened until now, content to dispatch its weaker cousins at Hannah's command, often perching itself vertically along the vertical Spire, where it has begun to leave claw marks from constant lookouts there. Its scales are dominantly chestnut, compared to the faint blues and greens of its subordinates.

I am surprised the woman only calls down one — maybe she sends them all, and this one, their leader, finally intervened. Its home is Atlas now, its tenure threatened as the Council before it. Harper lays weakened at its hulking fours, submissive prey for the advancing dragon, purring at the prospect of an easy meal.

A man in the east stands leaps over the railing, landing in a roll by the Phoenix. Luca's wings spread over Harper in a protective blanket, sword already drawn toward the Behemoth. The dragon is taken aback by the intruder, and snarls at the angel protecting its lunch.

"Wait!" Hannah calls, drawing the Behemoth's squinted eyes to her. "This is not in the rules! This man is trespassing!"

"Rules that ended," Luca shouts back, "the moment you brought this savage beast down here!"

"And yet, you had the Seed this whole time! What happened to honor?" The beast bows its head, still growling through the jagged rows of teeth, awaiting her order to resume. "Instead, you cast your dignity aside, and did not win Atlas fairly. Therefore, you have lost."

Caught between their public shouting match, the crowd falls quiet, awaiting their coveted bloodbath.

"So you have decreed! But it will not be shown that Luca, son of Tomas, first of a line of new Nephalim — *true* Nephalim! — stood by, and allowed you to break your word. Asking this woman to fight a Behemoth in her condition amounts to nothing less than a public execution! And I will abide no tyrant, she-devil. Light knows, I have done so for too long already."

The one goal in my remaining afterlife — to wipe the smirk off that succubus' face — is accomplished. But now my allies (*my friends*) are in danger, and that is a new problem that Tim's wife is too happy to take care of.

"If that is your wish, then I hope you have made your peace," she says, and looks at the dragon. "Kill them."

The woman turns her back, and the creature's head drops to an attack position. Luca's shoulders sink as the Behemoth draws a breath, knowing he can't withstand the intense heat from its lungs.

From my place in the stands, paralysis breaks. Launching from my seat, I begin pushing past the bodies separating me from the box. Looking to the Arena's northern end, I don't see Tim— that could easily be attributed to hurried glances and overwhelming desire to corner his wife.

The Behemoth facing Luca and Harper unleashes its volatile breath. The angel plants his sword between stones at his feet, hands at its hilt to shield the Phoenix with his wings.

The scream from Luca's mouth transcends pain, determined to hold onto honor until his final moments, stopping my urgency to catch Hannah as I hang on the outcome, holding my breath for their safety.

When the dragon pulls back, I expect ashes and dust where they stood, and anticipate my friends are scattered to the wind. A plume of roiling, black smoke lingers where intense heat bore down, cooking thin sand.

Hannah and Barrett are gone now, likely returning to the Spire, leaving Seraphina's corpse obscured by the stone chair. Members of the surrounding Brotherhood yell and guffaw at me to stop blocking their view of the clearing smoke below.

I jump back as a figure charges out of the plumes, drives his sword into the dragon's side with a scream. It lodges between the creature's ribs, prompting howls from the dragon.

Also emerging from the black, sweeping cloud comes Harper— the Phoenix is back on her feet, Mother's Star joined to the Seed, casting its strange hybrid glow.

The locket must have protected them.

The ailing Behemoth is taken by further surprise when a thick column of black air shoots over several bodies in the Arena's northern stands, arcing down the wall. It moves with ferocity, speed and brutality, wrapping under the dragon's chin. Like a gravity hook finding its anchor point, the smoke tube wraps around the monster's neck. The column weaves under the dragon's front legs, crossing over its lighter-shaded belly, securing each limb as it progresses. Tim's dark form binds the wings together, snapping them vertically as the Behemoth screams in pain, bowing on its haunches.

Luca wastes no time pulling his sword from between the dragon's rib. It sinks lower, grunting in discomfort until the roars and protests dull to a resigned purr. He draws his arm back and plunges the sharpest tip through its skull.

The alpha dragon's collapse shakes the entire structure— its off-center position sees the released wings strike the eastern wall as Tim withdraws. The webbed limb cuts a swath of sediment and debris through the base of the stands.

All three rows that were supported by that foundation sag. The men caught in its buckling levels push past each other to reach safety on the north and south portions. In the southern section's top row, the influx of Brotherhood and outlanders barreling toward our end makes escape in any direction impossible.

The Behemoth's collapse below whirls sand at Luca and Harper's feet as they back away from the dying monster. Tim returns to his human form at their side— the man who calls himself Death first lands as a totem, assuming his familiar human outline. The skin lightens, and his facial features take shape; the suit forms in the dancing plumes, finally solidifying into the celestial being I've known my entire life.

The three allies stand in a row along the northern wall. Harper eyes the dead dragon— screams from its brethren above fill the sky with the language of primitive creatures voicing their loss. Luca sheaths his sword as the white wingspan on his shoulders retracts at the swirling aerial horde.

For now, my friends are safe.

The bottom row's collapse on the eastern wall is sudden as the blade that Seraphina tried to use on Hannah. Several spectators are pulled down with the avalanche of concrete and stone. Screams pierce a rising cloud of dust and shrapnel with the men caught in the down slide soon falling silent at my stunned allies' feet.

The second row counted on the first to support its jam-packed weight, and tumbles as the structure gives, pulling down the top two rows. The third was empty on the east side after most of its occupants made it to the adjacent stands, and only serves to crush those who collapsed with the first two tiers, leaving a gaping wound into the surrounding district.

Hannah's inner circle has collapsed, and all that remains is to pry the last of her cold, dead fingers off the supreme realm. Crowded between the shaken populace crammed in the south, I look down at my allies, who return their own affirmations.

Luca bows his head with a smile, looking back up at me.

Harper casts a lone, sullen nod. Mother's Star glows with verdant fury, illuminating her saviors' expressions.

But it is not until I look at the man who calls himself Death that I notice something is wrong. Tim's eyes are wide, his finger raising to warn me of something terrible, formidable and imminent— *something present with me up here.*

Before I can turn my frown to the object of his shock, a hand clamps over my mouth from behind me. I can't scream or call their names. I'm dragged backwards, pulled through the shoulder-to-shoulder survivors. Another set of hands grab me— I kick with my feet, only to be restrained at the ankles.

I cannot see my attackers, but they are legion, a maw of darkness opening to swallow my soul. I try calling Tim's name, and imagine him dissolving into the column of smoke, raging through the blue sky to save me.

Nothing comes — only the short fuse in my breaths, snapping with each iteration.

I am pulled back, yanked down.

Dragged forward.

After that, the only thing I know is darkness.

CHAPTER THIRTY-EIGHT

WHITE LIGHTS.

The introduction of blinding Light pulls me from slumber. It is an assault on my being, weaponized to paralyze me at the same time it drags me out of unconsciousness. The scene is familiar— a dark room, a chair, a rope to hold me in place. The furniture is unreliable in balance — one leg is shaved away, giving the remaining tripod uncertainty it can maintain my weight and remain upright.

How did I end up here? That seems to be a recurring theme— like drifting from locale to twisted locale

(a hospital, heaven, light at the end of life's tunnel)

to end up in the worst place of all. All this time fighting for Light, and I am returned to the darkness I masqueraded within, unaware of what true darkness ever entailed.

It is here now, and I am terrified of it.

"Good," says a familiar voice, repeating equally familiar words. "You're awake."

Good, as it was in the Capitol when Stephen Hardwick left me in the same bad spot. I'm awake, as I was before my old partner tried to murder me.

I should have never trusted him.

As Tim's wife steps into the flood in my eyes, she is just another shadow of me— a mortal pretending to embody Darkness, mocking it with amateur impressions.

"I have to give it to you," she smiles. Coming into focus, the knuckles of her passing hand brush my cool cheek. "You almost had me, Miss Knox. Entrusting the Seed to my husband's champion? A brilliant display. Even more, turning the High Priestess against me? Ziz warned me to be vigilant, and now I am grateful for the Dark Lord's counsel."

I resolve to say nothing. The only thing left is to murder her, whenever such an opportunity presents itself.

"Although, there are some things that even the most brilliant mistress can never outmatch in the spouse, right? So much arrogance, you didn't even realize your only chance had slipped out from under you."

She lifts an object in her hand— it glows an evocative purity of white, but is no smaller than an earring's backing, affixed between the woman's forefinger and thumb.

The Seed of Light.

"All it took was making you believe it couldn't be taken. *Everything* has a price, Ramona."

How did she get it?

Despite our victory, Hannah now holds Creation's fate in her hand. She circles the wobbling chair.

"The Phoenix?" I ask, not wanting to know all the same.

Hannah snorts.

"Please— that basket case wouldn't do me the kindness if her life depended on it; not that she seems to value it very much."

"Luca?" I say, bracing for the worst news of my life.

Tim's wife smiles.

"So quick to point the finger at your allies— it's no wonder so few of them chose to defend Atlas. And from what? The right to choose our own free will, rather than serve gods who hold us to unattainable standards? Who, in their pettiness, left you comatose for over *two decades*?"

I have no more patience for her justifications.

"Oh, you mean the gods who created this universe, you witch? The ones who gave you life and loving parents, I imagine, and a husband who was faithful until the day you died? Even then, he told me it destroyed him. It ripped him apart, you ungrateful, stupid cunt!

"Do you know," I ask her, through gritted teeth and burning eyes, "what I would have given for *any* of that? I tell you, I wouldn't be caught dead doing this— *bowing* to some petty demon, all to satisfy your inadequacy over the fucking truth! You were never good enough for him—"

The speed of Hannah's knuckles meeting my cheekbone in an open plank of fingers sends my neck sprawling to the side. Hair is cast over my eyes and nose in fragments, strands glimmering under the Seed's glow, bringing out the contrast between the monster I thought I was and the one who took my place. I pray my neck is broken, and I can go onto the White Light.

Nope.

Still alive— still watching this bullshit play out.

Tim's wife doesn't even give me defeat, using her free forefingers to lift my chin.

"It must be difficult," she says softly. "Having such a limited worldview, watching it crumble like pieces of glacier into a cosmic ocean. So simplistic — and how like humanity! — to romanticize shades of gray. Evil must seem to be everywhere, when it is all you look for.

"I pity you, Miss Knox. Of course, no more than I pity myself— and not over Tim. The first mistake of a good woman is placing faith in men. They taste you, and swear yours in the only fruit they will ever want. But ask them to *wait* — to *delay* gratification when it's no longer readily available? Suddenly, an orange is worth more than an apple, and here we are— fighting over our interpretations of them. I have no desire to fight you, Ramona."

"No," I snipe. "Just destroy everything I've ever loved, at the moment I find it. Play your card or leave me the fuck alone."

This is the moment she has waited for — the opportunity to extinguish me like the little candle I am, and make a long, conniving speech to precede it.

"Soon. I wouldn't dare deprive myself of this moment, Miss Knox. I have waited for it for a very long time.

"When we first met, I told you why I chose this path. To amend that, it was chosen for me — never truly my choice. But over time, the Dark Lord's will became clear, even if his reasoning rarely did. And there has scarcely been a moment I regretted joining with him."

I bet he never mentioned what happens when their bodies separate. He is part of her, just as Tim's darkest manifestations once melded with mine to stop Hardwick.

We have to begin the separation process, Ramona.

We did, and I was left a shell on my bathroom floor, bleeding from a hole in my temple where all Tim's devilry escaped into the open. It destroyed me, putting me into deep sleep for a long time.

I wonder how Hannah will fare when Ziz no longer needs her.

Will it hurt?

Immensely.

But the Dark Lord will show no love in the aftermath of their physical parting. He will not wait at her bedside, nor surrender to higher powers for her freedom. He will not stand beside her as Tim stood by me, waiting for life to return. Ziz will sap the life from her, absorbing Hannah's essence into his own horrible form, and there will be no reversal or burden to undo the damage.

I wonder if the bitch knows.

"You and I are not so different," she observes, finally letting my head fall back under its own willpower and cupping the Seed in her fist. "I just wish you could have seen it sooner, Miss Knox."

As she turns to leave, I call her back — not by name, because she is a monster and deserves none other, but with my rage.

"You couldn't be more wrong!"

She wheels on her heel, facing me with those ice-blue eyes and that misplaced sense of injustice I hate so much about her.

"Because at the end of the day, I was always willing to lay down my life for those who couldn't defend themselves! I gave up everything, just like you did. The difference being, I wasn't stupid enough to expect some eternal reward!"

This last remark draws Hannah's lips in a tightly-puckered pout. There is no sadness, or even regret to it— she is devoted to her Dark Lord, in lockstep over the cost to her soul.

In the greater good's eyes, she is irredeemable.

"Sad, then," she says with a bleak smile, "that *this* was all that awaited you."

Hannah turns, disappearing into crawling emptiness. The Seed fades. My shallow breaths are drawn in, then forced out — as if meeting a door that does not allow the complete inhale entry to the lungs. The last of her steps evaporate, and I am alone in some deserted corner of the supreme realm, terrified for my soul.

When Hardwick abandoned me, I was quickly given company in the form of flames — they washed over the decrepit warehouse he left me bound inside. I called Tim's name as the chair collapsed beneath my legs, and slowly suffocated under tides of black smoke.

He is not here to save me this time. There will be no reincarnation when the flames come, no gorgeous room of stars where he will reveal everything in the only mirror I could ever face myself, a gift the man who calls himself Death had long kept.

I have been saving this for you, he said, gently leading me to a beach where the framed glass waited.

It will show you everything.

The moment between Hannah's silhouette being swallowed by darkness and the beast that slinks from its eternal depths momentarily following her departure is marked by the greatest fear I have ever felt as a conscious being. The room whose dimensions are shrouded in black void is filled by a yellow-eyed demon with great rows of teeth and the outlines of flesh wings. A great growl fills the room with no windows or doors or escape. The breath washing from the monster's nostrils saturates my personal space with wet, warm air as the creature's irises dilate in the dark.

A Behemoth. She left me as food for her pet — not the alpha male that Luca felled in the Arena, but more than I could ever hope to defeat alone. I scream as it slinks closer. I don't know how often dragons feed, but this one is hungry, and all too eager to please its mistress.

The eyes are my sole source of light, and not a great one — their yellow cast dances with the dim shadows, and I have one course of action as the Behemoth lunges for the chair.

Just as I dived over a wheelchair to dodge a bullet in the hospital, I force the uneven legs far right; the weakened prong snaps, and the backrest goes down. My head hits the hard floor, but adrenaline does not afford me the moment of recovery. The dragon's snapping jaws narrowly miss where my head was, passing over the broken chair.

Time to move, Ramona.

Hands still bound to wooden fragments, something tells me Behemoths aren't nocturnal, giving peace of mind long enough to pull arms under my rear, slipping legs through the opening between them. Vaulting to both feet using only my knees, I smash the backrest against the ground, splintering the chair's remaining piece. It shudders but doesn't break, and I slam it down harder as the Behemoth pulls its head back, searching the room for me.

One final thrust against the ground breaks the backrest in two. Rolling left, I fight shadow and Darkness and everything I ever mistook myself for, crawling on joined wrists as the mangled wood beats against my palms. I don't see the creature in pursuit, but hear its low growls, using these cues to roll away from their source.

My ribs hit a wall, and the crunching mandible of a beast ten times my size bashes on the surface above, sending unseen projectiles out the other side of its facade. Chunks of it land around me; my wrists smack the ground, dislodging the last pieces of broken back-rest from loops in the slacked ropes, pulling my hands free.

A streak of yellow glow pours through the reorganized wall, its combination of plaster and stone knocked outside. Just beyond it lies freedom, and escape from Hannah's depraved pet.

The Behemoth flails inside the structure. Thanks to Light, I make out columns and interior balconies. The floor is cleared of glass that previously inhabited it, but the crumpled fountain base sits on a circular marble floor that immediately rings familiar.

The Illumitory. The dragon's long tail has smashed away what remains of the fountain; it pulls down walls and columns, thrashing in the dark as I grab at the small opening, kicking my legs to pull through. The massive jaws close and open with ferocious grunts and squeals, nearly amputating an entire leg from the knee down as I tumble through the hole onto the Illumitory's lawn.

The creature pushes and prods at the pint-sized opening. Realizing it will not catch me, the dragon withdraws its snout from pursuit. Its howling ceases, and the Illumitory falls quiet.

As I turn around, the crimson sky over God's City enveloping everything I once loved about it, so too is my last shred of mercy gone.

The woman had her chance. I told her to take her followers and leave Atlas.

I showed her mercy, and received none.

The woman is going to die.

CHAPTER THIRTY-NINE

I WAS TWENTY-EIGHT years old when I met the man who calls himself Death. To my recollection, I was only a few years past infancy, incapable of reading and most rational thought; vulnerable from my parents' deaths, emotionally stupid in the way that only children and dysfuctional people can be.

I was just a scared child hiding under a dining table as Maya pushed a bookcase against the door to keep her recently rejected lover out. But Tim, the suited ghost who appeared underneath that clothed table, already knew everything about my life. He had been using his new powers as Death to investigate a personal injustice when he came across me, dying in a burning Georgetown warehouse. From there, he moved backwards, intervening at the ages of five, six, seven and twelve, appearing in ravines and my bedroom and a little white box where I was held after being caught stealing makeup.

I suppose he will never tell me which came first or last, but it doesn't matter any longer.

The first time will always be that little girl.

On the God's Road, the dragons shriek victoriously above; intuitively aware their master holds the Seed of Light. More than ten of them circle the Spire like overripe seagulls, squawking and snapping at each other mid-flight.

The ground is a different story. The outlanders outnumber the Brotherhood three to one and are less appreciative of their new digs than naturalized citizens, soiling the streets of nearly every district with their presence. They wield weapons brought from Earth that are more familiar than the swords and spears of Atlas, and no less dangerous.

The Brotherhood run security, telling the outlanders to settle down. The invaders scoff, flaunting their guns. One Brother smacks an invader upside the head— the newcomer relieves his pistol, and shoots the robed figure dead on the God's Road. His friends join in with toothless smiles and love of God and apocalyptic country, riddling the corpse with fresh bullets. The nearby Brotherhood's eyes widen, but there are too many of them to control, and they follow no law.

One of the Behemoths swoops down to mediate the conflict. Its footpads fight air as it descends, craning its accordion-like neck to snap up two of the outlanders. One screams before being sawed in half by razor-sharp teeth. The other loses his head as the dragon's jaw snaps shut over him, and beating wings lift the dragon skyward to rejoin its mates.

The surviving collective of outlanders involved in the Brother's shooting duck and yell, having bitten off more than they can chew. They scramble back to Devil's Corner as my name is called. My pounding heart is set on destruction, and it passes by me like Avalon's insect.

"Ramona!"

The woman never planned to go quietly— she would rather destroy Atlas than forfeit, burn the world down than admit defeat.

Maybe we should have just surrendered.

"Ramona!" Luca calls, grabbing me by the shoulder. Although larger and more capable, he does not look confident in our plan any longer. "Thank the Light. What happened?"

"No time," I pant. "Hannah has the Seed. We need to get it back." At Luca's widened blues, I nod. "It must have dislodged from Harper's locket when you fought the dragon. All that matters is getting it back."

The angel nods.

"Agreed. We will rejoin the others— they are safe in the Cathedral passage you found."

"All of them?"

"Tim, Harper and Quorroc. Nobody has been able to find Avalon, though. Nor his remaining students."

They must have seen the writing on the wall, and ported out of Atlas altogether. Or they're dead, taken down in some back alley by outlanders.

I have to hope for the former.

"Okay," I reply. "Let's join up with —"

We are interrupted by several sets of eyes that have noticed us. It begins with the Brotherhood in the vicinity tapping their comrades on the shoulder, pointing out the woman who should be dead in the Illumitory. From there, more Brothers are alerted; some recruit idle outlanders, telling them to help resolve a security issue. The dragons are signalled, and their shadows grow larger under my feet.

"Well, lookie watch we got here!"

Hannah's tribal-minded followers enclose Luca and I by the God City arch where I have stood, spellbound by all of Creation's hatred and self-loathing, winged monsters and wicked witches. There is no sign of the woman— only her people who know that we have been the cause of so much trouble, soon joined by massive dragons trembling the broken cobbles under their landing gear.

"Missus told us you was all taken care of," the speaking Brother quips. "Guesss you don't know when to quit, do ya?"

Luca's hand finds his sword's hilt, placing the strength to draw it in shallow reserve.

Rather than address the tightening circle of clashing factions and self-interested agents of chaos, Luca looks to me.

"When I tell you, you clamber over the wall behind us. Run for your life, sister. Run, and don't look back."

No.

"What? Luca, I'm not leaving you!"

Scanning the shrinking army we couldn't possibly hope to hold off alone, the angel doesn't meet my eye.

"It has been the greatest honor of my life to serve under you, Ramona Knox." He yanks on the hilt, pulling its gleaming blade to run parallel with his face, gripping it with both palms. "Go."

I can't do this to him.

"Luca," I say. "You don't need to do this."

The mob progresses slowly. Earthlings with raised barrels and Atlasians with pointed tips alike have us in their sights, salivating at our impending demise.

The angel doesn't answer verbally, grabbing my shirt by the collar, lifting me above his head. The fabrics stretch under his pull, but he does not let go. His wings spread beneath my kicking feet and protesting grunts and demands to put me down. Wielding his weapon outward to ward off Ziz's forces, the arm holding me up thrusts my body toward the top of the wall.

"Go, sister!" he screams. My own hands grab the brick barrier, one leg vaulting over it. Luca swings outward, cutting through a number of posturing Brotherhood; shreds of their robes follow the mutually crimson streaks from severed limbs and impaled torsos.

A set of gunshots escape the outlanders. A second follows it, grazing Luca's arm. He counters, dropping a mix of Brotherhood and invaders in a neat pile of lacerated corpses. A bullet strikes Luca in the rib, halting his momentum.

The angel drops to a kneel, wings instinctively contracting around his center mass to protect him. From my place on the proverbial fence above — one leg over each side, watching the slow march of Luca's end— he seems resigned as the cabal reinforced by dragons winds around him.

But the angel isn't done. He yells some indecipherable battle cry, pushing off one knee to balance, carving an arc across the entire front line of Brotherhood caught in the sword's path. They collapse to the ground at his feet.

"Ramona, go!"

The angel's final proclamation is met with several rounds of gunfire, spattering blood across the same wall I hold onto for dear life. The sword drops from Luca's open hand— he collapses to both knees this time; wings at full span, a stream of red saliva spilling between his teeth onto the road below.

I try to call his name, but only a low sob escapes my throat as the crowd parts. A Behemoth pushes between them, huffing before the angel. There is no Seed to shield him now, but I don't think Luca cares any longer.

The blast from the dragon's lungs blows me off the wall. I land hard on my side as its rage burns long and hot, cooking my friend alive.

I can't stay here. Luca is gone, and would have wanted me to finish this, not martyr myself to save him. Once the cheering and whooping on the wall's other side cedes, they'll remember the bitch who sat above the angel, watching their cruelty and murderous impulse take root.

I have to join the others. Fighting the breaths caught in my throat, there can be no mourning now.

When the time comes, I'll avenge Luca as well.

• • • •

AS THE ANGEL FORETOLD, Tim and Harper are in the tunnel below the Cathedral ruins. Its pieces are still shoved aside from the trap door. Had any of the woman's forces patrolled the area, they would have surely seen it. But no Brotherhood pursued me over the wall, appearing through the arch beyond which I fell, scrambling away from my fallen ally and his murderers.

Quorroc is not here — the man who calls himself Death tells me the Maester had some final preparations to make.

"What about Luca?" he asks. "I assumed he would have returned with you."

The mention of the angel is enough to send me into spirals. I close my eyes, lowering my shaking head.

"There are too many of them," I say. "Atlas is overrun with degenerates — all the bad apples the Council tried to keep out to begin with."

"What a damn mess," Harper muses. "So what do we do?"

I'm done pretending to have any of the answers. Hannah has the Seed, and all is lost.

"Time to find some hole to hide in before Ziz wipes out Creation, I guess. Look, there's no point fooling ourselves any longer. She won, okay?"

"So that's it? You're just going to give up?"

"What do you want me to do, Harper? The Council was wrong. I'm not special. I'm not extraordinary. I'm just a freak who made friends with Death and got to play on easy mode for a while!" The words burn my throat on the way up, and the bitterness may never go back in its bottle. "Face it. The bitch won."

The three of us fall silent, back in a cell where Harper strangled Tim. Her resentment has cooled toward him, and he is equally cold at the suspicion none of this would have happened if he never interfered in my young life.

"There may be another way."

The voice booming down the dark expanse does not belong to anyone in our party, but is immediately familiar. Its synthetic inflections emerge from deeper down the tunnel, the way Harper and I came on our way to claim the Seed.

The Avatar. Her arrival is accompanied by a sudden, wretched humming, followed by that horrible relay-flipping sound from Stone Mountain, and bright lights pouring up the tunnel. In seconds, Mother's Star is outshone by its creator.

"What way?" I ask, stepping forward.

The Avatar hesitates.

"My unit was designed to house the Seed of Light, and I have done so since the dying days of the First Age. Its power has residually spread to most of my internal network over such a long period — being hooked into every room and building through Atlas, this means the Seed has left deposits of concentrated Light in every corner of the city."

"What's your point?" Tim asks.

"Considering most of these points in the network are within my parameters of control, it means I can access them, and use those concentrations of pure energy to short-circuit the electromagnetic barrier that serves as an atmosphere to Atlas."

Harper squints, struggling to understand the implications.

"English, please."

"If the barrier is overloaded, anything caught in the field of impact — that is, anything that flies — will experience nothing less than fatal electrocution."

"Not even a dragon should survive that," I say. "That's the point you're trying to make, right?"

The Avatar is reluctant once again.

"Yes. But it does come with a caveat."

"What doesn't? Every action has a reaction."

"That is correct," she says. "Overloading the barrier will also destroy my circuitry, ceasing operations. In short, it will destroy part of Atlas' defense network."

This is it — our chance to disable the dragons, and one I never thought we would have. But after losing Luca, I am overly sentimental, and look back at Harper and Tim.

I'm done.

"You make this call," I tell them. "I don't care which of you makes it. Just make it. I...my heart's not in this anymore, guys."

Done making calls that only result in murder and mayhem either way. Done being damned if I do, and damned if I don't.

"Do it," says the man who calls himself Death.

I can't bear the responsibility.

"**Very well,**" the Avatar replies. "**I will require a few moments to designate the appropriate vectors. I would prepare to make your final stand. The outcome will be definitive and immediate.**"

I don't want to be a monster anymore.

CHAPTER FORTY

HANNAH IS ALONE AS she emerges from the Spire. Escaping her hideout in the carcass of Creation, the Avatar's final act smoked her out. It required no fire, but the crashing bodies of dragons. Barrett follows her out just in time to see its dying sacrifice, and all the destruction it entails.

The fifteen or so remaining beasts fall out of the sky like planes. One by one, they land in various places across Atlas.

One plunges into the shadows of Devil's Corner. I don't see it landing— only hear the snapping beams and collapse of whatever structure it plowed into at maximum velocity, sweeping brick and stone and plaster into the district's wailing remains. Another drops dead over the Cathedral ruins, while one more takes out the opening gate to the supreme realm. A fourth dragon dies when it tries to avoid swerving around Stone Mountain in its last moments. The prison narrowly escapes being cut in half as the Behemoth destroys the Dark Quadrant's outer wall. A second beast can't avoid its graceless descent — its body strikes the tower at its base. Stone Mountain buckles, leans and finally topples over, disappearing from my sight line. The prison's destruction is echoed by two hundred million souls escaping it, assuming the Arbiters weren't inflating the numbers. The souls themselves — black beads with no faces and terrible, tiny screams — collectively swirl from the prison's wreckage, meeting fresh air and escaping into a black hole of freedom.

A seventh dragon destroys what remains of the Arena, while an eighth and ninth jointly disappear over the supreme realm's borders, swallowed by the cosmos. The remaining six are gathered over the Spire; two collide in mid-air, but hit the ground on either side of the Seat. One destroys the Atlas-like statue to the Spire's periphery, another grazing past its symmetrical equivalent.

The final Behemoths die on the God's Road. They rotate as their falls culminate in cracking bones on the cobblestone. Harper is nearly flattened as one of the last dragons tumbles from flight— were it not for my arm reaching out, yanking her out of the landing zone, the Phoenix would be flattened.

The blond woman watches alongside Barrett — the old Maester is calm, despite the drained color from his toadstool of a face. Gone is the woman's maddening smile, replaced with horror at her massacred pets, and not an eternal reward to show for it.

"It's over, Hannah!"

Tim's voice rings across the gap dividing us from her. The man who calls himself Death exhibits a volume and confidence I have never seen of him. It takes a second to realize past his calm, measured composure, that this is a new side of him, a piece of the puzzle I have never seen.

Anger.

"Come along," he says. "You lost. It's time to stop fighting it."

But the blond woman (for all her tenacity and brutality) only clasps her hands, shaking her cocked head at the man she once married — there is nothing recognizable about that fact now.

"You don't understand," Hannah says. Her eyes water, but the voice remains steady. "The Dark Lord and I are one now."

"Then take him with you!"

A trail of moisture treads down her cheek, pulling part of her mascara with it. The black streak continues to her mouth corners — were she to smile, Tim might slap that grin off her face.

"He will not go. He is almost free — do you think after all this time and patience, the darkness will just go back in its bottle, Tim?"

The suited man is beyond conversation.

"I don't care. You got into bed with the Devil — you live with it! I was *ready* to face my punishment; you and your Dark Lord took that, and turned it into a mockery, because — why? You were jealous? You were stupid? You couldn't have figured it out: you were *gone*! Absorbed in the same fucking locket my friend Harper wears now!"

Tim's voice grows, and he has begun to pace back and forth.

"Tell me you remember that! Or was that one of Olivia's infamous lies?"

Of all the things he and I have said to Hannah over her short and violent tenure— all the taunts and jeers and slurs— this is the first to break her exterior. Beyond the fear of displeasing Ziz, she has played it cool, maintaining a minimal confidence. As the barbs in Tim's voice strike, her expression changes, embracing the one emotion I've never seen from her.

Sadness.

"Of course I remember that—"

"Then tell me, Hannah — what *happened* to you?"

An encore tear follows the first, dying on the same spot— the definition of insanity, as Hannah called it. Closing the distance between her and Tim, she stops in front of him, their faces only inches apart.

"I love you from Haven, to the stars. I meant that."

"If that's true," Tim replies, "then give me the Seed."

Even from behind him. I see the look — that nanosecond of her viscous, shit-eating grin. In the heartbeat before she unveils a dagger meant for her estranged husband, I try yelling his name, but the sound catches in my throat as Hannah pulls her arm back, thrusting the blade into Tim's midsection.

The man who calls himself Death is ready for the sleight-of-hand. She might have thrown him for a loop before, but he has left no contingency unchecked, no suspicion unturned. Dissolving into smoke, his black tendrils arc over Hannah's head, reappearing in human form behind her.

This prompts the morose Barrett to lunge forward, producing the same knife used to murder the Priestess. The elder lifts his arm; the knife travels, plunging down, and it seems like forever before it reaches the peak of my dread.

The loud sound that sends Barrett flying starts by tearing a hole in his neck. His body is catapulted toward the Seat as the Maester's lower face explodes in a mess. He falls still just past the Spire's double door.

Craning my neck back to see who saved Tim yields a very uncertain-looking Quorroc, holding a dead outlander's weapon. The elder's nervous hands hold the shotgun, in awe of its sheer power and recoil.

"First time?" I ask him.

Hannah, whose face is shades of Lovecraftian horror in its own right, turns and sprints from the scene, holding up the gown that drags behind her. She cuts right around the Seat's crumpled wall.

Harper is the first to attempt halting the blond woman. The locket flares; no longer imbued with the stolen Seed, its cast has returned to regular flames. Tim's wife ducks as the fireball flies past her, missing its mark and landing in one of the houses that dots the God's Road. The structure bursts into flames, spreading quickly to the next, and the one after that. Soon, all the white facades are engulfed in licking streams of red and orange, tunneling through their insides as the inferno works its way around Atlas' central plaza.

Tim morphs into dark form, giving chase through the relieved skies. I yell at Harper to remain with Quorroc as I give chase, feet pounding the cobblestone, making gains on the back of her dress. The smoke column shoots through thin air, weaving and twisting to achieve maximum velocity, easily outpacing the woman. She gasps and grunts and winces, turning sharp corners around the Seat's protective wall to avoid him.

Hannah veers a sharp right at the top of the God's Road into the Observatory district. The stone arch has settled into its jagged new form where dragons once rested on it. The nebula overhead makes the structure appear smaller than ever, even as she bolts up its gentle ascent, past the cross where she crucified Hardwick. The body on its crude, intersecting beams is nothing more than a skeleton now. Its left arm is gone, and the rest sags on the stake, almost tumbling where nails were driven through my old partner's palms.

As the smoke column arcs down, touching the courtyard, the man who calls himself Death returns to his regular appearance — the microbes of darkness solidify, amalgamated into a human silhouette. The color of its flesh lightens, lifts and fades to pink skin and hairs of his dark beard.

As I arrive at his position, stopping in front of the double doors left ajar into nothing, we share a glance, and proceed inside the Observatory.

Three go in, but not all will come out.

• • • •

THE FACT THAT THE BLOND woman chose the site of the Council's massacre to make her final stand is an irony not lost on me. Of all the beautiful monuments and timeless architecture destroyed in her siege on Atlas, the Observatory is relatively unharmed. Sandwiched between the destroyed Cathedral and Arena on either side of its enclave, the district is more victim of crippled integrity than physical destruction.

As Tim and I enter the long hallway past the doors — where the Royal Guard closed them to protect us from the monsters beyond its threshold, unaware the true threat was already inside — Hannah waits in front of the half-moon bench. The chamber draws into view, but the moment spent consoling our pounding hearts and sweating palms overrides any sense of victory.

The woman waits — her army of winged beasts and Brotherhood are gone, wiped out by the Avatar's sacrifice. Barrett is dead. Seraphina betrayed her, and Mykul is no longer here to defend her. All the walls that have kept us from winning — the bureaucracy and red tape of darkness — are cleared away, and all that remains is reckoning.

Hers. Ours. Light's.

Creation's.

The fate of all living things.

"Have you come to put me out of my misery?" she asks. "You'll have to forgive me — I was never very good at begging."

A thousand comebacks rest on my tongue. I have to remind myself that my part in this fight is over, as is Harper's.

This is Death's war now. Everything he has done and seen has led to this. Every terrible choice and wicked impulse of a human being forced into inhumanity has left his calm disrupted, his psyche broken.

And still, his voice is quiet, composed to the point of terrifying; no empathy left for his childhood sweetheart.

"The Seed, Hannah."

The woman smiles, reaching into her bosom, retrieving a familiar emerald light from her gown. Held at eye level is her final bargaining chip against annihilation.

"Oh— you mean this little thing."

Tim extends an open palm.

"Give it to me."

"Or what?" she asks. "That's right— or *nothing*! The fact of that matter is, dear husband; a cornered animal has nothing to lose."

Hannah lifts the Seed above her head, holding Creation at risk using nothing more than a panicked gesture.

"Not...another step," she says. Her blue eyes dance with the object's God-given glow, the effect washing over her face and shoulders in the rotunda's low light.

There is no upper limit to the woman's tenacity — she has every reason to quit after her inner circle collapsed; and yet, anything we could do pales in comparison to her Dark Lord. She would secure all of Creation for him, or die trying.

But Tim doesn't see it.

After all this time, despite his anger, he cannot see she would destroy us all.

"Please," says the man who calls himself Death. "Is this really what you want your legacy to be, Han?"

In spite of all her cruelty and unlicked wounds, she has just as much of a blind spot for him. For a second, her expression softens, and I believe he has gotten through to her. The arm holding the Seed buckles, dropping back to her side. Still unbunching from our pursuit, the gown slowly deflates, and will continue to do so until physics iron it out.

"Please, Hannah. It's time to stop this."

Head turned aside, looking to the place she first descended the stairs at the end from the checkered hallway, where her estranged husband first laid eyes on her for the first time in God knows how many decades, she is torn between morality and defeat, rebellion and acquiescence.

Returning to full awareness, there is no indication of further trouble; which makes the following seconds — as the Seed is vaulted into the air with her fist, and thrown at the ground as fingers open — the more shocking.

The tiny jewel smashes against the ground in a hundred fragments, pieces scattering outward in every direction across the Observatory floor as my mouth hangs open and Tim's eyes widen at the sheet of exploding Light. There is no immediate effect— that comes seconds later.

Light escaping as steam drifts back from the rotunda's far corners, sweeping in a circle motion from the outer edge. The constellation-laden glow is absent here, as is the verdant shade of its escaping life force.

Likewise, Hannah waits for the consequences to materialize. The punishment is delayed, but the dimmest soul could see the woman just opened Pandora's Box.

The ground begins to shake, early shocks of a devastating earthquake that cracks the marble flooring. Rumbling becomes louder than any Behemoth I have seen or heard. It is a twelve on the Richter scale, pulsing from the point of impact, pushing out the open doors into greater Atlas.

The half moon bench collapses as Hannah stumbles back under the repurposed floor. Tim and I fight for balance on the other side of a rising geyser shooting from below the supreme realm. The floor's center rises in the middle, giant halves of a former whole violently drifting apart. Walls are torn off in irregular, jagged halves. Main doors to the structure are ripped from their hinges. Beyond them, I barely catch the Spire topple in opposite directions. One part plunges forward, another to the side, while the base falls in on itself.

All of Atlas is breaking apart.

There is no more sign of Tim's wife. The rising rotunda rises like a wall in separate halves, obscuring angles of the giant chamber in a wave of marble and dirt and dust.

Stumbling and grabbing onto anything that will support our weight as the Observatory's dimensions rotate and change, the roof snaps off in quadrants, pulled apart at its common vertices. Its pieces plunge sideways, down and across as the supreme realm continues to self-destruct.

I try to yell Tim's name, but am either muted or dumbfounded beyond words, unsure if the syllable escapes into the symphony of crashing materials and groaning beams.

Tim!

The world revolts, and I lose sight of my guardian angel between the floors rising up and separating us. Soon, I am alone— caught amidst the slabs and debris of Creation, tumbling down from the heavens above.

The world buckles. It swallows everything, and I am being swallowed with it, falling into the darkness I have belonged to since birth.

As I depart this final frontier, legs kicking into oblivion and the stars surrounding it, my eyes are overcome — they are blinded by love I can no longer feel, optimism that is beyond me, leaving only a final, horrible impression.

White motherfucking lights.

The story will conclude in
The Book of Death:
Apocalypse

Acknowledgements

• • • •

THE LONGER A SERIES goes on, the list of people to thank for their help and insight grows more bountiful. As Atlas is my longest book, that list becomes longer. For the sake of brevity, I will try to list them here.

My editor Kindra Austin, for lending her expertise to this project. Kris Hack of Temys Designs for a stunning cover. Beta readers Capes, Leanna, Emma and Maranda for their time and diligence. My friend Candice for being the first to review and support this project, as with so many others. Kristiana Reed for her insights on classical pantheons. My Instagram community of authors and followers for helping me become a better author, offering advice and encouragement writing this tome.

On the personal side, my girlfriend Sara for putting this idea in my head, and helping to refine some of the wilder ideas. My daughter Skye for reminding me to never give up on my dream.

And you, reader, for your time and investment in this universe. The epic finale is almost here, and I hope you will want to return for one last trip around the afterlife next year.